Pyrate Crossover

ISBN: 979-8-9852206-4-3 and 979-8-9852206-5-0

Cover art and images by:

Roger C. Ambrose

& James R Whirlow

Pyrate Series Novels

by

Reidr Daniels

Pyrate Rising

Pyrate Assassin

Pyrate Crossover

Pyrate: Black Flag

Dedication

For My Sons

For their sweetness in their early years

For their independence in their teen years

For their achievements in their college years

For their success in recent years

But mostly, for their love and support through all the years

Contents

Novel   1

END   326

Notes   i

Characters   ii

Pronunciations   vi

Ships   viii

Locations / Places   ix

Acknowledgments   x

Preview: Pyrate – Black Flag (Novel #4)   I

Warning

The first section of Chapter VII includes an event that involves 'keelhauling'—a punishment occasionally (though rarely) meted out to sailors at sea. The practice dates back as far back as 700 B.C.

Due to its graphic nature, some readers may wish to skip or quickly scan that portion of the section. I say this because I value my readers, some of whom may find this event disturbing. My purpose in including it is to establish the lengths to which Pyrate Captain De Graaf is willing to go, in order to grow his reputation as the most feared of all pyrates. He is, after all, Captain Connachan's principal antagonist. I felt it was important to give this kind of insight into the man she was up against.

I apologize in advance if you are offended by the graphic nature of my description of the event. I've taken a further precaution by inserting a reminder warning at the beginning of Chapter VII.

Thanks for your understanding.

Reidr Daniels

Oh…one other note…

Though the current correct spelling of the word is "P-I-R-A-T-E", I've elected to use the olde English version: "P-Y-R-A-T-E".

Pyrate Crossover

A Pyrate Series Novel

Buckland Abbey

Devon, England

1600

He rubbed his hand softly on the seal. Garret's seal. This was as close as he'd been to her in more than a year. Though his trepidation over the letter's contents ran deep, it was at least confirmation that his beloved friend was still alive—at the time of its writing.

He placed the letter on his desk, rose from his seat, and walked softly across the thick Persian rug toward the dark, cherry-colored cabinet. Opening its glass doors, he pondered his choices. '*Brandy*', he thought. He poured a glass. Returning to his desk, he sat, sipped the gold liquid lovingly, and set the glass on the desk. He picked up Garret's letter, unsealed it, and began reading.

Isla Tortuga

Southern Seas

29 June 1599

Dearest Thomas,

I am afraid I am no longer the woman you may remember so fondly. Nor is William the same man. I have heard it said that some events in your life carry the potential to stain your soul. It seems all that has transpired since last we met has done precisely that. As things now stand, it is unclear whether we shall ever again be permitted to freely enter England.

I shall attempt to explain. By the time you finish reading, I trust you will understand how it is that life can transport you to places you never imagined, and shape you in ways you never thought possible…

I

Being infamous was both good and bad for Harker, thought Yauggan De Graaf. The good—Harker's legendary reputation as the most feared of all pyrates was now secure. The bad—he was dead.

Approaching the tavern in Santo Pedro, De Graaf recalled his prior visits here with Harker. The place was always quiet. And dingy. He frowned at the mass of people now pressed beyond the entryway and milling on the dusty street. '*What could possibly draw so many here to this decrepit little shack in this nondescript village?*' he wondered. Their presence threatened his desire for privacy in the matter at hand.

Those who saw him coming gave way. He pushed through the rest, unmoved by their grunts of annoyance. Entering the smoke-hazed tavern, his deceased partner's image flashed through his mind. Though he missed Harker, he recognized this was a new era—an opportunity to claim his partner's throne.

Watts and Dodd shared a rickety wooden table near the door, oblivious to the fetid mix of sweat, stale grog and smoke permeating the faltering old shanty. Santo Pedro was generally their last resort since it only ever offered the lowest price for their fish. Still, it always purchased whatever stock they had left to sell.

"Bloody mob," grumbled Watts, gazing into his tankard at the dregs of his watered-down beer. "No damn passage for the tavern girl."

Dodd nodded agreement. "Seems the locals were drawn here by news of that bloody pyrate's death—the one called Harker." He spat on the floor as though Harker's body lay there.

"That news be a week old," smirked Watts. "These bilge rats are just hearing it now?"

"Aye. So it seems." Dodd sipped his beer. "One of them blokes claims he once saw Harker right here in this shanty."

Their table jerked violently as a knuckled fist smashed hard on its top. "Your table," growled the fist's owner.

Watts looked up and down at the tall, dark-skinned man. Broad-shouldered and heavily muscled, he was dressed entirely in black from his bandana to his calf-covering boots. '*This beast was born of the damn shadows of the night,*' he thought. The long, greasy hair and full, black beard only darkened the beast's hardened face. The scars on it evidenced a history of savage combat. His piercing eyes and scowling brows promised imminent hostility.

Watts rose quickly, backing away. Dodd followed suit, abandoning both table and tankard. Watts looked back as the beast sat, sipped from Dodd's tankard, and began scanning the room. He avoided the beast's eyes.

The crowd flowed as bodies moved and pressed. Some of the pressing was intentional—women known to oblige patrons with physical favors offered openly provocative rubbing. One inebriated sailor stumbled backward, landing hard against the beast's shoulder. His beer showered the table. The beast erupted from his chair, grabbing the offender by the hair and whipping his dagger to the base of the drunkard's neck. "Lose your head again," he snarled, "and you shall find it searching for the rest of your worthless body." He shoved the man away, planting a heavy boot firmly on his buttocks. The man lurched forward, slamming into the two rugged-looking sailors he was with, both well-muscled and leather-skinned. Watts could see they didn't take kindly to the beast's treatment of their friend, nor to the spillage of their beer that his collision caused. He watched them approach the beast's table, hands clutching the hilts of their cutlasses. The beast had already retaken his seat.

"Vous paierez pour vos actions, cochon!" announced the larger of the two sailors.

Watts waited excitedly for the beast's reaction. But the dark man didn't flinch, or even look at the two Frenchmen. He simply drained Dodd's beer with his right hand….slowly. Deliberately. Watts noticed the beast gripped his dagger with his left hand, beyond view of the two would-be combatants.

"Sur tes pieds, cochon noir!" shouted the larger Frenchman. His words ignited a bustling shuffle of feet as patrons pushed away. Voices hushed in a sweeping wave. Watts watched the beast rise, keeping his dagger hidden. '*These two Frenchies are about to pay for calling him a black pig*,' he thought.

The larger Frenchman began drawing his cutlass. The beast thrust his left arm forward with concentrated aggression, hurling his dagger at the man's throat. The penetrating blade entered up the full length of its spine, causing the man's blood to bubble onto the front bolster. His accomplice, stunned and frozen, was hammered across the bridge of his nose by the beast's elbow. The crunching sound caused Watts to cringe as the man's head spun to his left, spewing blood. He crumpled to the floor. The beast's boot hammered forcibly onto his temple, re-drawing the shape of his skull. His body went limp. Silence smothered the tavern.

Watts glanced back at the Frenchman impaled by the dagger.

Now on his knees, his gaping eyes appeared to stare into nothingness. The beast withdrew his knife from the man's throat. Blood coursed through the opening. A back-handed fist to the temple toppled the dying man to the floor. The beast bent down and wiped his blade on the Frenchman's shirt—one side, then the other. Rising up, he scanned the stunned crowd. Watts again averted his eyes, feeling his body shake involuntarily. A young man who'd vomited was pushed away by another and slipped on his own bile.

The beast retook his seat as though nothing had transpired. He dragged the blade of his dagger back and forth along his thigh before raising and inspecting it. It gleamed even in the dim light. He skimmed his finger carefully along the razored edge. Watts and others watched in hesitant silence until the dagger was sheathed. Two men moved forward; hands raised to indicate they were no threat. The beast nodded and watched as they grabbed the fallen Frenchmen by their armpits. Blood smeared the hard, earthen floor as the two bodies were dragged out the door. Slowly, the tavern rediscovered its voice, although its energy had been sucked dry.

"Damn," whispered Dodd.

"Good we surrendered our table," Watts whispered back.

"And my beer."

Discussions among the crowd shifted from the demise of the infamous Harker to the beating they'd just witnessed. The two events were actually connected, Harker and the beast having been partners. But no one seemed to know that this beast had been alongside the dreaded pyrate when he was skewered…or that he'd sworn to take revenge on Harker's killer—Captain Garret Connachan.

II

Weeks earlier…

The deep-pink blush spreading slowly across the horizon drove a free-ranging rooster to shatter the calm. A dog barked in response, suddenly alert to the smell and distant voices of a handful of men. They were rowing their boat toward a ship anchored in the harbor of pyrate-infested Isla Tortuga, off the northern coast of Hispaniola.

"Harder," ordered the young, virile captain, William Tovery. He worried for the safety of his commander, Garret Connachan. She'd sent him to a pre-dawn exchange with a man called Prince, at a secluded location. But while he was there, the distant crack of pistol shots emanating from the harbor drove him to cut the meeting short. He was rushing back to Garret's flagship, *Pandora*, where she was staying. He knew only two others were on the ship with her. One was a former street urchin she'd rescued, named Scorpio. Garret preferred keeping the girl onboard *Pandora*, beyond reach of the village's poisonous culture, while the rest of her crew resided onshore during construction of their temporary quarters.

The only other person onboard *Pandora* was Spanish Viceroy Jorge Valdez de Barragan, a lauded military commander and fierce soldier. Originally their prisoner, he'd long since earned Garret and William's friendship. *'Surely he and Garret together would be able to defend themselves,'* thought William. He'd witnessed many times just how highly skilled Garret herself was in military arts.

"Hail, *Pandora*," William yelled as his longboat drew alongside. Dogs barked in response. Pigs snorted. The village's natural alarm clock was now fully engaged. "Is anyone onboard?"

High above, on *Pandora's* deck, an exhausted Captain Connachan was startled awake by William's call. Scorpio, asleep at her side, stirred. Garret moved the girl's head, placing it gently on the blanket she stuffed beneath it. Scorpio shifted her body.

Garret rose slowly, grabbing her sore arm; it was partially covered in dried blood. She walked past Musa and Caber who had earlier come to her aid. They, too, were beginning to rise.

"Hail, *Pandora*. Captain Tovery here. Declare yourselves." William shouted it with authority, now fearing the ship might well be occupied by pyrates. He and his men aimed their pistols at the rail in case shots from above were to answer his call.

"I am here Captain Tovery," Garret called out. "And safe."

The crew secured their boat and followed Tovery up *Pandora's* side. Their boots clopped along the wooden deck as they avoided the still-slick splatter of drying blood. William saw Garret and the others standing next to a canvas bag sewn loosely over what could only be a body. Coming near, he decided against reaching out to hold the young, auburn-haired Garret in his arms. She was his commander; it would have been out of place. He looked at her in sorrow. "Are you alright, sir?" he asked, properly acknowledging Garret as his superior.

"Everything appears to be in working order," she smiled, grimly. "Scorpio is unharmed."

William nodded toward the canvas-bound body, fearing the worst. Garret, on the verge of tears, sniffed and looked away, "The Viceroy," she said, her voice stuttering. William looked down in sadness at the heavily bloodied canvas covering the lump representing his departed friend. He prayed silently for God's blessing of the man's soul.

Scorpio was now up. Garret patted the girl's head. William turned to them, "What bloody Hell took place here?"

"Harker and several others assaulted us shortly after you left."

"I am sorry I was not here." William unnecessarily apologized, his mind quickly seeking to put the pieces together. "But…why just kill the Viceroy and leave?"

Caber stepped forward, "Only one bastard left on his own."

William looked around at all the blood. "So it would seem."

"By da time Musa and I come aboard, the Cap'n and the Viceroy had kilt all but one."

"De Graaf," specified Garret.

Caber continued, "Threw seven dead bastards overboard, we did. They be washin' ashore soon. It be a proper message to da rest o' Harker's crew."

"Harker too?" queried William.

"I ended his miserable life," interjected Garret.

"Truth be told, Cap'n, he be still hangin' on when we reached him," explained Caber. "We laid chains on 'im and threw 'im overboard. Thought it best he taste the sea's wrath."

Garret had nothing to add. William looked to Caber, trying to complete the puzzle, "You sewed up the Viceroy's body?"

"We did." Caber paused. "Both pieces of it." He shook his head, slowly.

William was aghast. "Damn," he yelled.

"His ear be missin'. 'Twas his arm was in pieces."

"De Graaf," explained Garret. "He took Jorge's ring as well."

"So De Graaf slew the Viceroy," William uttered in disgust.

"Not exactly," replied Garret, her eyes now watering. "Jorge was barely alive when I found him. He pleaded with me to end his misery."

"My Lord", gasped William.

"His dying wish," added Garret.

Thoughts and memories of his fallen friend weighed heavily on William. He could only imagine how Garret must have felt. Originally commissioned by Queen Elizabeth to eliminate the Viceroy, she and Jorge eventually became lovers, or so it seemed. He marveled at her composure in dealing with it all. He placed his hand softly on her shoulder. "I am so very sorry."

Garret turned to Caber. "Let us prepare for the Viceroy's burial. Now. His death must remain a secret. We cannot afford to have King Philip learn his friend was slain onboard an English vessel."

III

Though the beer was warm; the hands nursing the tankard were moist. De Graaf's ruminations on killing the two Frenchmen had yielded to those concerning the upcoming meeting with his partner's investor. He recalled Harker's words, '*Little goes on in and around Cartageña that the Phantom doesn't have his hands, eyes or ears on.*' That included the flow of cargo-rich merchant ships to and from Spain. The Phantom's information had proven immensely valuable to Harker, enabling him to outperform other pyrate captains. But with his partner now gone, De Graaf needed to secure the affiliation with the Phantom. After all, the door to the pyrate crown was open. Many would seek to claim it. Gaining the Phantom's trust would give his own sails the wind advantage. Still, he worried—both times he'd met the Phantom, Harker had led the discussion. He now faced negotiating a deal as a half-Black man in a white man's world.

Felipe de Heredia y Ortega and his two bodyguards muscled through the crowd outside the Santo Pedro tavern. Ortega, known to some only as Fantasma [the Phantom], stepped over the two bodies lying on the ground, where the crowd had yielded space. Almost an hour had passed since De Graaf dispensed with them.

Ortega was dressed as a seafarer, to avoid being perceived as anything other than that. In reality, he was wealthy beyond measure and politically well-connected. Some who were close to King Philip II of Spain drew on him for intelligence regarding activities in Cartageña and, more broadly, the Southern Seas. In return, they provided advance information on the movement of merchant ships. That was often accompanied by exclusive first rights to purchase goods being shipped to Spanish settlements on the Main and throughout the islands. But Ortega saw no harm in using the information to further his financial interests in covert ways—organizing outright thievery of some merchants' cargo. He chose to arrange operations of that ilk in small, out-of-the-way ports, a nondescript man in a nondescript village.

Santo Pedro was where he chose to provide Harker with information and up-front funding that would help the pyrate find and plunder sea-borne Spanish treasure. The return on those investments was significant. But given Harker's demise, his only choice was the pyrate's half-Dutch, half-Black accomplice—De Graaf.

His bodyguards waited outside as Ortega entered the once-again raucous tavern. Taking a moment to scan the crowd, he spotted De Graaf. Neither man acknowledged the other. Ortega simply approached De Graaf's table and pulled back the open chair. "So, The Patch is gone," he said, referring to Harker, who'd taken to wearing a blood-red patch over his dysfunctional left eye.

"It was a brave ending," De Graaf responded.

"No doubt." Ortega looked around. Not seeing a server, he pondered the leftover contents of an unattended tankard before him. He chose to pass.

"The score will be settled. In time," offered De Graaf.

Ortega had no interest in a discussion of revenge. He was here strictly to advance his financial agenda.

A young, half-caste girl approached from behind, placing a pewter tankard of beer on the table. Ortega slid two pieces of eight her way. As she reached for them, he gently caressed the back of her hand. She smiled at the generous payment, leaving her hand until the overweight and shoddily dressed, though surprisingly well-groomed, seaman withdrew his.

"Such a smooth hand," the girl noted.

Ortega smiled back. "Bless you, child." He turned to De Graaf as the girl left, "You asked that we meet."

"You know of the missing Viceroy from Inagua?"

Ortega sipped from his tankard and set it down. "Valdez."

"He now shares a home with The Patch."

Ortega wondered how he'd missed such important news. Had Cartageña's Governor Acuña known of the man's death and buried word of it?

De Graaf looked around. He reached inside his black doublet, withdrawing a small moneybag, looped at the top. He loosened the tie, reached in, and carefully slid something toward the Phantom under the palm of his hand. Ortega casually placed his own hand next to De Graaf's, palm down. The swap was executed smoothly. Ortega slid back his arm and moved his hand below the table. He turned and opened it, revealing a ring bearing the King's image. It was similar to one worn by Governor Acuña. Initials were engraved on the inside. He couldn't make them out in the dimness. He closed his hand and reversed the swap, saying nothing.

De Graaf discreetly returned the ring to its bag. "Valdez," he noted. "Does it interest you?"

"It has only modest value," Ortega sneered. He hadn't come all this way simply to buy a gold ring, even if it did carry Philip's image.

De Graaf pressed his case, "It has value far beyond the gold itself. The holder might use it to feign the King's endorsement of certain actions he wished to take."

"I am no fool," Ortega retorted. "Such actions could well lead to the holder being outed and imprisoned."

De Graaf frowned, returning the moneybag to his doublet pocket before taking another sip of his beer.

Ortega quietly processed the information he'd just been given. He relished the principal advantages he had over others—high intellect, and the ability to transform information into gold. He sipped his own beer and then set his tankard on the table. He leaned back. "There may be *some* opportunity here."

———

Warship *Mercilus* was mere days from reaching Isla Tortuga, battling the edge of a drenching storm spinning across the Southern Sea. Captain James Wenman, wearing an oiled overcoat to dispel the rain, stood on the foredeck alongside his master's mate, Lieutenant Ward. The rope around his waist, secured to the foremast, provided a degree of safety. Biting seawater showered over the bowsprit. His greased hair, knotted tightly behind his head, sluiced the water down the back of his coat. He loved a good, wet blow. It made him feel alive. Vigorous.

Wenman's legendary success against the Spanish Armada—amassing more confirmed ship-kills than any other captain—had brought the dashing young officer to the attention of Queen Elizabeth. At her request, he was now delivering her private, hand-written message to Garret Connachan, Captain of *Pandora*. Elizabeth had briefed him on Connachan's background.

"I hope this damn message is worth it," scowled Ward.

"What do you know of Captain Connachan?" Wenman shouted

above the wind and water.

"I hear she is not unpleasant to look at," Ward smirked.

"She signed on with Drake as a midshipman, even before reaching a suitable age. Disguised herself as a boy."

"I had not heard that!"

"Some retired colonel tutored her in the military arts. The old salt supposedly carved her into a highly skilled warrior." Water splashed his face mid-sentence. Wenman shook it off and continued, "Her Majesty claims Connachan's intellect and fearlessness in battle ultimately enabled her to come clean with Drake about her true gender."

"Heard she led the charge at Sagres," yelled Ward. "Got balls, she does."

"It seems Drake kept her gender secret until the day he announced her captaincy."

"Surely that ruffled the crew!"

"They say she had some strong supporters."

"Who?" shouted Ward.

"Ever heard of Drake's Black executioner? Name of Musa?"

"Who in England has not?"

"And some Scottish behemoth, known for tossing the caber."

"I should like to give *Connachan* a toss!" Ward yelled against a showering wave.

'*Not a bad idea,*' thought Wenman. '*It would be a delightful way to discover the contents of the Queen's letter.*' Though that thought crossed his mind, Wenman respected anyone who ascended to a captaincy on merit rather than birthright. He also knew the Queen was an admirer of Connachan, believing her to be a role model for girls who might aspire to positions of consequence. He was intrigued at the thought of meeting this unique young redhead with a 'not unpleasant' appearance. And perhaps giving her a toss.

A powerful gust of wind forced Wenman and Ward to wrap their arms around the taffrail.

"This bloody storm obscures our current position," shouted Ward.

"No matter, Lieutenant. Three days at most until we arrive."

"What do we know of Tortuga?" asked Ward.

"Spain appears to have little interest there. No soldiers. No Governor. It dances to its own jig."

"Some say it serves as a stopping point for privateers. And pyrates."

"Connachan is a privateer. Her only participation in Her Majesty's navy was against Spain's Armada. I never met her at the time."

"So she sails with the Queen's blessing?"

"She has in the past. And may still." Wenman couldn't be certain; the Queen hadn't shared her letter's contents with him. He knew it was in response to Connachan's earlier message. But he didn't know that Garret's message explained why she'd spared the life of Viceroy Valdez—a man she'd been commissioned to eliminate. After kidnapping Valdez, she'd decided to interrogate him first. That gave him an opening to forge a relationship that encouraged Garret to abort her mission. The Queen's resulting anger drove her to imprison both Garret and the Viceroy following their return to England. Wenman knew Connachan had been confined in the Tower of London but didn't know the circumstances.

"Are we certain Connachan will be on Tortuga?" asked Ward.

"Drake's brother, Thomas, assured the Queen that Connachan could be found there." Wenman was told it was Thomas who hand-delivered Garret's letter to the Queen sometime after she escaped the Tower.

"I imagine a warship bearing St. George's cross may not enjoy the welcome of any pyrates on Isla Tortuga."

"Fair point," yelled Wenman, his throat already becoming hoarse from all the shouting. "Let us approach under a flag of truce."

"Best you go ashore in seamen's clothes, sir, rather than in uniform."

Another wave crashed over the bow, soaking Wenman's face and coat. "God, how I love the sea!" he yelled. "Tis a fine day, Lieutenant."

"Indeed, sir. Though not for those in want of courage."

IV

Garret lay wide-eyed in the lightly swaying hammock. Though the creak of the ship's rigging this night was comforting, her mind was burdened. It currently offered recurring images of the dwellings being built just beyond the village on Isla Tortuga—images hazed by the gray dust that often hovered above the site. She even felt she could hear the virtual clammer of construction.

Her crew's work seemed frustratingly endless, especially given the buildings were intended to be temporary. Unfortunately, Master's Mate Blair was a perfectionist. He insisted the housing be strong enough to survive the sometimes-challenging southeasterly trade winds and heavy rain. And, in her mind, he was also paying undue attention to the two residences being built for her and Captain Tovery—as though any flaws in their structure might reflect poorly on his reputation.

The only hope of conclusion came from the belief of Blair's finishing crew that they would soon be ready for final inspection. Though not exactly homebuilders, their finishing skills were finely honed by years of work in and around the captains' quarters of sailing ships. Surely *they* would have a fair idea of when something was near completion.

Garret found the daily drum of building activity as numbing as an overly repetitive and poorly performed orchestral piece. Now six weeks since Jorge's death, the annoyance with her self-imposed confinement onboard *Pandora* was peaking. She felt an overwhelming need to set aside the haunting memories of the assault on her ship and get on with her life. Not just for her own sake but also for Scorpio's. Though their time had been put to good use, with Garret mentoring the girl on mathematics, navigation, naval strategy, philosophy and swordsmanship, Scorpio needed more. It was important she practice social mores, refining her skills at interacting with, and influencing, others. That was key to learning how to lead. Garret was confident Scorpio had leadership ability within her; it simply needed to be drawn out.

The dark of night always brought Garret another kind of blackness—one that filled her mind and soul, making sleep difficult. Sometimes impossible. And when it was interrupted, like now, she often gave in to wandering the deck, watching torchlights flicker in the village, replicating their image blurrily across the harbor. She even night-walked in the rain, hoping it might scour her soul of its gritty sadness. But there was no rain this night, she noted, as she wrestled with whether to get up.

Her mind turned to thoughts of the two lovers she'd lost, both tragically. It caused her to ponder the fragility of relationships. Would she ever find love again? Life on the oceans wasn't particularly conducive. But, having tasted the seafaring life, there was no going back to being a landsman. There seemed little adventure in that.

She thought about her homeland, particularly her relationship with Queen Elizabeth. The two had always found joy and commonality in sharing time together—successful women, leading men. It was during their last private meeting that Her Majesty had ordered the elimination of Viceroy Valdez, Spain's military leader in the Southern Seas. The objective was delivered verbally, to avoid any physical trace of royal involvement. Garret realized her returning to English soil with the Viceroy still alive, had put at risk the secrecy of England's complicity in his kidnapping. She also understood that her imprisonment, at the Queen's order, had potentially shattered their relationship. It needed to be rebuilt. She felt confident she could do that, provided Elizabeth would listen to her reasoning for keeping the Viceroy alive. It had sparked her to write the message Thomas delivered to the Queen on her behalf. She sighed at the thought that it might still be weeks, even months, before any response from Her Majesty would find its way to Isla Tortuga. Until then, the uncertainty of her standing with Elizabeth was just one more thing darkening this night and troubling her soul.

Her thinking turned to another letter—the one she'd asked the Viceroy [Jorge Valdez de Barragan] to write to King Philip II. She'd helped him write it. The words were still deeply etched in her mind…

Your Majesty, and my dearest friend,

I trust you are aware of my recent capture. I cannot apologize deeply enough, nor fully explain the shame I feel for having let you down in this manner. But I wish to inform you that I am well and being treated fairly by my captors. They have expressed a willingness to negotiate my freedom in exchange for certain considerations from you. Should you be willing to engage, please respond in the affirmative. Details shall follow.

For King and Country,
JVdeB

The exchange Jorge referred to was Garret's preferred alternative. The only other alternative that would guarantee her a path back to freedom in England was Jorge's execution.

It was Jorge's sealed letter that William was delivering, along with gold doubloons, to the man named Prince on the night of Harker and DeGraaf's assault on *Pandora*. Prince was a well-connected local figurehead and owner of Isla Tortuga's largest tavern, the Gente de Mar. He was the only one on the island who had the connections necessary to arrange delivery of Jorge's letter to King Philip. He'd demanded a handsome price for that service.

Between her letter to England's Queen, and Jorge's letter to King Philip, Garret sought to achieve favorable outcomes for all parties—an English foothold in the Southern Seas, freedom for the Viceroy, and her own positive re-engagement with Her Majesty. She'd hoped, too, that there might be some way to pursue a relationship with Jorge. But he was now gone—by her own hand.

A strong sway of the hammock turned Garret's thoughts to others she cared about—William and Thomas. She frequently beseeched God to watch over both. Since their days together as Drake's midshipmen, the three had formed a bond mirroring that of brothers. Though their relationship altered course once Drake revealed her true gender, she still regarded them as virtual brothers.

Her feelings for William, however, had grown deeper. He was a fine specimen of a man. Beyond his physical attributes, he was both intelligent and considerate, having been well-raised by loving parents. Thinking of him as a virtual brother made for an awkward transition to a different kind of relationship. Regardless, she had to constrain her emerging feelings for him. Doing otherwise could prove disruptive to the crew. '*Why was life so bloody complex and difficult?*' she wondered. '*Perhaps to strengthen me for even greater challenges ahead?*'

Sleep being futile, Garret extricated herself from the hammock, left her quarters, and headed to the main deck. She looked across the harbor. Now quiet in the dark of early morning, the little village seemed pleasant enough. But she wasn't fooled; it was a poor environment in which to nurture a pre-pubescent girl. Still, Scorpio had proven she could fend for herself on London's uncaring, unforgiving streets and alleyways.

Garret knew a time would come when some of the crewmen would resent Scorpio's presence onboard their ship—just as Harker and De Graaf once did with Garret herself. Most seamen still believed a woman's presence onboard ship was a bad omen—despite Garret's own example to the contrary. Worse yet was the likelihood that some bastard would attempt to take advantage of the girl.

Early on, Garret focused on preparing Scorpio to defend herself. She now understood how her own grandfather, Daniel, must have felt following the rape of his daughter—her mother. No doubt that was why Daniel decided the best way to protect his granddaughter was to provide her with the finest military training he could purchase…and raise her as a boy.

As she leaned against the taffrail, Garret's eyes were suddenly drawn to movement at the shoreline, backlit by village torchlights. A man was running headlong toward boats secured near the shore. By the time he reached them, a second man appeared, chasing the first with a pistol in hand. The first man paused beside a small boat. Seeming to sense he wouldn't be able to set it afloat in time, he ran directly into the water. Once up to his knees, he made a shallow dive. Garret saw a small splash of water light up near him, followed instantly by a pistol's blast. The shot had missed its target.

The first man swam frantically toward the nearest ship, his head never dipping below the water's surface. He was obviously a poor swimmer—one who clearly misjudged his own abilities. Garret sensed from his form that he would tire quickly, likely drowning before reaching his target. Unless someone were inclined to save him.

She glanced back to the man onshore. He was now walking away, no longer presenting any threat. She sighed deeply, pulling her sleeping gown up over her head and casting it onto the deck. Already barefoot, she climbed over the taffrail fully naked and dove toward the swimmer, whose pace had slowed noticeably. Her body entered the cool water seamlessly. After several strokes, she brought her head above the surface for a breath and slowed to tread water. She spotted the man some thirty yards distant. He now appeared to realize the peril he was facing. His strokes were quick and ineffective.

Garret was undaunted. She loved the water. Her grandfather raised her near a lake. She'd learned to swim before she was even old enough to realize it was a rare skill. But she now preferred swimming in saltwater; it was so much lighter than lake water, enabling her to glide through it at higher speed. She thought of Charles Prouten, Drake's master's mate. An excellent swimmer himself, he'd helped her further refine her skill. She now needed it more than ever.

Four strokes, breathe, four strokes, breathe. Water churned furiously behind her scissoring legs as Garret concentrated on her technique. She didn't look for the man; she simply listened for gurgling screams that might guide her to him. His arms were already thrashing.

Garret virtually skimmed the water. She heard a muffled choking scream. Altering direction slightly, she was next to the drowning man within moments. He was barely flailing but it was still too dangerous to reach out; he might grab on in desperation and pull her down with him. Treading water, she waited patiently until his energy was fully expended.

When the moment of capitulation arrived, Garret saw the resignation and sorrow in the man's eyes. He'd accepted his fate. His head sank quickly below the surface, his arms and hands following loosely behind. Garret drew herself toward him, arched her back, and headed under. She grabbed one of his trailing arms and pulled him near. The surface was already several feet above them. She kicked furiously to reach it. There was no resistance from the man; he was completely limp.

Finally breaking the surface, Garret gasped for air. She turned the flaccid body so that its back faced her, then placed her arms under the armpits, locking her wrists around the chest. Still treading water, she squeezed hard, forcing fluid from the body's mouth. It spewed out, clearing the lungs. Slime dribbled off the face as the unconscious body involuntarily coughed up more. Still grasping it, Garret leaned back and frog-kicked toward *Pandora*, damning the man's heaviness from the weight of his garments.

Barely conscious, the defeated swimmer who'd given himself up to the water…and the woman…seemed completely unaware of what was happening.

———

Seated among the rocks near the treeline, a bottled prize at his feet, De Graaf scanned the sheltered bay bordered by soft, white sand. Calming waves of docile, turquoise water lapped along the shore under a high, unfiltered sun. White-breasted birds chased and pecked at the receding waves. It was here that he and Harker met previously with the

Phantom. Far enough removed from the village of Santa Pedro, they were virtually assured of privacy.

A small boat bearing three men rowed toward shore. De Graaf rose and walked through sand that surrendered too easily to his boots.

The Phantom waited while his men disembarked and secured their vessel. Stepping out, he advanced toward De Graaf. The others waited behind. As the principals converged, the Phantom spoke first, without preliminaries, "You have the ring?"

De Graaf slowly withdrew a small bag from inside his doublet before reinserting it. The Phantom nodded, appearing to accept that the ring was in the bag. He stroked his beard. "I have a plan." The comment drew a small grin from De Graaf. "I am confident King Philip will reward not only its return," continued the Phantom, "but also any information regarding the circumstances of the Viceroy's death…and the name of his killer. The ring provides credibility."

De Graaf smirked. "Perhaps the King would pay even more handsomely if he believed the Viceroy were still alive." He knew Valdez couldn't possibly have survived the wounds he'd personally inflicted on him. But the only witnesses were Connachan and the little girl. He suspected they hadn't disclosed anything in order to distance themselves from any connection to the Viceroy's kidnapping. "We could then propose exchanging the Viceroy for gold."

The Phantom immediately shook his head from side to side, pushing his lower lip against his upper before responding, "Deceiving the King invites intolerable danger."

"Danger is my world," replied De Graaf. "Risking nothing brings nothing in return."

The Phantom paused. De Graaf turned, "Come. I have one

more prize." The two walked toward the rocks where he sat earlier. Next to it was a sealed glass jar. The thick fluid inside shone a deep orange-gold in the sunlight. De Graaf picked it up and handed it over. The Phantom turned it back and forth, his eyes focused on a dark item suspended in the ooze.

"The Viceroy's ear," explained De Graaf.

"Dios mío! Por qué? Cómo?" The Phantom thrust the jar back at him.

De Graaf laughed. "I sailed Asia with Drake. The natives there use honey to preserve bodies."

"But why would you do this?" The Phantom replied in shock.

"I bested a man of the highest military standing," De Graaf replied proudly. "This is my trophy." Grinning cockily, he added, "The Viceroy had no further need of it."

The Phantom remained stunned while De Graaf expanded on his thinking, "Perhaps the King could be convinced the Viceroy was taken prisoner for a ransom. The ear might suggest his captors are prepared to kill him if not well compensated for his return."

The Phantom took a further moment, "*Assuming* the King were to believe Valdez is still alive, he might indeed pay handsomely for his release. Still, others may try to convince him the Viceroy was slain."

"Which is why the ear is so valuable," countered De Graaf.

"The King will question whether this is indeed Valdez' ear."

"Look closely," said De Graaf, lifting the jar toward the Phantom's face. "The top of the Viceroy's ear is notched. A battle scar, no doubt. Surely those who knew him will recognize it." The Phantom didn't bother to look, apparently willing to accept the claim. De Graaf continued, 'With the ear and the ring, surely a man of your standing can convince the King the claim is credible." De Graaf knew the Phantom would take the bait.

"Perhaps we might provide the ear first," conceded the Phantom. "The ring could later serve as confirmation, if the King seeks further assurance and is willing to pay for it."

"So…*both* have value," De Graaf emphasized, enjoying the moment.

"Just so. Yet, once the King authorizes payment for the Viceroy's release, we shall need to claim that others attempted to kidnap him, and that he was killed in the process."

"Then surely the King would pay further, for the killers' names…or their capture."

"Let us sit awhile and think on this," replied the Phantom.

———

He awoke confused, swinging in an unfamiliar hammock, in unrecognizable quarters, on an unknown ship that creaked and swayed as though at-anchor. His memory came flooding back. Partially. He remembered being chased into the water and shot at. The shooter was a fellow sailor who accused him of cheating at dice. He remembered swimming to get away but everything after that was blank.

Naked but for his linens and the blanket covering him, he rolled out of the hammock and began searching for his clothes. They were nowhere to be found. He gave up looking and climbed the ladder to the main deck.

Scorpio stood next to Garret on the foredeck when she noticed the man exiting the crew's quarters. She nudged Garret, "He's coming." She pointed the way.

The man observed that the person approaching him was a woman. Conscious of being shielded only by his undergarments, he abruptly placed his hands over his privates. There was no real need; it was simply instinct. Still, he was unduly conscious of his disheveled appearance and skinny, pale body before this finely dressed, and not-unpleasant-looking, young woman.

"Good day, sir. I am Captain Connachan."

"Where am I? What am I doing here?"

"This is the *Pandora*. You are my guest. It seems you had too much to drink last night." She grinned.

"How did I get here? Where are my clothes?"

"You have many questions. I shall answer them while you eat."

———

"Land ho!" came the call from atop the mainmast.

"Where away, sailor?"

"Four points to larboard sir, if you please."

Warship *Mercilus* was nearing Isla Tortuga. Captain James Wenman scanned the double-blue horizon in the direction given. The dark, turtle-like hump he was told to expect was barely emerging. He was more anxious than ever to set foot on the island and meet the bright young Captain Connachan. "Bring her about, Mr. Poole," he called to his helmsman. "Trim the sails."

He turned to his Lieutenant, "Lower the cross. Ready the white, for rapid deployment on my orders."

"On your orders, sir," nodded Ward.

Before his departure from England, Captain Wenman had been reminded by the Admiralty of the navy's extreme interest in his reporting on the layout and activities of this surprisingly independent community. They understood it was a colony of seafarers, some of whom were pyrates. But any peopled location in the Caribbean islands that wasn't tightly ruled by the Spanish presented an opportunity for an English foothold.

Of the hundred or more pyrates known to reside on the island, some were said to have once sailed with the legendary Drake. Two in particular were now leading other pyrates—Harker & De Graaf. The Admiralty shared that when Drake announced Connachan's captaincy, those two, in particular, were furious. Harker was said to have later threatened Connachan's life in front of Tovery and others. It seemed odd, then, that Connachan should choose Isla Tortuga, the home of her archenemy, as her temporary base.

'We shall soon see what this curious *place has to offer*,' he thought. He was committed to documenting his findings thoroughly, including his interactions with Captain Connachan and her partner, William Tovery. The latter had curiously chosen a privateer's existence over a potentially promising naval commission. Wenman wished to understand the man's motivations.

As *Mercilus* began its final approach, Wenman headed back to his cabin, where the Queen's sealed message for Captain Connachan was secured in his ornate oak desk. He often speculated on the letter's contents. Unfortunately, there was no way of knowing. Holding the sealed parchment next to a lantern hadn't enlightened the writing.

He wasn't the only party interested in the letter's contents. The

Admiralty hinted at an opportunity for him personally if the matters at hand were to be shared with them—possibly even an assignment to one of England's newest and finest warships. So the stakes in deciphering the letter's message were high. If Garret were 'reasonable looking', as some implied, then seducing her was one pleasingly possible way of obtaining the desired information. '*A double win*,' he thought.

Wenman was envious of Connachan. Having a personal message from the Queen expressly delivered by the navy was compelling proof of Her Majesty's high regard for her.

Arriving in his cabin, he removed the key to the desk from a pocket inside his dress boot. He inserted it into the lock on the lower drawer, turning it counterclockwise. Sliding out the drawer, he saw his handful of naval logs, along with his formal orders and other personal documents. He withdrew the pile of six naval logs, placing them atop the desk and pulling out the one at the bottom. It was completely void of notes. Lodged between the last page and the back cover was the parchment with the waxed seal displaying the Queen's royal impression. He looked closely at the seal, trying to make out the specifics of the image. They weren't entirely clear, although there appeared there to be a crowned woman holding items in each hand. Unintelligible lettering encircled the edges. He walked the unsealed letter to the stern window of his cabin and held it to the light. Not surprisingly, the contents were still indiscernible. He returned to his desk, reinserted the naval logs in the drawer, and then closed and locked it. He stuffed the letter inside his doublet. His orders were to hand-deliver it to Captain Connachan or, in her absence, to Captain William Tovery… assuming they were still on this intriguing island.

———

Scorpio had earlier brought him his dried-out clothes, stiffened by salt. Now dressed, the man began devouring his salted pork and cheese breakfast like a famished dog. Garret poured him a cup of beer and took her seat across from him, in her quarters. Scorpio sat quietly, observing.

"You have not yet shared your name." said Garret.

"My apologies. I am Yosel."

Garret studied the man's appearance for the first time. His hair was black as coal and stringy under a dull gray bandana. His cheeks seemed a little drawn. He had large, dark eyes and a straight, distinctive nose. His beard was rugged and lightly graying, though not overly long. He was tall but slight, his bearing not in the least imposing. If anything, it was open; friendly even. "Yosel," she repeated thoughtfully. "The name is unfamiliar."

"Tis Hebrew."

"You are a Jew, then."

"Sephardic Jew. Portuguese." He tore off more dried pork with his teeth and chewed on it.

During her travels, Garret had learned that many Jews fled religious persecution in Portugal, ending up in the Southern Seas. Though she couldn't be sure she'd ever met one, she was certain they didn't eat pork; yet here he was devouring it. She also knew that many Jews converted to Christianity ('Conversos')…or feigned it, to avoid being caught up in the unsavory aspects of the Spanish-led inquisition. "A Converso?" she asked.

"My father was. And shunned by his own people for it. I have no religion but the sea."

"Do your crewmates call you by this name—Yosel?"

"Only those close to me. Others call me 'The Jew'."

"May I ask who was chasing you last night?"

"A shipmate. Claimed I cheated at dice."

"Did you?"

"No. He was sheeted to the wind by his beer."

"Which is your crew?"

"De Graaf's."

"The half-Black pyrate?"

"The same."

Garret let that sink in. Having admitted to sailing with De Graaf, Yosel was clearly unaware of the pyrate's assault on her ship. She sensed opportunity—if she could befriend him, and earn his trust, he might one day be in a position to provide her with information on De Graaf's plans. "You asked me earlier how you came to be on my ship," she noted. "Has it come to you yet?"

"Not rightly, ma'am."

"Captain, if you please," she corrected.

He nodded, "Captain. Yes."

Do you recall that the man who chased you also shot at you from the shore?"

"I do, yes." He tore off another piece of dried pork.

"Clearly, he missed." She smiled warmly. "You swam toward a ship that was beyond your abilities. The water began to claim you." Yosel's eyes darted back and forth beneath furrowed brows. Garret continued, "I saw you from my foredeck and dove in to assist."

Apparently, he remembered none of this. "You saved me?"

"I did indeed, Yosel." She used his name intentionally, to deepen their connection.

He stopped chewing and looked Garret in the eyes. Slowly, sheepishly, he responded, "Then I have much to thank you for."

Garret waved it off, "It was the only thing to do."

"Still, you could have simply let me drown."

"What purpose would that have served?"

He had no answer. "I shall repay you."

"God asks not for payment in return for his blessings. He asks only that we serve Him, by serving others."

Yosel put down his dried pork. "How may I serve you? Swab the decks? Clean the hold?"

"No, Yosel. But perhaps a time will come when I shall need a favor."

"By all means, Captain. Anything you need." He grabbed his cup, washed down the pork with a mouthful of beer, and smiled. A beautiful smile, thought Garret.

———

It was decided. De Graaf and the Phantom shook hands in confirmation. "I shall send an envoy to meet you in Santo Pedro two days hence, with the five hundred pieces of eight," said the Phantom. "Have the Viceroy's ear concealed in a locked chest. I shall alert you once the King responds."

"Just so," nodded De Graaf.

"One more thing," said the Phantom, looking into and through De Graaf's eyes. "Carefully examine the envoy's face. Seal it in your memory. When all is done, you will need to eliminate him, so there is no trace back to either of us."

"Understood," De Graaf nodded.

Ortega sat in the boat, watching his guards shove it into the water and jump in. He glanced back at De Graaf. '*The pyrate is no fool*,' he thought. '*His knowledge of our transaction is more valuable than his two mementos.*' Watching the hulking man walk away with the jar containing the Viceroy's ear, he knew that the envoy wasn't the only one requiring elimination. De Graaf himself was on that list.

Heading back to the village, De Graaf was pleased that the Phantom bought into his thinking. The man was well-educated. But there was a difference between the learning found in books and that to be had by observing the life unfolding around you. And in this pyrate-like world, De Graaf prided himself on being the keenest student. His life-skill had just trumped the Phantom's formal education. Still, one thing worried him—the Phantom's desire to erase any trail back to the two of them. If the envoy was to be eliminated, wouldn't the Phantom seek to remove *him* as well? The heat and humidity suddenly seemed oppressive. Sweat soiled his bandana and clothing.

His thoughts turned to Connachan—'the Witch', as Harker called her. His partner believed she either cast a spell or seduced Drake to gain her captaincy. Witch or not, there was definitely something dangerous about her. The woman was formidable, having out-dueled Harker when they assaulted *Pandora*. Though he didn't yet have a specific plan, De Graaf longed to spill her blood, taking her soul with it. He trudged on with a grin, sparked by the thought of dismembering her into more pieces than he'd carved from the Viceroy…and taking another memento.

———

Watching Yosel row ashore, Scorpio turned to Garret. "He seems like a nice man."

Believing that children, like dogs, had the ability to sense whether people were innately good or bad, Garret asked, "Do you think we might trust him?"

"Trust him with what?"

"He promised to provide information about his captain's plans...if he believes it might serve our interests."

"Is that not an easy thing to do?"

Garret looked directly into Scorpio's eyes. "Pyrates like De Graaf are ruthless with those who cross them."

Scorpio paused. "I hope he will be okay."

"He shall be fine. At least for now."

"Good...I suppose."

"When he has information to share, he will not bring it to me directly," added Garret. "He will send a messenger."

Scorpio had already moved on, to what she believed was a more pressing matter, "How long before we might go ashore?"

"Soon, dearest. Soon." Garret pointed toward her cabin. "Now, back to your studies."

"Yes, mum."

"Yes, *Captain*," she reminded the girl.

Scorpio stopped and smiled, "I love that you are the captain. I hope to be one someday." She dashed off to the cabin.

Watching the girl go, Garret felt a trace of pride in being her inspiration. She turned to look in the direction of the construction. Any day now, she and Scorpi would have a new residence at the rear of the other buildings, offering a degree of privacy.

Scanning the harbor, she saw Yosel drag ashore the small boat she'd provided. She knew he would face the most dangerous crossover of all—becoming a traitor to a tyrant. It was pure treason, but for the fact that De Graaf represented no country…only himself.

V

"Anchors at the ready," shouted Captain Wenman.

"At the ready, sir," came the response.

Warship *Mercilus* floated calmly into Isla Tortuga's outer harbor, unflagged and sails furled.

"Haul anchor, if you please."

"Haul anchor," shouted Lt. Ward.

Sailors scurried and chains clamored as one of the anchors was rolled out. It dragged the harbor floor briefly before bringing *Mercilus* to a jerking stop, further from shore than all other ships.

"Prepare to disembark, Lieutenant,"

"Aye, sir." Ward turned and left to instruct the crew.

Wenman peered out at the disheveled little village. Given everything he'd heard about Isla Tortuga, and the number of ships anchored here, he'd expected something larger; something more vibrant. '*A curious island indeed,*' he thought.

Seated at the longboat's stern, Wenman and Ward watched as six others rowed toward shore, where a growing crowd of villagers gathered.

"Judging by their look," said Wenman, "I suspect many are pyrates." In fact, several were members of De Graaf's crew. The pyrate captain himself, however, had yet to return from his clandestine meeting with the Phantom outside Santo Pedro.

"No doubt they are curious about our unflagged ship," replied Ward.

"Curious *and* guarded, I suspect."

William Tovery approached unaccompanied as the longboat ground ashore. The rest of his and Garret's crew were still immersed in constructing temporary residences beyond the village. Though this newly arrived ship was unflagged, he recognized it was of English naval design. It had been months since his friend Thomas delivered Garret's letter to the Queen, asking that her response be sent to Isla Tortuga. William prayed that this ship carried Her Majesty's reply.

Two men strode ashore like military officers, though not in uniform. William stepped forward to greet them, extending his right hand, "Welcome to Tortuga. I am Captain William Tovery, privateer."

"Good God," exclaimed Wenman, accepting and shaking William's hand. "What turn of good fortune is this? You are one of the people I have come to see. I am James Wenman." In a whisper, he added, "*Captain* Wenman; of the Queen's navy." A hushed murmur wafted through the crowd as those closest overheard. Concerns were shared quietly.

"Truly, it is not *surprising* fortune," replied William. "We are where we promised. And Tortuga is sparsely inhabited." William waved his arm across those assembled. "Mostly local villagers, transient privateers and ambitious merchants." William chose not to be explicit about the presence of pyrates, not in front of this crowd.

Nodding in Ward's direction, Wenman again lowered his voice, "This is Lieutenant Ward; Richard, if you will."

William shook Ward's hand. "Come," he said, placing his hand on Wenman's shoulder, "You must be thirsty for local offerings." His mischievous grin implied something more than mere liquids.

"I am indeed, Captain. May I call you William?"

"You most certainly may; there are no formalities here."

"Good. And I shall be James. Lead the way."

The crowd redirected itself down the dusty street like a flock of birds sharply altering course. Dogs and chickens accompanied them, as did a murmuring hum—robust discussion and general acknowledgment that this was a decent excuse to hoist yet another cup of grog…or two. Perhaps more.

———

Ortega was pleased to be back in his city of birth. Cartageña was thriving as never before. Following Drake's sacking of the city, King Philip was investing heavily in its reconstruction and defense. That included a military fortress, a castle-like governor's residence, restoration of the cathedral, and the erection of thick stone walls surrounding the city. All of that required labor and materials, which he and his network were arranging. He sat alone in his reading room, reviewing the latest statement of his financial accounts. It seemed De Graaf's idea might soon make a nice addition to his ledger.

Officially, he went by the name Felipe de Heredia y Ortega. And perhaps for that reason alone, he was rumored to be the grandson of the city's founder, Pedro de Heredia. No one bothered to refute that.

Unofficially, he was known by two other monikers. Among those conducting beneath-the-table business in Cartageña, he was commonly referred to as 'Sombra' Ortega [the Shadow] due to his extensive use of surrogates to handle his affairs. For clandestine operations that he, himself, conducted outside Cartageña, like his engagement with De Graaf, he insisted on being known only as 'Fantasma' [The Phantom].

Ortega purposely maintained a relatively low public profile.

But those in positions of authority understood he was the City's most powerful broker of merchant trading—legitimate or otherwise. It was said that nothing in the City changed hands without his palm turning silver. Early in his career he smartly redirected a portion of his burgeoning wealth into purchasing influence among members of King Philip's court—members who had the King's ear. It provided him extraordinary political power in Cartageña since the real locus of any major decisions impacting his city was Spain itself, ergo King Philip.

There was a knock on the door. "Ayudante Vegas," announced Abeo, Ortega's Black Master-of-Staff. Pedro Vegas was Ayudante de Campo to the General who served as King Philip's senior military advisor. He traveled often to Spain, making him an excellent conduit for Ortega.

Ortega rose, "Buenos dias, Ayudante."

"Buenos dias, Señor Ortega."

"Por favor," Ortega said, pointing to a chair, "toma una silla." He turned to Abeo. "Bring the Ayudante a cup of our finest port."

Vegas sat in the indicated chair, placing his hat on a side table. "Gracias. You asked to see me?"

"I understand you will soon return to El Escorial."

"Si; in two days. I am to provide the General with an update on the progress of our construction efforts, for his official report to the King."

"I trust your report will be positive."

"It will. We are ahead of schedule," Vegas said proudly. "My Blacks work tirelessly. I now have several hundred under my employ." Ortega knew the precise number of slaves engaged in reconstruction. They were the most lucrative of all the 'supplies' he provided.

Abeo arrived with an olive jar of port and two silver cups. He set one cup next to Vegas and poured out a portion of the jar's contents. As he turned to his master, Ortega simply waved him away.

Once Abeo had left, Ortega opened, "Tell me, Ayudante, how is it that you get the most out of your workers?"

Vegas grinned. "They prefer the joy of good health over the alternatives we can provide."

"I see." Ortega didn't believe beatings were the best form of motivation but was more than happy that Vegas did. After all, the more the Ayudante beat his Blacks, the more likely he was to need more of them. "Well, I am pleased to hear of your progress."

"There is one problem, however," noted Vegas, emphasizing the word 'one'. He looked at Ortega with a wry smile. "The supplies we require are more expensive than anticipated."

Ortega didn't care what the Ayudante thought about the inflated prices. Those in power received a fair portion of what he received in exchange for the supplies he provided. And Vegas himself was paid handsomely for his services. Middlemen like him were simply that—those who found themselves in the middle—never leading, simply facilitating. He redirected the discussion toward his original objective, "It recently came to my attention that the Viceroy from Inagua has gone missing."

Vegas was sipping his port. He lowered the cup. "Viceroy Valdez, yes. It seems he has been slain."

'*There it is,*' thought Ortega. Vegas' use of the word 'seems' confirmed that the military had no actual proof of the Viceroy's death. It presented an opening to proceed with the lie. He slithered through it like a snake, "Sources tell me the Viceroy is still alive."

Vegas set his cup on the side table. "That is most interesting news. Assuming it is true, of course."

"I have been approached by someone claiming first-hand knowledge. And proof."

"What proof?"

"I have no idea as yet, but I am assured one might purchase it."

"At what price?"

"Fifteen thousand pieces of eight," Ortega replied nonchalantly. Though the number was high, Ortega judged that the Viceroy's close personal ties to King Philip would support it.

"Dios mio! That is exorbitant. Especially for something of questionable existence, let alone provenance." Ortega chose not to respond; the ball was still in Vegas' court.

The Ayudante composed himself. "If credible proof exists, I shall need to arrange immediately for its purchase and delivery to the General." Ortega nodded without responding verbally. Vegas continued, "I shall see about the money. May I presume we can provide half up-front and the remainder on delivery?"

"I imagine that would be acceptable, though I cannot guarantee it." Ortega sought to maintain the ruse that he had no control over those who actually held the proof.

"I shall confer with my superiors," Vegas committed. "Might I expect delivery of the proof on the morrow?"

"I will see what can be done. Let us reconvene this evening. But please, keep my name out of this. I am nothing more than a messenger—a middle man, if you will."

"Of course. Thank you for bringing this to my attention."

Vegas took one final draw of his port. He rose from the chair.

"This evening, then."

Ortega watched Vegas leave. He felt comfortable using the man as a go-between for the ransom scheme. The Ayudante was well-positioned but ultimately expendable. When all was done, he too would be eliminated.

———

Leaving Santo Pedro, De Graaf stood at the bow of the *Death's Head*. The thought of the five hundred pieces of eight he received from the Phantom's envoy in exchange for the jar containing the Viceroy's ear made him smile. The ransom scheme—his own idea, as he saw it—was now underway.

Master's Mate Stevens joined him on the foredeck. "Where away, Captain?"

"The merchant lanes, Mr. Stevens. I am hungry to feast." De Graaf was anxious to further his reputation. He knew every conquest would deliver a message magnifying his status as one of the most feared pyrates terrorizing the South Seas. The nearness in time of his piracy exploits was important. The more frequent and recent, the better. Merchants aware of his reputation would be less inclined to contest surrendering their cargo. He would dedicate the next week, perhaps longer, to trolling for prey.

"The men, too, hunger for treasure," noted Stevens.

"Good. Make certain their weapons are as ready as they are."

"Indeed. I shall demand it."

As Stevens left, a stiff breeze and light spray swept off the water, causing De Graaf to blink. He reached into the pocket inside his doublet. The Viceroy's ring was still there. He checked it frequently these days, often subconsciously.

Scanning the breadth of the blue Caribbean waters undulating before him, De Graaf reflected on this life—freedom from would-be overseers, endless adventure, and the intoxicating feel of sheer power over others. Besides the Spanish navy, the only real challenge to that power seemed to be the Witch—Connachan. Word had spread of her having killed Harker, making her a seeming heir-apparent to his reputation as the most feared of all pyrates. The Caribbean Islands were not a large enough deck on which he and the Witch could co-exist. He was committed to bringing about her demise. He owed that to Harker.

———

"A new ship," announced Scorpio.

Garret walked to the taffrail, looking in the direction the girl was pointing. The unflagged vessel was anchored well beyond *Cutthroat*, De Graaf's consort vessel. "It appears to be an English warship." She scanned the harbor for any sign of *Death's Head*. It wasn't to be seen. Was that good or bad, she wondered. '*God forbid De Graaf overwhelmed this English warship and took her as his own. But then, why would he leave Death's Head behind?*' It seemed unlikely.

"I hope it *is* English," said Scorpio.

Garret nodded. "Friendly faces are always welcome."

Though she didn't say it, it occurred to Garret that English hands were *more than* welcome, given the possibility of having to face De Graaf again. But she felt confident the next time would not be a surprise. Surely Yosel would alert her in advance—provided he were aware of any assault De Graaf was planning.

"Might we go ashore today?" Scorpio asked.

"Patience, dearest." Garret judged they would soon reside onshore with her crew. At that point, De Graaf was less likely to attempt an assault. Still, she wondered about taking preemptive measures. Eliminating the pyrate would dissipate her concerns. But the thought of killing a man in anticipation that he *might* do something, troubled her. It would mark a definite crossover to the dark side, making her no better than a common pyrate. Still, the man had drawn first blood. She might well be justified in taking him off the board—at the very least to avenge Jorge's death.

The thought of Jorge brought a crushing sadness. She missed him dearly. Both him and Ambassador Pantas, for that matter. Two lovers, both assassinated, one literally by her own hand.

"I see a longboat coming."

Scorpio's comment jerked Garret back into the moment. She looked at the men approaching. One was William. The man next to him wasn't rowing either, suggesting he was more than a common seaman. The two conversed as six oarsmen propelled them toward *Pandora*.

"Permission to board, Captain," William called out as he ascended to the entry port. Formalities were in order.

"Granted," replied Garret.

William walked onto the deck, followed by the other gentleman Garret had noticed. William nodded, "Captain Connachan, allow me to introduce Captain James Wenman of Her Majesty's navy."

"A pleasure to meet you, Captain Connachan."

"And you, Captain Wenman." Garret turned slightly. "This is Midshipman Scorpio."

"Honored," replied Wenman. Scorpio nodded. "I must say,

Captain, you have a fine ship here," he continued.

"She is of my own design."

"Then I would add—she is as handsome as its designer."

Garret felt herself blush. '*Dammit*', she thought. '*I am a captain, not some mere damsel*'. "I thank you twice," she replied, "Once for each compliment."

Wenman smiled; a smile Garret liked. The man could easily be the prototype for an English naval captain. His long, dirty-blonde hair was tied in a knot behind his neck. He had a chiseled jaw, full eyebrows, and hazel green eyes. Though not dressed in uniform, he carried himself with the dignity and confidence of an officer. He was of good height and stature. Garret noticed his blouse fit rather tightly at his chest and hung loosely over his abdomen. She sensed that beneath his garments he was well-fit. His leather doublet was unbuttoned, an obvious effort to appear casual.

Wenman reached inside the doublet. "The Queen asked that I deliver this to you, in person. I understand it is of great importance."

"I imagine so," said Garret, grasping the sealed parchment. She placed it inside her own doublet. "Will you join us for a cup of port?"

"It would be my pleasure."

Garret turned to Scorpio, "You are such a fine lookout. Might I ask you to remain on deck while we converse?" Scorpio appeared disappointed but nodded agreement; the rest proceeded to Garret's cabin.

"Please, have a seat gentlemen." Garret gathered three silver cups and placed them on the heavy oak table. She unplugged a fresh ceramic jar of port and poured the dark liquid into each cup, finishing with her own. She raised hers. "To good health and good fortune."

"Queen and Country," Wenman responded.

"To all four," volunteered William.

After taking a sip, Garret sat, placing her cup on the table. "Tell us, Captain, what news of England?"

"The news is good, I believe," answered Wenman. "The war with Spain simmers but does not boil. Our allegiance with the Dutch grows stronger. Her Majesty presents herself in good spirits, though her health might claim otherwise, I am afraid. Those closest to her say her years as Queen have carved and rippled her face like a fallen pebble on water. She wears potions caked to her face like white mortar to stone. Still, the beauty of her personage shines through; emotionally and socially."

"I have fond memories of my meetings with her," offered Garret.

"As does she," confirmed Wenman. "She wishes you might be her guest again soon."

Garret wasn't certain how to take that. The last time she'd been on English soil, the Queen had her imprisoned. She wondered whether by 'guest', the Queen meant 'prisoner'. She supposed she would find out soon enough once she unsealed and opened the message.

"Garret and I are most anxious to learn what message Her Majesty has sent," William interjected.

Wenman raised his eyebrows. Garret noticed, guessing he was surprised that William hadn't addressed her as 'Captain'. "It is fine," she assured him. "William and I first met as mids aboard Drake's *Pelican*," she pointed out. "Having come a long way together, we are now the best of friends. We choose to use our first names when meeting in private."

Wenman bore a curious look. Garret clarified, "Best of…*friends,*" she emphasized.

It was William's turn to have his face involuntarily emote. Garret understood. She sensed his feelings for her ran deeper than those of mere friends, yet there was a line both were hesitant to cross. William took another sip of port, a longer sip than usual.

"Well," said Garret, patting her doublet within which was the letter, "we shall soon see what Her Majesty has in mind." She looked at William, "Unfortunately, the heart of the puzzle is missing, leaving a rather deep hole."

Seemingly ignoring her comment, Wenman shifted focus, "I should love to see more of your ship, Captain. Would you favor me with a tour?"

"By all means, as soon as we finish our port. I hate to let it sit."

"Yes, of course," replied Wenman. "It lives to be tasted. A fine selection, I might add." He held his cup aloft, nodding charmingly at Garret.

———

Captain Wenman awoke in Blair's cabin. He and William had spent the night onboard *Pandora*, the result of an excessive intake of port. His head throbbing, he rubbed his temples and swung out of the hammock. He recalled that Garret, too, had downed her fair share of port; perhaps more than she was used to. He'd taken advantage of that, and of William's need to relieve himself. He remembered moving in close and running his hand along Garret's arm, telling her she was the most amazing young woman he'd ever come across…on any land or ship upon which he'd set foot. She followed his comment with a demure smile, noting she was flattered and looked forward to…hearing more? of his…stories? travels? thoughts? In that moment, he was so pleased she hadn't withdrawn from his approach that he didn't pay full attention to her actual words. '*Unfortunate*,' he thought as he buttoned his blouse. Also unfortunate…Garret hadn't disclosed the contents of the Queen's letter. Hopefully she might, at breakfast.

William's knock interrupted his thoughts. "Are you up?"

"I am," he called out, stepping into his trousers. "A moment please."

"With Captain Connachan's compliments, you are invited to join us in her quarters."

"Excellent. I shall be there shortly."

Everyone lingered at the table after finishing their meal. Scorpio turned to Captain Wenman, "Will you be here long?"

"If by 'here' you mean onboard *Pandora*, the answer is no. But if you mean here on the island…" he turned Garret's way, smiling, "then my answer depends entirely on the Captain's needs and wishes."

"You are too kind, Captain," Garret responded. "I shall let you know what need I have of your services."

Wenman immediately hoped 'services' was sexual innuendo. "As you wish," he replied. He had hoped his response to Scorpio's question might prompt discussion regarding the contents of the Queen's letter. It hadn't.

William pushed back and rose from the table. "Thank you for breakfast, Garret. Our longboat has returned. We shall disembark shortly. Come the morrow, Mr. Blair and I shall return to discuss the readiness of your new residence."

Garret rose. "Excellent. Scorpio and I are anxious to go ashore."

Wenman followed William's signal, though not happily. He reached for Garret's hand, pulling the back of it toward him. "Thank you for your hospitality, Captain. You are most kind." He kissed the hand gently. Leisurely. Garret blushed. William rolled his eyes.

"Till the morrow, then," said William, placing his hat on his head and nodding at Garret.

"Till the morrow, William."

Once on deck, Wenman turned to William. "Odd that she made no mention of the Queen's letter."

"It is entirely her decision whether to share its contents."

"Just so. Perhaps I can be of assistance in providing any support she may need in acting on the Queen's orders."

"I have no doubt she will inform you if your assistance is required," William replied. The two descended into the waiting longboat.

"Push away, then," ordered the lead oarsman.

William pondered Wenman's curiosity regarding the letter. He hadn't shared that Garret let him read it before Wenman even awoke…

Dearest Captain Connachan,

Please be assured that your actions in the matter at hand have in no way pained me. Your comment regarding the growth of our empire in the West is well-founded. The exchange you suggest is one I shall pursue with our Spanish acquaintance. In the meantime, please remain safe. Further word shall be forthcoming.

It was precisely what he and Garret hoped for—the Queen no longer held Garret's actions regarding Viceroy Jorge Valdez against her. Though Her Majesty no doubt feared Garret's returning the Viceroy to England would implicate both her and her realm in the kidnapping, she now understood Garret's reasoning—King Philip might willingly provide England a possession in the Southern Seas in return for the release of his close friend. Of course there was now one major problem—the Viceroy's mercy death…by Garret's own hand.

William was aware Garret's relationship with Jorge had turned intimate. Ending his life must have been extremely difficult for her. Ironically, she ended up being the very assassin the Queen initially commissioned her to be. But with the Viceroy's death foreclosing any possibility of an exchange with King Philip, William and Garret worried the Queen would be waving a false flag by engaging with the King regarding such a trade. Best she stop waving. Immediately.

As they watched the longboat boat pull away, Scorpio turned to Garret. "Captain Wenman kissed your hand." It seemed more question than comment.

"Tis a common gesture."

"Does he love you, then?"

Garret laughed. "No, dearest. Tis a mere greeting when a gentleman meets or leaves a lady."

"But he seemed to take enjoyment in it." Again, more question than statement. It made Garret pause. Her interactions with Wenman were primarily captain-to-captain…though she did recall his display of interest in her the prior evening. *'It is not a favorable time,'* she thought. Still grieving Jorge's death, she wasn't ready for yet another relationship. Nevertheless, she recognized she now had three deep passions—sailing the oceans, drawing blood in battle, and enjoying intimacy with attractive men. The first of these was at the very core of who she was. The second was something she felt discomfited by but couldn't deny. The third was a guilty pleasure. And while she couldn't envision having a relationship with Wenman, she could definitely envision indulging her third passion with him.

VI

Ayudante Vegas was announced by Ortega's manservant, Abeo, the well-groomed Black man with the polished presence who managed his staff.

"Come," said Ortega. "Join me in my reading room." As he and Vegas took chairs, Abeo closed the door but kept his ear to it. He understood his master was a consummate dealmaker. Gleaning information about his dealings had proven valuable in the past…and might now. Though the conversation was muffled, Abeo knew enough to grasp the essence of what was being said rather than concentrate on every word.

"I trust you have brought the initial payment," said Ortega.

"Seventy-five hundred pieces of eight," replied Vegas. "My driver is delivering the chest to the rear entrance." He handed Ortega the key.

"Bueno. Muy Bueno," Ortega nodded.

"And the proof?"

"Unfortunately, that may take a few days. I suggest you delay your return to Spain." Though Ortega already had the honey jar containing the Viceroy's ear, he wanted Vegas to believe it would take time for his fictitious intermediary to connect with those supposedly holding the Viceroy. That would minimize any implication of his direct involvement.

"This is unacceptable Señor Ortega. The General awaits me."

"I am sure he does," Ortega responded, unperturbed. "And he will most assuredly commend you for waiting to obtain proof of the

Viceroy's life."

"Within the week, then," replied Vegas.

"We shall see," said Ortega, laughing inside at the would-be insistence of this mere middleman. In time, the man would pay dearly for such misbehavior. "I shall send word," he added loudly, waving his hand dismissively.

Abeo suspected the meeting within the study had ended. He stepped away smartly down the hall and around the corner.

Vegas exited the study and closed the door, sensing movement in the hallway. Nothing was there when he turned to look. He walked to the foyer, where Abeo ushered him out. Vegas looked at the slave wonderingly, not trusting him. He stepped outside. His driver was by the coach. Vegas lifted his head, questioningly. The driver nodded affirmatively.

As Vegas' coach pulled away, Ortega headed down the hallway to the villa's rear entrance. He opened the door and spotted the chest. "Abeo," he called out.

The man came running. "Si Señor."

"Find my guards." He pointed to the chest. "They will know what to do with this."

"Si." Abeo turned and rushed to find Ortega's two personal bodyguards. They were part of a larger team but unquestionably the most trusted.

Ortega smiled. Step one complete, he thought. He returned to his study, closing and locking the door. He walked to the bookcase, removed a heavy book, and grabbed onto the handle hidden behind it. Pulling hard, he opened the narrow shelving unit at the end of the bookcase. He squeezed through the opening, onto the landing behind, then lit the lantern hanging on a hook on the stone wall. He turned to close and lock the shelving unit before pulling the lantern off the hook. Carrying it high, he descended a dozen creaking wooden steps and traversed the cavernous tunnel. It ran six hundred feet, well beyond the rear of his main yard and gardens and into a heavily wooded area.

At the tunnel's end, Ortega ascended the steps, placing the lantern on another hook. He withdrew a key and unlocked the door that was similarly disguised on the other side as the end-section of a shelving unit. Grabbing the lantern, he entered the hidden storehouse containing many of his valuables.

The building was made of hard-packed earth, coated with a thick plaster of green-died lime. It was six yards wide and six long. The main door, through which his guards would bring the Ayudante's chest, contained multiple locks. He opened them and removed an iron crossbar. After exiting the door, he awaited the chest's arrival.

Ortega took in the soft, non-flowering vines covering the storehouse, making it almost invisible at a glance. Initially, they were too small to provide cover, so he'd chosen the green die to match the surrounding foliage. The color hardly mattered now that the vine had overgrown the building.

Ortega recalled the secret construction of the tunnel and building some fifteen years ago. The slaves involved had been segregated from all others during the project. Following completion, they were given poisoned beer to drink in celebration. Their bodies were buried in the woods not far from the storehouse. The building's location was now known only by his two most trusted, and handsomely paid, guards. There was no exterior handle on the door, and no way to open it from the outside. Ortega had installed the intricate set of interior locks and the crossbar to be doubly certain no one could ever enter the storehouse except through the private tunnel in his study.

Looking down the barely trodden path that wound through the woods, he smiled at his good sense in building this storehouse. It would forever remain his secret and special place.

VII

[Reminder Warning: This chapter includes a graphic description of a brutal punishment called 'keelhauling'. Some readers may prefer to skip over or quick-scan it.]

The *Santo de Cristo's* crew never saw it coming. During the dogwatch, their young lookout cruised in and out of sleep. In truth, his waking moments were only ever a handful of drowsy seconds.

Heavy clouds had enabled *Death's Head*, its sails darkened, to stealthily approach within a hundred yards of the *Santo de Cristo*. Two longboats and two smaller vessels bore twenty-five blackened-face pyrates toward the merchant ship. It floated low in the water, suggesting heavy cargo. The pyrates shared grins fueled by visions of soon-to-be-claimed treasure.

The best climbers scaled the ship's sides first, bearing grappling hooks secured to climbing nets. Reaching the top, they attached the hooks and spread the netting wide. The remaining pyrates, all barefoot, secured the boats to the netting and scrambled up the mesh, hanging just below the taffrail. At De Graaf's signal, they hurdled the rail and flowed onto the deck, swarming like armed fire ants. They found it devoid of crewmen, save for a heavily snoring helmsman who had earlier secured the ship's wheel, there being little wind and the sails fully furled. The man's dreams were abruptly ended for all time.

One of the pyrates ascended the mainmast to dispense with the lookout; it took only a moment. The remaining pyrates assembled behind Master's Mate Stevens at the entry to the crew's quarters.

De Graaf took two men with him to the officers' cabins. Having not shed blood in a while, he felt a pressing need to make a bold statement. With dagger in hand, he quietly tested the door to the captain's cabin. It was unlocked. His two men checked the cabin of the master's mate. It, too, was unsecured. De Graaf nodded and they breached the respective cabins.

One pyrate remained by the door of the master's mate's cabin while his partner deftly drew his blade across the officer's throat, followed by a soft gurgle of bubbling blood.

De Graaf approached the captain's bed and placed his dagger lightly at the man's throat, leaning in toward his face. He snapped the fingers of his left hand near the man's ear, to awaken him. Captain Jimenez' eyes opened slowly. His mind appeared to muddle through a thick fog of questions. Holding a finger to his mouth to indicate Jimenez should remain quiet, De Graaf prodded him to exit his hammock.

The Captain was completely naked. De Graaf laughed at the irony of the imagery. Not only was the man without clothes but he would soon be without ship, cargo, crew, and…life. He walked Jimenez toward the main deck, his dagger at the man's back. As they stepped onto the deck, Stevens' horde took it as their signal. They quietly descended into the dark quarters.

The crew slept almost side-by-side in gently swinging hammocks. The pyrates slithered among them like vipers. One man awoke. He jerked upward to gather his weapon. A short pike entered his chest. Most of the crew were hastily gouged and slaughtered without resistance. A handful were taken prisoner.

The pyrates and prisoners soon climbed the stairs, exiting the blood-soaked quarters. Captain Jimenez, held firmly by two pyrates, looked on. The raiders gathered round, their cutlasses still dripping blood. They assembled in silence, awaiting orders.

De Graaf grinned as he scanned his crew. "What bloody mess is this?" he yelled. The men laughed and cheered, thrusting their cutlasses high.

As the cheering dissipated, De Graaf called out another question, "Do we have enough prisoners to help us sail this prize?"

"Aye, we do," shouted one of the pyrates.

De Graaf pointed his cutlass at Jimenez, whose pants were soiled at the crotch. "Then I suppose we have no need of this sorry mess."

"Por favor," Jimenez pleaded, dropping to his knees. "Mi familia…mis hijos." Tears streamed down his face.

De Graaf was undaunted. He wanted this moment to be unforgettable—a tale his men would tell over and over until their death; a story no one could ever cleanse from their memory after hearing it. He'd planned an ending that two aging Dutch mariners had shared with him years ago. "Attach the blocks to the main yard," he shouted.

Pyrates quickly ascended the mainmast. They mounted pulleys at each end of the yardarm, ensuring they were properly secured before pulling the rope through. Stevens took one end of the rope and wrapped it around the sobbing captain. It was double looped under his arms, strapped over each shoulder, wound through each side of his groin, and tied to his wrists with a Carrick knot. De Graaf checked the knot. It wasn't going anywhere. He scanned his men's faces. "For ten pieces of eight," he shouted, "who will bring the other end of this rope 'round the keel?"

Few of the pyrates could swim. One stepped forward. "I will."

The volunteer stripped off his shirt and secured the rope to his waist before climbing the taffrail. He leaped feet-first, splashing into the water below. Bobbing up, he treaded water for a moment to regain normal breathing. He then took one deep breath, humped his back and went down headfirst, feet kicking furiously behind.

Heading to the ship's bottom he carefully avoided the calcified barnacles covering much of the vessel's underside. Pulling hard at the water, he continued kicking vigorously, fighting the tendency of the air in his lungs to propel him upward. Finally reaching the keel, his body begged for air. He pushed firmly against the keel, propelling himself upward but scraping his foot badly, leaving a trail of blood behind. His ascent up the other side was rapid. He breached the surface gasping for air. His fellow pyrates, looking down over the taffrail, erupted in cheers. He grabbed the netting that had been lowered and scrambled up and over the rail, onto the deck. His mates patted him on the back, once again cheering his effort.

De Graaf approached the swimmer. "Good man," he said, handing over the hard-earned pieces of eight. He turned to the crowd, pointing his cutlass toward Jimenez. "Now, let us see how well this Captain makes the turn."

The swimmer handed the now-unfastened rope to another man, who threaded it through the pulley and then secured it to a screaming Captain Jimenez with a second Carrick knot. De Graaf checked the knots; there could be no failure. Both proved secure. He nodded to the two men holding the sniveling captain.

"Curse you all!" screeched Jimenez as they wrestled him to the rail. In a moment he was hoisted up and pushed over the edge. The rope spun hard through the pulleys as he went in, head first, the water drowning his screams.

Several well-rasped hands pulled the rope, dragging Jimenez down the ship's side. Scraping along the barnacles and rough wood, his skin was savagely ripped away. He hit the keel, dislocating his shoulder. The pain forced his mouth open. His lungs gasped for air, in exchange for which they were instead flooded with salt water. Blood streamed away from every inch of his body as he was pulled roughly up the other side, scraping once more against rugged wood and hard-shelled barnacles. His skin peeled off in strips.

The bloodied slab of raw, sea-salted meat that was once Captain Jimenez, was hoisted out of the water and jerked up to the taffrail. Two men grappled the slippery red hulk and hoisted it over the rail. It fell to the deck in a squelching thump, unrecognizable as human. The soul that was still Captain Jimenez floated imperceptibly above the raw assemblage of roped-together limbs, organs and waste. Many of the crew chose to look away.

Now ready to place a defining cap on all the theater, De Graaf walked slowly toward the bloody heap. He planted his boot on what was once a man's back. It sunk in, oozing more blood onto the deck. He drew his cutlass, thrusting it high in the air and shouting the message he wanted delivered to every shore touching this ocean, "Let it be known this day—any man who dares challenge the pyrate De Graaf will drown in his own blood."

VIII

Business was buzzing in Isla Tortuga. The recent arrival of an unusual number of pyrates and privateers placed robust dark-market supplies in the hands of local merchants, leading to increased demand for the best food and alcohol, the finest clothing, new building materials, and other goods. Local establishments strained to cope with the heightened activity. The owner of the Gente de Mar, the man who called himself Prince, had arranged for several large boulders and rough-sawn wooden tables to be placed on the street outside his inn. They served as additional seating to capture the tavern's overflow.

Yosel, now beholden to Garret Connachan, sat on one of the new boulders, a tankard of grog in hand. As members of the crew of *Cutthroat*—De Graaf's original ship but now his consort—Yosel and his mates had remained in Isla Tortuga during the pyrate captain's visit to an undisclosed port [Santo Pedro]. A couple of crewmates were seated with him, enjoying their free time. The hot sun, accompanied by the stingiest of sea breezes, amplified the humidity…and the men's thirst. Their principal activity was drinking and spending away their freshly acquired treasure. Yosel, however, was different. Though he could barely pyrate with the least of them, he was everyone's intellectual superior. And he was no drunk. He was acutely focused on accumulating and securing wealth. In time, he hoped to establish a normal life in one of the larger cities—Cartageña perhaps. Or Sant Iago. He envisioned becoming a legitimate merchant, with a villa in the hills, a buxom wife, and a staff of servants. His gambling skills, honed to perfection through endless games of dice and cards, proved most helpful in transferring the wealth of his crewmates to his own account.

He cursed the drunken sailor who'd falsely accused him of cheating and nearly forced his drowning. But he'd put that incident behind him, now seeing the blessing in it. There was potential profit in serving as Captain Connachan's eyes and ears within De Graaf's pyrate horde. He could lean on his street-smarts and listening skills to acquire information Connachan would value. In time, he believed sailing with her might be more pleasant than pirating with the fiery and unpredictable De Graaf…at least until he could afford the city life he dreamed of.

A heavy-set, scantily clad woman strolled out of the Gente de Mar onto the street. Her mere presence suggested the competition inside the tavern itself was too fierce. Approaching Yosel and his mates, she placed her hands under her largely exposed breasts, giving them added prominence. One of the men grabbed her by the arm, pulling her onto his lap.

"Shiver me privates," she remarked, "you appear to have an offering for me." The pyrates laughed. One spewed out the grog he was drinking in a shower-like stream.

"I be bringin' ye a more than ample offering, wench," replied the sailor.

"Well then, I should like to see the proof of that." More laughter and snickering.

"Oh, ye shall see it all right; and then wish it were the same with all men."

She rose from his lap, pulling him away toward the tavern door.

"He shall pay a fair piece for that one," said Yosel.

"Especially when she discovers he be lying to her," laughed the grog-spewer.

The lighthearted interruption had distracted Yosel's thoughts. He now turned to thinking how best to acquire intelligence for Connachan. The first step was clear—finding his way onto De Graaf's flagship, rather than remaining among the consort's crew. *Death's Head's* inner circle was where the desired intelligence resided.

———

It was quiet in the tavern at Santo Pedro; much quieter than when De Graaf last met the Phantom here. News of Harker's demise and the Viceroy's disappearance had grown stale. In its absence, there was no longer a compelling rush to gather and converse. There were only a few patrons present, none of whom looked familiar to De Graaf, although they certainly recognized him.

He nursed his tankard of grog while awaiting the appearance of his partner in the ransom scheme. With the Phantom on his side, De Graaf liked his chances of a large payoff. Harker had insisted the man was savvy in the ways of generating wealth.

Slowly, inconspicuously, he reached into the left side of his doublet, confirming the ring was still there. It had been a month since he'd handed over the Viceroy's preserved ear, which was already serving as false proof of the man's existence. It would also assure the King of their supposed sincerity in ending the already-dead-man's life.

Ortega arrived shortly, accompanied by two guards. He entered alone. As always, the guards remained outside, keeping watch for undesirables. Ortega preferred not to be surprised by the appearance of Spanish soldiers.

Spotting De Graaf, Ortega hailed the server for a tankard of beer. No fan of it, especially the watered-down version in this place, he felt it necessary when presenting himself as an ordinary seaman. He took a seat across from De Graaf. They proceeded to speak in their customary code so that no one within earshot would comprehend the true nature of their discussion.

There was one item of transactional information Ortega didn't plan to share—his receipt of the initial payment from Ayudante Vegas in exchange for the Viceroy's ear. His mission today was simply to take possession of the Viceroy's ring. "You brought the piece?" he asked.

De Graaf patted the right side of his doublet. The ring was on the left side but he'd decided that, at this point, he didn't want even the Phantom to know its exact location. Trust needed to be earned.

"Good," Ortega nodded back. "I too have something of value." The remark drew De Graaf's full attention. "I have sent word to our friend in Spain, along with the honey jar." [The jar containing the Viceroy's preserved ear.] "I trust we shall soon receive what we seek."

The owner brought Ortega his tankard. He took a swallow. The taste was a little weakened, as expected. He actually respected the tavern owner for that. After all, business was slow; the owner had to make money somehow. Ortega slid a silver piece onto the table. The owner took it and left.

"How soon?" asked De Graaf.

"The seas and skies set the table."

"Just so." De Graaf paused. "I shall await your notice."

"Shall I again send it to Isla Tortuga?"

"Yes. Prince will see that I get it."

"I have heard this man is a pompous ass. Perhaps not the most trustworthy of messengers."

"You know him well," De Graaf grinned. "But he fears me."

Ortega sipped his grog. "I shall need the piece [meaning the ring], as further proof."

"It is secure with me."

"If we wish to expedite our business, I must have it in hand when the messenger returns from Spain. Our Spanish friend will want it immediately…and pay handsomely for it."

"How handsomely?"

Ortega placed his left hand on the table, spreading out all four fingers and the thumb, suggesting five thousand pieces of eight. He'd told Ayudante Vegas the captors wanted fifteen thousand for the ear alone but De Graaf didn't need to know that.

"I shall need my portion up-front."

"Half now, half when the transaction closes."

De Graaf mulled it over. That was a little more than a thousand up-front. "Fifteen now. The balance later."

"That, sir, is well more than half. Thirteen now," Ortega countered, "twelve later."

The look on De Graaf's face suggested he was proud of having out-negotiated him. But Ortega smiled inwardly. This man was no Harker when it came to negotiations. De Graaf had simply accepted at face value that the ring was only worth five thousand. Ortega made a mental note to take full advantage of the man's naivety in the future.

The two men shook hands. They would leave the tavern separately but meet within two hours at their usual hidden cove, to exchange thirteen hundred pieces of eight for the Viceroy's ring.

———

"Damnation!" he swore as the messenger left in haste. King Philip shook his head at the stream of conflicting news regarding Viceroy Jorge Valdez de Barragan's disappearance. The military reported weeks ago that Valdez was captured by Englishmen. Later rumors emanating from the Southern Seas suggested he was slain.

A letter from Queen Elizabeth claimed she held a 'prize' she would consider offering up in exchange for English rights to Las Virgenes islands. Though originally claimed for Spain by Cristobal Colon ['Columbus'], no meaningful presence had yet been established there. Elizabeth's phrase—*'a friend of Your Majesty'*—suggested the 'prize' was Viceroy Valdez. That was consistent with his military's claim of English captors. But prior to the Queen's letter, a message purportedly from Jorge himself arrived compliments of a man called 'Prince' on Isla Tortuga. Unfortunately, it lacked clarity…

Your Majesty, and my dearest friend,

I trust you are aware of my recent capture. I cannot apologize deeply enough, nor fully explain the shame I feel for having let you down in this manner. But I wish to inform you that I am well and being treated fairly by my captors. They have expressed a willingness to negotiate my freedom in exchange for certain considerations from you. Should you be willing to engage, please respond in the affirmative. Details shall follow.

For King and Country,

JVdeB

Philip wished Jorge had been more explicit concerning his captors. Were they indeed English? And were these 'considerations' he referred to the Las Virgenes islands suggested by Queen Elizabeth? He thought that likely. Yet the messenger had just announced the arrival of an Ayudante from Cartageña, who claimed the Viceroy was being held by *pyrates*. For ransom. They'd sliced off and sent the Viceroy's ear as proof. He'd asked whether there was a notch in the ear. Evidently, there was. Still, there was no certainty it was Jorge's. It could have been notched purposely to match his. He needed further proof of the pyrates' claim. And if they were indeed his captors, then why would Jorge have written that they were treating him fairly?

Philip contemplated how best to find the truth. But whatever the case, Jorge was likely still alive. Perhaps he was initially held by the Queen's minions, then later captured by the pyrates—something Elizabeth might not have known when quilling her letter.

The only other possibility, assuming Valdez wasn't already dead, was that these pyrates simply knew the Viceroy was being held by the English and were setting up their own ruse.

Ultimately, he would ensure the Viceroy's return, no matter the cost. After all, the unlimited stream of gold and silver from the Southern Seas easily covered all his needs and desires.

Philip sat at his desk, signing the third of three messages. The first had been sent previously to Queen Elizabeth, expressing his openness to her proposed exchange. The second, to his General, authorized him to pay the fifteen thousand pieces of eight the pyrates demanded. He offered even more for additional proof that they held Valdez—specifically, the ring he'd given Jorge upon assigning him

Military Viceroy for the Southern Seas. A further payment would be made for the Viceroy's return.

This third letter, just initialed, was his response to Jorge…

My Dear Friend,

I am in receipt of your recent letter. There is no need for shame. Your people have informed me of the circumstances of your detainment. While it troubles me to learn of your present situation, I am pleased to hear there is a path forward. I welcome a specific proposal from your new associates. However, to ensure that I am dealing with you, and not some imposter, please include in your response a description of the item I gave you when last we met.

For España,

P

This letter would be sent to Prince, on Isla Tortuga. If Valdez were alive, and received the letter, he would know the item to which Philip was referring was the ring.

All three balls would now be in play. Philip smiled—the truth would soon show itself like a true maiden on her first bedding.

IX

Tropical rain and an accompanying wind were particularly bothersome this day. Garett and Scorpio entered their newly completed residence soaking wet, shedding their coats. William Tovery and James Wenman followed, as did the men carrying chests containing Garret's and Scorpio's belongings.

Master's Mate Blair had earlier set a fire, to warm the place for their arrival. He nodded to Garret. "Welcome, Captain. I am pleased to present the fine work of my construction crew."

"I love this place," interjected Scorpio.

"As you should," replied Garret. She turned to Blair. "You and your men have done exceptional work," she said, scanning the masonry and woodworking. The place had a comforting feel.

"Thank you, sir." Blair waved his arms. "The living space is designed for food preparation and reading. There are modest separate quarters for you and the girl, and for the cook."

"How thoughtful. Thank you, kindly." Garret had no plans for the cook to live in the residence but didn't mention it.

"I am pleased you approve. Captain Tovery's residence is alongside and will be completed within days. No provision has been made for Captain Wenman, however. He was not in our plans."

"'Not to worry, Mr. Blair. Captain Wenman may use the cook's quarters."

Wenman smiled. William frowned.

"As you wish," nodded Blair. "Good day, then. I shall be available if you need anything."

"Excellent. Thank you again. And please, pass along my thanks to your men. Feel free to give them a day of revelry…upon completion of Captain Tovery's residence, of course," she nodded toward William.

Blair nodded and left.

"Well William," Garret opened, "what think you?"

"I believe you and Scorpio should have exclusive use of this place. Captain Wenman can share *my* residence."

It wasn't the response Garret expected. Clearly, William wasn't pleased by her offer to house Wenman. "Of course," she replied. She looked at Wenman, who appeared a little perturbed. He nodded a resigned acceptance.

"A cup of port, gentlemen?"

"Better than stepping back into the rain," replied William.

"Agreed," said Wenman, moving toward the table. He pulled back a chair. "Will you join us at the table, Scorpi?"

Garret smiled at the man's thoughtfulness. William rolled his eyes. Scorpio took the chair. William opened a chest, withdrawing a corked olive jar and three pewter tankards.

Wenman pulled out a chair for Garret. William placed the tankards, uncorked the container and poured the port. As he sat, Garret raised her tankard. "To an abundant life in the new world. And to those who make it so."

William and Wenman raised their tankards. "To abundance and the men," responded William.

"To *you*, Garret, for making it so," offered Wenman, smiling.

William again rolled his eyes, turning his head. The three drew heartily from their cups.

"Shall we discuss the import…" A loud, repeated knock at the door interrupted. "…of the Queen's message?" asked Wenman.

"Enter, if you please," said Garret.

"Sorry to bother you, sir," said the messenger. "De Graaf's ship has arrived."

———

The bitter, gray cold of the northern sea blasted him with a biting crosswind. Ayudante de Campo Vegas hated the oceans. He wished his current military assignment would end. Though the Caribbean islands and Spanish Main were beautiful, the frequent traversal of treacherous waters between there and Spain churned the contents of his stomach. Longing for the stability of dry land, he would seek to terminate this misery once the King's major construction projects in Cartageña neared an end.

An earlier opportunity might arise at the conclusion of this ransom business. Perhaps Señor Ortega might reward him by offering a role as his security advisor. He was well equipped to protect the old man's interests and activities, surely more so than his current guards.

Vegas' sources in Cartageña claimed Ortega was known as 'Sombra' Ortega (the Shadow) for his under-the-table dealings. There was even speculation he was the man known offshore as 'Fantasma'. But there was no proof; anyone conducting business with such a man was unlikely to out him. And Ortega was surrounded by fiercely loyal men. It was as though an invisible shield masked his every move.

It concerned Vegas that Ortega might actually be more than just an intermediary in this ransom scheme. He might well be the instigator. But again, there was no proof. And frankly, Vegas didn't care. As long as he got something in return, he would let it all play out.

As for the transaction itself, Vegas hoped Ortega could

negotiate a lesser payment to the Viceroy's captors than what he was now delivering on the King's behalf. Perhaps the shadowy Cartageñian might split the remainder with him.

Ocean spray, propelled by a sudden surge of wind, showered Vegas. He cursed the oceans and headed below deck.

———

Death's Head's arrival spawned a frenzy of activity on Isla Tortuga. Villagers streamed to the shore, anxious for the stories and treasures these arriving pyrates would share. Yosel was among the onlookers. In preparation for De Graaf's return, he'd paid Prince, to write the pyrate captain a specific message, and let him deliver it…

Captain De Graaf,

In honor of your return, I offer my finest beer and fairest maiden for your pleasure, at my expense. Perhaps we might discuss the purchase of your cargo.

Your most humble servant,

Prince

Gente de Mar

Yosel had also paid Prince for the beer and maiden…for good reason; delivering the message would give him access to De Graaf. And with that, he sought to negotiate his transfer from the pyrate's consort ship, *Cutthroat*, to his flagship. It would better position him to obtain intelligence for Captain Connachan, who promised to reimburse his expenses.

De Graaf and Master's Mate Stevens walked toward the village center. Yosel jostled through the surrounding crowd, hailing De Graaf loudly, "Captain. A moment, if you please."

De Graaf stopped to look in the direction of the sharp voice rising above the crowd's hum. A tall, skinny man with a rough, graying beard approached waving a folded piece of parchment. The sailor looked familiar. As Yosel pushed through, Stevens stepped between them, shielding his Captain.

"I have a message for you," Yosel said, looking first to De Graaf and then at Stevens. "From Prince." De Graaf didn't react. "May I read it to you?"

De Graaf looked around, then nodded to Stevens.

"Back off!" Stevens yelled to the crowd. "Now, you bastards."

Men began shoving away. De Graaf waited until there was sufficient space. He turned to Yosel, "Proceed."

Yosel broke the seal. He glanced at Stevens before opening the note and then looked to De Graaf.

"He can hear it," nodded De Graaf.

"If I may, sir," Yosel began. When he was done reading, De Graaf smiled and thanked him.

"One more thing, Captain, if you please."

"What is it then?"

"I have valuable skills to offer. As you see, I can read the written word. I also have experience managing accounts. I sail on *Cutthroat* but welcome an offer to join you on *Death's Head*.

De Graaf studied this brash man's face. "Where are you from?"

"Born in the islands. My father fled Portugal when I was young. I speak Portuguese. Spanish too."

"A Jew?" De Graaf asked, thinking it likely—many had fled Portugal, and this man had the look.

"I am, yes."

"Converso?"

"I practice no religion, believing only in a man's right to be free."

"How long have you sailed with my crew?"

"Long enough, sir."

De Graaf looked to Stevens, "Do you know this man?"

"I know *of* him. Others call him the skinny Jew. They say he be smarter than most."

De Graaf returned his gaze to Yosel. The man claimed to be skilled with numbers and was arguably smart. He wondered whether the Jew might prove valuable in his dealings with the Phantom. He grinned, "How much will you pay me to serve on my ship?"

"My first share," Yosel offered without hesitation.

"So be it. Make note of it, Mr. Stevens."

"Aye."

As the men walked on, De Graaf soaked in the crowd's admiration, Prince's generosity, and the thought that others might pay handsomely to serve with his crew. For the first time, he felt like the new ruler of this emerging pyrate world…taking Harker's crown.

X

It was the first time she'd been allowed to use a real sword. Countless lessons with a wooden prop had finally earned her this opportunity. Scorpio held the weapon with both hands. The hilt was warm to the touch, having sat in the sun. She gripped it carefully, never taking her eye off the target—a papaya atop a tree stump. The objective was to slice through it completely, without it tumbling ungraciously off the stump. The sweep of the razor-sharp blade needed to be perfectly horizontal, at high speed.

Confident and focused, Scorpio didn't intend to disappoint Garret. Legs wide and stable, knees bent, she held the sword back to her right side. She aligned her right wrist perfectly with her forearm, at the precise height of the papaya's center. She locked her left elbow, took a slow breath and held it for a split second. Head steady and torso stable, she began her swing and blew out her breath, twisting her hips. Her eyes watched the slicing sword decapitate the target. The papaya's upper half spun skyward, with speed. The bottom half momentarily wobbled on the stump, and then rolled off slowly.

Her sword now motionless and level on her left side, Scorpio didn't move—except for her eyes; they turned slowly toward Garret. A grin escaped. Her mentor nodded, with obvious pride. Scorpio relaxed. She repositioned the sword in front of her, placing its point on the ground and both hands atop its hilt.

"I believe I am ready, Captain."

"Ready for what, Scorpi?"

"For the defense of my country!"

"Good answer," Garret replied.

"May we eat now?"

"I suppose you have earned that."

"I believe I have also earned the right to be called Scorpio."

"Oh," remarked Garret, recognizing her shortened moniker for the girl suddenly seemed childish. "Of course you have." She paused. "Perhaps you might prefer a different name altogether. Tis certainly your right."

"I shall think on it," Scorpio replied.

As they headed indoors, Garret's mind dialed back to the day she'd wielded a wooden sword against her grandfather's and sent his flying. The very next thing she'd done was tell him she was hungry. The joy of that experience touched her now as though she was reliving the moment. She could feel Grandfather Daniel's presence…and love.

William walked in as Garret and Scorpio lunched. "Best of the day, Garret. You as well, Scorpi." The girl grimaced at the name. William grabbed a chair and sat. "I have given much thought to our dilemma. No doubt you have as well."

"Indeed," replied Garret.

"We cannot mislead Her Majesty about the Viceroy's death." Garret concurred. "But suppose we engage her in a modest deception?"

"The thought has crossed my mind. Quite risky, I venture."

"Just so. But hear me out."

"Of course."

"We inform her that the Viceroy has perished at the hand of pyrates. She may well have heard that by the time our message reaches her. But perhaps she might join us in suggesting to King Philip that there is word Jorge may still be alive. Would that not create an opening for further dialog? And could we not then offer the King our services in getting to the truth of the matter? Would there not be value in that, even if the unfortunate truth is later confirmed…by us?"

"Your thoughts have traveled further than mine." Garret paused to think. "The idea has merit. But perhaps we are best served by offering both Her Majesty and the King our services in capturing the person responsible for the Viceroy's death."

Garret noted William's look of bewilderment. "Yes, of course," she acknowledged, "he died a mercy-death at my hand. Yet no one but you, Scorpio, Musa and Caber know that. The Viceroy's deadly wounds were already inflicted by De Graaf." She leaned back. "Surely we can attach blame to *his* bloody hand."

William nodded repeatedly as he took this in. "I suspect De Graaf believes Jorge died by his hand anyway."

"No doubt," agreed Garret. After a moment, she changed direction, "There is one thing I have not yet shared with you."

"Which is?"

"Jorge's ring—the one given him by King Philip." Garret paused to let that sink in.

"Do you have it?"

"Jorge's forearm was separated in the course of battle. The ring was gone when I found his hand. De Graaf must have slipped it off and taken it with him."

William shook his head. "The bastard."

"Just so. Perhaps if we can recover the ring, we would have a valuable prize for Her Majesty to return to the King."

"A most desirous outcome…*if* we could pull it off."

"Then let us plan for it, William."

"Shall we invite Captain Wenman to our planning? He seems most anxious to know what is going on."

"Do you trust him?"

William paused. "I am…uncertain."

Garret noticed his hesitation. "Is there something more?"

William met her eyes. "I fear he may have designs on you."

"How so?" Garret asked, though well aware of Wenman's interest; he'd made subtle overtures whenever they met. And frankly, she welcomed them. He was a handsome man who was, unknowingly, helping her recover from the loss of Jorge. She selfishly wanted more of Wenman's attention—though not necessarily romantically.

"He asks many questions about you. And your relationships with others."

"What others?"

"Specifically…me."

"I see." Garret wished to end that line of discussion. Her feelings for William were still evolving—from colleague, to friend, to close friend, to near-brother, to potentially something more. It was the 'more' she couldn't define. In truth, she was trying to bury it, recognizing that further progression might well disrupt relations with their crew. Again, she changed course, "Do you think he can help us?"

"Besides carrying our message back to the Queen?"

"Yes."

"Perhaps…if we are to engage De Graaf."

"Just so."

"We shall first need to receive the Queen's response."

"Then let us keep Wenman close." As she said it, Garret

envisioned Wenman's strong arms wrapped around her body. The thought was more carnal than loving, and she knew it. Wenman was a plaything. A good one.

"Indeed," replied William, disrupting her thoughts. "But in your case, not too close."

___

As he left, William sensed that Garret had clearly taken a liking to Wenman. He decided he no longer liked or trusted the man—he was an impediment to his own relationship with Garret.

___

Standing on the porch of his Cartageñian villa, Señor Ortega breathed in the sounds of construction that daily serenaded the residents of this growing city. For him, it was the music of money. Every tool, every piece of wood, everything that delivered stone, all the food and supplies the workers consumed...*all* of it added to his growing purse. Money flowed down on him like a waterfall, bringing immeasurable joy. He sensed this was how King Philip himself must feel, but without all the stress the King had in fighting both political and physical wars. Surely Philip would envy *his* life.

Looking out over the sun-drenched harbor, Ortega raised his silver cup, carefully sipping the koffei. As its major exporter to all ports in the Spanish empire and beyond, the beans' explosive popularity was adding nicely to his treasurehouse. Next to slaves, koffei ranked alongside the more profitable products he distributed, like molasses, beer and sugar cane.

The barking of dogs momentarily broke his train of thought. His thinking turned to another love...intrigue. And right now, the most intriguing activity was the possibility of separating King Philip from some of his personal wealth by leading him to believe his precious Viceroy was still alive, and available for purchase. This was like playing cards with the King. Besting Philip by winning this hand would bring a level of joy paralleling that of his koffei's gold.

Surveying the harbor was now a daily ritual as Ortega impatiently awaited the return of Ayudante Vegas, his go-between in the ransom scheme. Every ship entering the harbor raised his hopes that it might deal him the trump cards in this royal game.

In the meantime, he needed to finalize how to dispose of Vegas once the transaction was complete. He believed his best option was to have De Graaf assault him on open water. That would leave no trace back to him personally. But then eliminating the pyrate—the only other man with intimate knowledge of the scheme—was even more challenging. De Graaf was feared by everyone, including his own crew. Perhaps for the right price, an ambitious and capable pyrate who coveted De Graaf's crown would undertake his assassination. Ortega felt one of his trusted guards could infiltrate Isla Tortuga to find such a pyrate. It warranted further consideration.

———

"Good morning, fair lady," said Captain Wenman. "I see you are well-armed. Might I pass?"

Scorpio smiled at him, "You may, good sir." She brought her shining sword to her side, placing the point in the dirt and leaning on it slightly with her right hand. She waved toward the house with her left. It was now common for the handsome young Captain to visit at this time of day. Though she personally favored William, she understood how Garret would be attracted to this chivalrous navy man.

"Thank you, kindly," Wenman smiled back. He approached and knocked on Garret's door. "Wenman here."

"Enter."

Wenman opened the door, pleased to see Garret from behind, standing in a sheer silk night-dress, gazing out the window. The streaming light disclosed the curvature of her form and highlighted her auburn hair. He'd never seen her looking so vulnerable. Not averting his eyes, he quietly closed the door. "You are a most pleasing vision, m'lady."

Garret turned slowly. He watched the image beneath the silk unfold differently. Delightfully. Her nipples pressed pointedly against the delicate fabric, as if targeting him. "A true gentleman might redirect his glance," she toyed with him.

"A true gentleman might be unable to."

"Then perhaps he must pay a price for his naughtiness."

Wenman quietly secured the door, not wanting Scorpio to inadvertently surprise them. He advanced toward Garret. "Any price, my fairest. You need only name it."

Garret grinned at Wenman's emerging rise. "I believe the last time you came, you promised a story of your exploits."

"Military? Or personal?"

"Choose carefully."

"Military then," he smiled. "It involves the worthiness of my sword."

"Please, share it with me." She moved toward him.

"Tis made of the finest material," he said softly.

"I have no doubt."

Garret was now face-to-face with him. That rugged, handsome face with the dark eyes. She placed her hand softly on his thigh and moved it gently toward the item in question. She felt it stir. "It appears to have a mind of its own," she said, smiling up at him.

He pulled her close, pressing her firm buttocks with both hands. "It wishes me to engage."

"By all means then. Engage."

XI

The Gente de Mar hummed with a level of activity suggesting village residents were up and active. William Tovery arrived at the tavern alongside Musa and Caber. The three were respected, though not always trusted, by the brigands who frequented the place. Some had sailed alongside them under Admiral Drake.

The trio was unlikely to suffer from any differences the pyrates might have with them. Musa's imposing size, and his reputation as an executioner, gave men pause. But it was his constant companion, the black-handled axe with its long string of notches, that delivered the most visual warning. And Caber's enormous bulk, combined with the red-headed Scotsman's fiery temper, left any would-be combatants preferring to keep their distance.

Though muscled and strong, William wasn't as physically imposing as his companions. Still, he was known for his skill with a cutlass—perhaps second only to the surprising Captain Connachan, who was supposedly among England's finest swordsmen. Many, however, doubted a mere woman was worthy of such acclaim.

William was here to see Prince. He hadn't yet heard from the tavern owner regarding Viceroy Valdez' message to the King. The man was paid handsomely to arrange its delivery. William's eyes connected with those of Prince's niece, Catherine—the server. She came quickly forward, having taken a liking to the virile young privateer. "Welcome, Captain. A tankard of beer?"

"Perhaps for these two," he said, nodding toward Musa and Caber. "I prefer a visit with your uncle." The girl pouted behind smiling eyes and nodded toward the stairs.

"Wait here," William said to his mates. He ascended quickly and knocked on the door behind which Prince conducted his business. "Captain Tovery here."

"Enter, if you please."

As he walked in, a caramel-skinned tavern girl rose from Prince's lap, wearing nothing above her waist. "I apologize for interrupting." William looked directly at Prince, to avoid staring at the young woman.

"Not at all, sir," replied Prince, hoisting his trousers.

The woman pulled her blouse from the floor but didn't bother putting it on as she walked to the door. She winked at William and blew him a kiss. Prince was not in a position to notice.

William turned briefly to watch the woman leave before turning back to Prince, "I am most anxious to learn of any response to the letter you were paid to deliver."

"As am I, Captain. In fact, the second payment for its arrival is foremost in my mind. So you can appreciate my own interest in it."

"Of course. But having heard nothing, you can understand why I might wonder whether you have taken me for the fool."

"Not in the least, sir. No, I assure you, I have not. The letter was sent on a fine merchant ship the day after your payment. I have little doubt we shall soon have a reply."

William probed further. "Have others inquired about the nature of our business?"

Prince paused briefly. "No. The matter is private."

"Excellent. Then I shall continue to wait, though not patiently."

"I understand," Prince confirmed.

"What ship shall I expect to arrive with the King's reply?"

Prince appeared reluctant to say. "The *Federico*," he whispered. "A three-masted merchant. Captain Suarez."

"Thank you." William turned to leave.

"If you see my lady friend," called Prince, "ask her to rejoin me. Her visits bring more pleasure than those of others."

As William left, Prince recalled his long-ago visit with Harker and De Graaf, who'd paid him for information about Captain Tovery's business. He'd chosen not to disclose that to William; no good could come of it. Besides, Harker was now dead, so it hardly mattered.

Descending the stairs, William thought about the next steps. The King's response to the Viceroy's letter, if it came at all, would give Garret an open line of communication to Philip. That held promise. She could choose to inform him of the circumstances of the Viceroy's death and offer her services in bringing De Graaf to justice. No doubt the Queen would vouch for Garret's integrity. But the sequencing of Garret's messages back to the Queen, and to King Philip, would require careful orchestration.

The caramel-skinned woman who'd earlier left Prince's room bumped into William near the bottom of the stairs, her blouse parted to her navel. "Pardon me," she smiled, "Might I be of service?"

William smiled back. She smelled fresh. He knew that was more mask than reality. Despite the temptation, he couldn't shake the thought of her having been with Prince. He nodded up the stairs. "His majesty anxiously awaits your return."

The woman frowned, drawing back her blouse to expose the taught nipple of her right breast. "He will be done shortly. Shall I save you some?"

"Just be well," William replied. For her sake, he hoped she might one day find joy in something other than her current calling. As she pressed softly against him, he brushed by, headed to where Musa and Caber sat drinking.

———

From his table at the back of the Gente de Mar, De Graaf watched Captain Willam Tovery exit the tavern with Musa and Caber. His stomach turned at the presence of these men in what he regarded as his personal pyrate village. He didn't think Tovery had spotted him through the crowd but fully expected his two henchmen would let him know he was there. He didn't care. He had no fear of these three. Even if they knew he'd participated in the assault on *Pandora*, there wasn't much they could do about it; they were outnumbered by his men.

As for Tovery's commander—Garret Connachan, he was sure that he and the Phantom could lay blame for Viceroy Valdez' death at her feet, and then claim a nice fee from the King for her capture.

De Graaf looked at Yosel, who sat across the table drinking beer. The Jew's intelligence and street smarts had proved helpful these past few days. He seemed to know most of the crew personally…and what they were thinking. Tapping that information would help identify any crewmen who might be a threat to overthrow him. He had no interest in putting up with such malcontents. He knew the type; he and Harker were of that same ilk.

Yosel's skill at math might also prove helpful. The more he thought about his last meeting with the Phantom, the more he believed the Cartagenian had undervalued his services in their ransom scheme.

He hoped to reopen that discussion at their upcoming meeting. Having Yosel there might lead to a better outcome.

He scanned the tavern to ensure no one was listening, then leaned toward Yosel, "I welcome your thinking on a matter of great concern." Yosel leaned in. "Understand…this is between you and me alone. If word leaks, you will find yourself missing a cherished appendage."

"You have my word."

"Good. Now then, I have a business partner." He paused to sip his beer. "We are negotiating over…certain goods I possess. This man has valuable connections to the lone buyer, though not directly."

"Have you agreed how to share the proceeds?"

"Not fully. What say you?"

"Do you intend to share equally?"

"Yes."

"I presume you have certain expenses—maintaining the security of the goods, for example."

De Graaf's thoughts turned to the Viceroy. The man was dead. The ransom was based on the myth that he was still alive. There was no expense in that…or in securing the Viceroy's ring. "No," he responded.

"Surely you had such expenses at some point?"

De Graaf shook his head, no.

Yosel looked surprised but continued, "Is your partner aware of that?"

"Perhaps not."

"Then might we *suggest* to him that you paid for the storage and protection of the goods in question?" De Graaf knew that wouldn't work. Again, he shook his head.

"What about transportation of the goods?"

De Graaf appreciated Yosel's exploration of the possibilities but knew he couldn't justify expenses of that kind. "None."

"What about the cost of *acquiring* these goods?"

'*Indeed,*' thought De Graaf. The acquisition cost was high. Eight of his finest men gave their lives assaulting *Pandora*. He needed to secure replacements—though the skills of those he lost couldn't possibly be matched. What's more, some of the deceased had rare skills (carpentry came to mind). Such replacements might well demand above-normal shares of any treasure. He answered Yosel's question, "Those costs were high."

"Then you have the right to recover them from the proceeds, before the calculation of shares."

"Just so," exclaimed De Graaf, smiling. He patted Yosel on the shoulder heartily. "You are a good man." They bumped tankards and drank.

———

He hated to leave Isla Tortuga. He'd come to deliver the Queen's message to Captain Connachan but unexpectedly found himself deeply drawn to the young privateer. Their relationship had stretched beyond amorous—turning physical, though such moments seemed too few and too fleeting. The presence of the girl, Scorpio, prevented anything more. Still, he had a duty to perform. Carrying Garret's message back to Her Majesty was time sensitive.

To Wenman's chagrin, Garret hadn't shared with him the contents of either the Queen's message or her own sealed response. He hadn't pressed her on it, not wishing to jeopardize their relationship.

Still, he was perplexed—what could be so important that she wouldn't share it? It underlined just how much Garret was in control—of both him *and* their interactions. Was she truly in love with him or simply using him for unknown purposes? The irony of the latter grated him. He came here thinking he might have to seduce her, to learn the contents of the Queen's message; yet she may well have turned the tables, seducing *him* for her own pleasures. If that were the case, then bully for her—she was a powerful woman with high intellect and master skills. Especially in the hammock.

Standing at the stern, grasping the taffrail, Wenman watched Isla Tortuga sink into the horizon. He vowed to return, and quickly. If the Queen's business with Garret was important enough to send him to the South Seas as her private messenger, then surely she would have him return to Tortuga immediately with her response to Garret's letter.

"Full sails, Lieutenant," he called out to Ward. "Let us beat the wind."

A vessel appeared in the distance, seemingly headed toward the Windward Passage. Wenman ordered the firing of a single cannon shot to acknowledge the ship's presence, without implying any harm. In human terms, it was a mere wave hello.

After a minute or two, the Spanish ship responded. It was headed to Cartageña, carrying Ayudante de Campo Vegas…and fifteen thousand pieces of eight from King Philip, for the purchase of Viceroy Valdez' ring. The two ships were virtual cousins—both bearing items coincidentally linked to the Viceroy.

Ayudante Vegas watched the distant, fully sheeted *Mercilus* meld with the horizon. His own ship was also fully sheeted. *"The world moves at a rapid pace,"* he thought, *"though too slow for my liking."*

He looked forward to his upcoming visit with Señor Ortega, also rumored to be the man known as 'Fantasma'. He was confident he might purchase the Viceroy's ring from Ortega for much less than King Philip authorized. He would suggest to Ortega that they settle on a lesser 'official' amount for the ring, and then split the balance of the King's funds. Ortega would then have no choice but to support Vegas' later claim to his superiors that all fifteen thousand pieces of eight had been spent on the ring. Surely Ortega would go along with the plan…yielding a handsome payday for both of them. He expected to gain some goodwill with Ortega in the process.

XII

In the days following Captain Wenman's departure with Garret's letter to the Queen, William encouraged Garret to leave her residence and enjoy some of what the village had to offer. For too long, he thought, she hadn't ventured much beyond where the construction crews were building their residences—work she reviewed regularly. It would soon be completed.

He noted that the balance of her time was spent schooling Scorpio on everything from navigation, mathematics, languages and philosophy, to the military arts. She'd turned down his offers to visit the pulsing heart of the village—the Gente de Mar tavern, where her men engaged in all manner of social activities. She claimed no interest in witnessing the sad state of affairs of the women there, trading bodily favors for money. She'd also expressed concern over exposing Scorpio to pyrate culture.

Nonetheless, William persisted, claiming the crew needed to see her as one of them, rather than aloof and above the fray. And though he hadn't told her, he knew the men were growing restless. They were sailors, not home-builders, with a preference for pillaging treasure from Spanish ships and villages. The further removed from that they were, the more restless they were becoming. William hoped that by mingling with the men in the taverns, Garret might pick up on those signals herself, without his raising the issue.

Deep down, he worried Garret's inner nature was not to pillage at all. But unless she wanted to make an ongoing life *here*, as a hollow citizen in this meaningless village, she needed to start planning a fresh hunt for treasure.

He'd found some solace in her having agreed to visit the town center on one occasion, to shop in the few local stores. But she hadn't agreed to join him at the Gente de Mar. Until now.

On the path toward town, the two captains were trailed by Caber. Garret was comforted by Musa's staying behind with Scorpio, to further her training. The girl had no experience handling an axe, and who better to teach her than the man whose mastery of the weapon was obvious from the parallel rows of notches on its handle? One row reflected deaths in battle; the other commemorated executions for which Musa was handsomely paid by English authorities.

"Has De Graaf been seen in the village recently?" asked Garret. She'd heard the pyrate's reputation was recently embellished by his capture of a Spanish merchant, during which he dispatched its captain in the most gruesome of ways…a 'keelhauling', they called it.

"Yes," replied William, "The tavern may well be his base of command when not onboard ship."

"And yet, he has made no attempt to threaten you or our crew."

"Not surprising, really. Unless provoked, he maintains a certain calm; like his mentor, Harker. 'Tis the method of the lizard—complete stillness before the strike."

"If he is there when we arrive, he may be challenged to maintain his calm, knowing that I took Harker's life."

"Perhaps. But Harker's demise has boosted De Graaf to the top of this piratical heap. Besides, the assault on *Pandora* was initiated by Harker, not you. You simply proved to be the superior warrior."

"I shall have difficulty maintaining my own composure. His attack on Jorge was savage and unforgivable. At some point, he must pay for that."

"I have no doubt he will. But I assure you, any confrontation between you will not be by surprise, nor in the tavern. The unwritten code of pyrates calls for open and fair battle between captains, and would-be captains, to determine leadership of a crew."

"I am not looking to lead his crew."

"Of course not. Yet some of his men once sailed with the Admiral and recognize you as a formidable privateer. They may be open to following you instead."

"Follow a woman?" Garret prodded, as a reminder that most sailors regarded women onboard ship as a bad omen.

"You have proven yourself, Garret. Both during and after sailing with Drake." They reached the edge of the town square. William continued, "My bigger fear is that some drunken pyrate who never sailed with Drake, nor knows of your exploits, might choose to challenge you. If so, Caber and I shall deal with him."

"Would that not suggest I am incapable of defending myself?"

William stopped walking and faced her. "You are a leader, Garret. Men expect that those loyal to you will deal with threatening behavior by others. Your own actions should be limited to dealing with other leaders, not lesser miscreants."

Within moments, the three found themselves entering the Gente de Mar, drawing a murmur among its patrons. Garret wore her green bandana, a beige-colored blouse, a leather doublet, and off-white trousers. She'd purposely left her blouse sufficiently open to make it clear she was a woman, but not enough to arouse the men. She sought to demonstrate that women were more than mere sexual objects. Her cutlass was in evidence and she'd tucked a sheathed dagger into the rope holding her trousers in place. She looked as much a pyrate as any in the tavern, though her clothes were cleaner, and in better condition.

Catherine approached. The pretty young server was now a constant presence in her Uncle Prince's tavern, though not one of its 'geese'. That was the tag sailors used when referring to tavern-women who tended to flock around them, for money.

"Welcome, Captain Connachan," said Cath. "I have heard much about you. Tis a pleasure to serve you. What will ye have?"

Garret was surprised the girl knew who she was. Apparently, her reputation traveled well. "Beer, if you please."

"A moment, then," said Cath, turning and walking to a broad wooden counter near the back.

Four men at a table rose, offering up their seats. Garret didn't notice; she was scanning for De Graaf. The men rising were members of William's crew. He nodded his thanks and motioned Garret toward the table. She ended her scan and moved that way.

It was only a moment before Cath arrived with a container of beer and three tankards. Having noticed Captain Connachan scanning the room, the girl sensed she might be searching for De Graaf. She was aware of their rivalry. "The Black pyrate is not here, Captain," she offered quietly. "Not at the moment."

Garret was amused by the server's intuition. "You are very observant," she noted.

"I am told you are as well. Perhaps we have that in common."

Garret withdrew a gold coin and placed it in the girl's palm. She held her hand for a moment, feeling a sense of empathy for her. "If you ever need my assistance, you need only get word to my crew."

"Thank you, Captain."

"Call me Garret."

"Thank you, Garret."

"And you are?"

"Catherine. Most call me Cath."

"Tis the name of a princess."

"Perhaps princess only of this tavern," she grinned.

Most of the men had turned silent, focusing on the young woman who'd vaulted to the highest level in the world of privateers. Some held her in awe. Others believed the rumor that she'd simply seduced Admiral Drake to gain her captaincy. And some believed, as Harker had, that she was actually a witch, not only seducing Drake but also toying with his mind.

Garret sipped her beer and once again scanned the room. She made eye contact with several onlookers. Most, in turn, averted their own eyes. Those who knew her simply nodded.

She raised her tankard high. "Please, gentlemen," she called out, "continue to make merry."

The hearty buzz of conversation soon resumed. William leaned forward. "As I said, nothing of consequence will occur here in the tavern."

"Not so, William," she chided. "That young server may well prove to be an asset, in time. That alone is of some consequence."

———

Every time he entered Señor Ortega's villa, Ayudante Vegas was awed by the audacious display of opulence. Twenty-foot-high pillars framed the entryway of the grand building. Inside, the floors were made of polished Italian marble, while the staircase to the second level curved upward from both sides of the foyer. Large artworks meandered colorfully along the walls. Statuary of varying sizes were present throughout. In all his travels, he'd never seen anything like it. He remined at the grand entry while Abeo, the manservant, went to inform Señor Ortega of his arrival. His thoughts turned to his strategy for negotiating the purchase of the Viceroy's ring.

Ortega himself strolled into the foyer with a presence that seemed to fill the room. "Welcome back, Ayudante," he announced in full voice, his smile stretching almost the width of his face. "Tis wonderful to see you again."

Vegas sensed the man's joyous attitude reflected his nearness to the money he was about to receive. "Thank you, Señor Ortega. The pleasure is mine."

Ortega draped his arm across Vegas' shoulders, "I trust you bring good news. And perhaps something more," he winked.

"I have indeed. Our Spanish friend was in good spirits."

"Excellent. Please," Ortega responded, pointing his arm down the hallway, "join me in my reading room."

After the two men entered Ortega's study, Abeo closed the door and placed his ear against it, to decipher the conversation.

Ortega filled a silver cup with fine port and handed it to Vegas, who sat across the desk. The moneyman filled his own cup and pulled back his ornate, high-platformed chair. Vegas recognized the elevated chair provided Ortega a power-position; his height advantage could make any guest feel inferior—especially those lacking strength of character or some other source of power.

Ortega raised his cup. "Salud!" The Ayudante responded in kind. Ortega sat. "Where shall we begin?"

"The King has agreed to payment of a ransom."

"Excellent."

"Still, he questioned whether the ear we delivered is in fact that of Viceroy Valdez. He wants further proof that the Viceroy is being held by those with whom you speak." He was careful not to say, 'those *for* whom you speak', though he half-suspected that was the case.

"A wise decision," Ortega nodded.

"In particular, the King wishes to see the ring he gave Señor Valdez when appointing him Military Viceroy for the South Seas. If these captors hold the Viceroy, then surely they have the ring."

"Most assuredly," Ortega replied.

"Then you believe they have it." It was a statement, not a question.

"We shall find out, shall we not?"

"Indeed."

"Pray tell, what price will the King pay?"

"Up to ten thousand pieces of eight." Vegas worried that might be a little low to start the negotiation, but he wanted as much room as possible to work with.

"That is unlikely to prove fruitful," sneered Ortega.

"How so?"

"These men apparently put their very lives at risk to capture the Viceroy. They may view such a paltry offer as a gesture of bad faith."

"This payment is only for the ring itself. The King will put forward an additional payment for the Viceroy's release."

"You are an intelligent man, Ayudante. Yet I wonder at your

understanding of men who would do such a thing as this. They are not likely to be patient. And they are clearly ruthless." Ortega sipped his port. "If the King's offer insults them, they may well send him yet another…more meaningful…piece of the Viceroy's body."

Vegas shuddered at the thought. "I see." He sipped his port. "What amount do you believe would avoid insulting them?"

"As we discussed previously—fifteen thousand."

Vegas already had the King's approval to pay that amount. Still, he wanted to show strength. And dialing down that number would leave him a pile of discretionary money. "With all due respect, Señor, the King himself is not a patient man." He leaned back. "He is fully capable of inflicting revenge on those who would cross him."

"A powerful man, no question," Ortega replied. He offered nothing further. Vegas understood why—offering a lesser amount would undermine his negotiating advantage.

"Certainly a man with such fine skills as yours can negotiate without risking further harm to the Viceroy."

"My skills serve me well in the merchant trade but are untested when working through channels to present an offer to vicious men."

Vegas nodded. "Fair point." He could see Ortega was no fool. The man was clearly well prepared. Perhaps a subtle slight of Ortega's abilities was in order. "Considering how such constraints severely diminish your skills, what amount do you believe is in order."

Ortega frowned. "Choose your words carefully, Ayudante." He sipped more port. "Perhaps I might counsel them that twelve thousand pieces of eight is a generous price."

"*If* they have the ring," Vegas responded, emphasizing the word 'if' to test Ortega's reaction. He increasingly sensed the man was more closely aligned with the captors than he was letting on.

"Indeed…*if*. But I shall need a reserve, in the event this amount is unacceptable."

Vegas stood fast, "The King has authorized no more than ten thousand pieces of eight."

"So you have said. But surely the King is willing to pay more. If not, you would have begun the negotiation at a lesser amount."

Vegas flashed a smirk to suggest he still held the upper hand. "Well played, Señor." He raised his tankard as if to toast Ortega. "It is as though you were bargaining for yourself, rather than on behalf of the Viceroy's captors."

Ortega leaped from his chair, planting his hands firmly on the desk. "I resent your insinuation! I am merely assisting the King. If you are to make such accusations, then I must insist on dealing with someone of higher standing. Your General, perhaps."

Vegas realized he'd pushed too far, reminding himself that he hoped to ultimately come through this with Ortega's longer-term support. He rose slowly. "I meant no offense, Señor. It was an ill-advised attempt on my part to counter your obvious negotiating skills."

The tension hung heavily before Ortega responded, "I accept your apology." He retook his seat. Vegas mirrored that.

"Twelve thousand pieces of eight then," the Ayudante nodded, taking another sip of the port. An exceptionally fine port, he thought. "Now, at the risk of losing my commission for sharing this—His Majesty has authorized up to fifteen thousand. I feel I must return with some portion, to assure him I have negotiated well." Ortega appeared perturbed but seemed to understand. Vegas continued, "If I may be so bold, I propose we split any remaining balance. You may consider your portion as payment for your valued assistance in the matter. But we shall need to be aligned on what the actual purchase price was." He sensed that his implication they defraud the King was not a hindrance.

Ortega rose, extending his hand. "We are agreed, then. I shall do my best."

Vegas rose, accepting the hand. "Excellent. I shall await the ring's delivery."

After Vegas left, Ortega remained at his desk, reflecting on both the discussion and the Ayudante. He hadn't liked Vegas' suggestion that his negotiating skills with the Viceroy's abductors had limited range. Nor did he appreciate the man's tone. Still, he might need the Ayudante's services if he were to later obtain additional payment for the Viceroy's release—despite the fact that the Viceroy was already dead.

If needed, he believed he could ultimately pin blame for the Viceroy's death on the Ayudante, suggesting the man's insistence on offering less than the full fifteen thousand was the basis for the pyrates' decision to execute Valdez.

On the whole, the meeting's outcome brought some comfort. De Graaf had already agreed to only twenty-five hundred pieces of eight to deliver the ring. The Ayudante would soon deliver several times that amount…to his great benefit. He leaned back, draining his cup of port.

Ayudante Vegas' mood was buoyant as his coach pulled away from Ortega's villa. Keeping payment for the ring to twelve thousand meant he could split close to three thousand with Ortega…and score beneficial points with the man. Word of the lesser payment would never reach King Philip. After all, Ortega just accepted a bribe; he needed to be discreet.

Having had his ear to the door of the study the entire time, Abeo gave the Ayudante credit for his skill in negotiating with Ortega—the finest practitioner of the art. But he himself now had valuable information for which others might pay well…perhaps affording him the ability to orchestrate his freedom. But who those payors might be, and how to find them, were questions for which he needed answers.

XIII

Dark, lumbering clouds pinned heat and humidity close to the ground as they entered the aging shoreside village of Santo Pedro. Yosel walked alongside De Graaf in silence, carefully observing the rag-tag place. The putrid scent of aging fish wafted by on a light breeze as they neared the tavern. "The fish move more slowly here than they do in the water," he chuckled. De Graaf laughed.

Despite the surroundings, Yosel looked forward to meeting the man De Graaf referred to as 'the Phantom'. Hiding behind that moniker suggested he might actually be well-known across the islands. Or perhaps well-connected. Maybe both. It promised to be an interesting afternoon.

The first droplets of rain and an uptick in the wind portended a coming storm. De Graaf hoped that wouldn't delay the Phantom's arrival. He knew the suspicious Cartagenian wouldn't be pleased that he'd brought someone with him. It hardly mattered, though; he wanted Yosel at his side. The Jew had helped him prepare for this negotiation.

De Graaf was surprised to find the Phantom's two bodyguards already posted outside the tavern door. He was used to waiting for the man. In keeping with their shared desire to maintain privacy, De Graaf didn't acknowledge the guards. He made only brief eye contact.

Stepping inside, De Graaf scanned the dimness. Finding the Phantom seated at a table in the rear nursing a tankard, he signaled the barman and proceeded there. Yosel followed. Ortega nodded hello, saying nothing.

There was only one open chair, which De Graaf pulled back.

Yosel pulled one from a nearby table. Ortega studied the stranger.

"My crewmate," offered De Graaf. "Yosel."

"No names. Please," replied Ortega.

The barman brought two tankards of beer. De Graaf proffered payment. The man left.

"Any news?" De Graaf asked.

Ortega glanced at Yosel, hesitating. De Graaf noticed his discomfort. "Speak freely. Our conversation goes no further."

Per their custom, the two principals spoke in a primitive code.

"Our Spanish friend [King Philip] has put something forward. But less than we hoped," Ortega lied.

De Graaf wasn't pleased. The last time they'd met, the Phantom assured him they'd receive five thousand pieces of eight…and split them evenly. He'd been given thirteen hundred up-front; the remaining twelve to be paid upon delivery.

"Your second portion will be one-third less than agreed," said the Phantom. De Graaf couldn't do the math. He shook his head in wonder. Ortega clarified, "Seven hundred, not twelve."

The math was off. De Graaf felt Yosel nudge his foot but didn't openly react to the prod. He looked the Phantom in the eye. "You toy with me," he growled threateningly.

Ortega paused before leaning in. "A rounding, my good man. A mere rounding."

De Graaf let the Phantom's explanation hang in the air, unwilling to let him off easy. Yosel was right, he thought. The Jew had earlier suggested this skilled negotiator would not only attempt to reduce their previously agreed-upon payment, but that he'd also negotiate a more favorable payment from the King. De Graaf leaned forward, bringing their faces mere inches apart, "Do not attempt to play me the fool. It will bring your end."

Ortega pulled back. "You must understand…my dealings with merchants are generally for much larger amounts. We round-off liberally." He sipped his beer. "I apologize for any misunderstanding."

"I have no patience for your petty games. I shall accept nothing less than we agreed. In addition, I must cover my expenses in acquiring the 'stone' [the Viceroy's ring]. They are significant."

Ortega maintained his composure. "What expenses?"

"Nine men were involved. Eight did not return. I shall need another thousand, for restitution."

Ortega paused. His eyes turned to Yosel, accusingly. He took another sip of beer and returned his tankard to the table. "I, too, have expenses. The channel along which my word travels is hungry."

"Take those expenses from your share," De Graaf challenged. He watched the Phantom squirm and look to the door for his guards.

Ortega leaned back. "Let us not quibble," he said. "Twelve then, plus your expenses."

'*Yosel was right*', thought De Graaf. By giving into his demand, the Phantom unwittingly confirmed he'd negotiated a higher ransom from the King. "I misspoke," he said. "It should be two thousand for the eight men I am now missing."

Ortega hesitated. De Graaf raised his tankard, grinning menacingly. Ortega nodded, raising his tankard in agreement. He leaned back. "Let us discuss our next steps."

De Graaf short-circuited him, "I have a plan."

"By all means." Ortega waved his hand upward, inviting more details.

De Graaf leaned in, whispering. "We request a gift [additional payment] in exchange for the final prize [the Viceroy]. Once it arrives, we explain that the prize has expired—at the hand of an English pyrate. We offer to capture and hand over this pyrate in exchange for the gift."

"I shall think on that," Ortega replied. "Let us reconvene in one week to discuss it further. I shall bring your money at that time."

"I shall take it now."

"I do not carry such amounts with me."

De Graaf again felt the nudge of Yosel's foot. He organized his thoughts. "Twelve now, the expenses next week. Either that or my crew will accompany you home to collect full payment." He watched as the Phantom scanned the tavern, no doubt wondering whether any of the men inside might be part of De Graaf's crew.

"Twelve, then. At our usual place."

Ortega's guards followed as he left the tavern, greatly displeased with Yosel's involvement. The man had clearly influenced De Graaf's renegotiation. He was now just one more loose end to clean up after the ransom was concluded.

De Graaf and Yosel took possession of the Phantom's silver an hour later. It was a joyous moment, but for the unwelcome rain. They decided to return to the tavern. Their small boat with its rigged sail wasn't equipped to challenge storm-threatened seas. They hid the chest of silver and proceeded back to the village, drenched but happy.

"Your finest port," De Graaf called to the barman as he and Yosel retook the table they'd shared earlier with the Phantom. The barman brought two tankards, this time with a small olive jar containing port. He smiled at the payment. De Graaf filled both tankards and raised his toward Yosel. "To my consigliere," he said. "with whom I shall soon be floating in liquid gold."

Yosel raised his tankard. "To floating in gold," he nodded, his mind churning with mixed emotions. Though he shared De Graaf's joy, he pondered his obligation to Captain Connachan, the man's nemesis. He felt a certain closeness to the fine young woman for having saved his life weeks ago. Sharing the knowledge of De Graaf's plan with her would mean betraying his own captain. Yet he knew De Graaf could just as easily turn on him. '*C'est la vie*,' he thought. '*Loyalty flows in and out with the tides*.' He would savor this moment but his future wouldn't be clouded by it. He owed a debt to Connachan, not De Graaf. Besides, he had no desire to live a pyrate's life…bearing the promise of one day swinging from the gallows. No, he would be a merchant. Or perhaps a financier, much like the Phantom.

———

"We have word from the King," William announced, rushing through Garret's door without even a knock. He'd come straight from the Gente de Mar, where Prince had given him King Philip's letter in exchange for the second payment they'd agreed to. He handed Garret the unsealed letter—Philip's response to Viceroy Valdez' message indicating he was being held captive, though in good hands. That letter was intended to open the door to possible negotiations for his release. At the time Valdez wrote it, no one anticipated he'd be dead before the King's response arrived.

"Thank you, William," said Garret, taking hold of the letter.

She didn't share William's enthusiasm. The letter only brought a flood of memories of the man she'd loved. And she doubted its value at this point. Without Jorge to respond, she would need to enter direct communication with the King. That would be awkward.

Garret found herself holding back a tear, her emotions still unexpectedly raw. She turned away from William to hide her sorrow, broke the letter's seal, and opened it. Scanning it quickly, she observed that the King, just like Queen Elizabeth, was artfully vague.

My Dear Friend,

I am in receipt of your recent letter. There is no need for shame. Your people have informed me of the circumstances of your detainment. While it troubles me to learn of your present situation, I am pleased to hear there is a path forward. I welcome a specific proposal from your new associates. However, to ensure that I am dealing with you, and not some imposter, please include in your response a description of the item I gave you when last we met.

For España,

P

Garret knew 'the item' Philip referred to was the ring he'd given Jorge upon his appointment to Military Viceroy for the South Seas. Though not in her possession, she could easily describe it from memory, enabling her to move the dialogue forward…if she choose to. She turned back to William. "There is opportunity here, but we must await Her Majesty's guidance. Hopefully, Captain Wenman will deliver that shortly."

———

Queen Elizabeth sat sipping now-lukewarm tea while anticipating the arrival of Captain James Wenman, who had just returned from the South Seas. His timing was fortuitous, she thought. She recently received a response from King Philip to her own letter proposing an exchange of interests, wherein he indicated an openness to exchanging Las Vírgenes islands for the 'prize' she claimed to hold—Viceroy Valdez. But first, Philip insisted she send him the specific item he'd given 'his friend'. She had no idea what that item was. Surely Captain Connachan would know. Hopefully, she'd asked Wenman to deliver it.

"Captain Wenman, Your Majesty."

Elizabeth set down her cup and approved his admittance. Wenman entered the room where she privately received visitors. He bowed in a grand, sweeping gesture.

'What a fine specimen of a naval officer this captain is,' Elizabeth thought. The same thought struck her every time she saw the man. He was handsome, well-groomed, and had a commanding physical presence. It was, in part, why she originally chose him to deliver her message to Garret. She hoped the two might develop a working chemistry. Together, they were a powerful young couple of military advisors. She thought it best they meet each other and form a bond she could later exploit, in service of her beloved country.

"I thank you for your gracious acceptance of my audience, Your Majesty."

"Tis a pleasure to see you again, Captain. I trust you bring fair news."

Wenman approached, extending his hand. "I have this letter

from Captain Connachan. I am afraid I have no knowledge of its contents."

Elizabeth was mildly disappointed; Garret hadn't shared with Captain Wenman what she'd written. It suggested she didn't fully trust the man. Or was she simply being cautious?

Elizabeth accepted the letter, anxious to ask the question she needed answered. But, in light of Garret's own hesitation, she felt a need to be less direct than she might otherwise be, "It has come to my attention, Captain Wenman, that the principal in question had an item of special meaning to our Spanish friend."

Wenman shrugged his shoulders. "I apologize, Your Majesty. I do not understand."

"I see. That is unfortunate." She meant that in two ways. First, it meant he didn't have the item King Philip requested. Second, it confirmed her suspicion that Garret didn't trust Wenman. She was curious about the latter. "Tell me, what were your impressions of Captain Connachan?"

"I find her to be an exceptionally gifted young woman." '*In so very many ways,*' he thought to himself, recalling their most intimate moments.

"How so?"

"Her intelligence, of course," he replied. "Her thoughtfulness. The military prowess of which her crew speaks."

"Is that all?" Elizabeth smiled coyly, inviting Wenman to open up at a more personal level."

"Pardon the thought, Your Majesty…I must admit, I found her quite engaging."

"Engaging how?" She toyed with him. He blushed. She had her

answer, no matter his verbal response.

"A gentleman can never be certain how a woman feels," Wenman smiled, graciously.

Elizabeth laughed. "I have no doubt she was attracted to you, Captain."

"I shall accept your undue confidence in me," he nodded.

"Give me a moment while I see what this 'engaging' woman—as you refer to her—has written." Elizabeth broke the seal and opened the letter. She was pleased to see Garret was well versed in the art of choosing her words carefully.

Your Majesty,

I thank you for your understanding in this matter. I shall await your further instruction. However, I must inform you that our prize [inferring Viceroy Valdez] *has now expired. Prior to that, I had reviewed and approved a message the prize delivered to our Spanish friend* [meaning King Philip]. *Assurance was given of the condition of the prize at that time, and noted that further communication would follow regarding a possible exchange. Given current circumstances, the best I might offer in lieu of the prize itself, is the party responsible for its expiration.*

I remain your most humble of servants,

GC

Captain, Pandora

The news was discomforting. Elizabeth looked to Captain Wenman. Perhaps he could help Garret apprehend the perpetrator of the Viceroy's demise. His immediate return to Isla Tortuga was therefore crucial. She was certain he'd be more than happy to do just that, considering his just-shared feelings for the woman. "I have further need of your services, Captain." She folded the message. "It is most important that you return to Isla Tortuga post-haste. I shall shortly provide you my reply to Captain Connachan. You shall afford her any support she requires in executing the mission I shall assign her. Your later return to England will, therefore, be at her complete discretion."

"Understood, Your Majesty. I am more than happy to be at her discretion."

XIV

Having just seen Garret and William enter the tavern, Cath went to her tiny room in the back to retrieve a sealed message. She'd been handed it two days ago, here at the Gente de Mar, by a man she recognized but didn't know. He'd also given her two reales, asking that she discreetly deliver the message to Captain Connachan and maintain the secrecy of its existence.

Cath was a keen observer of the tavern's patrons. This man was noteworthy for his interactions. Unlike most regulars, who came and left with the same crewmates, this one sat table with anyone and everyone. He differed from his pyrate brethren in other ways as well—taller, thinner, less muscled, more intelligent, and surprisingly well-spoken. An intriguing man, she thought. He hadn't shared his name but she'd heard others refer to him as 'The Jew'.

She tucked the note inside her blouse and reentered the busy main room. Garret and William were seated near the center, along with the large red-headed man others referred to as Caber—his real name was difficult to pronounce, or even recall. She poured three tankards of beer and headed their way.

A drunken, burly pyrate grabbed her arm as she passed, causing some spillage. "I shall have one of those," he said, gruffly.

"They are for someone else, good sir."

"Let them wait." He pulled her arm toward him.

Spillage be damned, Cath thought. She showered the beer onto his heavily bearded face like a frontal wave. He arched back awkwardly, unsuccessfully avoiding the spray. His crewmates at the table laughed uproariously. "I hope you enjoyed your beer," Cath said.

"I shall collect your payment when I return." His mates laughed even harder.

Confident she had enough friends here to keep the drunk from retaliating, Cath continued to Garret's table. She smiled as she set down the two remaining tankards, "There was a small storm along the way. I am afraid I had to unload some cargo."

"I imagine that particular storm has a small thundercloud," Garret smirked. The metaphor sailed innocently past the young server.

"From a man whose name I do not know," Cath whispered, cautiously drawing Yosel's letter from her blouse and leaning it against the tankard. She turned and left, thinking it best to draw away the attention of any onlookers. Garret stealthily slipped the note inside her doublet and sipped her beer.

A rustling noise preceded the high-pitched shriek that sliced through thick tavernous air. The drunk Cath showered moments earlier now held her arm angled up tightly against her back. Garret sprang from her chair, causing it to fall back hard against the ground. She rushed to the girl's aid. "Unhand her, you fool," she instructed the richly muscled drunkard.

The pyrate looked menacingly at Garret as Cath grimaced in pain. "What business is it of yours?" He slurred his words. The tavern quickly turned silent.

"You shall find out soon enough. Unhand the girl."

The drunkard let Cath go, his anger now focused on Garret. His grin suggested he welcomed the opportunity to show her how strong men handle foolish women. He stepped toward her, emphasizing his significant advantage in size and weight. Those nearby noisily pushed back tables and chairs to make room. Caber and William were now standing. William placed his arm against the barrel-chested redhead.

Garret recognized the man as one of De Graaf's crew. She sensed she was on her own. William or Caber's involvement would lead to an all-out brawl, which could easily end badly, her friends being seriously outnumbered by De Graaf's men.

"I take no orders from witches," the man growled. He spat on the ground. "I prefer to have my way with them." His mates laughed.

Garret maintained eye contact, her mind racing through options. The man's legs were too close together to permit hard contact with his groin. The lessons of the old colonel, who'd spent countless hours training her, suggested her next best target was the throat. She began speaking to distract the drunkard while seamlessly folding the fingers of her right hand, readying the knuckles.

"Witches or no…" Garret never intended to finish the sentence. As the man listened, she cast her forearm in the direction of his neck. Her knuckles crushed his larynx with lightning speed. His eyes went wide as he choked, staggered backward, and thrust his hands to his neck in a chaotic dance. Drawing her dagger with her left hand, Garret stepped forward, sweeping the butt end crushingly into the drunkard's temple. He crumpled to the floor in a heap.

With the room virtually lit by the whites of patrons' eyes, Garret stood atop her opponent. She pressed her boot hard on his neck. "Witches or no," she repeated, "we have *our* ways."

The bastard lay barely conscious. Garret reached down, pulling his dagger from his pants and withdrawing his cutlass. "Here is how witches have their way with reckless men," she said, driving her boot hard against his testicles. The men who saw it cringed and groaned as the drunk wailed in agony.

"Now then," Garret said to Cath, "might we have our third tankard?"

———

Back in her cabin, Garret pulled the note Cath had given her from her doublet and laid it on the table. She didn't recognize the seal.

Scorpio drew near. "Who is it from?"

"We shall see in a moment."

"I have decided," Scorpio redirected.

"Decided what?"

"My name. You told me I might choose one."

"Of course I did," Garret reassured her. She was surprised the girl had acted on it so quickly it. "What have you chosen?"

"I was reading about the French noblewoman who lived two centuries ago—Jeanne de Clisson. She turned pyrate to avenge her husband's execution."

"Just so."

"They called her the 'Lioness of Brittany'."

"They did indeed."

"I should like to be a Lyonesse—Lyonesse de Tortuga," she exclaimed, slashing an imaginary sword high in the air.

Garret smiled. "A member of the cat family. Kat for short, then?"

"Well, to you and our friends, I shall just be 'Kat'! En garde!" the girl responded, taking a fighting stance and pointing her would-be sword at Garret. Hint taken, Garret drew her own invisible cutlass. They maneuvered, thrusted, parried, and laughed their way around the small residence, not hearing the knock at the door.

William entered amid the chaos of the faux battle, "I hope I am not interrupting your lesson."

Garret and Kat nodded a good-humored truce.

William looked to Garret, "I simply wondered whether you have yet read the message."

"Oh, yes," replied Garret. "I mean…no. I have been distracted by the Lyonesse here." Garret nodded toward the girl.

"The lion?"

"Lyon*ess* de Tortuga, if you please." Kat took a sweeping bow, introducing her new self. But to you…'Kat'."

Garret walked to the table, picked up the note, broke its seal, and took a moment to read it. She looked at William, note still in hand. "Do you remember the man I told you about—the Jew who was drowning not far from *Pandora*? Name of Yosel?"

"I do, yes."

"The letter is his." She read it aloud.

Captain,

I have befriended the man in whom you have interest. [She told William Yosel was referring to De Graaf.] *He has traded an item of your good friend for much value. The buyer is a phantom.* [She gave William a curious look, not understanding that reference.] *Together, they intend to implicate you as the perpetrator of your friend's demise, to extort even more value. You might expect a clandestine visit, followed by a voyage to your friend's homeland.*

Y

Garret set the letter on the table. "There is cause for concern."

"Indeed."

"Do you remember my telling you De Graaf took Jorge's ring?"

"Yes, of course."

"That must be the item Yosel refers to. De Graaf plans to extort payment from someone who values it highly. King Philip, perhaps?"

"More importantly, he intends to lay blame for Jorge's killing at your feet."

Garret nodded. "Then apprehend me and turn me over to Spanish authorities."

"Precisely."

Garret drew back a chair and sat. "I hope Yosel will provide more clarity regarding De Graaf's plan."

"Hopefully in a timely fashion."

"We must be alert to the pyrate's movements."

"Most definitely. This may well be your only notice." William paused. "Perhaps we should set sail for a period of time—at least until we receive further instruction from the Queen. Or…we disrupt De Graaf's plans by eliminating him first."

'There is wisdom in William's words,' Garret thought. They were delivered with genuine concern for her safety, much like her grandfather might have spoken them. "I appreciate your concern, William. You are right—time at sea might do us all some good."

———

They sat in the reading room, sipping the fine port Ortega had poured and toasting the culmination of their exchange—silver pieces for the Viceroy's gold ring. Ayudante Pedro Vegas opened the small box Ortega pushed his way. He withdrew the ring, noting its surprising weight. Turning it in his hand, he observed King Philip's image imprinted on its face. It appeared to have sufficient relief to be used as a seal for letters. He returned it to the box, closed the lid, placed it back on the desk, and took another sip of Ortega's port. The man obviously knew how to find and select only the best-available. It was most pleasurable to be sharing it with him here in the villa.

"I presume the item is as warranted," stated Ortega.

"It is indeed. His Majesty shall be delighted to have it."

"Excellent." Ortega raised his silver cup toward Vegas, nodding slightly before sipping.

"He will be even more pleased by the Viceroy's safe return," Vegas pointed out.

"Yes, no doubt." Ortega placed his cup on the desk. "I am assured the Viceroy remains in good health."

"Minus his ear, of course," chided Vegas.

"Of course."

"How do you envision making the final exchange?"

"I believe it should be done at sea, at night. It will be most private that way."

"Private indeed," replied Vegas, wondering at Ortega's motivation behind a clandestine night-time exchange. Was there something the financier wished to hide? It fueled his suspicion that Ortega might well be the orchestrator of this ransom, not merely the man at the end of the captors' communication channel.

"Of course, we shall need to negotiate the ransom amount," Ortega noted.

"By 'we' you mean—you and I?" Vegas tested, anxious to see

whether Ortega might slip up. The correct answer would be 'no'—the negotiation had to be with the Viceroy's captors. But if Ortega were to say 'yes', it would virtually confirm he was more aligned with the captors than he wanted others to believe.

"You toy with me, Ayudante."

'*The man is no fool*,' Vegas thought, recognizing he needed to avoid upsetting him. "I misspoke. The negotiation will surely be between us and the Viceroy's captors."

"Indeed."

"What amount do you imagine they have in mind?" queried Vegas.

"I shall need to confer with the intermediaries."

Vegas sensed Ortega's words were carefully chosen, to avoid any hint of his direct contact with the captors. "How will you guide their thinking on the matter?"

"What value does any life have?"

"Surely some have less than others."

Ortega leaned back. "A man such as the Viceroy is a true prize, is he not?"

"He is indeed."

"I understand at one point he was a Maestre de Campo, in charge of a tercio—three thousand men."

"You are correct."

"Then perhaps one could argue he is worth three thousand times the wages of an average soldier." Vegas took that in without comment. "What is it you pay an average soldier? Or what might his family be paid upon his death in battle?"

"I am in no position to disclose such information. But I shall share your thoughts with the King when I deliver the ring."

"My guidance to the King would be at least thirty thousand doubloons," Ortega volunteered. Vegas was stunned at the enormity of the amount. Ortega rose. "I wish you well on your journey, Ayudante."

Vegas took one last sip of his port, rose, and picked up the box. "I shall proceed with all haste. The King has limited patience." He paused before adding, "And great wrath if he is crossed."

Leaving Ortega's villa astride his prized black stallion, Ayudante Vegas cringed at the thought of another back-and-forth voyage across the oceans. And still another after that, with the Viceroy in tow. He prayed that voyage would be his last. But he imagined it would all be worth it, if he could lay hands on a share of the ransom money. It might enable him to begin a new life—one in which he might be in position to afford the same fine port as Señor Ortega. Though he doubted the man was to be trusted, there was no choice but to do so. Certainly not at this point.

XV

As fast as *Mercilus* was sailing, it simply wasn't fast enough for Captain James Wenman. He'd pressed the crew for every square yard of sail, anxious to get back to Isla Tortuga. And to Garret.

Standing at the ship's bow enjoying the wind against his face, he reflected on his conversation with the Queen. He was disappointed that she, like Garret, chose to be discreet in her remarks. One comment in particular left him perplexed. As best he remembered it, it went: '*I understand the person in question had something of special importance to our Spanish friend*'. He tried parsing it out. First, who was this Spanish friend? It had to be someone of importance. Perhaps a spy in King Philip's court? Who might that be, he wondered. Or, for that matter, what about the King himself? He'd one heard a rumor that Philip proposed marriage to Queen Elizabeth. Could he be this 'friend'? It seemed unlikely— the two had gone to war against each other not that long ago.

Secondly, who was this other '*person in question*? That was simply impenetrable. He sighed, resigning himself to the fact that he was unlikely to break the Queen's code, certainly not without Garret's help. He would insist she bring him into the loop. She was, after all, sharing other things of importance with him. He smiled inwardly at the thought of her naked body, oblivious to the brisk wind flowing through his hair. "More speed, Lt. Ward," he shouted.

———

The familiar streets of Cartageña were dark as he headed back to the villa. They were not quiet, however. Dimly lit taverns beckoned with the sounds of bawdy activities—though not for men of his color.

Abeo had just met with some of the slaves he knew. He'd done that with several lately, seeking information about the disappearance of Spain's military Viceroy—Jorge Valdez—the man he'd overheard Ayudante Vegas discussing with his master, Señor Ortega. He was careful to insert the subject in casual conversation, to avoid being too conspicuous. Thus far, all he'd heard were conflicting rumors. Some said the Viceroy was dead. Others said it wasn't known whether he was dead or alive. Yet all agreed Valdez had been kidnapped, apparently by English pyrates.

Harker, the most notorious pirata since the death of Drake, appeared to be the prime suspect, though he was now reputedly deceased. The name of his partner also surfaced on occasion—a man named De Graaf. This pyrate was still alive, as far as anyone knew.

De Graaf reputedly frequented the 'refugio de piratas'—Isla Tortuga. The pyrate haven was a long way from Cartageña. There was no way Abeo could travel there, to confirm De Graaf was involved, and maybe holding the Viceroy captive. And, to his knowledge, pyrates were unlikely to travel to Cartageña; the risk of imprisonment and execution was too high. So, unless he could find a slave on some shuttle ship to Tortuga, the island card was unplayable. Though his contacts might help him find such a slave, time was rapidly descending the hourglass. Still, that was not the whole card game. It was but one hand.

His mind turned to a different path—finding someone willing to pay richly for information regarding the ransom scheme Señor Ortega and Ayudante Vegas had planned; a person who might know people with access to King Philip himself. A high-level merchant, perhaps. Or a military officer. He sensed the latter was his best option since many of his slave friends worked on construction projects overseen by the military. If one had a favorable connection with an officer, he might serve as a conduit to securing a reward for information on the ransom scheme. It was imperative he pursue that immediately or the value of his information could fall just like that sand in the hourglass.

———

Death's Head and its consort, *Cutthroat,* sailed within two hundred yards of each other, cruising the merchant lanes for prey. De Graaf was happy to be back on the blue Caribbean waters. It was where he belonged, feasting on his favorite meal—Spanish merchants. Bent over the table in his cabin, he studied one of the many maps he and Harker confiscated during their assaults. Some maps were notably better than others. He questioned the skill of several cartographers plying their trade in these waters. The maps he found most helpful were those crafted by the Belgian, Mercator. The man's style and accuracy were arguably the best.

Sliding a heavy, three-inch-diameter magnifying lens along one of Mercator's maps, De Graaf pondered assaulting a Spanish village. It had been a while since he and Harker led a land-based assault, parting Nombre de Dios from its treasures. Gold and silver were often more prevalent in villages than on merchant ships. Unfortunately, villages that made finer meals were becoming more difficult targets, requiring significantly more men.

A knock at the door disrupted his thoughts. "What is it?" he asked harshly.

"Yosel."

"Enter, then." He liked the Jew but despised being disturbed.

Yosel entered. He pointed to the map. "Where are we headed?"

Ordinarily, De Graaf would only share that with Master's Mate Stevens. But Yosel had earned his trust, proving helpful in negotiations with the Phantom. "A village perhaps," he replied, still bent over, eyes focused on the map. Moments later, he stood up. "What brings you?"

"I have given thought to the next step in our negotiations."

De Graaf withdrew his hand from the glass. "Sit," he said. Yosel pulled up a chair. De Graaf sat as he spoke, "The negotiation is now in the Phantom's hands. Have we something more to offer him?"

"No," Yosel admitted, "But he is a master of the craft. No man could extract more from King Philip than he. It would benefit us greatly if we knew just how much."

"Indeed," replied De Graaf, though he sensed that was futile.

"Were I negotiating with the King," offered Yosel, "I should consider the magnitude of resources he put at the Viceroy's disposal—ships, sailors…supplies. A sizeable investment. I believe the Phantom would estimate the Viceroy's value relative to such resources."

De Graaf nodded without responding. He wished to hear more. The Jew had obviously come with a specific objective in mind.

Yosel continued, "Any man of wealth pays a fee to those who manage his money. Investments with minimal risk merit only a small fee; perhaps five percent. Those with greater risk demand more." De Graaf accepted that. Yosel went on, "For investments bearing the highest risk, the King might easily pay one-fifth of the amount."

"Go on."

"It would be reasonable to assume the Viceroy is worth at least fifteen percent of the assets King Philip placed at his disposal." De Graaf didn't fully comprehend but let Yosel continue. "If we knew the size of his fleet, and number of men at his command, we could estimate the value."

"I suppose."

"Gathering that information would better prepare us for our negotiations. The order of magnitude alone is valuable."

De Graaf nodded. "Perhaps one of our crew once sailed with Valdez' fleet…or knows someone who did."

"Fair point," replied Yosel, "I shall look into that." He nodded toward De Graaf's cabinet. "Might I have a taste of wine?"

"Of course." De Graaf rose, walked to the cabinet, and withdrew a dark green olive jar. As he returned, Yosel spoke.

"Consider the ransom's path."

"By all means." De Graaf set out two cups and poured the wine.

"The Phantom must use a go-between with connections to the King himself," noted Yosel. De Graaf handed him a cup. "Perhaps a merchant of high standing."

De Graaf scoffed. He had no respect for merchants. He'd captured many of their ships and found none to be men of high standing. "More likely a military officer. Surely the King holds them in higher regard than any merchant."

Yosel didn't necessarily agree but went along anyway, "Who is the highest-ranking military officer in Cartageña?" De Graaf shook his head; he had no idea. Yosel continued, "Perhaps the one overseeing the King's construction projects?"

"I suspect the officer in charge of the military would assign someone else to oversee construction, in case anything went wrong—

someone to take the blame."

Yosel laughed. "Which of these two would be more likely to travel to Spain—reporting to the King on the construction's progress?"

"The one most familiar."

"Precisely." Yosel sat back and sipped his wine.

"We need to find this man."

"That should not prove difficult."

"We are not exactly welcomed in Cartageña," De Graaf noted.

"*You* are not," replied Yosel. "There is no doubt of that. I, on the other hand, do not exactly bear the likeness of a pyrate. My presence in the city would go unnoticed."

De Graaf liked the idea; the Jew's skill at mingling with others was admirable. It could prove most helpful. He lifted his cup. "To Cartageña then," he grinned.

Yosel left De Graaf's quarters in fine spirits. This outcome was precisely what he'd sought to come away with—a visit to the city he hoped to one day make his home.

———

It peaked all of his senses—the breaking of stone, clatter of tools, and barking of hucksters selling their wares; guards shouting orders above the construction site's pervasive clamor; horses hauling creaking supply wagons and casually dropping batches of bowelled scent; airborne dust smothering the future residence of Cartageña's Governor and pitting Abeo's tongue. He coughed, covering his eyes at the puff of wind. Ortega's manservant had come to find his friend, Babatundé. The hulking Nigerian's daily obligation was to move building stones into position. Despite his forced existence, the man had an irrepressible spirit, engaging nature, and a fine sense of humor. If anyone could earn favor with his overseers, it would be him. Babatundé's fellow slaves lovingly called him Babu.

Abeo spotted Babu and his friends at their lunch break, seated on a stone pile, eating papaya and laughing. Babu rose to greet him, "Blessed to see you, arakunrin [brother]." He reached out and hugged Abeo. "It has been too long. I thought you must have passed to the other side."

Abeo laughed, "No such good fortune."

"You look well. Your massa favors you." Massa was the word Babu had come to use for 'master'.

"He has no choice—he prefers I not spit in his food." Abeo winked.

It was Babu's turn to laugh. "But you do, no?" he chuckled.

"Yes. Often." Everyone in the group joined in the laughter.

"May we have a moment alone?" Abeo asked.

"Only if you promise not to spit on my papaya."

Within minutes, Abeo had everything he needed. Babu did indeed have a friendly relationship with one of the guards. And he agreed to let the soldier know that Abeo held valuable information, for sale. The men hugged and separated.

"Allah be with you, Babu."

"And with you."

XVI

The head peeking through the door belonged to Master's Mate Wakefield. "Might I enter, sir?"

"Please," replied Captain Tovery.

Wakefield walked in. "I am pleased to report the men's residences are finally ready."

The news wasn't unexpected; William walked the site daily to observe the construction. Wakefield's report was simply official notice that the men were waiting to break down their lean-tos and move into the buildings, each of which could house up to twenty at a time.

Nonetheless, William was anxious to get the men back to the sea, hunting Spanish treasure. It had been far too long, and their mutterings over the last few weeks worried him. Unfortunately, he and Garret still had unresolved differences on the matter.

"Thank you, Mr. Wakefield. Please inform the men that the next three days are theirs to enjoy. We shall convene and assemble outside the residences on Sabbath morn."

"Thank you, sir. They shall be delighted."

"There is nothing better for the spirits than a little freedom and frivolity. I hope the taverns can handle the load."

"The geese as well," Wakefield winked, referring to the tavern women.

"Indeed," William laughed.

Wakefield turned to leave. William stopped him. "Please, join me in a celebratory drink."

"Thank you, sir."

William took the olive jar sitting on his table and poured its contents into two tankards. He handed one to Wakefield and raised his own high in the air. "To a job well done."

"Job well done," Wakefield echoed. He took a sip and raised his cup. "And to you, Captain, for your guidance and leadership."

"I thank you. But of course, I cannot drink to myself."

"Then I sip alone." He did so.

"What think you of the presence of these pyrates in the village?" William asked. He now sipped his own beer.

"I imagine some may be decent men. A handful perhaps," replied Wakefield. "The remainder are serpents…ones you would not wish to cross paths with on a moonless night."

"I presume you include De Graaf in that group."

"Most assuredly. His second, Mr. Stevens, is no better. Two others of similar ilk have emerged."

"How so?"

"Their recent victories at sea have cheered the taverns, bringing them a certain standing. Some claim both are as brutal as De Graaf, though others are doubtful."

"Who are these men?"

"One calls himself Attila, after the historic general. They say he has Dutch blood, like De Graaf. He is a large man. His hair is fair in color and flows long. He has a combat scar—a slash crossing his lip." Wakefield drew an imaginary line from his right cheek to his lower left jaw. "He fancies a sea-blue bandana. Perhaps you have seen him?"

William shook his head, "Not that I recall."

"The other man goes by the name of Beauclere. French, of course. Not a particularly big man. Older. His hair has grayed. He crewed with Le Pen, the pyrate captain slain by De Graaf. They say

Beauclere has never forgotten that killing." Wakefield paused to sip his beer. "He is a man of refined manner. Well-dressed. To see him, you might think him a merchant. But he is a hyena, dressed as a gazelle."

"I see. I shall need to stay alert to these men."

"The pyrates they lead appear to hold them in high regard, if not fear them."

William pondered that comment, suspecting Attila and Beauclere led by fear. He thought of Garret; she led by example. The same was true of their mentor, Admiral Drake. Although the Spanish considered Drake a pirata, he was the finest of England's commanders. He never led by imposing fear in the minds of his men. Still, there was no doubt that fear could be a highly effective motivator—fear-of-death in particular. That appeared to be the emerging style of successful pyrate captains. Their brutality brought fear both to those who followed them and those who learned of them from others. Fear was not only their reputation, it was also their lead weapon. They could intimidate merely by wielding that reputation rather than a cutlass. "What of their skills?" William asked.

"Attila is a warrior of unimaginable strength and skill. One might liken him to Musa in that way, though his demeanor is completely different."

William nodded, taking in the thought of this man. How was it that he hadn't come across him yet? Surely the man stood out.

"Beauclere is not a man of great physicality," Wakefield continued. "He has his minions for that purpose. He is known to be intelligent and observant, with a mind like a hunter's trap."

William altered course a little since he'd originally opened the conversation with something else in mind. "Tell me, do you believe there are men who sail with these two pyrates who may be inclined to join us if presented that opportunity?" William knew he and Garret would need more men, in time. Finding good ones on Isla Tortuga would facilitate their recruiting.

Wakefield paused. "I doubt that, sir. Perhaps a few; no more. I believe chances are better that Attila and Beauclere might attract more of ours than we of theirs."

"How so?"

"Our men bemoan the construction work while others grow fat on Spanish treasure."

William nodded, grudgingly accepting Wakefield's conclusion. It was now perfectly clear—his men needed to sail. And soon. Further, he and Garret would need Captain Wenman's help if they were to challenge De Graaf. There was no way around that.

———

He was convinced the threatening queasiness within his upper chest was the ocean's curse. His strict diet of wine and bread seemed pitiful medicine for this unrelenting plague. Ayudante Vegas rose from the table in his cabin and strolled to the chest where he kept his books. He'd long ago discovered that well-authored ones helped break the connection to in-the-moment physical concerns, transporting him to a place of interest and comfort. He selected one about the first crusade, a military success of Christian forces over infidel Turks. Returning to his chair, he opened it at an earmarked page and began reading. But his mind soon yielded to the irrepressible pull of the wealth he hoped to amass as Señor Ortega's intermediary to King Philip. He dreamed it would bring him a lavish life in Cartageña. He'd just decided his future would be in that bustling city, rather than in Spain. It would mean one less crossing of these dreaded oceans.

Vegas' thoughts turned to the ultimate release of Viceroy Valdez. He was convinced King Philip would offer up gold doubloons rather than silver pieces of eight, as a grand display of his support for the Viceroy. After all, Valdez was more than a mere military officer. He was Philip's dear friend—dear enough to call the King by his first name. The only question was: how many doubloons? He hoped the King might seek his counsel on that. If so, he would suggest well more than Señor Ortega had in mind. That would enable him to pocket a sizable portion…and eliminate the need for yet another voyage.

Unable to concentrate on it, Vegas closed his book. He rose, went to his cabinet, unlocked the drawer, and withdrew the Viceroy's ring from its small box. He slid the ring on his finger. It was much too large. Viceroy Valdez' hands were clearly forged on the battlefields of the Netherlands. It was said that his favored weapon was a two-handed broadsword, one mirroring the Scottish claymore. Heavy and sharp on both edges, it was especially deadly. His practice and use of the weapon no doubt contributed to his fingers' girth, explaining the oversized ring.

Vegas hoped to one day meet the man whose freedom he was enabling. Perhaps the Viceroy might reward him handsomely for his efforts. He easily slid the ring off his finger, returning it to its box. He locked the drawer and put the key in his doublet pocket. Visions of gold filled his head—better medicine for his nausea. At least for now.

———

They passed in the night, though too far apart to be seen. The

English warship *Mercilus* bore Captain James Wenman, with the Queen's message for Captain Garret Connachan. The Spanish caravel *Zuñiga* carried Ayudante Vegas, with the Viceroy's ring. It wasn't the first time the two had crossed paths, though on neither occasion was there any meaningful interaction. Nor should there have been. It was simply coincidental distant crossings between ships of two countries not currently at war. At least, not officially.

Captain Wenman was awakened by Master's Mate Ward, who had the middle watch. "What is it, Lieutenant?"

"Sorry for the bother, Captain. I am afraid I feel rather ill. I am unable to finish my watch."

"What signs?"

"The runs, sir. Bloody ones. And constant."

Wenman rose, grabbed the lantern and proceeded to light it. Ward looked exceedingly pale. "Have a seat. I shall fetch the doctor."

"I may not be here when you return. The runs may take me elsewhere."

"Indeed," nodded Wenman. "Then let us meet here soonest." He exited for Dr. Stafford's quarters.

The man snored like a wild boar. Wenman knocked loudly. The snoring continued. He tried the door. It was unlocked. He walked in. "Doctor Stafford," he said, gently nudging him. No response. Wenman slapped the man's face. The snoring stuttered to a halt. The startled doctor swung at Wenman, barely missing him. "Tis I, Doctor. Captain Wenman." Stafford bent up from the waist, shaking the fog from his head.

"Your assistance is required. Lt. Ward is ill."

Stafford struggled to climb out of his hammock, grumbling as he did so. He hated life on a ship; it was meant for much younger men. Given a choice, he would be back on dry land, practicing in his village. Only his damn misfortune had brought him here. He should never have agreed to bleed the Admiral. His failure in that cupping led to his unmerciful assignment to this Godforsaken ship. While Wenman waited impatiently, Stafford put on his coat and grabbed a bag containing his instruments and medicinal vials. "Lead the way then," he groused.

Ward was on the floor, shaking, when Wenman and Stafford arrived. Vomit pooled by his head. Small bits remained on his chin.

"Help me get him to the hammock," said Stafford. The two dragged him over and struggled to hoist him into the bed. Stafford threw a blanket over him and wiped his face. He placed his hand on Ward's forehead. "He runs a fever. Fetch me some water."

Wenman grabbed a nearby olive jar and poured water into a cup. He handed it to Stafford. The doctor held up the Lieutenant's head to help him drink. He used the remaining water to wet a cloth, placed it on Ward's forehead, and asked for a spoon. Wenman retrieved one as Stafford reached into his bag and pulled out a vial. He poured some of its contents onto the spoon and once again raised Ward's head, giving him the medicine. When Ward finished, Stafford placed his head gently back on the hammock and returned the vial to his bag.

"What is it, Doctor?" asked Wenman.

"A fever of some kind. Tis difficult to be more specific."

"What medicine have you given him?"

"Laudanum. It will calm him. He requires rest and fluids."

"Can you attend to him, then?" Wenman had no desire to be Ward's aide; he had more pressing responsibilities. Stafford mumbled something he couldn't make out. "Pardon me?"

Stafford appeared to rethink what he'd just said. "I shall have my assistant watch over him. I worry he may be contagious."

"I see," Wenman grimaced. "Please have your assistant move Lt. Ward to his own quarters, as soon as he is able."

"Most certainly, Captain."

Stafford picked up his bag and left. Wenman watched him go. He didn't care for the man. His manner wasn't pleasing in the least. Nor did his skills appear to be that good. It was a sad comment that the navy saw fit to place only the poorest of physicians on their ships. Then again, he supposed he was lucky to have one.

Wenman glanced back at Ward, who was already sleeping. Stafford's comment about possible contagion worried him. He was well aware that sailors in the South Seas occasionally contracted tropical diseases unfamiliar to European medical practitioners. The spread of those afflictions sometimes led to deaths among the crew. Strict measures were required. Ward and the doctor's assistant would need to be locked down and guarded. He could ill afford the spread of a potentially deadly disease…if that hadn't already begun.

XVII

The city's charm demanded that Yosel stop to breathe it all in—its buildings, its people, its vibrancy. He noticed Cartageña's nearby Cathedral was still under reconstruction, several years after Drake's assault. The Governor at that time supposedly paid 'El Draque' one hundred-ten thousand silver ducats to cease his shelling. He was no longer Governor.

Walking the narrow streets, Yosel sensed the balconies were close enough for tenants on either side to exchange goods. He smiled at the dazzling array of colors covering doors, walls and terraces—blue, gold, orange and aqua being common. Pink bougainvillea seemed to bloom everywhere. Morning glories added white, yellow and other colors to the mix. Hibiscus contributed purples and reds. A tasty feast for the eyes, he thought.

The city's residents also represented a broad mix of colors… and cultures. Here he was, a Jew rubbing shoulders with Catholics and others with strange religions. He smiled at the ease with which the people mixed here. How different it must be from the days of the inquisitions in Europe that drove his father to flee. Throughout the Southern Seas there were numerous Indigenous peoples, including Caribes and Zenŭ, whose ancestors lived here for centuries before the Spanish ever arrived. Blacks enslaved and imported from Africa were also prominent, particularly at the many construction sites. And, inevitably, there were people of mixed race and color, filling in the complete spectrum of shades between black and white.

Yosel noted the prodigious activity along the city's perimeter, where enormous stone walls were being erected. In places, they were beyond forty feet thick, studded with castellated bastions. It seemed as though building those walls was an endless project…by the time they were finished, the original sections would already be crumbling badly and in need of repair. Or under attack by some other bold pyrate.

The city was obviously thriving, despite its challenges in recent decades. Drake wasn't alone in having assaulted, pillaged and burned it. Ironically, it was constructed on top of an indigenous city that was itself decimated by Spanish Captain Pedro de Heredia, who thirsted for all the gold the area was known to harbor. But the Spaniards later became the target of both French and English pyrates, including Roberval, Cote and Hawkins. Still, the city now flourished under King Philip's reinvestment and fortification efforts. It was most definitely a Spanish prize. Philip seemed determined to maintain it as the foremost trading center in the Southern Seas. Yosel was convinced it was a place where he could make a good life for himself, in time. He genuinely hoped it had seen the last of any assaults.

De Graaf's ship had anchored beyond the city's view the night before. By late morning, Yosel bade De Graaf farewell, disembarking for Cartageña alone on a skiff. He was to return to the same place at week's end, hopefully with critical knowledge concerning the military ships known to shuttle back and forth between Cartageña and Spain. He sought to find and engage a military officer open to providing information regarding the specifics of any cargo arriving on military vessels. For a price, of course.

A nearby tavern appeared to be a promising place to begin his search. It was near what looked to be a fortress under construction along the harbor's coast. It might well be frequented by military men overseeing the building project, or otherwise involved in the comings and goings of ships.

Two Indigenous-looking children ran toward him, kicking up dust from the street. Yosel suspected they were seeking a handout. They reached him with arms extended, pushing to outmaneuver each other. He sensed his skin color had brought them his way. After all, it seemed the fair-skinned people in this society held the biggest claim on money. "Fácil," he said, attempting to calm the boys down from their struggle for position. He reached into his pocket, giving each a small coin.

"Gracias, señor." They almost didn't finish the phrase before dashing off to spend their newfound wealth.

Yosel walked on, entering the surprisingly bright tavern. The afternoon sun streamed through a lone window, exposing the muddled drift of miniscule airborne particles. Though not full, the place was active and noisy. He walked to the serving table, behind which was a broad array of olive jars, bottles and tankards. The server nodded his way but was attending to another man—one dressed in uniform. '*How convenient*,' thought Yosel. Anxious to engage a soldier, he stepped to the man's side. "A good day for quenching one's thirst," he said, indifferently.

"Indeed. The dust in my throat requires frequent flushing."

The man's breath suggested this was not his first drink. "You are part of the construction then?" Yosel asked.

"Tis my fate, unfortunately. Not the military life I imagined."

The man was undoubtedly Spanish, though not necessarily of European birth. His less-refined accent implied he was either born in the Southern Seas or had spent so much time here that his manner of speaking had devolved to a more local dialect. "You are from here?"

The soldier took a long moment to study him. Yosel knew when he was being taken for a Jew. He sought to set the man's mind at ease. "Converso," he said. "Born in San Juan Bautista."

The soldier nodded and paused to sip his drink. "My father was from Cadíz. A sailor." He turned his head back to his tankard. "I was born here. I had no desire to sail. Perhaps I should have."

"Sailing can be a difficult life," offered Yosel. The server filled a tankard for him. He offered a coin. The server pocketed it and walked toward another patron.

"More difficult than this one?" the soldier replied, clearly referring to his miserable life on a dusty construction site.

"The seas can be an angry maiden."

"You are a sailor, then?"

"I sail with merchants, maintaining their accounts."

The Spaniard spit on the dirt floor. "Merchants," he said. "They live to take advantage of us." Yosel nodded as the man continued. "Our money comes hard, yet they take it from us so easily."

"Just so," Yosel agreed, "They pay a small price for their cargo, then charge us unfair prices." The server glanced their way. Yosel suspected he was listening to their conversation. He leaned closer to his new friend, lowering his voice "Would it not be interesting to know what cargo comes into the city? And how much is paid for it?"

"You keep the merchants' accounts. Surely you must know this."

"I know the accounts of those for whom I sail. But much greater cargos arrive daily."

The Spaniard nodded. "The supply ships carry vast quantities."

"The King's ships as well. The value of their cargo is likely well beyond anything we might imagine."

"Ahh. Spain's gold. Cartageña's very blood." The soldier raised his tankard in mock praise, taking a healthy swig.

"So it is." Yosel sipped his beer and pressed on. "Have you seen gold being loaded onto the ships?"

"When the caravans bring it, many of us are called to stand guard."

"It must be a sight."

"Many are called to help. Others flock to watch. As the days pass, and the gold is boarded, you can see the galleons sink ever lower into the water from its weight." The man took another sip.

"It takes more than a day to load a galleon?"

The soldier laughed, which Yosel interpreted as a reaction to his apparent naïveté. "Every load taken from the storehouse is weighed and counted in the presence of guards, beyond view of the people."

"Have you seen them weigh it?"

"I am not of sufficient standing. Had I been born in Spain, I would." He finished his beer.

Yosel quickly waved at the server and pointed to the man's tankard. He pulled a coin from his pocket and placed it on the counter next to the man's cup. The soldier looked at him. Yosel noticed the drunken fog in his eyes. "I am new to the city," he explained. "Let me buy you one. As a friend."

The man didn't protest. Yosel stayed quiet as the server poured the beer and took the coin. When he moved away, Yosel watched the soldier lift the tankard to his lips before continuing, "Being a counter myself, I find much joy in the process. Do you know the man who weighs and counts the gold? I should like to meet him. Perhaps I might be of help.”

“I know him, but not as a friend.”

“How would I find him?”

“His name is Sanchez.” He spat on the floor disrespectfully. “A short man. Rotundo.” He spread his arms wide as if to display the man’s sizeable girth. “He fancies a yellowed wig, to announce his importance.”

“What is his calling?”

“Tesorero.”

‘*Of course*’, thought Yosel. ‘*Who else but the treasurer would be charged with such a role*?’ Another thought ran through his mind— the Tesorero would be involved in *any* financial transaction authorized by the King.

Feeling he’d gleaned all he could from the soldier, Yosel sought to end the conversation. “I must leave, mi amigo.” He patted the man’s shoulder. “To find a place to stay before the dark takes hold.”

“Gracias, señor,” the soldier replied, raising his cup and then drawing it to his lips.

———

“You do not understand,” exclaimed William, his voice rising. “The men thirst for action!”

“I cannot risk missing Captain Wenman’s arrival with Her Majesty’s response,” argued Garret.

“Wenman be damned. He may never arrive.”

Garret winced. “Wenman be damned?”

“Not damn the *man*. Damn the waiting. If we fail to hunt for treasure, we shall lose not only the crew’s hearts and minds but also the men themselves."

Garret stared at him in silent anger. William thought now was perhaps the best time to share what he'd been hearing from the crew, thinking it would finally convince her of the need to join him. "I am afraid the men believe you have gone soft, Garret."

"Gone soft?"

"Tis a male thing. They believe you have lost your desire for action." He lowered his voice, "Because of the girl."

"You're talking mutiny, William!" Garret exclaimed. "Mutiny!"

"No Garret. It's survival."

"Have you gone mad? We have no letter of marque. Would you have us become bloody pyrates?"

"There is no choice!"

"We *do* have a choice," she protested. "And as long as I am in command, I shall make that call."

"Damn you, Garret. You have lost complete touch with the men. They are not home builders. Nor landsmen. They are adventurers thirsting for Spanish treasure. Without that, I assure you, we shall lose them to captains who share their thirst."

"To *pyrate* captains?!!"

"Yes. And they have choices beyond just De Graaf."

"Good God, William. We cannot simply turn pyrate!"

William hesitated. Turning pyrate was precisely where he was headed. Yet he'd only ever sailed on behalf of England, with long-term ambitions to earn a Captain's post in the Queen's navy. So how could he possibly support a turn to the dark side, he asked himself…again. But with supplies and funds now running low, there was really no choice. Either turn pyrate or lose the crew. And without a crew, he and Garret would be stranded… mere villagers in this Godforsaken place. She needed to grasp that. Now.

"Call it what you will, Garret. Either we pyrate for treasure or we stay here—catching fish for a living."

"I will not have you speak further of this," Garret ordered. "We are privateers, not pyrates." She turned away. "With no commission from Her Majesty to plunder ships of any nation," she added.

"You are either with me or without me," William barked, half in frustration, half in resignation.

Silence followed. Garret's glare seemed to burn his soul. He stared back with no intention of cowering. After moments that posed as forever, he turned, walked to the door, and opened it.

Garret realized William was on the verge of ending everything they had shared for so long. He was the boy she once partnered with as a midshipman; the young man she came to know as a friend…while still presenting as a young man herself. And now, he was the man she admired, and enjoyed partnering with. At times, she felt drawn to him as something more than just a friend. She'd often had to resist sliding into a more intimate relationship with him. In truth, they were as close as a man and woman could be, without being lovers. How could she simply let him walk away? "William," she called out.

William stopped at the sound of Garret's voice but couldn't turn to look at her. His disappointment was overwhelming. He sensed this was the end of their relationship—of any hope that they might remain partners…or something more. But his mind was set. She'd chosen not to join him. It was over, but for this final farewell.

Before the yelling started, Kat sat quietly reading in the bedroom. But reading had become impossible. The end of the shouting and harsh words implied an even more significant ending. A bitter one. Tears began etching lines down her cheeks. The two people in the world she cared about most were on the edge of giving up on their friendship. It was too much. She burst out of the room and ran straight to William, grasping his waist. "Do not leave," she sobbed. "Please."

Garret looked on, tears unexpectedly welling up in her eyes and threatening to spill over. Her last word, William's name, had simply fallen from the air, uncaught by any supporting words—ones that now materialized in her head: 'do not leave me'. But her lips couldn't form them. Her parched throat couldn't sound them.

Tears cascading down her cheeks, Kat grasped William even tighter. He placed his hands on her, gently pushing her away as he bent at the knees, leveling his eyes with hers. "I have to go, Kat. You take care of the Captain. She needs you now, more than ever."

"No," Kat sobbed, "you cannot leave us."

"But I must, m'lady. There is no alternative for me." He wiped the girl's tears gently with his hand. "There are times when one must decide the course of their own future. Even when that may not be easy. One day you will understand." He drew her toward him, hugging her firmly.

Kat felt the warmth of William's heart blanket and comfort her in that moment. And then he stood. She watched him nod at Garret, not letting his eyes linger on her for even a moment. He turned his back…and left. The door closed quietly. She and Garret were suddenly, achingly, alone. Together.

———

The stiff breeze dusted the weather-worn seaside village of Santo Pedro. It was almost devoid of activity with the local fishermen out to sea, as usual in the later morning. De Graaf had come here to meet with the Phantom while Yosel weaved his magic in Cartageña. He still didn't know that the man most people referred to as 'Fantasma' was actually Cartageña's premier financier, Señor Ortega, who artfully shielded his identity. Aside from the tavernkeeper, the two schemers were alone.

"Where is your friend?" Fantasma asked.

De Graaf knew he meant Yosel. "Seeking treasure elsewhere."

"I see. No matter." Fantasma sipped his beer and set the tankard on the table. "Our messenger has set sail."

"With what message?"

Fantasma lowered his voice, "The Viceroy can be purchased."

"Of course, but at what price?"

"We discussed how one might arrive at an amount."

"I am not understanding."

"I proposed a means of determining the Viceroy's value, to guide the King's thinking."

"You toy with me," De Graaf growled.

"I assure you, I do not. Setting an arbitrary price for such a man does not help our cause. Best we let the King set the value. We can only plant the seed."

"Men who deceived me are no longer among us."

"I assure you, the proceeds will fully satisfy your appetite." Fantasma leaned in, "But we must now align ourselves on the circumstances of the Viceroy's demise."

"We agreed to blame the English privateer—Connachan."

"Yes, but we must be specific regarding Connachan's supposed actions. In order to be believed, they must contain an element of truth."

"You appear to have something in mind."

"I do. Where is Connachan now?" asked Fantasma.

"Isla Tortuga."

"Then we can suggest that is where the Viceroy is being held."

"Isla Tortuga is my home. I choose not to invite Spain's navy."

"I see."

De Graaf leaned forward, "We can claim the Viceroy was held at sea, and later slain there by the Witch."

"The Witch?"

"Connachan."

"Connachan is a woman?" Fantasma exclaimed.

"She sailed with Drake. Some claim she seduced and cast a spell on him to gain her captaincy."

"An interesting woman."

"She is Hell's own fire." De Graaf leaned back, sipping his beer.

"If this is to be our story, then the element of truth must be an actual assault at sea—one that can be verified," Fantasma suggested. "Has a vessel been attacked recently by pyrates in nearby waters?"

De Graaf recalled his attack on the *Santo de Cristo*; perhaps that would suffice. But in giving it more thought, he remembered keelhauling the ship's captain. The event was so brutal that the story traveled quickly…and he himself was identified with it. So no, that wouldn't work if they were to lay blame on the Witch. He responded accordingly, "Not that I am aware of."

"Then we must orchestrate an attack."

"I can arrange that," De Graaf replied, welcoming the thought.

"Best it happens soon."

De Graaf was not to be played the fool; Yosel taught him that. "Such action comes at a price," he said. "I shall need payment in advance, to oil the planks."

Fantasma sipped his beer. "How much?"

"Several men are needed. And maintaining the secrecy of our involvement will require even further payment."

"Of course."

"Two thousand pieces of eight."

"One thousand," replied Fantasma. "Half now."

"Fifteen then, all in advance."

Fantasma paused. "As you wish. But this must later be deducted from the King's ransom."

De Graaf knew the proceeds from capturing and stripping a vessel's cargo would easily cover his expenses. So the fifteen thousand up-front was pure bonus money. Nor did it carry any risk of loss… unlike the King's ransom, which might never be paid if they were unsuccessful in pulling off the final step of their deception. He put down his tankard and extended his hand. "Agreed."

XVIII

While King Philip continued the session with his General, Ayudante Vegas sat alone in the anteroom, revisiting his uncomfortable expulsion from the meeting. Things hadn't gone as well at El Escorial as Vegas hoped. Yes, the King was pleased to receive the ring he'd given his close friend, Viceroy Jorge Valdez. But he expressed great displeasure that he was now being asked to pay an exorbitant ransom for Valdez. He'd shouted that his combined military forces had sufficient capability and resources to find and free the Viceroy, begging the question: 'why should he have to pay a ransom'? Cowered by the King's outrage, Vegas failed to respond. He simply endured the continued outburst until it subsided. It hadn't ended quickly; or well.

Vegas took solace in the fact that the King's poor health may have contributed to his extended rage. Still, he worried for his future. The King might easily take away his rank…or worse, imprison him and have someone else retrieve the Viceroy. If that were to happen, he might never again see Cartageña, or run his hands through the pieces of eight and gold doubloons he'd amassed over time and hidden in the woods behind his home.

Hoping to avoid an unfavorable outcome, Vegas had assured the King he would find and return the Viceroy without any further expense on His Majesty's part. That brought on his abrupt dismissal, with no clarity regarding his fate.

He suddenly found it exceedingly hot in the closeness of this small, windowless room with just one chair. A lone art-piece hung from the wall—one Vegas imagined the King had tired of and hence banished to this virtual closet. The wooden painting showed a court

jester peering through his fingers with a foolish grin on his face. He felt
uncomfortable with the jester's stare as he sat there interminably,
awaiting his fate. He wondered whether the beads of sweat emanating
from his forehead were generated by the heat…or by his fear.

The fog of this puzzle was finally lifting for King Philip. The
ring Ayudante Vegas just delivered was all the assurance he needed
that he was now dealing with the Viceroy's true captors. The message
from the Viceroy himself, delivered by a merchant sailing from Isla
Tortuga, appeared to be a dead end. Yet, it confirmed Jorge was alive at
the time it was written, and that he'd been on that island. The place was
a known haven for pyrates, privateers and dark-market merchants. So it
was entirely possible that a band of pyrates had captured Jorge. But
then, what was he to make of Queen Elizabeth's message that she had a
'prize'—or, as she put it, "*a close friend of Your Majesty's*", whom she
would gladly exchange for Spanish-held territory in the Caribbean Sea.
That prize *had* to be Jorge. And if it were, then these were *English*
pyrates. Or more likely, English privateers who kidnapped the Viceroy
under orders from the Queen herself. It infuriated him that she might
take such aggressive, unfounded action at a time when the two
countries weren't actively at war. At least not a declared one.

All of these clues pointed Philip to three conclusions. First, that
the Viceroy was still alive; second, that he was being held by English
pyrates; and third, that he might well be in captivity on Isla Tortuga.
His primary objective now was to preserve his friend's life. It seemed
the best way to assure that was to follow through with the ransom
payment the Ayudante proposed, despite his dislike of the man.

Philip also decided to send Rodrigo de Cuero to Isla Tortuga, to determine whether the Viceroy was still being held there. The man had served him well in the past. He was a seasoned intelligence gatherer. He was also a highly effective assassin. It was de Cuero whom he'd commissioned to take the life of Indonesian Ambassador Pantas years ago. At the time, the Ambassador was plotting with the English against Spanish and Portuguese interests at Ternate. The assassination went smoothly, with no repercussions for Spain. So Philip had complete confidence in de Cuero to infiltrate the pyrate island and gather the necessary intelligence. The spy would accompany Ayudante Vegas to a Caribbean port near Isla Tortuga, and then find his way onto a merchant vessel bound for the island, posing as an ordinary seaman.

Philip also decided to order his fleet in Inagua to stand at the ready for a possible assault on Tortuga if de Cuero were able to discover the actual location where the Viceroy was being held.

One way or another, Philip would retrieve Jorge and obtain retribution from those responsible for his capture. He sent a messenger to find de Cuero and accompany him to El Escorial, immediately.

———

Amid all the construction site noise and dust, Babu sat with fellow slaves during their late-afternoon meal break. But on this occasion, Babu wasn't his usual talkative self. Instead, he ravenously devoured his food, anxious to finish. It was the day he and Abeo, Señor Ortega's manservant, agreed to meet. Abeo had promised him a reward for an introduction to a Spanish officer with whom he could share important information. Babu had already raised the possibility with a guard who seemed more friend than overlord.

While finishing a banana, Babu spotted the dark outline of a man framed by the dust-filtered sunlight behind him. His long, flowing silk coat gave him away—Abeo had style. His position as manservant for the rich Cartageñian gave him special standing in the slave community, drawing the envy of every slave Babu knew. But it wasn't simply Abeo's role; it was the man himself. He was intelligent, well-spoken, and thoughtful of others. He was both respected and well-liked.

Babu stood, welcoming Abeo with a hug. "You look well, my brother."

"Except for all the dust," Abeo frowned, attempting to brush some of it off his stylish coat.

"Come," Babu said, pulling him aside. They walked a few paces. "I have spoken with a friendly guard. He has agreed to meet you tonight, three hours after the sun has fallen."

"Excellent."

"He suggested the woods on the far side of the cemetery, behind the cathedral."

"Please assure him, I shall be there."

"You do not fear the cemetery's spirits then?" Babu grinned, flaring large, richly yellowed teeth…though some were missing.

"Only those of my ancestors," Abeo winked. "They have knowledge of all my bad deeds."

Babu laughed. "I hope you shall not meet any of mine!"

Abeo reached into his pocket, pulling out a few silver coins. "I thank you for this."

Babu took the pieces of eight, pocketing them quickly. "The guard's name is Fernando. I told him nothing of your relationship with Señor Ortega. Nor did I share your name. He knows only that you are my friend, with information you believe will interest the military."

"I am most grateful, Babu. If there is ever anything I can do in return, please let me know."

"I shall. You may be certain of that," Babu smiled and nodded.

The two men hugged once again, and parted ways.

Returning through the city streets, Abeo framed his thoughts on the meeting with Fernando. He worried his information might implicate Señor Ortega, leading to his arrest. If so, his own job as manservant would be in jeopardy. He knew he must be careful about what he chose to share, and what to ask in return. He thought it best to disclose only the involvement of Ayudante Vegas. He didn't like the man anyway—he was aloof and condescending. Whatever might happen to Vegas as a result of this matter was not his concern.

———

Lying in bed, drenched in sweat, Captain James Wenman sensed his fever was contracted directly from Master's Mate Ward. Doctor Stafford sat bedside, cloaked in a blanket. He administered a dose of laudanum.

"The medicine is in short supply," noted Stafford. "It should be restricted for use by officers only."

"How many of the crew are afflicted?" Wenman asked.

"I have not maintained a count, though I imagine twenty to thirty currently show signs."

"What of Ward? Has his condition improved?" Wenman asked, more out of concern for his own prognosis than for Ward's well-being.

"I am afraid he shows little progress."

"And you, Doctor?"

"I continue to suffer, although the laudanum provides comfort."

"Indeed." Wenman had one more pressing question, "Are there any who seem in perilous condition?"

"Yes. One in particular will surely pass today or tomorrow."

"How far along is he?"

"Tis difficult to say. I believe he caught the disease first, perhaps during our stop at Cape Verde."

"Two weeks ago, then."

"Indeed."

"Shall we all find ourselves in this man's condition after a similar passage of time?"

"I cannot rule that out."

"Is there nothing more to be done?"

"Flushing the system with water is the best we can do. And perhaps a cupping."

Wenman shivered at the thought. Years ago he'd seen a man cupped. The sight of his blood draining into a large cup had brought him a wave of nausea. "Hopefully cupping is a last resort."

"Perhaps I might cup one of the crew, to see whether it helps."

"By all means, let us do that quickly. Perhaps two crew members—the one who seems imperiled and another who has been ill as long as Master's Mate Ward."

"As you wish." Stafford placed the laudanum in his bag and rose, adjusting the blanket around his shoulders. He shuffled slowly to the door.

The old man is quite pale, thought Wenman. He was frail at his best. What if he were to perish? "One more thing, doctor…what of your assistant?"

Stafford turned to answer, "Mr. Snadden has not contracted the disease. Not yet anyway. Perhaps it is his youth and manner. He is a man of the Bible and obsessive in his cleanliness. Perhaps God shines on him."

"May he shine on us all."

"Indeed."

Stafford shuffled out. Wenman questioned whether he might ever see the doctor again. He decided he should call on Mr. Snadden, just in case. That might also present an opportunity to reserve sufficient laudanum for himself.

———

Orion's crew noisily set sails and hauled anchor at Captain Tovery's order. Though the ship had always been *Pandora's* consort, it would now be the flagship of William's two-vessel fleet. Though he felt uncomfortable taking her ships without her knowledge, there was really no alternative.

Blair had reluctantly agreed to serve as *Pandora's* temporary captain. Unlike Garret, he concurred…it was either turn pyrate or waste away on Isla Tortuga.

The sails pulled the two ships forward—their destination: the Windward Passage, between Cuba and Hispaniola. Given King Philip's heavy investments in Cartageña's refortification, the Passage promised a robust flow of merchant vessels. Excellent hunting grounds.

Standing at the bow, William noted the transition from aqua-colored harbor water below to sky-blue water beyond, and on to a wide layer of dark-blue sea defining the horizon. It was a beautiful sight, not only for its bright mix of color but also for the joy it brought—to finally be sailing again. Still, Garret's absence darkened his soul. She'd steadfastly resisted venturing into the clouded world of piracy. He drew some comfort from his agreement with Blair to avoid the kind of all-out piracy being practiced by others, like De Graaf. Their assaults would be limited to Spanish-flagged merchants. Any others were off limits. After all, he thought, they were men of honor—principled and thoughtful, just as Drake had been. And, at least for now, they would fly no colors, least of all the blood red that pyrates increasingly flew.

Standing on the shore, Garret placed her arm on Kat's shoulder, watching her two ships breach the harbor's edge. She'd learned this was the day of departure, though that information hadn't come from William. He'd elected to take both ships without her consent. She regretted it had come to that but didn't fully blame him, believing he was following his head, not his heart.

It was difficult to be mad at William. Her feelings for him ran too deep. She fought the ache in her heart as the ships entered open water. There was no guarantee she would ever see them, or William, again. The ocean was like that—it gave and withdrew like a wave washing ashore and then receding—forever separating sailors from their loved ones. And yet, despite the risks, the sea summoned men like a lady of the night, reaching deeply into their soul and tugging at it relentlessly. William had chosen his lady. It wasn't her.

"Will we see him again?" asked Kat.

"I am certain we shall," Garret replied, burying her misgivings.

"I shall keep watch, every day."

Garret pulled the girl close, knowing that Kat's feelings for William, though different from her own, also ran deep. After Jorge's death, the girl increasingly turned to William as a father figure. And William obliged, with stories, lessons and comfort, much like a real father might. But now, thought Garret, he'd taken a dark turn—crossing over to piracy. How could she justify his decision if Kat were to ask? She hoped the girl didn't. Thank goodness no blood red flag flew on either of the two ships, to draw her attention.

There was one other concern Garret wrestled with, apparently unlike William—her future with her beloved England. Relinquishing that bond was not an option for her.

————

Attila, the virile young pyrate captain, strode from the shore with two of his men. His eye was drawn to Captain Connachan, standing with her girl alongside. Having just watched *Orion* and *Pandora* depart, he was surprised Connachan wasn't aboard. That meant the Witch, as most pyrates referred to her, was now vulnerable. Here was his opportunity, he thought—to take her down and have it forever be known that he, not De Graaf, was the one who orchestrated her demise. It would add nicely to his escalating reputation. He deeply wished to surpass De Graaf as the most feared pyrate.

Unfortunately, he'd already informed his crew they'd leave on the morrow, to feast on Spanish treasure. Reneging on that wouldn't play well with the men. And there was no time to deal with the Witch himself. He embraced the two men alongside him as they strolled toward the Gente de Mar. "Well mates, it seems you shall not be joining me on the morrow. There is work for you here. And a generous reward. Let us discuss it over tankards."

XIX

The skiff bobbed in the water alongside *Death's Head*. Yosel secured it to the ship and ascended the netting to the taffrail. De Graaf was there to greet him, offering a hand and pulling him up through the entry port.

"Welcome back," smiled De Graaf.

"Thank you, Captain. It is good to be back…though Cartageña is a jewel I shall need to visit again soon."

"Perhaps you shall. It would be a fine mark on our names were we to take it." De Graaf grinned at the thought but recognized he would need to assemble an enormous force for such an assault. That required capturing several prizes and convincing a considerable portion of their crews to join him in a pirating life. Yet that was his ultimate goal—a fleeted warlord with sufficient forces to challenge any coastal town, or even a large city such as Cartageña.

Yosel nodded toward De Graaf's cabin. De Graaf understood— they should speak in private. "Come," he said, "share a drink with me."

Together in the Captain's quarters, Yosel and De Graaf discussed the Jew's visit to the city, over tankards of beer. Yosel informed him he'd initiated relations with Tesorero Sanchez, Cartageña's treasurer. Since he and Sanchez shared a certain financial expertise, they'd enjoyed several discussions on the subject. Yosel invited the man to dinners and extended their conversations to other topics of mutual interest. "The treasurer is particularly fond of beer," he explained. "And having consumed it, he boasts stoutly of his powers."

"What powers?" inquired De Graaf.

Yosel leaned in, "All ships entering the harbor must submit to his assessment of their cargo…even naval vessels; King Philip requires accountability for everything he sends to Cartageña."

De Graaf set his tankard on the table. "Anything else?"

"Caravans entering from Potosi's silver mines, or elsewhere, are similarly obligated. Truly, Sanchez knows more about Cartageña's flow of goods and capital than anyone."

"Can he be persuaded to share his knowledge with you?"

Yosel grinned. "I asked whether anyone had ever offered him a reward for information regarding large shipments of gold and silver."

"And?"

"He said no, though he appeared open to the idea."

"Excellent!"

"Excellent indeed. I told him I would soon return to Cartageña and remain awhile, to receive word of such activity…for his benefit."

"Fire the cannons!" exclaimed De Graaf.

Yosel sipped his beer. "I shall need someone to accompany me, as a messenger...and protector."

"Just so," acknowledged De Graaf. "The man will need to be discreet."

"I have given this much thought. An African would be best—a former slave who speaks little Spanish. He must deliver my messages to you without risk of interception." De Graaf nodded in agreement. Yosel continued, "I shall also need sufficient funds to reward Sanchez."

"How much?" De Graaf asked.

"I worry that the higher the reward, the more suspicious he will become, and the more demanding of a higher price." Again, De Graaf nodded. He liked the Jew's thinking. "Perhaps fifty pieces of eight for information on any naval vessel," suggested Yosel. "There may well be several. I should carry at least five hundred."

"So be it. I shall arrange for a chest and a sailor to accompany you back to Cartageña."

"Where shall I send the messenger when I have news?"

"The tavern in Santo Pedro. The Phantom and I agreed a few days ago to meet there every second week. The messenger can leave your sealed messages with the owner."

"I did not realize you had met with the Phantom. Is there anything you discussed that I should know?"

"We agreed to place blame for the Viceroy's death on Captain Connachan. The Phantom will tell his contacts the killing was at sea. For that to be credible, he asked that we attack a ship we can point to as the site where the Viceroy was slain."

"But how will you keep the crew from knowing the Viceroy was not actually onboard such a vessel? Their knowledge of that could undermine your story."

"Only my most trusted men shall accompany me."

Yosel sipped his beer and set down his tankard. "I have a thought."

"Which is?"

"Suppose you were to assault a small fishing vessel. After the attack, you alone investigate the hold and claim the Viceroy was chained there, among the fish." De Graaf leaned back, wondering where the Jew was headed. Yosel went on, "You order the men to kill the crew and burn the boat, to eliminate any evidence or implication of involvement in the Viceroy's death. They could be paid to later claim they witnessed Captain Connachan assault the vessel."

"But surely the men would imagine a generous reward for the Viceroy's rescue. They would ask why I chose to kill him instead."

"Tell them he was beaten and bloodied to the very edge of death…and that he was not of right mind; that he could not be trusted."

De Graaf grinned at the Jew's scheming, pleased that this man had come to his attention. He was worth his weight in gold.

———

All the sickness onboard *Mercilus* had delayed its return to Isla Tortuga. Captain Wenman felt fortunate, however. His condition was now improved enough that he could get a little air on deck, at times. Unfortunately, many of the crew were not so lucky. And more than a handful had been lost, including the old curmudgeon himself, Dr. Stafford. That left Stafford's assistant, Mr. Snadden, in charge of providing all medical services—something for which he was ill-prepared. On the bright side, Lieutenant Ward had recovered fully. He was now frequently on deck, leading those who hadn't yet taken ill or showed only mild symptoms.

Wenman had spent his downtime reading…and thinking about Garret. It seemed so long since he'd last seen her. He wondered whether she was still spending her days in the village and schooling her young friend. Or had she been drawn back to the sea for a period? If the latter, he hoped she would be back when he arrived. He looked forward to continued exploration of her physical attributes. It shouldn't be much longer now, and for that he was thankful.

———

Ayudante Vegas could scarcely believe his good fortune. A

mere week ago he'd sat in a cramped room, facing the possibility of imprisonment in a Spanish jail. But King Philip not only agreed to pay for Viceroy Valdez' release by his captors, he'd also seen fit to reward Vegas personally for his part in negotiating the exchange. He now accompanied the King's gold across the oceans to do just that. Standing on the main deck facing a brisk wind, he thought of the two locked chests the King entrusted to him. They were old and scuffed, with dulled brass handles at either end. Each measured around twelve inches by eighteen inches, and were about one foot in height at the rim. Together, they held well over forty thousand freshly minted Spanish doubloons; more than enough ransom money, Vegas thought.

He'd found that fondling handfuls of the gleaming gold yielded immense pleasure. But through all his playful handling of the coins, he failed to notice something unique about these particular doubloons. Because Philip was determined to find and execute the villains behind this egregious ransom scheme, he'd ordered the doubloons minted with a special character added beneath the Crusader's Cross—the tiny image of a ring. Tagging the coins this way facilitated tracking them after the exchange. Spanish authorities throughout the South Seas would be alerted to apprehend anyone who might use them for purchases.

Other thoughts rolled through Ayudante Vagas' mind as droplets of rain began pelting his face. He imagined the Viceroy would be deeply pleased by the enormous value King Philip placed on his life. Still, he wondered how many doubloons he should actually entrust to Señor Ortega, and on what terms.

Though he could hardly wait to meet the highly regarded Valdez, he harbored reservations about the riskiness of the exchange. How would the process unfold? There was no guarantee it would all occur without incident, especially given bloodthirsty pyrates were on the other end. His own exposure was significant. If anything were to go wrong, he would be held accountable. He felt a need to accompany Ortega on the exchange. And perhaps before that, he should be taken to see the Viceroy, to ensure the man was in good health…despite missing an ear. Could he even secure his own safety during such a visit? Further thought needed to be given to the process of concluding the transaction.

Also high on Vegas' mind was the uncertainty regarding Ortega, who could well be the ransom scheme's mastermind, not just a link in the communication chain. It was even possible he instigated the Viceroy's kidnapping. If so, what other deceptions might Ortega be capable of? The worst scenario Vegas could envision was the killing of the Viceroy, the loss of the doubloons, and he himself being implicated in a scheme to defraud the King—a sure recipe for his own execution.

In that moment, Vegas suddenly realized his life could be at stake in a different way as well. If Ortega had indeed planned this entire deception, he might seek to erase any trail leading back to his own involvement. That would mean eliminating anyone who knew of it—including Vegas himself. He would need to be alert to any attack the wealthy Cartageñian might orchestrate against him. Upon his return to the city, he would arrange for two of his finest soldiers to accompany him at all times.

His thoughts turned to one other worrying matter—the presence onboard of the King's agent, Rodrigo de Cuero. This was another man he didn't trust. The emotionless look in his eyes, the discomforting quietness of his presence, and the seemingly deliberate slowness of his movements, all gave Vegas pause. De Cuero was a man of few words—more inclined to listen than contribute to any conversation.

Though apparently ordered by the King to search quietly for the Viceroy's captors, Vegas doubted that was de Cuero's only mission. He seemed more than a mere intelligence gatherer. Within military circles, the King was rumored to employ assassins. De Cuero could easily be one of them. Was the man also tasked with keeping an eye on him, or perhaps even disposing of him if things went awry? It haunted Vegas. He would exercise extreme caution in sharing anything with anyone who might have de Cuero's ear.

———

Wispy clouds toyed with the slivered moon above Cartageña. The dark grounds behind the city's cathedral were scattered with worn wooden crosses and mostly off-vertical headstones marking the resting places of former believers. Ortega's manservant, Abeo, assumed the markers clumped closely together denoted family members. He avoided stepping on places where he imagined bodies lay beneath. His footsteps broke the cemetery's solemn silence but he could still hear distant, jovial voices emanating from the city's taverns.

The grounds flowing just beyond the cemetery were closely bordered by trees. Near the forest's edge, Abeo spotted a large rock. He chose to wait there for Babu's friend, Fernando—the soldier charged with guarding the slaves constructing the Governor's residence. Sitting on the rock, he reviewed what he intended to say, though he soon tired of waiting. He looked upward. Stars flecked the sky like a spray of pebble-shot holes in a distant black canvas, backlit by flickering candles.

The crunching sound of breaking twigs drew his attention. He turned quickly, spotting a dark figure emerging from the woods. Abeo noticed he wasn't in military uniform. That wasn't what he expected.

Abeo rose. The man came within two yards and then stopped, saying nothing. Unable to make out the face beneath the broad-brimmed hat, Abeo opened the discussion, "I am Babu's friend, Abeo." He extended his hand.

The man stood motionless, offering neither name nor hand. "You have information for me?"

"I do," Abeo nodded vigorously.

"What is it?"

"It concerns a conversation I overheard."

"Among whom?"

"Two men. I only recognized one—a military officer."

"Do you know this man's name?"

"I do. You yourself might recognize it. He is of high rank."

There was a pause. Abeo hesitated to provide the Ayudante's name, believing the soldier would pay handsomely for it. Instead, the man shifted course.

"What was the content of this discussion?"

"The two men discussed an exchange."

"Of what?"

"Money."

Fernando spit to his side in a demeaning manner. "Men exchange money every day. Why should this exchange interest me?"

"The amount is significant," he responded, looking from side to side to ensure no one
else was present.

"I need more. Do not waste my time." Fernando seemed more frustrated than interested.

"Several thousand pieces of eight."

Fernando went silent. Abeo couldn't tell what the soldier was thinking, but the drumming of his fingers against his leg suggested he was thinking so hard that he was unconscious of his own movements. It bode well for his willingness to pay for further details. Abeo waited patiently, relishing the moment.

"I need the officer's name. And the item being exchanged."

Despite Babu's assurance that Fernando wouldn't use violence to obtain the information, Abeo had tucked a small knife into his belt at the base of his spine. Slowly preparing his right hand to grasp it, if necessary, he responded carefully, "I can provide both." He let the words hang in the air, confident Fernando would grasp that he must extend an offer.

"You shall be fairly rewarded for your cooperation."

"Might I ask what value your commander may place on this information?"

"The only thing that should interest you is the value that *I* place on it." Again, he spat to the side. "Fifty reales."

Abeo didn't like being played the fool. He knew the information was worth several times that amount. He needed to reset Fernando's thinking, just like his master did in any negotiation. "For one hundred, I shall provide the exact amount of the transaction. For another five hundred, the name of the military officer. For an additional one thousand, I shall identify the item to be exchanged, which I assure you will be of enormous interest."

"That is a bold request," said Fernando, appearing to understand that he wasn't dealing with some uneducated slave. "You realize I could arrest you now and force you to disclose this information."

"I do. But Babu assured me you are a man of reason."

Fernando paused. He was proud of his reputation. "I shall confer with my comandante." He reached into his pocket and withdrew his hand to see what was there—a mere five reales and three pieces of eight. "This is all I have." He extended his hand with the coins. "Take these as good faith that I shall return with more. Let us meet here again at the same time, two days hence."

Abeo reached out and opened his hand to accept the payment. "I thank you, sir. I shall not disappoint you."

"You had best be certain of that."

As he left the forest and cathedral behind, Fernando suspected the information Babu's friend held could well be worth the payment he requested. Perhaps even more—it had the potential to advance his own military career. Yet the amount was beyond anything he could authorize himself.

He wondered exactly how Abeo had stumbled across such valuable information. It was unlikely to have come from a conversation held in a public place. Perhaps it was a private meeting where this slave would not have been observed by the other two men. It was even possible the two had met in one of their own residences. Perhaps Abeo served as a slave in the residence. He made a mental note to query Babu regarding this slave's occupation.

XX

In the wilds of the world, where prey leads predators follow. That was just as true on the surface of the world's oceans, particularly in the picturesque strait separating Hispaniola from Cuba. Sailors called it the 'Windward Passage'. Spanish traders frequented it to peddle their merchandise in the South Sea islands and on to the Spanish Main. Pyrates knew that Spanish naval presence in the Passage was sporadic, making these treasure-hunting waters both rich and vulnerable. The arrival of Viceroy Valdez at Inagua was intended to change that dynamic. But following the Viceroy's kidnapping, Spain's primary naval installation at Inagua was in disarray. Even worse, the Viceroy had already dispersed much of the fleet throughout the colonies, to protect villages from sea-borne raiders. As a result, the Windward Passage remained largely undefended. Pyrates lived large there.

Captain William Tovery, on *Orion*, and Master's Mate Blair, now in temporary command of *Pandora*, prowled the northern entry to the Passage, aiming to capture Spanish treasure. Gold, silver and jewels were high on the list of desirables. But there was excellent demand for other cargo as well—slaves and ivory from Africa; silks and spices from Asia; sugar and molasses from the islands themselves; and koffei beans and coca leaves now increasingly popular in Europe. Cargo such as this could be traded for prices favoring both pyrates and devious merchants who formed the foundation of the so-called 'dark' market.

Pyrates had other needs as well, including food, ships' supplies, and spare parts for their own vessels. So hunting proved fruitful in a multitude of ways. And every single ship had value to pyrates. Even other pyrate vessels might become prey. In that regard, pyrates were not unlike cannibals—prepared to eat their own given desperate need or reasonable opportunity.

Standing on *Orion's* main deck, scanning vacant waters over the port side, William found himself more anxious than he'd expected. It was his first time as commander of the two ships, and much was expected of whoever was in charge. It now occurred to him just how much pressure Garret must have felt at times. Not only did he need to locate suitable prey but he had to orchestrate a successful raid as well. Without both, he was likely to be scorned by the men. Perhaps even deposed. It reminded him of something he'd once heard Admiral Drake say—if you look behind and find no one following, you are not a leader. So he understood the need to earn his men's respect. This was unlike earning a post in the Queen's navy. Here, the *crew* decided who would be Captain, not the Admiralty. His anxiety was growing exponentially as time passed. He turned away from the taffrail and called out to the young lookout atop the mainmast, "What see you, Robert?"

The young man jerked at the sound of the call, peering down to see Captain Tovery looking his way. He quickly scanned all around him. There was nothing visible beyond blue water and a vivid sky painted with sweeping white clouds. "Nothing, sir."

"Thank you," replied William. "Keep a watchful eye, young man. Two pieces of eight, should you spot a prize."

"Aye, cap'n."

William proceeded to his cabin, conscious of the questioning looks on some of the men's faces. Once inside, he walked to the table where he'd laid out three maps earlier. His last reckoning placed him near the northwest coast of Hispaniola, meaning there was still much water to sail. He pulled aside the top map and looked at the one beneath it, though only briefly. He pulled that map aside as well and gazed at the next. A thought suddenly came to him—what about an assault on a small coastal village? If he were unsuccessful finding prey at sea, he might need to resign himself to an assault on land—an act of desperation, he thought. Still, he would scan the maps for a village that might prove easy to capture. Hopefully, it wouldn't come to that.

For nearly half the hour, William poured over his maps, his tankard of beer running down to its dregs. His right eye was feeling fatigued from lengthy scrutiny through his magnifying glass.

"Sail ho," screamed Robert, from the fighting top. The muffled sound snaked into William's cabin through his partially open door.

"Thank God," William said aloud, to himself. He raced to the deck. "Where away, Robert?"

"Behind us, sir. Five points to larboard from the stern."

Looking out in the approximate direction, William scanned the horizon, right to left, slowly. Sunlight glanced off a distant white sail. William squinted to enhance his focus. Given the angle of the ship, he noted what appeared to be two topgallants and two topsails, square-rigged on the foremast. He was unable to make out a third mast, absent which it was unlikely to be a warship. Probably a two-master, he concluded—a brigantine. Its pennant appeared burgundy-colored. Definitely not English. His heart raced. This was the meal he hungered for. It was approaching at an angle. "Come about," he yelled, seeking to meet his prey head-on. "All hands. Lively now. Luff the sails, gentlemen. Gun crews at the ready."

The rigging slackened, then tightened, as *Orion* began leaning toward its intended direction. That alone caught Blair's attention on

Pandora. He picked up the signals coming from the flagship and instructed his crew to replicate *Orion's* turn, in haste. *Pandora* would widen its position, however, to strengthen the attack.

William was now breathing rapidly. Reaching firing range couldn't happen quickly enough. Unfortunately, the wind wasn't in his favor, and time was a constraining factor—striking distance needed to arrive before the drowning of the sun. He paced the deck, his hands sweating.

His mind turned to Garret. There was no doubt she would not approve of his taking this prize without a commission from the Queen. But he desperately wished, at the very least, to earn her grudging respect for his skill in capturing it.

———

Happy to be back in Cartageña, Yosel had headed to Palacio Real, the inn and tavern where he'd met with Tesorero Sanchez on previous occasions. Having secured two rooms and arranged for a message to be delivered to the Tesorero, he decided to enjoy a fine meal. He left his room and knocked on the door of the adjoining one, where the African pyrate accompanying him was resting.

"Food?" he called out. He heard the big man stir inside.

Bora had been taken as a slave from a village near the west coast of Africa's Songhai empire. A man of the minority Bassa people, he was betrayed by one of his own who harbored ill will toward his family. He was taken by people of the Wangara tribe and sold to Spanish slavers. The slave ship was later seized by Caribbean pyrates who offered him an opportunity to join them as a free man. Understanding only the word 'free', he accepted. Within months, he found himself sailing on a different ship—one commanded by the infamous pyrate, Harker. De Graaf was the master's mate at the time.

Though Bora spoke little English, he understood important words, like 'food'. He opened the door, smiling at Yosel.

Descending the stairs to the tavern, Yosel scanned the room to see whether he recognized anyone. There were only two, neither of whom he'd engaged with previously. He presumed they were frequent customers. Bora followed him down the steps to an open table where they sat, awaiting someone to serve them.

It took longer than Yosel expected for the server to arrive; the tavern wasn't that busy. But the man finally came. "Might I speak with you separately, sir?"

Yosel rose, wondering whether his message had already been received by Tesorero Sanchez, and the server now bore his reply. But it wasn't that.

The server leaned in, whispering, "We do not serve people of his kind here." He nodded his head in Bora's direction.

Yosel didn't like the server's tone. On the other hand, he didn't wish to make things uncomfortable for him. "Is the owner here?" he asked.

"Not at this moment."

"Who is in charge then?"

"I am, if you please."

Yosel didn't like that answer. He hoped to discuss the situation with a gentleman of higher understanding. Still, he wasn't inclined to take his business elsewhere. "This man is my partner, not my slave."

"Still," the server shrugged, "his color."

Yosel looked back at Bora. The man's skin was black as night.

He turned back to the server. "His skin is deeply colored by the sun after many months at sea."

The server looked at Bora again, in apparent disbelief. "I am afraid…"

Yosel cut the man short. "You shall serve me *and* my sun-browned partner." He took his hand from his pocket and placed a doubloon in the server's palm. "Do you understand?"

The server hesitated, but the gold seemed to weigh heavily.

"I have no desire to make this difficult for you, my good man," said Yosel, patting him on the shoulder. "Should anyone ask, you may blame the effect of the ocean's sun for my partner's color."

The server recognized this would be the excuse he would give his owner, should one of the customers complain to him. " Just so," he replied. Yosel returned to the table and sat. The server followed, "What is your pleasure then, gentlemen?"

———

Not certain what disturbed her sleep, Garret opened her eyes. She looked around the room without raising her head. Kat was fast asleep on the bed across from her. There was no sound. Nothing was amiss. She closed her eyes but didn't immediately fall back to sleep. Thoughts began weaving through her mind but were suddenly interrupted by another noise emanating from outside the wall with the lone window. She opened and directed her eyes that way. There was a quick shadow of movement. A tree branch swaying in the wind, perhaps? But it had only moved in one direction.

Garret threw off the covers and rose from the bed, reaching for her cutlass with one hand and grabbing her boots with the other. She strode barefoot to the door of the cabin, trying her best not to wake Kat. Arriving at the door, she waited, placing her ear against the wall. She could barely make out a kind of shuffling sound. A wild boar perhaps? There were plenty on the island. She propped her cutlass against the wall and drew on one of her boots. As she began pulling on the second, the cabin door was forced crushingly inward, almost removing the hinge from the wall. She let go of the boot and grabbed her cutlass. Placing her back firmly against the wall, she slid into a crouched position, a mere two feet from the door. A dark boot appeared in the doorway, planting itself heavily on the ground inside. She watched the blade of a cutlass rise upward.

Kat, startled by the noise, jerked up from her bed and ran to the bedroom door. She screamed at the hulking, dark figure in a long coat filling the doorway, cutlass drawn and pointed. Her scream drew the large man's attention.

Garret spotted her opening. She slashed her sword upward from the ground, aiming for the man's wrist. Her half-swing cut deeply into the flesh above his wrist, stopping at bone. The intruder howled in pain, his cutlass decoupling from his grip. He stumbled forward and fell to his knees, grasping at his badly bleeding forearm.

Kat turned and raced to find her own sword. A second man rushed in behind the first, sword drawn. He swung in Garret's direction. His slash hit the wall above her head. Garret rolled away and scrambled to her feet, sword at the ready. Her assailant reached for the pistol in his bandolier. Garret thrust her sword toward him, forcing him to lean back. She charged at him immediately but the first intruder swung a leg at her ankle, causing her to lose her balance. She fell.

Kat dashed into the room, sword raised in her right hand. She screamed for all her might, drawing the attention of the man in the doorway. He glanced at her, giving Garret a split second to roll onto her front and get to her knees. The intruder turned back and came at Garret hard, his sword swinging crosswise at her head. Her own sword redirected the blow just enough that her opponent's blade tasted only a little of her blood. But her sword slipped from her hand, falling to the ground.

Kat, both hands now on the hilt of her sword, brought it crashing down on the face of the man on the floor. It cut through his cheek, lips and chin, spurting blood everywhere and causing him to jerk his one good arm to his face. She struck again, this time against his raised arm. He screamed in agony, writhing on the floor.

The second intruder raised his sword to strike Garret's head one last time. She sprang low, head first, toward his forward ankle. Grabbing hold and yanking hard, she compelled his back leg to slip from under him. He fell onto his backside, his head slamming against the ground. Garret snatched her cutlass and took to her feet, one of which was still bootless. She thrust the point of her sword directly at the fallen man's neck, within a hair of his larynx. Blood dripped from her head-wound onto his trousers. There was sudden silence, except for the gurgling of the man who'd burst through the door first, blood now bubbling up and out of his mouth and pouring down his left cheek.

"Who are you?" Garret asked of the second intruder. He said nothing. She pressed the point of her blade lightly against his throat, drawing a small bead of blood. "Who sent you?" The man's eyes darted toward his partner, as if to see whether he was coming to his aid. "There is no one here to save your rotten soul," she added in response to his movement.

Kat, taking a cue from Garret, stood over the first man with her sword at his neck. Blood flowed like lava from his wounds. His body was convulsing, though he appeared unconscious.

The man at the point of Garret's sword looked directly at her, uncertain what to say. He'd been sent by Attila, the pyrate captain who hoped to embellish his reputation by ordering Garret's execution. Attila had warned the two would-be assassins that, were they to be foiled in their attempt, they should lay blame at De Graaf's feet; make him the fool. Here, now, on the edge of his life, the words came quickly. "De Graaf," he stuttered.

Garret suspected the man was lying; she knew De Graaf was man enough to take her on himself. She pressed a touch harder on her sword, drawing a little more blood from the man's neck. "Speak truthfully or breathe your last."

The intruder's eyes spoke his fear. "De Graaf," he said again. "Spare me," he added.

"What good could come of my sparing you? Will you not simply strike again?"

The man whimpered like a beaten child, "Never."

"Your word is of no value to me." She pulled back her cutlass.

The man grasped at his neck to stem the bleeding. He whispered, painfully, "What can I do?"

"How much were you paid?" demanded Garret.

"Two doubloons."

"Do you have them?"

"My boot."

"Which one?"

He pointed to his left foot with his free hand.

Garret knelt to one knee, placing her cutlass near the man's groin and pushing it gently inward, letting him know it was there. With her free hand, she reached down the inside of the boot, her fingers feeling for a pocket. She withdrew her hand, holding two doubloons.

"Is this all I am worth?" she asked, rising to her feet but keeping the point of her sword firmly at the man's crotch. He didn't respond. "How much is *De Graaf* worth?"

The intruder looked again to his fallen partner, who had stopped moving. "Less than you," he answered.

Garret turned to Kat, "Is he breathing?" She was referring to the first assailant.

"I cannot be certain."

"Keep your sword at his throat. Reach down and place your hand against his neck, like so." She demonstrated. "Keep your hand there to the count of ten and tell me whether you feel anything."

Kat followed the instructions. "Nothing, mum."

Comfortable the first intruder was done for, Garret spoke again to the man at the end of her sword, "I shall pay you twice what De Graaf has given you. Four doubloons; the two here in my hand and two others when you take his life." She knew the math didn't exactly hold up, but sensed this man wasn't smart enough to know the difference. The two doubloons he'd brought were now hers. So it was, at the very least, a half-truth. The other two doubloons would come from his dead partner's boot, where she assumed he, too, had hidden them.

"De Graaf is surrounded by his men."

"Find a way," Garret yelled back, "or I shall find you." She threw the two doubloons out the door. "Now, leave your sword and your pistol, and go. Come back for the remaining doubloons once the deed is done.”

The intruder rose and stumbled out the door in haste, picking up the doubloons as he went. Garret knew he wouldn’t return…nor would he follow through on killing De Graaf. Nevertheless, her message would be sent.

Kat rushed to Garret’s side. “You are bleeding.”

“Tis but a scratch,” Garret replied, placing her hand on the girl’s shoulder. “You were fierce in the face of battle.”

“Lyoness de Tortuga!” Kat smiled, though tears of relief spilled onto her cheeks.

“Indeed you are,” responded Garret. ‘*The girl showed more bravery than some of my crew.*’ She thought. “I am so sorry you have had to witness such brutal actions in your short life.” She was referring not only to the events of this night but also to the action onboard *Pandora* the night Viceroy Valdez was slain.

“I saw many bad things in London,” Kat replied. “They stay with me, but do not control me.”

Garret understood. The little street urchin had grown up in the very pits of the city’s dark side.

“Why did you let him go?” Kat asked, referring to the departed intruder.

“He fears me now. He will not come at us again.”

“But De Graaf will.”

‘*The girl is wise beyond her years,*’ thought Garret. She had little doubt De Graaf would challenge her again. But she was unaware this assault was Attila’s design, not De Graaf’s. Both pyrates had her on their kill list. Her life wasn’t about to get easier anytime soon.

XXI

"Pull the lines," he shouted. "Ready the sails." Captain Juan la Roja had seen a thin, dark line of clouds forming in the distance—a storm coming. He had no idea a far more lethal tempest was bearing down on his ship. The *Visser*, his two-masted buss, was designed specifically for ocean fishing. Having enjoyed two fruitful days, its hold was half-filled with fish. La Roja already looked forward to a handsome payday upon his return, so there was no sense in risking the oncoming weather. *Visser* came alive as some of the crew drew in the fishing lines while others worked the rigging. La Roja took the helm.

The buzz of activity onboard kept la Roja and his men from spotting the fast-approaching *Death's Head*. It was fully sheeted, with the wind in its favor and its crew fully prepared for their assault. Cannons were loaded with grapeshot, to rip open the sails and take down the crew without badly damaging the ship itself. De Graaf's plan, the one he'd initiated with the Phantom and then finely tuned with Yosel, was about to unfold. But none of his men knew the deception that was about to transpire. One thing was certain, however—none of the *Visser's* crew would survive to tell the real story.

As the pyrate ship came within range, its appearance was finally picked up by its prey. Captain la Roja, hoping for the best, immediately ordered the raising of a white flag, hoping to appease the pyrates by surrendering. His fish, as valuable as they were, were not worth the lives of his crew nor the loss of his vessel. He'd been assaulted once before and surrendering had played out well—he and his crew survived. Unfortunately for him, this particular predator was of a different nature. It was barely of the same species.

De Graaf was upset by the white flag's appearance. Firing on a surrendering vessel was frowned upon, even by pyrates. They rightly believed such a practice would only encourage future prey to fight rather than surrender. But De Graaf's plan demanded an assault. And this was precisely the kind of ship he needed to attack—a fishing vessel with a cargo hold. Besides which, his crew could use the target practice.

"Guns at the ready," he yelled. "No quarter to be given."

"At the ready, cap'n. No quarters," came the reply from Stevens.

"Fire at will!"

A sudden shower of small iron balls streaked forward like a dark cloud, exploding ahead of an orange flame trailed by smoke. Hearing the pyrate's call, the men on the *Visser* dropped to the deck, grabbing anything they could, to hold on. Those who failed to drop quickly, including Captain la Roja, were peppered and shredded by grapeshot, forcing their fall. The remaining sailors held on as the ship came under a second volley. Pistols were fired down on them by De Graaf's sharpshooters positioned high in the rigging. Two more men aboard the *Visser* yielded their lives. One of the crew, shaking and in tears, stood up with his hands raised in surrender. He was quickly dropped by pistol shots to his chest.

De Graaf and six of his most trusted men jumped into a longboat and rowed to the now seemingly lifeless *Visser*. When they reached it, De Graaf was first over the side, cutlass drawn. He had only one thing in mind—getting to the hold. On his way, he skewered a crewman begging for his life, thrusting the sword so firmly that it pierced through the back of the man's neck. He withdrew it quickly and headed down to the hold, while his men ensured the rest of the *Visser's* crew were done for.

De Graaf was surprised by the quantity and variety of fish he found in the hold. It seemed a shame to waste them. But it was necessary. He waited long enough to make his tale plausible before hastily returning to the deck. His men looked at him intensely, anxious to learn of the value of their prize.

"Burn the ship," he barked. The men stood looking at each other, not understanding why they would do such a thing.

"Burn it," he screamed.

The men spread what little gunpowder they had. Two offered up the grenados they'd brought along. He had them lay those at his feet. One handed him a lit torch before they all disembarked. They waited in the longboat for De Graaf to set the vessel aflame, most swearing under their breath at the sheer insanity of it all.

De Graaf was confident there would be nothing remaining of the *Visser*. He lit the two long-fuse grenados one at a time, throwing them down into the hold. He torched the sails and then lit the long-fuse leading to the gunpowder.

The explosions began earlier than De Graaf expected, launching him off the edge of the vessel and into the water, yards beyond the longboat. His men rowed toward him. They pulled him in and continued rowing to a safer distance, watching the explosive fire rapidly envelop their prey. The *Visser* burned robustly, as if in anger, smoke billowing upward in a dark cloud. The beleaguered vessel would soon begin its descent to its final resting place.

One of De Graaf's men posed the question they were all thinking, "Why cap'n? Why we be burnin' this 'ere ship?"

He turned to face the man. "There was nothing in the hold but the Viceroy of Inagua." The men appeared shocked. They'd all heard stories about the Viceroy's kidnapping and rumors of his death. De Graaf waited, letting it sink in before continuing, "He was beaten and tortured to the point of meeting the devil. There was no mending him, and no way to return his body without undue scrutiny. Burning the ship leaves no evidence that could lead to our execution by the Spanish." The men nodded—more out of respect for De Graaf than for truly agreeing with him.

De Graaf went on, "You are all witnesses here. On pain of death, you must say nothing of this, other than what I tell you now." He looked each man in the eyes, sequentially. They all nodded in his sight.

"On pain of death," he reiterated for emphasis; there could be no misunderstanding. "In time, unless I find word of this has traveled beyond our crew, you shall each receive twenty pieces of eight. At that point, you will be free to share the story. But here is the version you must tell."

He paused momentarily, making certain they were all attentive. "Let it be known that we found English pyrates onboard this vessel. We shall say they held the Viceroy prisoner but beat and tortured him to death." Again, he scanned the men's eyes individually, waiting until each nodded agreement before moving his eyes to the next.

"One last thing," he said. "And this is most important. We shall lay blame for the Viceroy's death at the foot of the Witch...Captain Connachan."

"But she was not even…" began one of the men. His words turned to a gurgle as De Graaf's dagger entered his throat. The man slumped forward. His mates looked away. They all knew who Connachan was, and that this wasn't her doing. But the promise of money…and fear of death…spoke loudly. Convincingly.

De Graaf turned to look again at the hulk that was once the *Visser*. Its flaming mainmast crumbled as the carcass slipped beneath the surface, returning its fish to the sea. He grinned at the ease with which this necessary deception had played out.

———

It was the kind of victory Captain William Tovery, privateer-sans-commission, hoped for. The Portuguese merchant flying Spanish colors quickly responded to *Orion's* warning shot by raising a white flag. Being flanked by *Pandora* as well no doubt contributed to the merchant captain's decision. The takeover ended the way Admiral Drake always preferred, thought William—bloodless. In that way, the victory itself was a tribute to the deceased Admiral.

Now standing before the Portuguese captain…as a freshly minted pyrate…William was as magnanimous as was his mentor, "I thank you for your decision not to engage, Captain."

"The safety of my crew is my primary concern," replied Captain Luis Drago.

"I commend you for that. We are nothing without the support of our men."

"Indeed."

"I can assure you, we shall take only what we need. You must understand, however, that I shall also offer your crew an opportunity to join my own, as free men."

"That is certainly your right." Drago nodded, glancing at the faces of his men. "I ask only that you leave me with sufficient men to sail my ship."

"We shall take less than ten," William replied. Another thought occurred to him. "Are there slaves onboard?"

"I have no interest in slaving," replied Drago, "Tis a barbaric practice."

"Just so. I only ask because, were there any, we would extend them the same offer to join us."

William's men worked well into the night, transferring goods and supplies from the captured ship into *Orion's* hold. They were assisted by the three members of Drago's crew who elected to join the English pyrates. William was surprised so few had done so. He suspected it was because Drago was that rare leader who appreciated his men rather than abused them. The harsh discipline typically dispensed by merchant captains tended to squeeze the very souls out of their sailors, leaving them mere empty vessels.

Sitting in his cabin following a light meal, William shared tankards of beer with Drago. Amid the creaking of the ship and swaying of the lanterns, they swapped seafaring adventures. William was careful not to disclose more than was appropriate regarding the Queen's missions.

Drago was particularly interested in hearing of William's voyages with Drake, and what he'd learned from the famous Admiral. While the Spanish King viewed Drake as a pirata, Drago admired him for having circumnavigated the globe. It was a remarkable display of seamanship that hadn't gone unnoticed by any seafarer, no matter their country of origin. And though Drake was only the second to sail the globe, he was the first captain to actually survive such a voyage.

For his part, William sought to learn more about the inner workings of the trading world. Over much beer, the two men forged an affinity for each other. As the evening wore on, William posed a pointed question, "Tell me, my friend, would you consider joining me…as a privateer?"

Drago shook his head. "It is not in my blood to be a warrior."

"You a religious man, then?"

"No. Not in the truest sense."

William leaned in. "I am prepared to have you be a full partner. We could use a man with your knowledge and skills. We could also use your ship," he admitted.

"You say you are a privateer, yet you have taken my ship as a pyrate."

"Only out of necessity," replied William.

"Still, does such action not make you a pyrate by definition?"

William leaned back, taking yet another sip of beer. Thoughts of Garret filled his head. Would *she* now think him a pyrate? He looked up at the ceiling. "Perhaps there is a middle ground."

"How so?"

"I have only ever operated as a privateer, under the Queen's purview. Yours is the first ship I have taken without England's support." He leaned in again. "Keep in mind, there was no damage to your ship or your crew."

"I thank you for that."

"You must understand—until I receive a new commission, I must keep my men fed, paid and happy. But I am committed to taking only Spanish-flagged vessels." He placed his tankard on the table. "Or Portuguese ships, since you are now under Spanish rule."

"I see. Not privateer yet not wholly pyrate."

"Precisely. And you are Portuguese yet not wholly Spanish." William leaned back again. "Do you not have anger toward Spain?"

"I am a simple merchant captain, not a man of politics."

"But surely you must bear some resentment over your country's inability to possess complete freedom."

"There is truth in that," Drago acknowledged, after sipping his beer.

"Then join us. I cannot imagine you enjoy being a servant captain to a Spanish overlord who is likely ruthless in *financial* ways."

Drago grimaced. "The man is a bastard."

"I can assure you, the pay you receive as a Spaniard's underling is unlikely to match your fortunes as a free privateer."

Drago took a deep breath. "Allow me to give your offer further thought."

———

This time, Abeo didn't have to wait for Officer Fernando to arrive; the military guard was already waiting for him in the dark, beyond the edge of the cemetery. He imagined Fernando had brought the reales with him. In return, he would share the information he'd overheard Ortega discussing with Ayudante Vegas regarding their ransom scheme. Though he would never betray his master, he was more than happy to offer up Vegas.

"Buenas noches," said Fernando. He didn't extend his hand.

"Buenas noches."

"My comandante has agreed to the terms you requested."

Abeo was surprised there was no negotiation. He realized he should have asked for more. Perhaps there might still be an opportunity to do that. "You have the money?"

"I do. But first, tell me what you know."

"Where is it?"

"Nearby."

Abeo tried to discern the look on Fernando's face but the dark wouldn't permit it. Was the guard speaking the truth?

Fernando continued, "So…who is this man you recognized? The military officer."

"May I see the money?"

Fernando hesitated briefly. "Follow me," he said. He turned, walking slowly in the dark. Abeo followed for about twenty yards. Fernando leaned down behind a tree, pulling out a small box with tarnished brass handles on either end. He opened it and stood with the box at his feet. Abeo saw the silver reales. They glinted in the light of a slivered moon filtered by the moving branches of the trees above. Still, this couldn't possibly be the full one thousand he requested.

"I need the name," said Fernando.

"Do I have your word I shall be paid for each item I share, and that I may walk away freely when this matter ends?"

"You have my word. But understand, if you lie to me, this will end badly for you."

"I understand," Abeo nodded.

"The name," Fernando repeated.

"Pedro Vegas."

"The Ayudante?"

"The same."

"You are certain of this?"

"I am."

"And his intent?"

Abeo looked around before responding, "To deceive the King."

Fernando nodded. He'd brought a second box of coins in the event the answer to the first question warranted it. "Tell me, what was the amount of the exchange?"

"Have you brought additional silver?"

"I have."

"The two men discussed thirty thousand doubloons," offered Abeo.

Fernando seemed staggered by the number. "You are quite certain that was the amount?"

"I am."

"What could possibly warrant that kind of money?"

Abeo shuffled, sensing this was his moment to ask for more. "I am afraid the circumstances have changed. I shall require another thousand reales to provide that information. It is of major significance."

"Do not play me the fool," Fernando fumed. "Tell me now or I shall take you directly to the comandante."

Abeo hadn't expected that. He looked around to see whether Fernando had brought other soldiers with him. But it was too dark; he could make out nothing but the forest itself. He reached to the small of his back, making as if to scratch it, though readying his hand to draw the knife tucked into his pants. That, and the name of the Viceroy were all he had to ensure his continued existence. "May I see the rest of the silver?"

"Do you not trust me?"

"It is not that I mistrust you." He looked around before continuing, "It is the strange circumstance I find myself in."

"The second box is there," Fernando said, pointing to the base of a tree, five yards away.

Abeo looked that way, spotting what appeared to be a brass handle. He turned back to Fernando. "Babu assured me you are a man of honor." He let out a breath and gave up the final piece, "The payment is a ransom for the Viceroy of Inagua, who is being held captive. That is all I know."

Fernando hesitated for several moments. Finally, he walked to the second box and pulled it forward. Two men emerged from the shadows. "These men shall help you collect your boxes."

As he watched the Black man depart, Fernando contemplated the true value of this information. Though most believed the Viceroy was dead, there were rumors he was still among the living. If those rumors were true—and they now appeared to be—then this was indeed good fortune for him personally. It meant he might well be at the very forefront of recovering the Viceroy. What's more, he could disclose the existence of a ransom scheme orchestrated by Ayudante Vegas…and perhaps others. He smiled at the thought that he might soon be elevated to a role that would no longer require overseeing slaves in the incessant dust and boredom of the construction site.

———

The movement of the sea against the ship had always caused his stomach to flutter. It also gave his throat an eerie feeling. Ayudante Vegas suspected it was something to which he might never become accustomed. Still, he was buoyed by his belief that this would be his final trip across the ocean. Now, more than ever, he was convinced the leftover proceeds from the earlier purchase of the Viceroy's ring, combined with his share of the doubloons soon to be exchanged for the man himself, would enable him to leave behind his military career for a handsome life in Cartageña. Nothing could get in his way now—he had the King's support and more than enough doubloons to close the deal with Señor Ortega. It was only a matter of how the exchange itself would take place. The only other detail to lock down was how much of the King's offering he and Ortega would choose to split between themselves. In doing that, Ortega would never be able to give him up without incriminating himself.

His thoughts turned once more to the other, less favorable, possibility—that Ortega might wish to eliminate him, to keep word of his own involvement from leaking out. Convinced Ortega was capable of that, he'd committed himself to employing his own security guards. But he preferred an option that would enable him to avoid living in constant fear for his life—eliminating Ortega altogether, after the deal was done. Yet how would he orchestrate it?

He sensed Ortega would be most vulnerable in transit, leaving his residence behind. He could have two men stake out the man's villa. Pyrates perhaps? The sailors and merchants in Cartageña spoke of such men often in the taverns. One pyrate, in particular, was widely discussed—a man named De Graaf. But Vegas had also heard other names of that ilk, including Attila and Connachan. Some claimed

Connachan was a woman. He couldn't see how that would be true, though it mattered little. He would try contacting this De Graaf, or Attila. Though it wasn't clear where they were based, it was common knowledge that pyrates frequented Isla Tortuga. Since King Philip's agent, Rodrigo de Cuero, was headed there, perhaps he could pay him to make inquiries; maybe even arrange an introduction. He headed to de Cuero's cabin, to see whether the man was open to the idea.

XXII

Mid-morning sun filtered into De Graaf's cabin at the ship's stern. Unlit lanterns swayed gently as *Death's Head* held anchor in the hidden harbor. Yosel and Bora had returned from Cartageña half an hour earlier. The Jew, looking a little disheveled, sat across from him, a tankard of beer in hand. The two were updating each other.

De Graaf was exuberant about sinking the *Visser*, and soon laying blame for the Viceroy's death at Connachan's feet. Thoughts of watching her swing from the gallows gave him great pleasure.

Yosel shared news of his discussions with the Cartageñian Treasurer, Sanchez. Apparently, no ships of real interest had arrived at the city—at least none carrying the kind of coinage De Graaf and Yosel expected might serve as ransom for the Viceroy. Nonetheless, Yosel had rewarded the Tesorero handsomely for the information he was providing, as a display of continued goodwill.

"Are you certain we can trust this man?" De Graaf asked.

"There is never any certainty when matching a man's word to his actions," Yosel admitted, "but I fully expect he shall bring me word when the right vessel arrives. He has nothing to lose and much to gain."

"He may well bring you news, yet he might also expose you to the authorities."

"That was my initial concern as well. So I made clear to him that my interest would continue well beyond this one event. I believe he now sees a fruitful future in providing me with ongoing information that would benefit both his interests and mine."

De Graaf sat back, letting that soak in. He saw the parallel between Harker's reliance on the Phantom for valuable information and

Yosel's relationship with the Tesorero. "This is most interesting. It bodes well for our current plan. And it does indeed open the door to future opportunities." He raised his tankard toward Yosel. "I applaud your handling of the matter."

"You may wish to delay that compliment until we actually obtain the information we need."

"Just so."

Yosel changed topics, "Are we still to meet with the Phantom on the morrow, as planned?"

"We are. But since the King's ransom payment has not yet arrived, the Phantom may not have information to share with us."

"Still, we could further discuss the ransom amount."

"The bastard seeks to buy us cheaply." De Graaf grumbled, failing to mention that the Phantom had already given him twelve hundred pieces of eight as payment for capturing and destroying an appropriate vessel, which ended up being the *Visser*. De Graaf had only promised his fellow attackers twenty each, to keep quiet about the event until the right time. So there would be plenty left over. Though he chose not to share that information, he was nevertheless committed to taking good care of Yosel; the Jew was valuable.

"We should demand a specific number," offered Yosel.

"Say more."

"Not a share, as we have before. Let us demand a minimum amount, below which we shall claim all the effort and risk surrounding the exchange itself is not worth it.

"You have a number in mind?" De Graaf sipped his beer.

"Twenty thousand."

"Pieces of eight?"

"Doubloons."

De Graaf was shocked. He shook his head in disbelief.

"This is not simply about a Viceroy," explained Yosel. "There are many of those. This particular one is said to be the King's most favored friend."

De Graaf nodded, feeling this was just one more example of why he needed Yosel's continued counsel.

———

Looking out from the bow, Captain James Wenman wondered what the circumstances were surrounding the three ships huddled in the distance. As far as he could determine, only one was flagged. It appeared to be a Portuguese brigantine. He suspected the other two ships might be pyrates who had bested her. If that were the case, *Mercilus* was ill-prepared to bring needed assistance to the besieged ship. Now nearing the end of its voyage, several of its crew had already died from fever, while many more were still suffering from its effects. Wenman himself wasn't fully recovered. He ordered the trailing of anchors, slowing his ship's progress without it being obvious to the three distant ships. He wished no confrontation but felt obligated to display the full confidence of the English navy, hopefully encouraging the apparent pyrates to flee.

It was Blair, onboard *Pandora*, who first glimpsed the oncoming vessel. As it neared, he could see it was an English-flagged warship. "Damnation," he uttered aloud; not that anyone could hear. He never wanted to be a pyrate in the first place, and now that he was, this warship threatened his very existence. "Damn Connachan and Tovery," he groaned. Immediate action was required. "Ship ahoy! Alert *Orion*," he yelled. "Prepare to set sails." He knew he couldn't call for their unfurling unless and until instructed by Captain Tovery.

William was in his cabin on *Orion* with Captain Drago when he heard the knock. The two were continuing their dialog on partnering. "Enter," he said.

It was Wakefield, William's Master's Mate. "Sorry to bother you, sir. An English warship approaches."

William rose immediately, sensing the seriousness of the matter. "I shall be right there." Wakefield left quickly. William headed to the door, turning back to look at Drago. "Let us continue this discussion at another time," he said. "For now, you must signal your ship to set sail with us." He hustled to the deck, the Portuguese captain following closely.

"Full sails. Lively now," William ordered, rushing to join Wakefield at the stern.

"There sir," said Wakefield, pointing in the approaching ship's direction.

"Definitely English," replied William. He wondered how best to play this out. Looking closely, he sensed there was something familiar about the vessel. "Do you recognize this ship?" he asked Wakefield.

"Only its English design."

"We agree then. Prepare to sail."

"Aye, sir," replied Wakefield. "Prepare to sail," he shouted.

Men who'd already scurried up the masts and along the yards, were furiously unfurling the sails. Others readied the clewlines. As

Orion's sails were secured, they created a series of cracking sounds, like gunshots—the massive sheets capturing the stiff wind. His ship's sudden lurch caused William to lose focus for a moment.

Hearing the distant call of Captain Tovery on *Orion*, the men onboard *Pandora* expected and heard an echoing call from Blair. The consort set its sails almost as quickly as the flagship.

Captain Drago signaled his crew to set sail and follow. The brigantine, however, was unresponsive. Unfortunately for him, Drago's crew appeared unaligned to the task at hand.

As *Orion* began turning broadside, William walked along the starboard side, peering intently at the seemingly familiar warship. Suddenly, it hit him. It was Wenman's ship. "Stow the sails," he demanded. There was no need to flee.

Wakefield was confused but relayed the call. The crew responded.

Bewildered by the sudden reverse in *Orion's* tactics, the men on *Pandora* shook their heads and followed suit. The two ships were now both in broadside position but the wind had forced a fair gap between them.

Drago watched in frustration as his ship, now almost fully sheeted, was moving away. He sensed his crew saw this as their opportunity to escape, even though it meant abandoning him.

Onboard *Mercilus*, Captain Wenman didn't like what he was seeing—the two pyrate ships had turned broadside…an obvious effort to make a stand rather than retreat. The Portuguese-flagged vessel, on the other hand, appeared to be fleeing. It was now decision time. What was he to do? Given their separation, the pyrate ships had him partially flanked. Already broadside, they also had an unacceptable advantage, although they hadn't yet opened their gun ports and rolled their cannons. He worried there wasn't enough time to turn broadside himself, in order to return effective fire. Barely out of range, he ordered the firing of his bow chasers as a warning shot—a display of willingness to engage. That might at least buy the Portuguese merchant more time to make good its escape.

William was shocked to see Wenman's bow chasers light up. The sound of the shots followed closely as the two small cannonballs headed his way. Either Wenman had lost his mind or he'd failed to recognize Garret's ships.

William hoped he was wrong—maybe this wasn't *Mercilus* coming at him. Or perhaps it *was Mercilus* but captained by someone other than Wenman. He knew he had to choose immediately—wait or not. Wait to see whether the warship would press its attack, which could prove costly, or take a chance on it being Wenman and hoist the white flag to seek quarters. If he did seek quarters, and this wasn't Wenman, he could well find himself at the mercy of the warship's captain; and maybe end up losing his two ships. Worse yet, he could be taken prisoner and tried for piracy. For a brief moment, he considered fleeing. But that was not his nature. Not with two ships. What a fool he would look to his men were he to turn tail.

The choice seemed clear—prepare for the worst and ready his ships for battle. Still, on the chance that this was indeed Wenman, he would send a message, hoping for a favorable response. "Signal the warship," he called out to his flagman. "One word—Tovery". He then turned to Wakefield, "Ready the cannons. Ports closed."

More shots headed *Orion's* way. The flagman, who was just beginning to wave his signals, ducked to avoid any possibility of being hit. The cannonballs came much closer this time, though still splashing harmlessly into the sea.

Drago's brigantine was now several hundred yards away in hasty retreat. Feeling deserted, he came alongside William, shaking his head in wonder at Tovery's decision not to return fire immediately.

Blair stood on *Pandora's* deck, also questioning William's inaction. In his mind, this was suicide.

———

There was no way to tell how old Kat was. Neither she nor Garret had any idea what year, let alone what day, she was born. Yet there were modest indications she might be coming of age. Garret recalled how her own grandfather had gone to great lengths to celebrate *her* birthdays. They might sail on the lake or hunt fox. Her favorite occasion was the last birthday before she'd left to join Drake for the first time. Grandfather Daniel had arranged a visit to their country residence in Scotland, a modest creekside cottage in a valley surrounded by rolling, velvet-green hills. A handful of Scotsmen in blue-green tartan kilts played their bagpipes on the grounds outside the cottage. She'd never before heard the wailing of the pipes. They brought the hills alive, seemingly drawing their notes from the mist and the nearby babbling brook. Cloaked in warm garments, she felt the cool Scottish air fill her nostrils with a freshness she'd never known. She remembered a calm coming over her at the time, bringing with it a longing to be at one with the land and the flowing waters. She and her grandfather had supped by the fire that night, feasting on something the Scotsmen called haggis—a mix of sheep's organs, onions and spices, boiled inside the lining of the animal's stomach. She savored it like no other meal before. Her grandfather also used that occasion to introduce her to a golden-colored drink brought from a monastery in Fife. The Scots called it usquebaugh. Her grandfather said the word meant 'the water of life'. The English, he said, called it whiskey. It stung her throat, making her cough as she drank it. Grandfather Connachan had laughed aloud. "No, Garret," he'd said, "you must sip it slowly; it is a most precious gift…from God himself."

Now, here on Isla Tortuga, with Kat perhaps nearing a comparable age, it seemed only fitting to extend her a similar celebration—honoring her coming passage into the next era of her life.

Though there was little to offer here, Garret decided to take the girl into the village for the first time. Although the streets of this pyrate haunt bore an element of risk, there was something to be gained by exposing the girl to the realities of the world in which she currently lived. Garret was confident Kat could now handle herself here, for the most part. Her prior existence as a London street urchin left her with the ability to sense impending danger. And she'd proven to be an excellent student on the use of both cutlass and dagger. What's more, over the last several months she'd reached a goodly height, been tested in battle, and demonstrated her courage. These signs suggested the girl was ready.

The two of them were dressed for their visit. Taking a page from her grandfather's book, Garret had done her best to style Kat with the rakish look of a cabin boy, rather than a young girl coming of age. The girl was entirely comfortable with that. Having lived in London's back alleys, she felt more comfortable in trousers than dresses anyway. For her part, Garret wore a white headband, beneath which her auburn locks were tied in a tail. She wore a dark blouse under a brown doublet, concealing her breasts as best she could. She had no desire to draw men's attention.

Both Garret and Kat wore a bandolier across their chests, containing a pistol. Their cutlasses were holstered at their hips. Each had a dagger sheathed beneath their belt, concealed in the small of their back. Their trousers were dark in color, their boots black. By intent, nothing about their appearance signaled femininity, other than the lack of facial hair. Garret knew she would be recognized for the woman she was; it just wouldn't be blatantly obvious. And there would surely be no confusing her for one of the geese who typically flocked around the seamen. She donned her black cavalier's hat as they left their cabin.

Kat could hardly contain her excitement while they strolled the busy street. She soaked in the many voices and the sounds of animals running freely. Street merchants barked at passersby, seeking to engage them in a transaction. They'd just left a small dry-goods shop offering the basic necessities of life. It also sold various curios and trinkets intended to catch a shopper's eye. She'd noticed small wood carvings by one of the island's artisans.

As they stepped through the door of a larger shop selling general supplies for seafarers and their ships, Kat's eyes were drawn to a colorful green-winged parrot with a bluish face, orange eyes and a mostly white beak. One of its legs was lightly attached by a string to the top of a wooden stand. The bird made long eye contact with her. She tugged at Garret, drawing her attention to the bird. "Might we buy it?" she asked.

"If you could purchase but one thing, would it be this?"

"It would indeed," Kat responded, without hesitation.

'*Ah, the passions of youth*,' thought Garret. She smiled at Kat, not wishing to diminish the enthusiasm of a little girl from the young woman she was becoming. "If you wish, then."

The two walked on after purchasing the parrot. It perched itself comfortably on Kat's shoulder, its leg attached to her belt by a string. Kat fed it with seeds the shopkeeper provided. He hadn't given the bird a name. Kat would think on that.

As morning dissolved to afternoon, Garret took Kat to the Gente de Mar. It was still early for pyrates to be descending on the place; most preferred living the night and sleeping through the early day, recovering from the night's revelry. The tavern's interior seemed bright, catching the sunlight as it did. Garret stood near the entryway, waiting for the server to approach. It was Cath. The last time Garret was here, she'd come to the girl's aide when a drunken sailor gave her trouble.

"Tis good to have you back, Captain," said Cath.

"Tis good to see you as well." She turned slightly. "This is my friend, Kat." The two girls nodded at each other. Cath was a few years older but about the same height. Unlike Kat, she showed her feminine side in a manner designed to catch the eye of customers. Her uncle—Prince, the tavern owner—had counseled her to dress in such a fashion if she wished to obtain the most generous of tips from the men. Her modest bosom, swelled and lifted by a tight corset, was clearly the focal point she intended it to be. Her partially open blouse revealed small but plump breasts with an invitingly smooth channel running between them. The softly pointed yellow pendant of her necklace hung atop the channel, directing the men's attention.

"Tis a pleasure to meet you, Kat," said Cath.

As the young server turned toward Kat, Garret could see she wasn't entirely certain whether Kat was a boy or a girl.

"Is there something I might bring you?" asked Cath.

"Fruit, if you please. And two cups of wine."

"Any boucan?" Cath asked. Some of the locals had taken to roasting, smoking, and hang-drying strips of the island's wild boar. It proved popular with the tavern's customers.

"Perhaps a few strips, thank you."

"Give me a moment then."

"We shall be outside," noted Garret. She thought it best to sit outdoors today. It would enable her to see who was approaching—always best to be prepared, especially in light of their recent incident.

As the two ate their meal and drank wine from pewter tankards, Kat breathed in deeply. "This is the best day of my life. I am happy here."

"I am glad," replied Garret. "You deserve to be happy."

Kat broke off a tiny piece of the crisp boucan, placing it near the parrot's feet. The bird cocked its head as though determining whether it might eat this new 'seed'. It chose to look away. Kat gave it a real seed instead.

When they were done, Garret rose, "Shall we walk by the shore?"

"I would like that very much."

As they were about to leave, Cath came by. "I am sorry, Captain. I almost forgot. I recently received this message for you." She handed Garret a sealed note.

"Thank you." Garret gave her a silver piece in return. Cath left.

"Is it from William?" Kat asked, hopefully.

"Not likely." Garret unsealed the note. It was another message from Yosel, the Jew she'd saved from drowning. His words were cryptic.

My friend,

You are in danger, though not of the kind you might imagine. There is blame to be placed. Avoid the authorities. I cannot be more specific.

Y

XXIII

'*I do not like this Jew,*' thought Ortega. '*The man is a schemer, albeit an intelligent one.*' Yosel's presence always brought more challenge to the negotiations with De Graaf than Ortega preferred. He suspected the Jew had prepped the pyrate for this meeting beforehand.

De Graaf's just-concluded remarks about his attack on the *Visser* now drew Ortega back into the moment, with a different concern, "We cannot afford any loose ends. How can you be certain these men will remain silent about sinking this fishing vessel?"

"The promise of a generous payment…once we are ready to have them spread the word."

"Still…" grumbled Ortega.

"I assured them that any leak will bring them *all* a painful end."

As De Graaf spoke, Ortega's mind wandered to the other loose ends—De Graaf himself, Yosel…and Ayudante Vegas. He'd already initiated a plan to deal with them through a pyrate named Beauclere, whom he'd been informed held a grudge against De Graaf for having slain his former captain (Le Pen). Ortega extended an initial payment to eliminate the three, at the right time. Beauclere hadn't asked why; he seemed more than happy to end all three if it paid handsomely to obtain revenge on De Graaf. For Ortega, that would erase any trace of his involvement in the ransom scheme.

When De Graaf finished commenting, Ortega's focus again returned to the present in the Santo Pedro tavern. "I see," he replied.

De Graaf altered course, "Any word of the King's payment?"

"Not yet. I imagine soon."

"I have given our shares further thought."

Ortega first glanced at Yosel, the likely seed of those thoughts. His eyes then returned to De Graaf. "Tell me."

"We are partners, yes?"

Ortega was inclined to disagree—De Graaf was simply a tool. "Suppose we are."

"I say we are," De Graaf growled. "Let there be no mistake."

Ortega chose not to react.

"That would mean sharing equally," De Graaf added, for clarity.

"Minus what I have already advanced you," Ortega noted.

"Of course." De Graaf leaned in before continuing, "But I am not in this for my good health, which will be at great risk during the exchange…even greater once the King learns the Viceroy is dead."

"We are both at risk," countered Ortega.

De Graaf leaned back and sipped his beer without responding.

Ortega noticed Yosel was watching him intensely though he failed to observe the Jew's foot stealthily tapping De Graaf's. Being a seasoned negotiator, Ortega simply waited for the pyrate's response.

Finally, De Graaf leaned forward, "Partnership aside, I have decided that I must be paid no less than half the value of my own life."

'*Damn the Jew!*' thought Ortega, glancing Yosel's way. He turned back to De Graaf, "The worth of a man who faces death daily cannot be very high." He steeled himself for the expected response—one he was certain he wouldn't like.

"Twenty," said De Graaf, implying 'thousand'.

"Pieces," Ortega confirmed, as in: 'pieces of eight'.

"Doubloons," De Graaf parried.

Otega could almost feel the color peel from his face. Only the

Jew could have planted such an egregious number in De Graaf's head. He sought to obliterate the suggestion. "Out of the question! Let me…"

De Graaf raised his hand, interrupting. He leaned in slowly, eyebrows drawn, teeth bared, bringing finality with his words, "*That* is my price."

Ortega sat motionless. Speechless.

De Graaf sat back. "Minus what you have advanced me, of course," he said nonchalantly, waving his hand in the air.

Yosel grinned.

————

Incensed, Pedro de Acuña y De los Monteros rose from his desk, shaking his head at the scheme his General had just exposed. The Governor of Cartageña was horrified that a military officer would defraud his own King.

General Gonzalo Serezo, the city's ranking military officer, continued revealing what he knew, "One of my men uncovered the plot—Officer Fernando."

"Do we have any proof?"

"Not yet, Your Excellency—only the word of the slave who claimed to overhear a conversation."

"A conversation among whom?"

"Two men. He recognized one as Ayudante Vegas."

The Governor was shocked. He knew and liked the Ayudante. The man oversaw all construction projects in Cartageña authorized by King Philip…and they were progressing well.

"The Ayudante's frequent trips to Spain, to report on the progress of the King's projects, give him the means to take advantage of His Majesty in this way," General Serezo explained.

"How can this happen under your very nose?" Acuña shouted, reacting out of fear for his own standing. If the King were to learn of this treachery, he himself risked being recalled…even imprisoned.

"At least I have identified the deception before it plays out," Serezo offered defensively.

Governor Acuña stepped away from his desk. "We must have evidence." He paced the floor. "Ayudante Vegas has the King's ear. We cannot accuse him without proof."

"Perhaps we might search his residence for messages he may have received."

Acuña shook his head in disagreement. "It would show our hand. I could face the King's rath."

"What about using criminalés?" offered Serezo. "The place could be searched and vandalized. It would look like ordinary theft."

"Such men are more likely to run off with prizes than bring us evidence." Acuña paused for several moments. "Perhaps one of my guards might pay a visit. He could inform the Ayudante's manservant that I am in need of certain papers Vegas was to sign."

"That may indeed be best."

Another thought occurred to Governor Acuña, though he didn't share it. He could confront Vegas personally. If he were innocent, he would react with unrestrained shock over the accusation. If he were not, however, he might show visible signs of guilt—perhaps a cold sweat— and reject the charge sternly, without any shock. The Ayudante's reactions would enable Acuña to assess the man's guilt, regardless of any evidence. He could then have his guards pressure a confession. But if Vegas were to prove adept at controlling his emotions, he would quickly cover his trail…making it impossible to incriminate him.

Governor Acuña walked to the window. He noticed several ships anchored in the harbor. That sparked another thought. He turned back to General Serezo, "If the Ayudante brought back ransom money authorized by the King, surely it would be accounted for by the required inventory audit."

"Indeed," nodded Serezo. "Tesorero Sanchez would know."

"Precisely," Acuña nodded. "I shall meet privately with the Tesorero."

———

With no white flag being offered by the presumed pyrates, Captain James Wenman of the *Mercilus* continued firing warning shots. The two targets remained broadside, sails furled, gunports closed. *'What on earth are they thinking?'* he wondered.

The trailing anchors slowing his approach were unlikely to prevent coming within range of the pyrates' cannons momentarily. There was now no choice. Although his thirty-six cannons offered sufficient firepower, only a handful could be manned by his decimated crew. And the guns were useless unless he could turn *Mercilus* broadside. Those thoughts dictated his decision. "Ready about. Hard to port," he screamed at the crew. The spanker was hauled to aid the rotation of the stern. With the winds providing sufficient speed, the ship turned even faster than it would have normally, as the drag of its anchors redirected some of the forward momentum into the turn. But *Mercilus'* sharp heel meant its cannons would fire harmlessly into the sky until the turn was virtually complete.

In those anxious moments, *Orion's* and *Pandora's* gunports hammered open. Their already-loaded cannons were briskly wheeled into position and secured. The gunners awaited Captain Tovery's call.

William had never faced a decision this grave—opening fire on an English warship. Were he to fire, he would be forever branded a pyrate and hunted by the English Admiralty. Despite having crossed the line into piracy with the seizure of Captain Drago's vessel, that action alone wouldn't ignite the Admiralty's revenge. Firing on the *Mercilus* definitely would. Still, it was either that or face being fired upon first, at the peril of his own ship and crew.

"Your orders, captain?" the gunner's mate asked impatiently.

Though William could taste his mate's growing frustration, he hesitated to respond, hoping for a different outcome. It was then that *Mercilus* opened her gunports, forcing his hand. "Fire at will!" he said, in resignation.

The resulting roar was deafening. Multiple cannons from both *Orion* and *Pandora* spit fire and cloud, launching an attacking horde of cannonballs at their target. Within moments, the side and railing of the *Mercilus* were battered hard, spraying slivers of shattered wood across the deck, deeply piercing two of her men. Sails were torn through, as was one unfortunate sailor. Many of *Mercilus'* cannons had been rolling forward into position when the jolt of the pyrates' volley caused them to break free. Men crushed and pinned by the backward roll of the great guns screamed in agony.

None of *Mercilus'* cannons were ready to fire, despite Wenman's desperate call. He knew the delay in returning fire would prove costly. More far-off blasts assured him of the imminent arrival of the next volley. He threw himself on the deck, grasping for anything he could hold onto. His warship shook hard with the onset of newly arriving black iron spheres, many again ripping into his ship. One shot hit the mizzenmast squarely above the parrel, causing the top third of it to begin its descent. It pulled hard on the rigging, crashing powerfully onto the deck and down onto the skull of Captain James Wenman, killing him instantly where he lay.

Below deck, *Mercilus'* gunners were finally able to secure three brass cannons, firing a feeble response at the pyrates. They missed their targets altogether. Lt. Ward, now in command of the flailing warship, ordered an immediate retreat. His diminished crew jumped to their nearest stations, scrambling to engineer a turn away from the battle.

The freshly minted pyrate captain looked on from *Orion's* bow. The retreat of Her Majesty's warship brought William mixed feelings—relief and sadness, pride and doubt. The sight sparked joyous cheers from his men on deck and those high in the rigging. Cheers emanated loudly from *Pandora's* crew as well.

William ordered one last firing of the cannons to send *Mercilus* on its way. He glanced up at the sky, refraining from joining his crew's celebration. He clearly understood what the future now held for him…and probably for Garret too.

———

Walking the deck of the King's transport ship, Ayudante Vegas estimated it would be at most a week before he would once again walk the streets of Cartageña. And not long after that, he would strut them just as any wealthy man would. Daily, he'd descended into the ship's hold, to spend time with the shiny gold doubloons that offered the promise of life as a free and wealthy man. They occupied his mind constantly, to the point where he was nearly oblivious to his usual distaste for ocean travel.

He envisioned himself buying a fine residence; perhaps one with a view of the harbor. He imagined having any young woman he cared to choose, from among the many that would throw themselves at him freely. He dreamed of eating the finest roast boar and drinking ports that could match the best of Señor Ortega's collection. He would build an enormous library to hold his cherished books and display the most colorful artworks of the day. There was no end to his desires. Of course, all of that depended on his ability to retain a meaningful portion of the King's doubloons, to add to his already-buried cache of silver reales and pieces of eight.

Of the forty-thousand-plus doubloons King Philip had entrusted him with, Vegas felt certain he could retain at least five thousand for himself. He could now negotiate with Señor Ortega from a position of strength. If necessary, he would infer that he was aware of Ortega's direct involvement with the men holding the Viceroy, since he was now convinced Ortega was in fact the real mastermind behind the ransom scheme. The man's hands were literally dripping with guilt. Though he wouldn't directly threaten to reveal Ortega's involvement, he would make it clear that the time for bargaining was over.

That wouldn't be the end of the matter, however. Recognizing his life would be at some risk if Ortega sought to wipe clean his trail, Vegas was ready with his own plan. He headed to the ship's stern, to meet with the King's spy, Rodrigo de Cuero. The man's mission was to travel to Isla Tortuga, to search for the Viceroy on the possibility that he was being held captive there. He was set to disembark at Ciudad de

Puerto Rico, where he would hire on with a merchant ship headed to Tortuga. That would provide him suitable cover for his clandestine activities there. Vegas had already suggested to the spy that he would pay him a fee to engage a pyrate on Isla Tortuga for a special assignment. De Cuero had asked for time to consider the request.

"Buenos díos, señor," said de Cuero as Vegas approached.

"A good day, indeed. We are making excellent time."

"So we are."

"Have you made your decision regarding the item we discussed?" Vegas inquired.

"If I may, I should like to propose an alternative."

"Which is?"

"Allow me to personally handle this assignment."

The Ayudante paused, sensing Ortega, the intended target, might be well connected with King Philip. If so, could he trust de Cuero to keep silent regarding the man's assassination? Yet, now that he'd opened the door, how could he back out? It would make de Cuero suspicious of his intentions. He felt a need to proceed with caution. "Might I count on your silence regarding this assignment?"

"On my honor."

That was good enough for Vegas. "The mastermind of the Viceroy's kidnapping is known to me, though I have no evidence to prove it—certainly nothing I could share with the King."

"I see. And what is your plan, then?"

"To eliminate this man."

"That seems a strange request. Could he not be arrested instead and challenged to prove his innocence?"

"If I were able to provide proof of the man's treasonous act, he would be executed anyway."

De Cuero offered no response.

"So? Are you in or not?"

"What is this man's name?"

"I shall provide that following the exchange of the Viceroy. I cannot risk anything getting in the way of that."

De Cuero paused briefly. "I am in," he said, extending his hand. "Of course, we shall need to agree on an appropriate fee."

"Just so," replied Vegas, shaking the spy's hand.

As he left the ship's stern, Vegas replayed the conversation in his mind. It was all coming together nicely, he thought. Ortega would soon be his minion, tasked only with delivering the Viceroy…before being eliminated.

XXIV

Sitting outside her island home, Garret glanced at Kat who was reading nearby. The girl looked content. That was a good thing. Her own mind, however, was occupied with regrets over her parting discussion with William. There was no telling when or if he and the crew would return to Tortuga. She didn't want her argument with him to be the last words they might ever share. They haunted her. And the more they did, the more she found herself drawn to him. Though never her lover, he'd always been her closest friend. They'd shared quarters as midshipmen under Drake, fought enemies shoulder-to-shoulder, and, together with Jorge Valdez, escaped from would-be captors in England. But their relationship wasn't just about shared experiences. As they'd grown into adulthood, she'd become attracted to William's intelligence, his demeanor, and, admittedly, his physical appearance.

That last thought made her think of Captain James Wenman, the last man with whom she'd been intimate. He, too, was smart and physically appealing. His arrogance, however, was off-putting. While she'd long ago learned to enjoy the sensual pleasures men could deliver, her experience with James taught her that love was not a necessary ingredient. The man was of no interest to her beyond what he could provide sexually. As she thought about it, she could almost taste his lips on hers, sense the softness of his hands on her breasts, and feel the warmth he brought inside her. He was a compelling plaything. But she recognized that, if there were any man at all for her in this semi-nomadic life, it could never be James Wenman.

William, on the other hand, was at least a possibility. '*Does he feel the same way?*', she wondered. Unfortunately, the deep chasm now between them threatened to keep them separated. Hopefully, when he returned, they could share their feelings openly and bridge the gap. She recognized that might mean bringing her fling with Wenman to a close. No doubt the ambitious naval captain, upon arrival, would immediately seek to restart from where they'd last paused. She needed to steel herself to resist his overtures if she were to initiate a more meaningful relationship with William.

The closing of Kat's book interrupted her thoughts. The girl had obviously completed her assigned reading for the day. Garret admired her willingness to learn. Not having had that opportunity when living along London's alleyways, it was clearly something this girl-come-young-woman welcomed. With her studies over, it was time to enjoy each other's company.

"Might we go to the village, mum?" Kat asked. Ever since their first visit, she'd been anxious to stroll the main street again.

"We may indeed. Do you fancy bringing Mr. Blue?" It was the name Kat had given her parrot, after its blue-colored face.

"Yes, of course. Of course I do." Kat walked over to where the bird was perched.

"Of course," the bird squawked. Garret and Kat looked at each other in shock. Did the bird really chirp that? "Of course," it echoed. The two women laughed heartily.

"He speaks!" shrieked Kat.

"So he does," agreed Garret.

"Of course," squawked Mr. Blue. "Of course."

Garret made a mental note not to have the bird around during any future sexual engagement.

———

Why the two pyrate ships chose to end their engagement with the beleaguered *Mercilus* was beyond Lt. Ward's understanding. Inexplicable as it was, he was thankful for it. What concerned him most about the encounter was the loss of Captain Wenman. The man had been in high standing with the Admiralty, which bode well for Ward's own continued climb through the naval ranks. Would that progression be stalled now that he and Wenman had been scuttled by pyrates?

There was another concern haunting him as well. Looking back as the gap between them grew, it appeared the two ships were those of Captain Connachan. How was that even possible, he wondered. Captain Wenman had strong feelings for the woman. And Ward had the distinct impression she'd even given him her favor. So why would she assault a merchant ship and then turn on the English-flagged *Mercilus*? And how could he possibly complete Wenman's mission to deliver the Queen's message to Connachan on Isla Tortuga? He had no idea what it was.

Ward focused in on the man standing on Orion's bow, who appeared to be looking his way. '*My God,*' he thought, '*Could that be William Tovery? Had he, too, turned pyrate? God damn them both. They shall pay a heavy price for their actions.*' But that would have to wait. First, he needed to limp away, replace *Mercilus'* broken mizzenmast, and return to England for proper repairs and further instruction.

The following morning, the crew of the *Mercilus* -- including the sick and wounded -- assembled on deck. Acting-Captain Ward praised the deeds of his former commander. The preacher closed with a prayer. Four men shouldering a broad plank began their march to the larboard side as the crew stood in salute. The great guns of warship

Mercilus roared as the men lifted one end of the plank. Captain James Wenman's body, wrapped in a canvas bag draped with an English flag, slid effortlessly overboard.

"You shall be avenged, Captain," Ward said under his breath. "I promise you that."

Wenman's body, encased in its canvas home and wrapped by heavy chains, was warmly embraced by the blue Caribbean waters. Inside the breast pocket of his doublet, the ink on Queen Elizabeth's letter to Garret Connachan melded with the saltwater. The parchment slowly accompanied Wenman's body to the sandy bottom, its undisclosed contents dissolving into eternity.

———

The red-flagged ship *Demise* rocked quietly in Isla Tortuga's harbor, its cargo-hold heavy with spoils segregated for each man's account. The village itself chimed with the sounds of laughter, singing and shouting as Attila and his crew celebrated the conclusion of their successful voyage. Drink, debauchery and uninhibited revelry flowed like a roiling river from the Gente de Mar. Attila worked the crowd, boisterously mingling with his men and luxuriating in their fawning congratulations. On this night, he sat alone atop the pyrate world.

As the night aged, Attila spotted one of the two men he'd assigned to eliminate Captain Connachan during his absence. He motioned him to join him upstairs in a private room, anxious to hear the details of their assault. Attila entered first. The would-be assassin followed, closing the door but purposely avoiding the latch.

"So?" opened Attila, "What news?"

"Diggs no longer walks the earth," the man offered. "His incompetence foiled our assault."

"Damnation!" Attila rubbed his chin. "What of Connachan?"

The man hung his head, mumbling, "She remains among us."

Attila erupted, "You bloody bilge rat." He walked up to the man, placing his broad chest against him. He peered down at him and growled, "I have clearly misjudged you."

The failed assassin stood motionless, unable to muster a response, his eyes riveted to the floor. Attila contemplated what to do next. There was no choice, really—the man needed to be silenced, to bury any knowledge of the plot and deflect any possible embarrassment for having authorized a botched assault.

The fool suddenly shuffled back as though he'd just read Attila's thoughts, drawing his cutlass. Attila stepped back himself and grinned, slowly drawing his own weapon. "You make this easy, stoute hond," he smirked, spiking his word-jab with Dutch.

The room was too small to circle. Attila lunged with lightning speed. His opponent awkwardly deflected the blow. Attila reset. The man reached with his left hand for a dagger sheathed at his back but fumbled the grasp. Attila read the man's misdirected focus as an opening. A slashing upward blow sent the fool's cutlass airborne, hammering against the wall. Though staggered by the motion, the man finally managed to grab and draw his dagger. He flung it hard, piercing Attila's left shoulder. Furious and unwavering, Attila didn't bother withdrawing it. He crashed his sword down hard on the left corner of the man's skull, cracking an incision clear to his brain. Blood spewed out as if to escape the man's fate. His shriek was short, suspending itself abruptly. His knees buckled. He fell to the floor in a folding heap.

Unable to resist, Attila bladed the man across the back of his neck. Blood sprayed freely, splattering Attila's clothes and face. He paused to admire his kill before turning to the nearby credenza. He grabbed a cloth by the washbasin, wiped his face and cutlass, and then carefully withdrew the dagger from his shoulder, wincing in pain. He pressed the cloth hard against the bubbling blood.

Attila sat patiently for minutes on end, waiting for the blood to coagulate. Someone needed to clean up this mess, he thought. Prince would not be pleased. But surely a few doubloons would pacify him.

When enough time had passed, Attila knelt next to the corpse, searching for coins. Gathering up two doubloons from the man's boot, he stood up and stepped over the body, exiting the door. He walked to the landing and scanned the crowd below. Prince's powder blue coat stood out; he was alongside the table where tankards were filled, no doubt keeping a fervent eye on the amount of each pour. Attila descended the stairs and pushed past several drunkards to reach the owner. "You have something to take care of in my room," he whispered in Prince's ear. "It needs to be done now."

Prince noticed the blood on Attila's clothes. He understood the implication. After many years serving a pyrate clientele, there wasn't much he hadn't seen or handled before. He accepted the two offered doubloons.

Attila grabbed a tankard of beer and a woman's arm. She turned angrily but then smiled at the rugged, blond-haired pyrate. They proceeded up the stairs.

———

"I thank you for joining me, Tesorero," said Governor Acuña.

"It has been far too long since last we met, I am afraid."

"It pleases me to be here, Your Excellency," Tesorero Sanchez replied as he looked around. The two men sat alone on grand chairs in the green-cloaked gardens at the rear of the Governor's residence. The grounds featured shrubs carved as animals and a wide color-spectrum of flowers, all bordered by hedges and covered lovingly by a canopy of strategically positioned palm trees, their fronds swaying casually in the light breeze. Lit torches, a three-quarter moon and countless stars brought light and life to the sculpted gardens. "Your grounds are stunning," Sanchez concluded.

Acuña nodded his thanks and changed the subject, "I must say, Tesorero, your work has been excellent. I review your reports regularly, with great interest."

"Thank you, Governor. I take pride in my work."

"As you should," Acuña commended him. He paused while his manservant, Abeo, poured the fine wine Sanchez had brought with him. A newly arrived French merchant had gifted it to him earlier this day.

"I trust your many construction projects are proceeding well," said Sanchez, wishing to extend the preamble.

"They are indeed. I am most pleased by the progress. My own new residence shall be completed early in the coming year."

"Excellent." Sanchez raised his cup in toast and sipped the wine.

Acuña sipped his as well. "I do have one concern, however."

The Governor's tone told Sanchez their preamble was over. "Pray, tell."

"I worry about the incomplete accounting for a large shipment of pieces of eight. The coins arrived two months ago on the King's transport ship. They were under the supervision of Ayudante Vegas. Your report notes their arrival but does not specify their purpose." The Governor drank from his cup, his eyes not leaving Sanchez' face.

"I recall that, Your Excellency. The quantity was unusual. The documents merely indicated the coins were assigned to the Ayudante."

Governor Acuña leaned back. "Did the Ayudante say nothing of their intended purpose?"

Suddenly feeling warm, Sanchez placed his cup on the table by his chair. "I naturally presumed they were for the construction projects he is overseeing."

"You assumed this?"

"Yes. Nothing in the documents suggested otherwise."

"Does it not strike you as odd that no purpose was provided?"

"His Majesty's wishes are not always made known to me."

"Understood," Acuña replied. "Perhaps I should speak directly with the Ayudante."

"That may be best."

"I must tell you, Tesorero, for any future shipments of this nature, complete documentation of the intended purpose is warranted."

"I shall make it so."

"And I should like to be informed immediately upon arrival of *any* large quantity of coins."

"I shall be quick to share such details with you."

"Excellent. Then we understand each other." Acuña raised his glass. "An excellent wine, no?"

"It is indeed, Your Excellency."

Tesorero Sanchez sat uncomfortably in his coach as it wheeled down the bumpy road on its way back to his residence. His discomfort wasn't solely physical; the Governor's intense questioning had brought on an unpleasant chill.

All this recent interest in the inventory of ships' goods was unlikely to be coincidental, he thought. First was that of his new friend and fellow accountant, Yosel. And now it was the Governor himself. Something was brewing; he was anxious to find out what. He was also suddenly impatient for the return of Ayudante Vegas. Whatever was going on, this man seemed to be in the middle of it.

XXV

It was nowhere to be seen. Scanning the sea from *Orion's* deck, Captain Drago was appalled that his crew had left without him. Perhaps they assumed he was already dead, at the hands of these English pyrates. If so, fear for their own lives would explain their escape during the chaos of the engagement with warship *Mercilus*.

Now on his own, Drago pondered William Tovery's offer to join him. Were he to accept, he would be free of the overbearing Spanish owner of his vessel; free to live life on his own terms. The downside was living a pyrate's life, likely meeting his end in battle or being hung for piracy. Yet he could just as easily lose his life as a merchant captain at the hands of pyrates less friendly than Tovery.

Being a pyrate wasn't in his nature. But then, William claimed to be a privateer, not a pyrate. The line seemed blurry at best. Still, what was there to lose? He was a reasonably young man…despite the recent emergence of a few gray hairs. He could always sail with Tovery and then later change his mind if things didn't sit well. With no ties to a wife and children, he was open to accepting Tovery's offer.

William approached. "Shall we pursue your ship, Captain?"

Drago turned, "No. Let it go."

"Does that mean you have decided to join us?" William asked.

Drago paused before responding, "It does, yes. I shall give this life a try…understanding, of course, that you are more privateer than pyrate."

"Indeed." William answered, despite knowing he'd already crossed that line. He looked out at the vast void of ocean, in the direction Drago's crew had headed. "You shall need a ship to captain."

"Let me first serve as your master's mate. Allow me to learn the ways of a privateer. My own ship would never have served well. It is too slow and too old for such service."

"True enough, from what I observed," William grinned.

"It may serve my interests to have my crew believe I was captured and forced into this life." He sensed that would be a reasonable defense, were he ever to be captured by the Spanish navy.

"Is there nothing onboard your ship that you feel compelled to go after? Something personal, perhaps?"

"I am a man of simple means, Captain. My maps and instruments are the things I cherish most. But they can be replaced. I did have Spanish coin in my cabin, though I suspect it was among the things your crew has already transferred to *Orion*."

William was quick to respond, "We shall return anything of that nature to you, of course. And I shall ensure that you receive a share of the proceeds from your ship."

"Thank you, Captain. Perhaps we might share another cup of beer, in celebration of my turning…privateer."

"Yes, indeed. Privateer."

———

It was just one more in the endless series of days that beckoned Garret and others to these remarkable islands in the Southern Seas. The bright sun lightened an otherwise deep-blue sky spotted with puffy white clouds. A calming breeze swayed the fronds of the tallest palm trees, with little impact on the dusty street below. Garret loved the way aqua-colored water gleamed in the sun against the shore's bright white sand. If this weren't Heaven, she thought, it would suffice until she arrived there…assuming that was to be her final destination.

Kat, seated across the table outside the Gente de Mar, was dressed in men's garb, looking much the young pyrate, from her black bandana to her boots. How far she'd come, thought Garret—from street urchin to privateer. Privateer without a ship, however.

The two were now alone, together, except for the presence of Mr. Blue, who crunched a seed he was given. The bird left powdery crumbs at its feet. It squawked. And squawked again, this time mimicking a word—'Pyrate'. Garret's eye was immediately drawn in the direction of the bird's gaze. A large man was just now exiting the tavern, with two others trailing behind. Something about him was striking. Perhaps it was the contrast between his blue bandana and golden locks. Or maybe it was the scar running down the right side of his face, across his lips, to the left side of his jaw. Battle-tested, she thought. And obviously a survivor. He had a menacing look—fierce eyes and a crooked nose that extended well beyond an average size. His bandolier holstered two wooden-handled pistols with enlarged butts, and a medium-length cutlass with a broad blade. He walked as though he were on a mission. One of the men behind him pulled his arm and pointed her way. The three men stopped. Garret knew it was best to show strength in such situations. She rose casually, her hand atop the hilt of her sword, legs apart in readiness. "Good day, gentlemen."

No response came. The three stood motionless, glaring at her.

"Is there something I might do for you?" she inquired.

"What price are you asking?" replied Attila. His men laughed at the implication.

"You have not the money I should require. Nor shall you ever."

Attila waited while his companions attempted to stifle their laughs. It was clear this woman wasn't intimidated. He'd heard she was strong of character. Now he was seeing it first-hand. "I have no need of money," he growled. "I simply take what I want."

"Well, you shall find no comfort here, I am afraid." Garret gripped her sword's handle, slowly but smoothly. Kat rose and stood beside her. She, too, grasped the handle of her cutlass.

Attila glanced at Kat, then back at Garret. "Does the young lad fight your battles then?"

"He has assisted me in the past." Garret thought back to Kat's help during the night of the attack on their cabin. She had no idea the intruder they'd slain was Attila's man. She believed he was acting under De Graaf's orders, as his accomplice had claimed.

"When the time comes," Attila growled, "you shall need more than a mere pup to assist you."

"Do you have a complaint with my presence here?"

"You are the Queen's dog. Tortuga is not meant for barkers such as you."

"I am here directly from the Queen's prison. Her guard felt my bite," Garret replied, nonchalantly.

"A fat prison guard is hardly a man." Attila spread his arms wide, thrusting his pelvis forward. "This…is a man." His men laughed.

Garret resisted a desire to comment on the inadequacy of his male parts. There was no need to further antagonize the pyrate. Perhaps if she were alone, she would have uttered what she wished. But, for Kat's sake, she sought to avoid a physical confrontation. She peered deeply into the man's eyes. "I have no need of men in this moment."

"One day you shall oblige me," warned Attila. "You can be

certain of that. For now, you are simply an amusement." He spat on the ground in her direction and turned, walking away with his men.

Garret returned to her seat, as did Kat. "Did you not fear him?" the girl asked.

"Fear is not our friend, Kat; it is our enemy. We must welcome the fight if we are to avoid it." Garret noticed Kat appeared not to understand. "You shall learn this, in time," she assured her. "Now, let us finish our lunch."

"Pyrate," squawked Mr. Blue. The two young women laughed.

———

The ship bringing Ayudante Vegas home slowed as it entered Cartageña's busy harbor. He stood on the deck, anxiously awaiting the anchor to take hold so that he might disembark this vile vessel. At his request, four of the captain's men had already brought his two chests to the deck. The four now stood behind him, ready to lower the small but exceedingly heavy containers into a boat. Together, the chests bore the King's ransom—specially-minted doubloons to be exchanged for the release of Viceroy Valdez.

Tugging at the anchor's suddenly hard grasp, the ship shuddered to a stop. It bustled with men tightly furling sails and otherwise preparing for the conclusion to their lengthy voyage.

Tesorero Sanchez waited onshore. He'd been informed of the arrival of King Philip's transport ship and suspected Ayudante Vegas would be onboard. The final piece of the puzzle could well be in hand, he thought. He'd brought along four of his staff. Two were now getting into a longboat to be rowed to the ship, where they would obtain the inventory records and begin their count and verification. The remaining two stood beside him, waiting for any boat that might leave the ship and head to shore. He had no desire to let anything slip past him. Governor Acuña had explicitly requested immediate notice of any significant coinage arriving at the harbor. He would not disappoint him.

Sanchez watched as two dark items were lowered by netting into a waiting boat at the base of the ship. A man dressed in military uniform descended the ship's side and stepped into the boat as well. This had to be the Ayudante, he thought. Who else would be permitted such an expedited exit from the ship? It suddenly occurred to him—he had no one here with military authority to stop the Ayudante and have him submit to his questioning. "Lorenzo," he said to an assistant. "Have the Capitán de Puerto attend me here. Now."

"As you wish, sir." The young accountant turned and ran off through the heavily trampled sand to the Harbor Captain's office.

'*Terra firma*', thought Vegas as his boat approached the shoreline, '*How blessed am I?*' With the boat nearing its grounding point, he noticed Tesorero Sanchez moving toward the area. He recognized him but had never been greeted personally by him upon his arrival. How nice, he thought, believing his reputation for having direct connections to King Philip was finally paying off. It stroked his pride. This was a most beautiful day.

The boat slid onto the beach. The Ayudante jumped out into the shallow water, glad to no longer be floating on top of it. His legs felt wobbly. The rowers pulled the boat further onto the shore and began unloading the heavy wooden chests.

"Welcome, Ayudante Vegas," Sanchez said, extending his

hand. "Tis my pleasure to greet you. I trust your voyage was swift and uneventful."

"Thank you, Tesorero. It was indeed. Though, not being a man of the sea, it was too long, regardless."

Sanchez laughed. He too disliked traversing the oceans. "Let us have a drink together, shall we?"

Vegas seemed flattered. "Of course. I shall join you as soon as my belongings are secured at my residence."

That was precisely the opening Sanchez hoped for. It allowed his follow-on question to appear quite normal. He nodded toward the chests. "What is it you have brought with you?"

"I am delivering certain goods at His Majesty's request."

"Might I inquire as to the nature of these goods?" replied Sanchez. "It is, after all, my responsibility."

The Capitán de Puerto and two of his men were now only yards away. Vegas saw them approaching. He didn't like where this was headed; it was unexpected. He'd previously brought significant coinage to Cartageña on behalf of the King without facing this kind of scrutiny. "His Majesty has not authorized me to disclose the contents."

"I understand," nodded Sanchez. "Yet I must insist."

Now that the Capitán de Puerto was at his side, the Tesorero's face turned somber and serious. Vegas knew he needed to be careful. The last thing he wanted was to be forcefully detained, which suddenly seemed a possibility. "Might I have a private word, Tesorero?"

"Anything you have to say, you can say in the presence of these officers." The comment ended their verbal chess match.

Reluctantly, Vegas opened up, "The contents are His Majesty's doubloons.”

“For what purpose?”

Vegas pulled Sanchez aside, by the arm. “We must discuss this privately,” he said softly. “I assure you, the King would insist upon it.”

“As you wish,” replied Sanchez, “The guards will secure your chests while we proceed to my office.”

“Thank you, Tesorero.”

Vegas was relieved, feeling he’d bought himself more time to consider what to tell Tesorero Sanchez. He hoped their walk would be long enough to fully think that through.

———

The signalman left his position on *Pandora’s* main deck and rushed to Acting-Captain Blair’s quarters. The door was open. He knocked anyway.

“Enter,” Blair called.

“Thank you, sir. *Orion* has flagged us. Captain Tovery requests your presence.”

“Thank you. You may go.” Blair set a weight on the maps and rose from the table; ‘*Garret’s table*,’ he thought. He walked to the chair where he’d placed his coat and cutlass. Donning both, he left his quarters and soon disembarked for his meeting.

“Welcome aboard, Mr. Blair,” said William as the aging Master’s Mate stepped through the entry port.

“Thank you, Captain. I trust we are sharing supper. I am quite famished.”

“Indeed we are. But first, I would like you to meet Captain

Drago." William motioned to the Portuguese captain.

"Pleased to make your acquaintance," Drago said, extending his hand.

"And yours," replied Blair, wondering why the man seemed completely at ease despite being abandoned by his crew during the altercation with *Mercilus*.

"Captain Drago has agreed to join us," said William, "along with a few of his crew." He pointed toward his cabin. "Come."

The meat was dried, the cheese had been scraped of mold, and the biscuit was stale. The wine, however, provided welcome cover for the food's shortcomings. The three men drank heavily while discussing their altercation with the English warship. "This is most unfortunate," William concluded, "yet it was *Mercilus* that initiated battle. We were merely defending ourselves."

Blair didn't respond. He gazed into his tankard of wine, shaking his head from side to side. William transitioned, "Absent a commission from Her Majesty, we now have no choice but to sail on our own account. Capturing Spanish-flagged vessels may constitute high piracy but it will not bring us England's wrath." He sipped wine. "Engaging the Queen's navy, however, has unfortunate consequences."

"Captain Wenman's report of the incident will surely draw the ire of the Queen herself," commented Blair.

"The question is whether he recognized our ships. If so, Her Majesty's anger will be directed at Captain Connachan."

"And any accomplices," Blair lamented. "We shall all be branded pyrates."

"Perhaps so," replied William. "We can no longer assume

English warships will treat us as anything other than that."

The three men paused, all contemplating their fate. William was first to break the quiet, "There is no clear path of return to England. We shall have no access to our resources there, financial or otherwise. Once our current funding is gone…which day is fast approaching…we shall have to rely solely on hunting Spanish prey. Either that or prey on fish."

"We have no choice," Blair concurred. "None at all." He raised the tankard to his lips and drained his wine. He looked at William. "Captain Connachan will have no part in hoisting the red." He was referring to the color of the flags increasingly being flown by pyrates.

"That very thought was expressed when last we met," William disclosed. "Yet circumstances have changed. Once I share this news, I trust the Captain will understand."

"I prefer not to join you for that disclosure," Blair replied.

Drago interjected, "Dare I ask—who is this Captain Connachan?"

"She is our commander," replied William.

"*Pandora* and *Orion* are her personal ships," added Blair.

"She?" Drago responded with surprise.

"Indeed. She is all woman," William smiled.

"I have never heard of such a thing," offered Drago. "A woman as owner, perhaps, but never a captain. What woman would voluntarily place herself on a vessel crawling with men as unrefined as any man could be?"

"Prepare to be surprised."

"Are women not a bad omen onboard ship? What men would choose to sail with one, let alone follow her lead?

"Those who have seen her in battle," William noted. "The fiercest woman you shall ever meet. Schooled by Drake himself." He sipped his wine and continued, "She is intelligent, highly skilled, and…not unpleasant to behold."

"I welcome meeting her, then."

"That time will come soon enough."

Drago nodded. He drank from his tankard and returned it to the table. "I believe you are both honorable men," he offered, "though you clearly wrestle with your countrymen seeing you as anything but that."

"Honorable perhaps," responded William, "but facing a future that demands less-than-honorable actions—the uncommissioned taking of ships by force." He shook his head as though in disbelief.

"Well gentlemen," Drago responded. "I am fully invested. Let us turn the page on our prior endeavors and embrace a new future… together." He raised his tankard. William and Blair raised theirs in return. Only two of the men drank. Blair's tankard was already empty.

XXVI

Dust filled the air as a phalanx of horse-mounted Spanish soldiers thundered along the winding dirt path through the low-lying hills on the edge of Cartageña. They were headed to the villa and sprawling grounds owned by Felipe de Heredia y Ortega. The sun glanced off their silver-colored armor—helmets, breastplates and skirt; coverings for their arms and legs; and metal-encased boots. Dressed as though headed to war, even their horses wore armored headpieces. Three short-haired, gray-spotted hounds ran alongside the twenty-four soldiers. The dogs had proven useful in the past, tracking down native people and escaped slaves. Their barks and howls added to the cacophony of noise that now filled the rolling hills bordering the road.

Acting on the input of Tesorero Sanchez, Governor Acuña had issued the order to find Ortega and bring the man to him. Sanchez had pressed Ayudante Vegas for an explanation regarding the doubloons he was transporting on behalf of King Philip. The threat of imprisonment encouraged Vegas to disclose that Viceroy Valdez was being held captive by men requesting a prize in return for his release. What's more, the King's doubloons were actually a second payment—the first had been made in exchange for the Viceroy's severed ear. Vegas also shared that Señor Ortega was the man with whom he'd made that prior exchange. He indicated Ortega had been approached by the Viceroy's captors in the hope of establishing contact with King Philip regarding their demands. But he didn't go so far as to suggest Ortega might well be the mastermind of the ransom scheme.

The Governor's soldiers negotiated the final curve in the path and stormed through the open gates leading to the villa's expansive forward grounds. Ortega, and others inside his residence, heard the heavy commotion spiked by the barking of dogs. Abeo, his manservant, hurried to the front door, opened it, and peered out. Seeing the glint of soldiers' armor, he suddenly worried about having negotiated a payment from Officer Fernando in exchange for exposing Ayudante Vegas' involvement in a ransom scheme. His worries were both for himself and his master, Señor Ortega. Though he hadn't given up his master's name, it was possible the Ayudante had. Abeo suddenly wished he'd never sought payment from Fernando in the first place. The military's involvement could well upend what his fellow slaves currently saw as his much-blessed life under Ortega.

Abeo watched as the rising cloud of dust, and the up-and-down movement of the horsemen, flowed toward him like a rogue ocean wave. The soldiers were far enough off that he doubted they'd seen him open the left side of the great door that stood sheltered from the sun by the pillars and overhang marking the villa's grand entrance. The staff had gathered behind him in the foyer.

"As you were," he said, turning toward them. "There is no need for concern."

The staff looked skeptical but followed his orders and returned to their stations, albeit nervously. Abeo briefly pondered attempting an escape but the sound of the dogs dashed that thought. As a child, he'd witnessed dogs savagely attacking and tearing apart a native man on the run. That sight had never left him. He knew he must stay put, praying his participation in the disclosure of the ransom scheme was of little interest to these men. After all, Officer Fernando had no idea that he was Ortega's manservant. There was some comfort in that. He simply needed to maintain his composure in welcoming the soldiers.

The horses slowed their pace, drawing to a halt before the majestic entryway. The dogs were instructed to heal. Their barking withered away. Abeo strode onto the portico, closing the door behind him to keep the dust cloud from entering the villa.

The leader dismounted and approached, hand-on-cutlass.

"Buenos días, oficial," Abeo called out confidently, with a broad smile. The approaching soldier appeared more a collection of shining metal pieces come to life than a mere mortal. One of the dogs joined him at his side as he walked.

"Where is he?" the officer growled impatiently. The dog growled as well.

"I presume you mean Señor Ortega."

"I have no time for your foolishness." The officer pushed him aside and pressed through the doorway, into the foyer. "Dios mio," he exclaimed, never having seen anything as magnificent as this villa. Even the Governor's residence couldn't match its opulence.

Four of the officer's soldiers had also dismounted. They quickly followed their leader into the foyer, dust and all, their armor clanking. Once again, the officer demanded of Abeo, this time more sternly, "Where is he?"

"I am afraid I do not know, sir."

Having heard the soldiers approaching his villa, Ortega now stood motionless on the dark landing of his secret passage. He'd closed and secured the entry door disguised as the end-section of the bookcase in his study. He hadn't lit the lantern, worried its light might show through the door's seams. He placed his ear to the door but couldn't make out the muffled words of the conversation Abeo was having. He decided that, were a soldier to enter the reading room, he would quietly proceed along the tunnel to his storehouse, where they would never find him. His thoughts were suddenly interrupted by an officer shouting orders. The sound of clanking armor permeated the bookcase.

How on earth had this come to pass, Ortega wondered. Had the Ayudante exposed him? If so, why? What possible justification could Vegas have for disclosing the ransom scheme, since he too was mired in the deception? Had someone else come to learn of the scheme? In the end, it didn't matter. All that mattered now was to survive this intrusion and then surface later to weave an acceptable story. Perhaps he might reward the Governor generously for his continued freedom. He needed to give it all more thought.

The approaching clank of armor suggested a soldier had just entered the reading room. Ortega quietly removed the lantern from its hook but still didn't light it. He would try to feel his way along the wall of the completely blackened tunnel. But first, he needed to step off the landing without causing the wooden steps to creak. He tested the initial step, carefully increasing the pressure of his foot on an edge close to the rail. Unfortunately, the step didn't oblige him. Its creak seemed so much louder than he'd ever remembered it. He froze instantly, listening intently for any sound from the study. Each follicle of hair on his arms rose, pulling up the skin at its base. He felt a tingle along his spine. Sweat beaded up on his forehead. Had the soldier heard the damn creak? He felt trapped in the dark dampness. His heart thumped so loudly he could hear it. The clank of armor turned louder.

———

Death's Head smoothly entered Isla Tortuga's harbor. The night sky was heavily overcast, barring light from the moon and stars. But lights hung and swayed gently on lightly creaking ships anchored nearby. More lights dotted the shoreline. Distant voices broke the quiet. The village remained open for business despite the late hour.

Stevens approached from behind. "*Pandora* and *Orion* appear gone," he observed.

De Graaf nodded, "Damn 'the Witch' for even coming here. This be our island," he growled.

"Not likely we can share it for long," replied Stevens.

"I shall deal with her…for killing Harker.

"It seems you will have to wait until she returns."

"Hopefully soon."

"Eight fathoms, if you please," came a sounding.

"Anchors at the ready," yelled Stevens.

"Six fathoms."

"Hold anchor."

"Four fath…"

"Anchors away!"

The whirl of rope and splash of iron followed quickly. The ship slowed as its anchor searched the sandy bottom for grip. Its weight forced the issue. The ship rocked briefly, then held. They were home.

"Prepare to disembark," Stevens called out. A buzz of excitement enveloped the ship. Several whooped and hollered as the crew scurried along the deck and rigging, securing the ship.

"Barker, Withers, you have the watch," yelled Stevens. He grinned upon hearing the two men groan their disapproval. It was just the way of things—no matter who had the watch following arrival, it was a groaning moment. The men close-by laughed, saluting Barker and Withers. "Fare thee well, swabbies."

De Graaf and Stevens took the first longboat ashore, rowed by six of their men. Oppressive humidity soiled their blouses. No matter; De Graaf soaked in the moment—coming home to a well-lit village on a still, warm evening, with heavy treasure in his ship's hold. He breathed in deeply. He was a free man, sailing under his own orders and leading others, many of whom outright feared him. His reputation provided all the comfort he needed…and all the women he wanted.

The Gente de Mar was soon bustling. De Graaf and his men ordered beer and food and ogled the women—some comely, some with other attributes that drew men's attention. The place filled with boisterous singing, laughter and bawdy conversation, drawing pyrates from other crews to the revelry. Out of necessity, the partying poured onto the street, accompanied by celebratory pistol shots.

Prince was upstairs in his room counting money. Concerned with the rising commotion, he placed a bag of coins in a chest, locked it, and concealed it under a worn blanket. He pulled on his coat and cutlass, exited, and locked the door. Descending the stairs, he quickly spotted De Graaf. The large, half-Black man was hard to miss, even in a crowd of this size. Prince pushed his way through the horde, heading toward the back of the room where De Graaf had taken a table.

"Tis a pleasure to have you back, Captain. What can I bring you?"

"Perhaps that handsome niece of yours?" De Graaf grinned.

"I am sorry, sir; anything but that. The girl is still not of age."

"It shall be a most pleasing day when she is."

Prince shuddered. It occurred to him that he would have to send Cath to Hispaniola, to live with her mother's family. He had bigger dreams for her than mating with a pyrate—captain or not. "Perhaps a fine port and roast boar? Compliments of the inn, of course."

"That shall do…for two of us. My first mate will join me shortly. We are hungry beyond measure."

"As you wish." Prince motioned to Cath. She'd earlier watched him descend the stairs and knew to pay attention. She came quickly. The room was so loud that she placed her ear next to her uncle's face.

"Two tankards of our best port and roast boar for Captain De Graaf…and one more. Without interruption," Prince instructed. As Cath turned to leave, he grabbed her arm. "At our expense." The girl nodded and hurried off.

Prince turned back to De Graaf. "It will be here shortly," he assured him. "Our best customer comes first."

Stevens was busy relieving himself behind the tavern. He overheard voices of men he didn't recognize. Peering around the tree, he noticed they were speaking with members of his crew, sharing news of the recent death of one of Captain Attila's men. The rumor was he'd broken into Connachan's place with an overwhelming desire for her favors. He'd paid the ultimate price; she'd bested him despite his size advantage and the element of surprise. Her reputation had only grown.

Stevens pulled up his trousers and entered the tavern, not bothering to engage with the men he'd overheard. He pushed through the crowd, looking for De Graaf. Finding him near the back, he proceeded there, drew up a chair, and sat. "Interesting news," he said.

"Connachan has slain one of Attila's men…" He glanced over his shoulder briefly. "…a large man who breached her place in the dark of night. The killing has brought her praise…and respect."

"Only a coward assaults one who sleeps," De Graaf scoffed, "I shall challenge her in the light of day, before witnesses." It occurred to him to raise the question, "Her ships have put to sea. Did she depart after the attack?"

Stevens shook his head, "She is here without her crew. They say she has even been in the village…with a young one."

"Why would her ships leave without her?"

"No doubt Tovery & Blair are on a mission. Only they would be entrusted with her ships."

"Perhaps I should challenge her before they return."

Cath set two tankards of port on the table. "The boar shall come shortly, sir."

"I smelled it from the shoreline," De Graaf replied. "A scent second only to that of young women. Both are Heaven to those who have sailed for too long."

Cath smiled awkwardly without responding.

"Two servings will not suffice," Graaf yelled as Cath turned to leave. "Bring four…and join us, if you please."

———

Although he'd met with Sanchez on multiple occasions, this was his first time inside the Tesorero's office. It was austere but far from barren. Yosel noticed the walls were unadorned except for a framed map of the Caribbean Sea hanging off-kilter near the window. A simple desk and two chairs sat askew at the end of the room furthest from the entrance. Boxes filled with documents formed a haphazard gauntlet to the desk. Folders containing parchment were piled precariously high on both the desk and the shelves behind. From their many conversations, Yosel had judged Sanchez to be meticulous in matters of his profession. Somehow that trait failed to extend to the orderliness of his office.

"My apologies," Sanchez said as he stepped over a box. "Goods flow into Cartageña like rain in a windstorm. The documentation leaves no time to bring order to my office."

"No apology needed," replied Yosel.

"You may trust, however, that I know where every piece of information lies and can lay my hands on it within moments."

Yosel suspected that was true. He navigated his way to the guest's chair and sat across from Sanchez, who took his own.

"I have nothing in the way of drink to offer you. I find it dulls the mind—something I cannot afford when attending to my tasks."

"Of course." Yosel understood—when assessing the inventory of a captured vessel, he needed his full wits about him, unclouded by spirits. His fellow pyrates were always anxious to learn the final value and could easily turn hostile if he were to err.

"If I may, Yosel, I have a question of a most serious nature."

"I am at your pleasure."

"Since the beginning of our friendship, you have shown great interest in the arrival of large shipments of coinage. Unusual interest I might add." He shuffled through documents on his desk, avoiding eye contact. "And you have paid me well for the information I provided."

"I thank you for that."

"Yes, of course. Yet you have never shared the reason for your interest.”

Sanchez ceased shuffling his documents and leaned back. Yosel suddenly sensed he was in the middle of an inquisition. Why would the Tesorero bring this up now, and why here? Something was clearly driving him. Had Sanchez somehow learned of the ransom scheme? It pained him to think that could be the case, and that his now good friend might suspect his involvement in the plot. The two had bonded by reason of their shared profession. He sought to frame his response in a manner that might reinforce their common ground.

“You and I have analytical minds,” Yosel opened. “We seek to find understanding through numbers. The mercantile workings of a city such as Cartageña are complex. Yet we both know the flow of capital fuels the level of trade. New flows are the best indicator of future trade activity,” he leaned back and smiled, “and the potential for the accumulation of personal wealth. ”

“Indeed.”

“I hope to one day establish an import and export business here. Tracking capital flows helps me determine the level of investment I shall make, and the nature of the returns I might expect on that investment.” There was some truth in his statement—Yosel had a strong desire to establish a business here, as soon as his pirating prizes were sufficient to fund it.

Sanchez breathed a sigh, suggesting he’d taken the bait. He leaned forward, banged his fist on the desk, and smiled. “One day, perhaps you and I shall venture into business together.” He turned and reached into a deep box behind his chair, withdrawing a bottle of port. He placed it on his desk. Yosel was confused; only moments ago Sanchez claimed to have no drink to offer.

The Tesorero must have observed his confusion. "It is not for the moments of business." He reached back into the box for two small pewter cups. "Yet it is excellent lubrication for celebrating friendship." He set the cups on the desk, opened the bottle, and poured. They each took a cup.

"To friendship," Yosel said, raising his cup. Sanchez echoed the toast. They sipped the port.

The Tesorero set his cup on the desk. "I must say, while the flow of capital hints at future economic activity, everything is not always as it seems."

"How so?" Yosel asked.

"Let me share with you a most confidential matter—one I trust you shall keep secret."

"You have my word."

"Are you aware that the Viceroy of Inagua, Jorge Valdez, has gone missing?"

"I am. I heard he was killed by pyrates."

"That is often said in the streets, yes. Yet some say he was kidnapped but not slain." He sipped his port. "In fact, some men have come forward, claiming to hold the Viceroy captive. They have offered his release…for a price." Yosel expressed contrived shock. Sanchez continued. "We have detained a man who is involved in this scheme."

Though calm by nature, Yosel could feel his body temperature rise. Who was it they detained, he wondered—the Phantom? If so, he and De Graaf might be implicated. He drew his cup to his lips.

"This man has traveled between here and Spain, handling the negotiations," Sanchez explained. "At one point, he delivered the Viceroy's severed ear to King Philip."

Yosel again feigned shock. But he was relieved; the man Sanchez spoke of couldn't be the Phantom.

"The King could not be certain the ear was the Viceroy's," continued Sanchez, "so he asked the man to bring him the Viceroy's ring, for which he provided fifteen thousand pieces of eight."

Yosel hid his surprise at the amount. He and De Graaf had come away with so little of those funds. "This Viceroy is apparently of great importance to King Philip," he noted.

"He is indeed. And this man leading the negotiation, an Ayudante, claimed all fifteen thousand were used to purchase the ring. I suspect, however, that he kept some for himself…judging from his reactions under my questioning. He shall soon face a formal inquiry on the matter, at the Governor's request."

"I see."

"Even more interesting," Sanchez went on, shuffling through parchment on his desk, "is that the Ayudante recently returned with…," he pulled out one page and read from it, "…forty-one thousand, three hundred five doubloons." He passed the parchment across to Yosel and leaned back. "Payment for surrendering the Viceroy."

Yosel contained his emotions. This was the exact information he and De Graaf sought. He simply shook his head, saying nothing.

"Governor Acuña is in command of the situation," said Sanchez. "The doubloons are now secured in the storehouse…under heightened guard."

"This is most fascinating," replied Yosel. He sipped his port. "What measures are being taken to secure the Viceroy's freedom?"

"Ah. That is the reason I am sharing this with you."

"How so?"

"The Governor does not trust the Ayudante to lead the exchange. At least, not on his own. He proposed that I accompany him. The Ayudante could explain to the Viceroy's captors that I am there in my capacity as Tesorero, charged with the security of the doubloons."

"I see. But what has that to do with me?"

"The more the Governor and I discussed his proposal, the more concerned he became for my personal safety. With this much gold at stake, there is great risk that things may not proceed as planned. Happily, he has decided I am too important to be placed at such risk."

"Well, that is certainly comforting."

"Yes. And that is where you can be of great service to us."

"How so?"

Sanchez leaned forward, "We feel you could stand in my place, as my representative. You are relatively new to Cartageña and therefore unlikely to be recognized by the Viceroy's captors. I imagine they would accept you as my authorized second."

Yosel paused to consider the possibilities. The Phantom must have used this Ayudante as his go-between with the King. If the Ayudante were to be subjected to tough questioning, he might well implicate the Phantom. If so, would the Governor demand that the Phantom participate in the exchange and set it up as a trap? And how would the Phantom react to Yosel's involvement? Would he sense he'd been double-crossed and point a finger his way? Clearly, he and De Graaf needed to discuss all this. Should they inform the Phantom? Could they even trust him? Things were suddenly more complicated and tenuous than he and De Graaf had envisioned.

Sanchez broke the lengthy silence, "It appears you have a concern, Yosel. Let me assure you—the Governor has pledged his forces to your personal safety in the matter. They shall be nearby and ready. You need only witness the exchange; then you are done."

"I see."

"Of course, you shall be rewarded for your service. I suggested one hundred doubloons. The Governor has agreed to that."

"That is most generous of you," Yosel replied, despite believing his life was worth so much more.

"A deal, then?" Sanchez raised his cup in readiness.

"So be it," smiled Yosel, raising his own and downing the remainder of the dark liquid. He set his cup on the desk "Tell me, Tesorero, do you have any idea who will be on the other end of this exchange—those who will bring the Viceroy?"

"Not at the moment. The Ayudante has identified a certain individual, though it is unclear whether that man is simply a messenger or one of the Viceroy's captors. The Governor sent his soldiers to this man's villa but they have been unable to locate him."

"I see," replied Yosel, now certain that the man the Ayudante fingered was the Phantom. "Well, I trust you shall let me know whether he is considered dangerous before I meet him."

"Rest assured, Yosel, he is not."

XXVII

Governor Acuña turned over the parchment he'd just been handed. He dismissed the messenger and broke the seal he didn't recognize. The letter was two pages long. He glanced quickly to the bottom of the second page, to see who signed it. It was Felipe de Heredia y Ortega—the very man he'd sent his soldiers to arrest. He returned to the first page and began reading…

Your Excellency,

I was informed by my staff that your men arrived at my residence while I was away. The officer in charge explained to my manservant that you wished to see me concerning a matter of great interest. I believe this may have to do with a transaction which I was on the verge of sharing with you. Specifically, I have been in discussions with Ayudante Pedro Vegas regarding the exchange of money for the release of a friend of King Philip who is being held captive.

Allow me to explain further. My involvement comes about through a channel of communications, the origin of which is a group of men who claim to hold the King's friend prisoner. They contacted me through their sources, believing me to have sufficient standing in Cartageña to ensure their message might be delivered to the King himself. I have participated in these discussions to learn all I can regarding the captors and, hopefully, to execute a successful exchange on the King's behalf.

Acuña read this with a certain cynicism. It seemed as though Ortega was making excuses. He continued reading…

You may wonder why it is that I chose not to bring this to your attention earlier. Please know that I gave that considerable thought when I was first approached. I deemed it best to shield you from any potential injury to your reputation should the transaction fail in any way. On the other hand, assuming the transaction is successful, you shall be able to inform others that I have been acting on your behalf, in secret. In that way, any success will inure to your personal benefit.

Acuña's skepticism softened; there was wisdom in Ortega's thinking. He knew the man well and understood he was highly regarded for his intellect and level of influence in the merchant community. He began to think Ortega's actions and reasoning were appropriate, under the circumstances. The letter closed…

I would be most pleased to meet with you to discuss this further, at your discretion.
I remain, your humble servant,
Signature appended

Acuña ripped the message into small pieces, thinking it best to dispose of any trace of his own advance knowledge, in the event of any failure. Rather than send Ortega a written response, he would send a messenger to the man's villa, asking that they meet in private on the morrow, at his own hidden retreat, far from the harbor. The messenger would provide Ortega with a map for his use in that regard. Sealed, of course.

———

By the time she and Kat arrived at the harbor, *Pandora* and *Orion* were both at anchor. Men were already rowing longboats ashore. Garret noted that neither ship was flying the Queen's flag. She hoped that was because William had no desire to be viewed as a threat to the pyrate community, rather than some indication that he was no longer associating himself with their homeland.

"It shall be so good to see William again," said Kat, filled with excitement.

"I believe so," replied Garret. But inside, she felt a queasiness. She worried how her upcoming encounter with William might play out, given the severity of their argument prior to his departure.

The two young women were surrounded by a large, animated crowd that was still gathering onshore. Crowds of this size weren't uncommon when two- or three-masted vessels were arriving. Such ships generally brought cargo and money that had a way of flowing through the community, benefiting many. As she scanned faces and figures, Garret noticed some were familiar—two in particular. One was her archenemy, De Graaf, whom she surmised must have arrived in the dark of night, like the scourge he was. Otherwise, she would have noticed the commotion.

The other familiar figure was Captain Attila, the pyrate who recently confronted her and Kat outside the Gente de Mar. It wasn't clear whether either pyrate had noticed her. She was yards behind both. They seemed intensely focused on the longboats now approaching.

Looking back to her ships, Garret observed heavy cargo being unloaded—no doubt prizes from another ship. That only heightened her unsettled state. With *Pandora* and *Orion* no longer sailing under the Queen's authorization, any assault William might have made would be deemed high-seas piracy. Not only that but she, as the ships' owner, would be accountable. A sickening vision of swinging at the end of a noose on Execution Dock along the Thames flashed through her mind. She could envision no other outcome upon returning to England.

As strong as her feelings were for William, his apparent piracy threatened to tear them apart. The possibility of a favorable reunion was dimming like light from a ship hastily departing at night.

"There he is," Kat said excitedly, pointing in the direction of William's approaching longboat. Garret looked that way. She noticed there was another man in the boat who was not rowing. That was odd. Only the captain and master's mate would ordinarily be granted such privilege. The other man's skin appeared darker than William's, though definitely not black. He wore what appeared to be Spanish or perhaps Portuguese garb. She couldn't be certain which.

As the boats hit the sand, William immediately stepped out into the water lapping against the shore. The other man joined him. Being far removed, Garret raised her arm, waving it lightly to draw William's attention. There was no enthusiasm in her motion, though Kat was suddenly jumping and waving vigorously. William must have caught a glimpse. He and the other man headed their way, clumps of white sand covering their dark, wet boots.

"Good day, sir," William said with a grand smile. It was proper recognition for Garret, as his commander, though she hardly felt like it in that moment. She nodded, without returning his smile.

Kat couldn't contain herself; she gave William a hearty hug.

"My goodness," said William, looking down at her. "You hug more like a cabin boy than a young girl—and look like one too," he kidded.

"Good day, William," Garret said dryly. She refrained from extending her hand. Despite his warm smile, an awkwardness hung between them like a menacing, pregnant cloud.

William brushed away the discomfort, "Allow me to introduce Captain Luis Drago, our new partner." He turned to Drago, "This is Captain Connachan."

"Good day, Captain. Welcome to Isla Tortuga," said Garret, this time extending her hand. Drago accepted and shook it. He didn't bow, however. She understood—William had prepared Drago well, aware that she preferred being greeted as a captain, not as a woman. She smiled at William for having done that. The dark cloud between them lightened a touch.

Garret was confused by William's use of the word 'partner' to describe Drago. She was anxious to hear more about that. She turned back to Drago, "Perhaps we might celebrate your arrival with a drink at our local tavern, the Gente de Mar."

"That is most kind of you, Captain. I would be honored."

Again, she thought, William had schooled Drago well. He'd addressed her as Captain. She turned and led the way, not noticing that De Graaf and Attila had both, separately, been observing them closely.

Drago turned and whispered to William, "The captain's corset seems harshly tied."

———

Far from the easiest road he'd ever traveled, this one seemed barely wide enough for his coach to squeeze through. Native shrubbery and budding trees brushed frequently against its sides. Now nearly an hour on, Ortega wondered why it was that Governor Acuña wished to meet so far from the city. The smothering vegetation was making him feel a little claustrophobic.

The carriage suddenly jerked to the right and began climbing a rise in the path. The shrubbery thinned. Cresting the rise, Ortega could see the broad expanse of sand leading to the ocean. He breathed in the air's saltiness.

The coach slowed and turned sharply to the left. As it did, a small building emerged. Its white wall almost blended with the sand, making it difficult to see, except for two weathered, aqua-colored shutters flanking a lone window. As the coach neared, Ortega knew he must be looking at the side of the Governor's retreat. Its front faced seaward. A few distant islands dotted its view.

The horses drew to a halt. With puffs of sand still drifting by, the coachman jumped down and opened the carriage door. Ortega exited, his hair blowing in the light breeze. Nearby boobies squawked at his arrival. A wave of serenity washed over him like clear water running onto a sandy shore. He now understood—this was a place the Governor could come to rest mind, body and soul, far from the demanding pace of a leader's life in the city.

The Governor came forward, barefoot. His loose white-cotton shirt and tan-colored trousers gave the appearance of a common man, though he was anything but. Ortega suddenly felt overdressed.

Acuña smiled, extending his hand, "Bienvenido a mi humilde casa de playa. Tis small but has much to offer."

Ortega shook the hand, "It is most charming, Your Excellency. Thank you for having me."

"Come, let us sit beneath the trees." Acuña turned and walked toward two wooden chairs on which the paint was abundantly peeled. Ortega followed. A servant exited the beach house with cups of port, trailing well behind.

The two men sat facing the sea, their chairs angled slightly toward each other. A small wooden table rested between them. "I cannot remember the last time I found myself in such a setting," remarked Ortega. "It is quite calming."

"I find it helps the conversation flow—much like the water."

The servant handed each man a tarnished metal cup. Acuña continued, "Please, you must remove your boots and feel the sand's warmth on your feet."

Ortega complied. "I was pleased to receive your invitation," he said, wriggling his toes in the sand. "We have much to discuss."

"Tis a grave matter at hand. I appreciate the thoughtfulness expressed in your letter. Maintaining privacy serves my interests as Governor. And yours, of course."

"Of course."

"Would you be kind enough to share what more you can regarding Viceroy Valdez and his captors?"

"My sources tell me he is being held at sea, on a fishing vessel. The pyrates who hold him removed and delivered his ear, to assure the King he is their prisoner." Acuña appeared shocked. Ortega continued, "At His Majesty's request, these pyrates later provided the Viceroy's ring, as further confirmation it was indeed Valdez."

"I am told the King sent fifteen thousand pieces of eight."

Ortega sipped his port, hiding his surprise. That information could only have come from King Philip himself...or Ayudante Vegas.

He recalled settling with Vegas on twelve thousand outright. The Ayudante then offered to split the remaining three thousand, to which he agreed. Ortega recognized that if Vegas was the source of the Governor's information, then their stories needed to align. Was the Governor testing him? Surely Vegas would have claimed he paid the full fifteen thousand for the severed ear. "Yes…fifteen thousand."

"I suspect the Viceroy's release will command a higher price."

"So I imagine," Ortega responded, wary about what Acuña did or didn't know. He immediately wondered—had Vegas already returned from Spain with the ransom payment and communicated the details to the Governor? He placed his cup on the table. "Before he left for Spain some time ago, I told the Ayudante the King must decide the amount."

"The Ayudante has recently returned, with doubloons in hand."

"Excellent," replied Ortega. "Then we shall soon enjoy the pleasure of the Viceroy's company."

"The question, as you must know, is just how much these pyrates expect to receive."

"Who can say?" he replied. "My sources tell me they were displeased with the fifteen thousand but accepted it anyway, believing the final payment would be substantial. I imagine they might seek several times that amount."

"It would be best to settle on the amount now," said Acuña.

Ortega worried this was a test. "I do not see how that is possible. I am in no position to counsel these pyrates."

"Tell me, Señor Ortega, do you know who leads them?"

"I have only heard rumors."

"And what do those rumors suggest?"

Ortega remembered De Graaf's proposal about placing blame, "The name Connachan has been floated."

"An *Irish* pirata?"

"She sails for England."

Acuña's eyes widened. "She? This must be a tale."

"I assure you, Your Excellency, the woman exists. She once sailed with El Draque—the most heinous of pyrates. They say she presented herself as a boy when signing on as a midshipman."

"Fascinating."

"Some suggest Connachan is a witch. They claim she used her powers to seduce El Draque. In return, he granted her a captaincy. When the Admiral died, she set sail on her own account."

"Have you any idea where she might be found?"

Ortega knew she'd been on Isla Tortuga at some point. If he disclosed that, the Governor might send warships to the island. But De Graaf was based there. Any conflict could obstruct his own ability to lay hands on the doubloons. "I cannot say. Pyrates travel like ghosts in the night—the only time one learns where they are is when they choose to make themselves known."

"Of course. Well, it appears you shall have to negotiate with this 'witch', on our behalf. How would you propose we do that?"

"I shall contact my sources. Is there an amount you believe His Majesty will find acceptable? It would allow me to test their response."

"Let me think on that," replied Acuña. "You understand, of course, that we must be extremely careful in securing the King's doubloons until we take possession of the Viceroy."

"Yes, of course."

"How would you suggest the exchange take place?"

Ortega sipped his port and placed his cup on the slightly sloped table. "At the last exchange, two of my guards accompanied me to a place the pyrates suggested—a secluded location along the coast. Three of them met us there." His story was a complete fabrication.

"Then you will recognize these men when you see them again."

"I am afraid not. It was too dark. They wore black hoods, with holes for their eyes and mouth. I did not recognize their voices."

"Was this 'witch' among them?"

"She may have been. But the only one who spoke was a man."

"Did you fear for your life?" Acuña wondered aloud.

"No. They needed my further help with the Viceroy's exchange." He picked up his cup and sipped. "I had no fear."

"I assure you, this time will be different, it being the final payment. For the safety of the doubloons…and yours, of course…we shall require an armed detail nearby."

"Were I a pyrate," Ortega volunteered, "I would choose to make the exchange at sea. After all, that is their home, where they are best prepared for any threat."

"Their home and their killing field," Acuña replied. "We should propose an alternate venue."

"They may be unwilling."

"One more thing," said Acuña, as though he hadn't heard Ortega's comment. "Will these pyrates recognize you?"

"I believe so. My face was not covered."

"Then we shall be unable to send an imposter in your place."

"Perhaps someone might be disguised to look like me."

The Governor shook his head, "Too risky. You shall have to lead the exchange. But first, you will need to negotiate the amount necessary to secure the Viceroy's release."

Ortega suppressed any visible sign of the humor in his having to negotiate with himself. He probed again, "How much has the King provided?"

Acuña hesitated. "You suggested these pyrates will expect several times what was paid for the Viceroy's ring. The King's generosity will accommodate that."

Judging by the ease with which the Governor said it, Ortega was certain King Philip provided more than sufficient resources. "I shall open discussions. It would help if I could provide an initial number."

Governor Acuña paused. "Let us first hear from them."

Returning to Cartageña along the same dusty trail he'd traveled to meet Acuña, Ortega contemplated the upcoming exchange. The Governor expected the release of Viceroy Valdez at the same time as the doubloons were delivered. With the Viceroy long since dead, that was impossible. He pondered having De Graaf seize the doubloons while they were in transit to the site of the exchange. He worried, however, about the risk to his own life during such an attack. De Graaf might well prefer he be eliminated in the process. And even were he to survive, the Governor might suspect him of having leaked transit information to the pyrates. Worse yet, if the attack were successful, the doubloons would be in De Graaf's possession. Why would he even bother to hand over Ortega's share? The more he thought about it, the more he disliked that strategy.

Another less risky possibility crossed his mind. He could inform the Governor that the pyrates were demanding a partial payment up-front, with the balance due upon the Viceroy's release. He and De Graaf could then split the up-front payment with minimal risk and later claim the Viceroy had been slain onboard the *Visser*. He and De Graaf had already prepared for that. The more he thought about it, the more he preferred this approach. Fewer doubloons but less risk.

Now nearing the outskirts of Cartageña, Ortega felt excited about what was to unfold. This could well lead to more money than he'd ever laid hands on at any one time. What's more, it would mean victory over the King in this virtual chess match they were playing. He breathed in deeply, pleased that he and De Graaf were scheduled to meet in Santo Pedro on the morrow. That would expedite things.

'*Life is good*,' he thought. '*God favors me*.'

XXVIII

"I have related news," William said. "You may find it rather discomforting." The other four looked his way—Garret, Blair, Portuguese Captain Drago, and Kat. All were seated at a table outside the Gente de Mar, discussing the seizure of Drago's vessel.

Garret hadn't said much. She was seething inside. Without any commission from the Queen, William and Blair's capture of Drago's ship was high piracy—something she couldn't condone. Her anger was rising by the moment. And now William was about to share something even more discomforting? How much worse could it be? She readied herself, looking directly into his eyes.

"We had an unfortunate confrontation shortly after transferring goods from Captain Drago's ship to *Orion*," William continued. "It was entirely unprovoked, I should add."

"Spanish navy?" Garret asked.

William looked her in the eye. "No," he replied. "I am afraid it was English."

Garret lost any semblance of patience, "My Lord...an English warship?"

William diverted his eyes, peering down at his hands tightly grasping his tankard of beer. He nodded, affirmatively.

"Please assure me you were not foolish enough to fire on it, William."

He looked up. "We had no choice, Garret. It fired first. Surrendering would have led to our imprisonment...as pyrates."

"I cannot believe this!"

"We tried signaling the warship but it was not to be deterred. It continued firing. I had to consider the well-being of the crew.”

“Just so,” concurred Blair, shaking his head in agreement. “No choice.” He looked away as Garret glared at him.

“Have you lost your minds? They may well have recognized our ships. *My* ships,” she shouted in disgust, rising to leave.

“That is quite likely, under the circumstances,” William conceded.

“What circumstances?” Garret yelled.

William hesitated. “I regret to say…it was *Mercilus*.”

For a split second, complete silence fell at the table. Kat broke it, “Not Captain Wenman?”

William turned to her. “Yes Kat, Captain Wenman’s ship.”

“Is he alright, then?” Kat asked worriedly.

William placed his hand on the girl’s shoulder. “I cannot be certain. The ship retreated.”

Garret, now standing, felt the full heat of her rage. Thoughts and questions flooded her mind like two angry rivers converging at a waterfall. For Kat’s sake only, she tried to control her fury, speaking in a measured pace, “Why fire on James’ ship? Why not a white flag?”

“At the time, we were unaware it was *Mercilus*.”

“And why would he retreat?” Garret’s voice turned shrill, beyond control.

“His mizzenmast was shattered. The ship was completely vulnerable.”

“But you were outgunned. Could he not have stood and fought?”

“*Mercilus* seemed ill-prepared. We unleashed full cannons, leveling great damage. His crew may have suffered deeply as well.”

William's answer was greeted with a cold stare. He offered nothing more.

Although James Wenman was her plaything, Garret had no tears. He was not her lover. She could accept the certain loss of his sexual favors. But the realization that she and William would surely be branded pyrates pained her. She breathed in deeply to gather herself, then exhaled through clenched teeth. "If James had recognized you initially, he would have held fire." It was a tenuous expression of faint hope that her ships hadn't been recognized.

"We cannot assume we went unrecognized," said William. "We were being watched by someone at the stern as *Mercilus* retreated."

"You understand what it means if you *were* recognized," Garret stated, trying hard to steady her emotions.

"Yes. The Admiralty will consider us pyrates."

"Her Majesty as well!" Garret exclaimed, banging the table hard with her fist. "She was our only hope. And now we have no way of knowing what message she may have sent us. Unless *Mercilus* inexplicably returns to Tortuga," she added sarcastically.

Neither William nor Blair responded.

As she turned to leave, Garret vented her full anger, almost shouting, "We are afloat without sails! Nothing can guide us through such turbulent waters, gentlemen. Magellan-like waters!" She turned to Kat, "Come. We must take our leave."

Following Garret and Kat's departure, Captain Drago offered an observation, "That is one unhappy hurricane. I should not like to be on your side of the sea."

"I knew this would not sit well with her," explained William.

"She and Captain Wenman had relations with each other."

"That, yes," offered Blair, "…and the piracy thing, of course."

————

Two barking, sand-colored dogs ran toward him chasing something unseen, leaving their trailing dust lingering in the air. De Graaf kicked the lagging animal. It stumbled but deftly recovered and hurried on. De Graaf spit at it as it left. Turning back, he could see the small Santo Pedro tavern where he would soon meet with the Phantom, moving them one step closer to concluding their ransom scheme. Yosel was to join them as well. The Jew and the Phantom were both coming from Cartageña, though separately.

Dressed fully in black, the hulking pyrate smothered the light as he entered the doorway. His summoning of the dark drew the gaze of the few customers inside, save for those who were already too much into the tavern's bitter fruit to care.

The tavern was dark inside at the best of times, owing to its paucity of windows. His pupils took a moment to adjust. He looked to the tables in the back. Yosel was already there. De Graaf headed that way while motioning to the owner, "A tankard."

De Graaf took the seat across from Yosel, anxious to be briefed before the Phantom's arrival, "What news from Cartageña?"

"My friend, Tesorero Sanchez, has informed me of the recent arrival of a Spanish ship." He scanned the room to see whether anyone might be listening. As far as he could tell, none were. Nonetheless, he leaned in and whispered, "It carried forty thousand gold doubloons.

De Graaf blew a copious amount of air through his lips. He whispered back, "For the Viceroy's release?"

"Yes. The gold was entrusted to an Ayudante. According to the Tesorero, this man is the messenger between King Philip and an unnamed man from Cartageña. I presume that man is our Phantom."

"To be sure," grunted De Graaf.

"Sanchez did not disclose the Phantom's name but it seems clear he knows him." As he said it, Yosel held up his hand, suggesting De Graaf hold his comments.

The owner arrived and set De Graaf's tankard on the table. De Graaf put down a coin and watched the man pick it up and leave. He turned to Yosel, "The Phantom's real name is unknown to me anyway." He sipped his beer. "Go on."

"The Governor is also aware that the gold is for the Viceroy's release. He and Sanchez want me to accompany the Ayudante when he delivers the gold to the Viceroy's captors. I am to present myself as the Tesorero's assistant, responsible for the safekeeping of the doubloons."

De Graaf was stunned. "How can this be?"

"The Governor wishes to avoid any harm coming to the Tesorero." Yosel sat back and sipped his beer. "And Sanchez has faith in me to act on his behalf."

"What good fortune is this?" He smiled at Yosel. "You, sir, are as sharp as my cutlass." He sipped his beer. "Is the Phantom also expected to participate in the exchange?"

"I suspect he will, with the Governor's blessing."

"Then we must alert him to your involvement. He cannot be surprised by your presence."

"Just so," agreed Yosel. He leaned forward. "There is one cloud on the horizon, however." He looked around and then back at De Graaf. "The Governor insists the gold be handed over at the same time as the

Viceroy is released. This is not an easy problem to solve."

"We shall have to disguise one of our men as the Viceroy."

"Were I the Governor," replied Yosel, "I would send along someone who could identify the Viceroy. If he does, and if that man sees the ruse, there could well be a bloody confrontation. We must ensure the balance of power rests with us."

"Indeed." De Graaf again sipped his beer. "One thing is certain…we cannot have the exchange take place onboard *Cutthroat*. The Spanish navy would pursue me until the end of my days."

Ortega left his two men outside and entered the tavern. Within moments, he spotted Yosel and De Graaf, both of whom still knew him only as 'the Phantom'. It was just the way he wanted it. He walked their way, pulled back a chair and sat. "Good news, gentlemen, the…" Yosel raised his hand, silencing him. The owner approached.

"Beer, sir?"

"A tankard, if you please."

"As you wish." The owner turned and left.

Ortega lowered his voice. "Our Spanish friend's payment has arrived. It now resides with the Governor. Perhaps four thousand reales." He was unaware what the real amount was, but this seemed a safe number to share with these two brigands. He had no idea Yosel already knew there were actually forty thousand doubloons, according to Tesorero Sanchez.

"I need a moment with my mate," De Graaf responded.

Ortega looked at Yosel in frustration. The Jew was a problem whenever it came time to negotiate. If De Graaf wished to confer privately with the man, he would make the two of them get up and leave to do that. He nodded his head toward the door. The pyrates rose and stepped outside.

The two henchmen who accompanied Ortega to the tavern were waiting outside. Yosel and De Graaf moved beyond earshot of them. They noticed one of the henchmen peering inside the tavern, likely to ensure their boss was okay.

"I doubt the Phantom knows how much gold the King has sent," Yosel opened.

"Should we tell him?"

"He would surely be delighted to know. But he will find it hard to believe we would have such information."

"Perhaps we share a lesser amount with him."

"No. We need him to negotiate with full knowledge."

"Fine. I shall tell him," said De Graaf. The two walked back into the tavern and retook their seats.

"We have sources in Cartageña," De Graaf opened. "Well-placed sources," he added. "They tell us the King has shipped forty thousand doubloons for the Viceroy's release." He sat back and smirked.

Ortega was shocked—both at the order of magnitude and at the fact that these two pyrates might have better sources in Cartageña than he did. From the little that Governor Acuña had shared with him, he expected five or six thousand doubloons at most. This was beyond even his imagination. "May I ask who your sources are?" he inquired.

"They are highly positioned and credible," Yosel assured him.

There it was, thought Ortega—confirmation that the Jew was De Graaf's not-so-hidden weapon in these negotiations. The man's confident response suggested his sources were indeed credible. He would give these two the benefit of the doubt. "If your sources are accurate," he responded, "we can negotiate for a significantly higher amount than I was led to believe was available. Might I suggest we negotiate for less than the full amount, however, to give your sources reasonable cover. Say, thirty thousand"

"Leave ten on the table?" De Graaf said it so loudly that Yosel nudged his foot, to settle him. "*Your* ten," De Graaf grumbled at Ortega.

Yosel stepped in, directing his comments to the Phantom, "You are right. We must protect our sources. Let us agree on thirty."

Ortega nodded. He looked at De Graaf, whose trust in Yosel seemed to win out.

"So be it," said De Graaf.

The three men raised their tankards. Yosel and De Graaf drank. Ortega merely wet his lips; he was no fan of the common man's drink.

De Graaf turned his eyes to the Phantom but tilted his head toward Yosel, "We have been discussing the nature of the exchange."

"I have a plan for that," Ortega quickly replied. De Graaf leaned back, suggesting the Phantom should proceed. "On my recommendation, I believe Governor Acuña may agree to issue half of the payment up-front, without actually seeing the Viceroy. The balance would be held back for the man's later release. We could accept this initial payment and then, prior to the exchange, announce that the prize has been lost…at the hand of this so-called witch—Connachan. The sinking of *Visser* has already set the foundation for that."

"But that would mean leaving behind thousands of doubloons," replied De Graaf.

"Just so. But," Ortega raised his index finger, "with no risk."

He leaned forward. "We shall claim the witch received the initial payment. Both the money and the Viceroy's death would then be on her head, not ours."

"Perhaps the Governor might offer the balance of the doubloons for the witch's capture," said De Graaf.

Yosel interjected, "Or…we might still obtain the balance of the doubloons by mounting an assault on their location."

"I cannot…" began Ortega. Yosel again raised his hand, halting him. The owner approached.

"Another round?" he asked. Business was apparently slow. No one suggested they wanted more. He walked away.

Ortega continued, "I cannot support an assault on the location of the remaining doubloons. It could lead to my coming under suspicion since the Governor has told me the ransom funds are secured in the storehouse." He paused. It was clear De Graaf wasn't buying his suggestion to settle for just an initial payment. He conceded, "If we are to proceed with an exchange for the full thirty, we must offer a suitable location."

"Not onboard my ship," De Graaf replied.

"Of course," Ortega replied. "We shall need a location the Governor will find acceptable."

"I have a proposal," said Yosel, leaning in. "Let us suggest the meeting of two longboats, just beyond sight of the city's harbor. In the dark of night, of course."

"Say more," replied Ortega.

"We can dress someone who, from a distance, and in the dark, might easily be mistaken for the Viceroy." Yosel then began moving his fingers on the table, representing the two boats. "Our boat would approach head-on to their broadside, with the imposter in the back, making him less visible." Ortega and De Graaf both nodded. Yosel continued, "Once our boat is within a few yards of the Governor's, our men could set it aflame and jump overboard. The Governor's men would then be faced with abandoning their own boat or colliding with a wall of flame."

De Graaf smiled, "Not unlike what Admiral Drake has done in the past…though at a much-reduced scale."

Yosel continued, "We would have a third boat nearby, cloaked entirely in black as to be invisible. The men in that boat would be huddled beneath the cover. Once the Governor's men abandon their vessel, the men of the third boat would shoot them in the water, douse any flames, pick up our own survivors and retrieve the doubloons." He sat back in his chair.

Ortega looked to De Graaf, "You are fortunate to have this man."

"Indeed." De Graaf now leaned in. "You will be surprised to know the Governor's representatives have asked him to be among those who will accompany the doubloons to the exchange."

Yosel and De Graaf left the tavern together, well after the Phantom. Yosel was pleased at having everyone agree to his proposal. At completion of the exchange, with Tesorero Sanchez his friend and future partner, he could soon return to a more normal life, establishing a business in Cartageña.

De Graaf was also pleased. He knew he could count on the Jew. The man was sharper than anyone he knew—including the Phantom.

———

"I have met with Senor Ortega," said Governor Acuña, placing his cup of port on the table between himself and Tesorero Sanchez. "I believe we can trust him. However, unlike in your case, we cannot have someone stand in his place when meeting with the Viceroy's captors. His face is already known to them."

Sanchez nodded. He had come here at the Governor's request. They'd already discussed security measures for the ransom doubloons. The Governor was pleased to learn that the number of guards at the treasure-house had been doubled.

"Do you have the final count for me?" asked Acuña.

"I do. It is just under forty-one thousand doubloons."

"That seems an odd number."

"Just so," Sanchez replied. "I have no idea how the amount was determined, other than the coins themselves fitting snugly inside the two chests. Ayudante Vegas indicated the entire amount is available for use in obtaining the Viceroy's release."

"I see. Perhaps one day I shall have the pleasure of meeting with the King to understand his reasoning regarding the amount." He reached again for his port. "Tell me, what news have you of this man with whom you spoke—the Jew?"

"He has agreed to present himself as my representative. He was most appreciative of the payment we offered in that regard."

"And, once more, you have complete confidence in him?"

"I do."

"Excellent. Then let us proceed as soon as we hear from Señor Ortega regarding the amount these pyrates are requesting and the location of the exchange."

"The Jew is out of town at present, though soon to return. I shall inform him the moment he is back. When do you expect to hear from Señor Ortega?"

"Very soon. He knows I am anxious to retrieve the Viceroy."

———

The girl had a special mastery of her short sword. William watched in admiration as Kat went methodically through her practice routine—at times in slow motion and at other times at battle speed. She was truly gifted, partly due to her natural athletic ability but also from having been schooled by an exceptional teacher. Garret sat nearby, pointing out certain nuances she observed in Kat's movements. William waited until there was a natural break. Kat artfully sheathed her cutlass with a twirled flair. William smiled and clapped, "Well done, m'lady."

"Thank you," Kat replied, taking a grand, sweeping bow as would a knight in the presence of his Queen. It was all in keeping with her recent decision to present herself as a young man. That included her manner of dress, the swagger in her movements, and the way she behaved in general…almost mimicking William himself. All of it was designed to be perceived as male by those who didn't know her. It could only work to her advantage in this male-dominated environment.

Garret rose, acknowledging William's presence. Though still unhappy with his recent piratical action, she'd become more accepting of it. More understanding. What was done, was done. Setting aside the tug of personal feelings she had for him, she recognized her future, as well as Kat's, depended on William's continued partnership. They were in this together. *All* in. "Thank you for coming, William. We have much to discuss."

"My pleasure, Captain."

For his part, William was uncertain how he would be received by Garret at any given moment. Their original friendship had been the strongest he'd ever known. And at times, over the past two years, it even hinted at becoming more intimate. But her recent anger toward him threatened to fracture their relationship beyond repair. It was as though he were now walking among seashells, trying desperately to avoid crunching them under his boots, to avoid awakening her anger.

"Come, let us walk." Garret gestured to the path leading to the village. She turned. He followed at her side. Kat lagged behind.

"I have given our situation much thought," Garret said. "It troubles me greatly." William, head down as he walked, could almost hear the seashells cracking, despite there being none on the ground. "Still, I am inclined to agree—we must now accept an altered destiny."

William stopped, raised his head, and peered into her eyes. He knew how hard it must have been for her to say that. She was a woman of honor and integrity; a servant and agent of the Queen herself. Moreover, just like him, she was fiercely loyal to England.

Garret stopped as well, returning his stare. Their eyes remained locked. The songs of birds, hum of insects, and distant clatter from the village wafted gently over them. William couldn't find any words to meld with the shared moment, rather than break it. He had no desire to complicate their relationship but every desire to deepen it. Gazing into her eyes, he felt an ardent longing for Garret; a desire to be with her— always. Still, he suppressed the urge to share his feelings.

Garret searched for the meaning in William's eyes. She saw

sadness, and longing, and maybe the hope for a better life—perhaps together. She'd neither expected nor intended her words to affect him this way. Yet here she was, caught in a moment that pleaded for more than she felt ready to give. This man, whom she'd known and liked since he was a child and fellow midshipman, meant more to her than anyone. She'd known the passion of prior relationships with Pantas and Jorge, and the sexual pleasures once afforded her by James Wenman. But this man, this ever-friend, offered something different—something she didn't fully comprehend. Was it comfort? Partnership? Was it a level of caring beyond any shown by others? She reached slowly for his hand and took a step toward him, keeping her eyes on his. She tilted her face upward. "There is danger along this path," she said, softly.

William sensed an openness he'd never before felt with Garret. "Then let us walk it together," he responded, without even having to think the words. He grasped her other hand, firmly, stepping in to feel her breasts against his lower chest. It was not a time for more words. He lowered his head, pressing his lips against hers. She moved her arms to his back, drawing him close.

Kat glanced their way after having followed the movements of a nearby squirrel. She savored the moment. The two people she most cared for now shared something she'd long hoped for.

Nearing the village, the cluttered sound of many voices, excited ones, caused Garret, William and Kat to quicken their pace. They found the area well beyond the Gente de Mar bustling with energy. That seemed unusual, it being before noon. A crowd was still in the process of forming. Men were rushing toward the source of the noise. Some were oddly or barely dressed; awakened by the commotion, they wished not to miss any of the action.

Garret heard a clash—the definitive sound of two men at swords. Voices cheered and oohed as she and William pushed among the onlookers. Sunlight glinted off raised swords, despite the dust rising around the combatants. '*Who were they?*' Garret wondered as she peered between men's heads. The two now-weary warriors circled, their clothes dirty, torn, bloodied, and drenched in sweat. Their thrusts were slow, their cutlasses heavy, and their wounds many. It would end soon, thought Garret.

The bigger man, perhaps desperately seeking to end the contest, made an all-out rush toward the smaller one. His sword was gripped in both hands and raised high above his right shoulder—as high as his wounds would permit. He brought it down almost vertically with all the might he could muster but was awkwardly wide of his moving target.

Having deftly stepped aside, the smaller man spotted his opening. He thrust the blade of his cutlass deeply into the left side of his opponent's chest, at heart level. The boisterous crowd suddenly turned silent. They had favored their large crewmate—the bladed combatant, not this newcomer. The skewered man fell to his knees, dropped his cutlass, and raised his hand barely above his shoulder, in submission. But he wasn't about to be given any quarter. The smaller man threw aside his own cutlass and pulled back his short-coat, exposing a jewel-handled dagger. It gleamed in the sunlight. Though partially obscured, Garret sensed she recognized it. The man smoothly withdrew the deadly instrument from its sheath. Like a skilled assassin, he thrust it backhanded into the pyrate's neck, just below the larynx, causing his opponent's eyes to bulge open in disbelief. They remained open as the dagger was rapidly withdrawn, pulling him face-forward onto the ground. His body jerked and shook in the dirt for a few moments as the crowd looked on in awed silence.

When the body finally lay still, two pyrates stepped forward, hands open. The victor nodded to them, acknowledging their right to retrieve their fallen mate. They took the dead man by his underarms. His boots left a parallel trail in the dirt as the men dragged his body away.

The crowd began dispersing slowly, sharing thoughts on what they'd just witnessed. Some exchanged coins. Garret grasped the arm of a sailor passing by—one she recognized as being from her own crew. "Do you know these two men?"

He nodded toward the body being dragged away, "That one sailed with De Graaf." He turned to look at the other man, now painstakingly wiping away blood from the blade of his obviously treasured dagger. "The dead man claimed this other was a spy, sent by the Spanish. He asked too many questions."

"Do you know this man's name?"

"De Cuero, I believe."

"Thank you." Garret handed her crewmate a silver coin. "Your next grog is on me."

Much of the crowd headed to the Gente de Mar, where watered-down beer would facilitate continued discussion of the event.

"Shall we go?" asked William, wondering why Garret was staring at the victor.

"Take Kat with you. I wish to speak with this man."

"He does not appear to be particularly friendly."

"I am fine. Give me a moment. I shall meet you outside the tavern."

William put his hand on Kat's back. "Time for a drink." Kat followed his lead.

Garret stepped toward de Cuero, watching as he lovingly wiped the distinctively Asian dagger's blade with an oiled black cloth—something only a man of meticulous nature would do. "My name is Connachan. Captain Connachan." She offered her hand.

King Philip's spy didn't look up, nor respond.

"Such a fine weapon. I have never seen anything like it," Garret lied. Her first lover, Ambassador Pantas, owned just such a dagger. In fact, she suspected this very one might well have been his. "Might I have a look?"

De Cuero turned his head toward Garret, questioningly. He'd heard of an Englishwoman masquerading as a pyrate. This must be her, he thought. If there were any truth to her reputation as a skilled warrior, he was not about to hand over his dagger. It wasn't something he would do for anyone, let alone her.

"I prefer not to share my weapons."

As he spoke, Garret's eyes focused on the dagger. Being this close to it, she was virtually certain it was the one Pantas once owned. "Where did you purchase it?" She hoped the question would defer any suspicion de Cuero might have over her knowledge of the dagger's provenance.

De Cuero looked down at the weapon fondly, taking his time.

Garret sensed he was searching for an answer. "It has been in my family for generations."

"I see." It seemed obvious from the man's hesitation that he was covering the truth—this wasn't a family heirloom. Nor had it likely been purchased or given by a friend. If it were either, he would have said so without hesitation. Her mind spun. This liar could very well be the King's spy, as his deceased opponent had suggested. He also had the characteristics of an assassin. His painstaking oiling of the blade was but one example. She sensed a strong likelihood that de Cuero might be the very assassin who'd taken Pantas' life on the dark streets of London years ago. This dagger was the proof. She thirsted to learn more about this man, and perhaps trick him into admitting his deed.

De Cuero stepped away to recover his cutlass. He began cleaning it with the now-bloody rag he'd first used on the dagger.

"Might I buy you a drink?" Garret asked.

De Cuero didn't answer. He carefully wiped blood from the cutlass. Garret waited. Finally, de Cuero turned her way. Garret could see he was sizing her up—as a woman? A potential adversary? She couldn't be certain; his face was expressionless.

"Perhaps tonight," de Cuero responded. " I must first attend to my wounds."

Garret joined William at a table he'd secured outside the Gente de Mar. Kat was with him. "So," asked William, "what do you make of that man?"

"He strikes me as one who lives by the sword. Perhaps even *for* the sword. And he is most cautious with his answers. He could easily be the King's spy."

"If he is, then it cannot be long before the Spanish decide to invade this pyrate-infested island."

"Perhaps. Yet there is little to be gained here, beyond revenge."

"Revenge can be a powerful motivator," William replied, indirectly inferring Garret's own revenge-taking on the village of Santiago del Príncipe, for which she once traveled far out of her way. He continued, "You realize, of course, that if the Spanish were to assault Tortuga, we would be forced to stand with men such as De Graaf and Attila. Would we not?"

"Defenders of the red flag," Garret smirked. "Who would have imagined that?"

"Yet that is precisely where we are."

"Is there not a different color?" Garret asked with frustration wrapped in grudging acceptance.

"Perhaps. On some black day."

XXIX

Six men were assembled around the large oval table in Governor Acuña's well-appointed office. Their sole mission was to finalize the exchange of King Philip's doubloons for Viceroy Valdez. Of the six, only Señor Ortega knew the Viceroy was no longer among the living.

Ayudante Vegas, seated across from Ortega, glanced at him frequently, uncomfortable about being in the same room with him. The two had met on prior occasions to arrange payment for the Viceroy's ear and ring. But Vegas was deeply concerned about having withheld a portion of the King's initial payment for Valdez' ring—a portion he and Ortega had shared. He worried what Ortega might disclose to the Governor about that, if he hadn't already. And if he had, did the man's account line up with his own? There was danger ahead if their stories weren't perfectly aligned.

Governor Acuña, now standing, opened the discussion, "Gentlemen, you are well aware that we are here to discuss something of utmost importance to King Philip—the release of his dear friend, Viceroy Valdez. I have asked General Gonzalo Serezo, leader of our provincia's military forces, to take us through the plan he has prepared." He directed his arm toward Serezo.

"But first, I should like to introduce Capitán Don Francisco Rivera de Mendoza." He moved his arm toward Rivera. "He served with the Viceroy both in the Netherlands campaign and also at Inagua. He is the only man among us who knows the Viceroy personally and can attest to the fact that the man offered by his captors is indeed

Valdez." Everyone acknowledged the two military men. "Finally, I have asked Tesorero Sanchez to join us." He nodded toward Sanchez. The men looked his way, acknowledging him.

Acuña continued, "Before General Serezo shares his plan, it is important you understand that one of two things will happen. If we are fortunate in arranging the Viceroy's release, we shall all be lauded by His Majesty. And handsomely rewarded, I imagine." He smiled at the thought. "However, should anything go awry, and the Viceroy be lost in the process, we shall all face the King's wrath." He looked at the men in turn. Each nodded their understanding. "So then…let us use our time here to agree on every aspect of the General's plan. There must be no holes in our thinking and strict adherence to the plan."

Ortega was now deeply concerned. His own plan, devised with the pyrate De Graaf, included disguising someone as the Viceroy for the purpose of the exchange. He hadn't expected the presence of Valdez' associate, Capitán Rivera, who would easily recognize an imposter once he was close enough. It caused Ortega to regret the decision he'd made at his last meeting with the Governor. He'd suggested an initial partial payment to the pyrates, as a display of goodwill, but acquiesced once the Governor pushed back. If only he'd pressed harder, he thought, he and De Graaf might already have the initial payment in hand, without any risk whatsoever. Now, there was significant risk involved. The disguise of the would-be Viceroy would need to be compelling enough to avoid premature discovery of the ruse. But at some point, the pretense would be discerned, and chaos would then unfold. At least the Governor had agreed to conduct the exchange in the dark, well beyond Cartageña's harbor. It was an environment pyrates thrived in. But they would most assuredly need to be better prepared if they hoped to come away with the thirty thousand doubloons everyone had agreed to.

Ortega's thoughts were interrupted by Governor Acuña. "General Serezo, would you please review the plan with us now."

"Thank you, Your Excellency," Serezo said as he rose. He scanned the others' faces. "We have agreed with the pyrates' request to conduct the exchange in a meeting of longboats, well beyond the harbor." He pointed to a specific position on the map laid out on the table. "No weapons are to be carried by either party. Nonetheless, we can expect they will have pistols hidden in their boat. We will as well, since we must be in a position to defend ourselves."

Ortega interrupted, concerned about the risk to his own life. "Surely it cannot be your intent to initiate, or otherwise invite, fire. Such action would place the Viceroy's life at extreme risk."

"Of course, Señor Ortega. If you would be so kind as to let me finish," the General responded, clearly perturbed by the interruption. "The two chests containing doubloons shall be placed on benches, between the rowers. We shall open both, to display the contents. We shall then ask that the Viceroy be identified by Capitán Rivera. Once this is done, the Viceroy shall step across to our boat before the chests are handed over. We shall then depart." He looked to Ortega, "Without any aggressive action being taken, of course."

The General reached into his pocket, pulling out a doubloon. "There is, in fact, no need for aggressive action." He grinned, anxious to share a little-known secret. He held up the doubloon. "You see, gentlemen, on the King's orders, these doubloons have been minted with a mark that will enable us to identify them once they appear in the marketplace at any Spanish port. So, we shall inevitably recover them…*and* the men who bear them." He scanned the men's faces. "Therefore, during this exchange, we shall be focused solely on preserving the life of the Viceroy, not on securing the doubloons." He looked to the Governor, handing him back the floor.

"Are there any questions or concerns, gentlemen?" Acuña asked as Serezo sat back down.

"Have we decided who will be in the longboat?" Ortega asked.

General Serezo responded, looking first to Capitán Rivera. "The Capitán, of course." He returned his gaze to Ortega, "I have asked the Governor that you be present as well, Señor, since you are the only one these pyrates know."

"They know *of* me, General," Ortega clarified, hoping to reinforce the impression that he was merely an intermediary.

"Of course. Still, your presence is required." Serezo leaned back and continued, "We shall also have with us a member of the Tesorero's staff—a Jew named Yosel." Tesorero Sanchez nodded his acknowledgment.

"The remainder of the men shall be from within my ranks," said Serezo. "They shall serve as oarsmen and handle the two chests."

A brief silence followed. "Any other questions?" asked the Governor.

"Only the day and time," said Tesorero Sanchez.

"Three days hence. At two of the clock, in the morning," Serezo replied. "We shall gather one hour beforehand, at the harbor."

"Well then, gentlemen," Acuña said, rolling up the map to signify the meeting was ending, "may God be with us."

Ortega returned to his villa, pleased with the fact that he had all the information needed to ensure there was no hiccup on De Graaf's side. Three things in particular were of critical importance. First was the presence of weapons onboard General Serezo's boat. Happily, there was no intent to use them; they were a defensive measure only. Second, and most unfortunate, was that Capitán Rivera would be present. At some point, he would recognize that the man purported to be the Viceroy was actually an imposter. And as soon as he did, it was likely shots would be exchanged. He would inform De Graaf to place a hood over the imposter's head, to buy themselves time. The third and final piece of valuable information was that the doubloons had been specially marked for future identification. That meant they would need to be exchanged outside Spanish ports or in dark markets.

Ortega was aware that De Graaf had already secretly encamped in the forest outside Cartageña. He would send him word of these details in a sealed message to Yosel, who was currently residing in the city. Though he would have preferred to meet the Jew in person, Ortega recognized he couldn't afford to risk being seen with him, given the Jew's involvement with the Tesorero. He began crafting the message to De Graaf in his mind. He would put quill to parchment the moment he returned to his villa.

———

This is not a good time, dearest," said Prince, "Not in the least."

"Of course, Uncle," replied Cath. "I understand."

"Then what is this private matter to which you so urgently need to attend?"

"My friend is desperately ill," Cath lied. She'd just been given a sealed letter and asked by the messenger to immediately deliver it to Captain Connachan. She didn't care to disclose that to Prince. "She requires my immediate attention."

"Well then, be quick about it. You are too skilled at separating thirsty pyrates from their pieces of eight to be gone for long."

Now walking the narrow path to Garret's residence with the sun bordering the horizon, Cath pondered the nature of the relationship between Captain Connachan and the Jew, whose message she carried. Yosel was a member of De Graaf's crew, not Garret's. So why would he be leaving Garret sealed messages? Could it be he was interested in leaving De Graaf's crew to join hers? Or, she smiled inwardly, was it simply his misguided way of initiating a relationship with Captain Connachan? They couldn't possibly be lovers. Of that she was certain.

She soon reached the clearing where Garret's crew had constructed its new residences. She asked a man passing by for directions to Garret's place. When he questioned her motive, she displayed the sealed letter.

Garret's residence was located behind, and sheltered from, the other buildings. '*The privilege of rank*,' thought Cath. She admired how this young woman managed to ascend to the leadership of all these men. It gave her a feeling of hope, leading her to think about how she, herself, was also effective in bending men's will to her designs. Though it was something she had in common with Garret, they clearly bent men differently…at least at this point.

The horizon began swallowing the sun as Cath knocked at Garret's door. "Aawck! Pyrate!" squawked Mr. Blue, Kat's parrot.

Cath recognized the sharp sound of the bird that frequently accompanied Kat to the tavern. "Captain Connachan," she called out, "'Tis I, Cath."

The door opened almost before Cath finished getting the words out. Garret was grasping the grip of her cutlass, in standard precaution. "What a pleasant surprise. Enter, please."

"Pyrate!" squawked Mr. Blue. "Pyrate."

"Enough, Mr. Blue," scolded Kat. "Not a pyrate."

"Pyrate," the bird squawked again, less loudly. It looked away.

"What brings you?" asked Garret.

"I have a letter from the man they call the Jew. His messenger asked that I deliver it right away." She extended it in her hand.

Garret accepted it. "Would you care for a cup of beer?"

"Thank you, no. I must return. My uncle is displeased that I left the tavern. It is a busy time."

"I see. Next time, perhaps."

"It would be my pleasure, mum. Good evening then." Cath turned to leave. "To you as well, Kat." The girl smiled at the use of her new name. Cath left. Garret closed the door.

"Aawck! Pyrate!" squawked Mr. Blue, loudly.

Garret unsealed the letter. It was three pages—lengthy, compared to Yosel's prior messages. The last page was a hand-drawn map with the cross of Christ marking a particular spot along the shoreline, near a small bay. A second cross, this one an X, marked De Graaf's encampment further inland. Her eyes widened as she began reading the first two pages.

"What is it?" asked Kat.

Utterly absorbed by the letter's alarming content, Garret didn't respond. There was a ransom plot afoot for the release of Viceroy Jorge Valdez, her former captive-turned-lover. '*He is deceased, for God's sake*,' Garret whispered to herself. And yet here was news of a deception plotted by Yauggan De Graaf, the very man whose actions had led to Jorge's death. The pyrate was proposing to exchange Jorge for King Philips' doubloons. He would receive them at sea and then row ashore to the location Yosel had marked with the Christian cross. She smiled at the Jew's humor in using that symbol. She recalled how he sometimes presented himself as a Converso even though he wasn't. In truth, he wasn't religious at all.

Garret continued reading. "My God," she exclaimed, seeing that De Graaf eventually intended to place the Viceroy's death at *her* feet. The pyrate clearly had no scruples. He would bring the full wrath of Spain's revenge on her head, even if it meant risking an invasion of Tortuga.

Finally, Yosel noted that he would dress in all-white clothing, to identify himself. Clearly, he had no desire to become an accidental fatality if Garret and her men attempted an assault on De Graaf.

She laid Yosel's map on the table and folded up the other two pages, placing them inside her doublet.

"What is it?" Kat repeated.

"Nothing of concern." Garret had no desire to worry the girl with this matter. "I shall require time to consider what has been written here. Be about your business."

While Kat turned and picked up a book, Garret sat, looking at Yosel's map, thinking to later compare it to her own maps. Any action to intercept De Graaf, she thought, would best occur at the landing site, the point furthest from his encampment. Given a distance of roughly one hundred yards between the two locations, and the possibility of additional men staying at the campsite, the assault would need to be as silent as possible. It called for crossbows. Even so, De Graaf's water-borne men would surely be carrying pistols. An early, overwhelming barrage of arrows would buy her time before returning pistol-fire would alert any men at De Graaf's encampment. She would need to plan a two-directional assault.

The larger matter at hand was what to do once her men succeeded in overcoming De Graaf's crew and recovering the gold. There were two parts to that. First, what to do with the doubloons—treat them as captured treasure or return them to the Spanish as a gesture of goodwill? She knew her crew would strenuously object to the latter. But perhaps the Spanish would reward them for the doubloons' return. That might even facilitate discussions with King Philip regarding the exchange of the islands that both she, and now the Queen, sought for England. It was a path that might also restore her once-positive relationship with Her Majesty.

The second part: What to do with De Graaf? Turn him over to Spanish authorities, or take her revenge on the bastard for giving rise to Jorge's demise?

XXX

The Gente de Mar was overflowing on this rather dark night. Rodrigo de Cuero, King Philip's spy and assassin, took a seat at a table outside and waited for a server. He felt his hair being toyed with by the warm breeze. His well-practiced, blank expression hid the frustration he was feeling. His sole reason for being on this pyrate-infested island was to uncover the whereabouts of Viceroy Jorge Valdez—the mission assigned him by King Philip. But thus far, he'd learned nothing of any value. If anyone knew anything, they certainly weren't sharing it.

He'd also made inquiries about the pyrate De Graaf. Ayudante Vegas had provided him handsome funding to engage the pyrate's services for some special project he had in mind. But here too, he'd made no progress; De Graaf was not even on the island.

He hoped Captain Connachan would arrive soon. After all, he'd come here at her invitation. In preparation, he'd sought information about this so-called witch from village residents. The word was that she was a privateer who once sailed with El Draque—the pyrate so deeply despised by King Philip. Her two ships were anchored in the harbor, having recently returned from an attack on a Spanish-flagged, Portuguese vessel. That alone made her Spain's enemy. So she was fair game. De Cuero was unaware, however, that he was missing one important piece of information that no one had shared…or even knew.

Garret approached the tavern alone. She almost didn't recognize de Cuero. The sweat-laced, scruffy appearance following his battle with the pyrate he'd slain earlier, had given way to a still-rugged yet polished look. It was his well-trimmed beard with a light streak of gray up the middle that gave him away. His black, curly hair flowed beneath a dark bandana. He wore a black long-coat, likely to conceal weapons he was carrying, she thought.

De Cuero nodded as she neared his table. He rose to welcome her, as any schooled gentleman would. Garret pulled back a chair, noticing the turning heads of De Graaf's nearby crewmembers. She sensed they didn't like de Cuero any more than they liked her. No doubt they were curious why she and de Cuero were even meeting; the man was rumored to be a Spanish spy and she was an English privateer-cum-pyrate. If anything, De Graaf's men would be expecting them to cross cutlasses, not tankards of beer.

"Welcome, Captain" de Cuero opened. He waved to gain the attention of a nearby server. "Allow me to splice your mainbrace." The phrase was commonly used to serve beer to a ship's crew but, by the way he'd delivered it, Garret felt a wave of sexual innuendo.

"It shall be my pleasure," Garret responded, returning the not-so-subtle implication with one of her own. She sat. "My compliments on the skill you displayed earlier today. Most impressive."

"My opponent, too, was skilled," noted de Cuero. "I now carry his marks with me…for all time."

A server approached. "Beer, Captain?"

Garret looked to de Cuero. "It was my intention to honor your victory by purchasing a beer for *you*."

"But I now have mine," he replied, "Perhaps the next."

Garret turned to the server, "Yes, beer if you please. And boucan."

"Bring another for you then, sir?"

"Just so," nodded de Cuero.

The server left. Garret looked to de Cuero, "Have you tried boucan?"

"I have, yes. A most surprising delight."

"So it is." Garret was happy to engage in trivial conversation, for now. But in time, she hoped to verify that this current holder of what she believed to be Pantas' jeweled dagger, was indeed the man who assassinated her first lover. She intended to ply him with beer in the hope that he might ultimately boast about his prior exploits, and accidentally provide a damning hint.

"You are English," remarked de Cuero.

"And you, Spanish."

"Does that not bother you?"

"Are we not both children of God?"

"Different Gods, perhaps," de Cuero replied. He was Catholic, at least by way of his ancestors' beliefs and observance.

"We may distinguish God differently," agreed Garret, "yet I assure you, he does not do so with us."

"You are religious, then."

The server interrupted, placing two tankards of beer and a plate of boucan on the table. De Cuero drew the last of his current tankard and handed it to her. Garret gave her a silver coin. The server left.

"I believe there is a God," Garret responded belatedly to de Cuero's remark. "Though he sometimes acts in ways we do not understand." Pantas' assassination was one top-of-mind example.

"Some say God has a purpose for each of us," de Cuero replied. "Though I agree, it may be something others do not understand." He smirked as he said it, perhaps subconsciously.

Garret read his face. He could well be Pantas' assassin, she thought. She watched him take a strip of boucan. "Have you brought your dagger? I should like to see it."

De Cuero reached inside his coat, withdrew it, and placed it lovingly on the table, handle sideways. He kept his hand on the grip.

"May I?" asked Garret, moving her hand toward it.

De Cuero studied her eyes. He pulled back his hand, slowly.

Garret placed a finger on either side of the hilt and carefully drew the dagger toward herself, without grasping it. Best not to prompt fear in de Cuero's mind, or draw the attention of onlookers, she thought. "Magnificent. The artistry appears Asian."

"It may well be."

Garret perused it further. There was now no doubt—it was the one Pantas always carried, commissioned by the Sultan himself for his favorite nephew. Yet, for Pantas, it was merely an ornament—a display of fine Indonesian artistry. "Would you be interested in selling it?" Garret asked, thinking it best to portray her interest solely as that of a buyer.

De Cuero shook his head. "No. It is my prize."

'*There it is,*' thought Garret. It was the slip she'd half-expected. He'd made a different claim in the afternoon—that it was a family heirloom. "Your prize?" she pressed.

"A gift, really. Given by…a friend." De Cuero stumbled with his words. The truth was that King Philip allowed him to keep the dagger after he'd shown it to him as proof of Ambassador Pantas' assassination.

"An exceptional friend, apparently…" remarked Garret. "…one who would part with such a priceless piece."

De Cuero seemed uninterested in extending that conversation.

"It is not for sale," he said curtly, reaching across the table and pulling
it back hurriedly.

A sudden chill coursed through Garret's very soul—the
certainty that she was now face-to-face with Pantas' assassin. The
dagger might not be for sale, but she was determined to possess it. Its
current owner would have no need for it in his afterlife.

———

Yosel arrived at the small beach on a single-occupant skiff. He
slid the vessel across the relatively firm sand to the treeline, finding De
three of Graaf's boats already hidden among the trees. He headed along
the narrow path leading inland with the aid of a small, squeaking
lantern. "Bloody Hell!" he cursed, attempting to wave away the
devilish flying insects attracted by his light and inclined to bite.
Walking briskly and occasionally stumbling along the rugged path, he
soon heard the sound of pyrates' voices.

De Graaf and his men sat by a crackling fire, drinking watered
beer. Their self-made clearing in the woods wasn't far from Cartageña
but it was virtually inaccessible by anything other than boat, the forest
being too dense. They'd landed at the secluded beach several days ago
to carve the narrow path about a hundred yards inland, and set camp.
This was now the base for their upcoming ruse—supposedly
exchanging Viceroy Valdez for the King's doubloons. The devious
transaction would take place well beyond view of Cartageña's harbor.
Afterward, they would return here to count and divvy their prize.

Yosel entered the clearing. "Damn these bloody insects," he

scowled. "They are the cursed of the earth…forced to suck the blood of others."

De Graaf chuckled, "The jungle's *own* Pyrates." His men laughed.

Yosel didn't see the humor in it. "I have good news," he said, slapping an insect biting his neck.

"We are anxious to hear it, replied De Graaf."

The men listened while Yosel laid out the specifics of the note he'd received from the Phantom's messenger, detailing Governor Acuña's plan for the ransom exchange and release of Viceroy Valdez. When he finished, De Graaf turned to his men, "God is on our side, gentlemen." Heads nodded in response. He turned back to Yosel. "Your ability to obtain such information is bloody remarkable."

"I have been most fortunate."

De Graaf paused to think. "Given the number of men in the Governor's boat, we shall send only six in our approach-boat, including our imposter."

Stevens, who would be posing as Viceroy Valdez, pulled out a double-breasted black coat with bold brass buttons and held it in the air for all to see. "What think you, gentlemen? Shall I make a good Viceroy?" The pyrates laughed.

De Graaf continued, "The Governor's men will not fear a group of only six." The pyrates concurred. "Our second boat shall stay concealed beneath the black canvas and maintain a proper distance as to be nearby but undetected. I shall lead that boat. Seven of you will accompany me."

"Be aware that I shall be in the Governor's boat," Yosel interjected, "I have no desire to put my own life at risk."

"Of course," nodded De Graaf.

"I have worn white clothing, so you will all recognize me." Yosel opened his dark cloak for the men to see. "I shall discard my coat once the action begins."

"Excellent," said De Graaf.

Yosel spoke directly to the men, "When the approach-boat is set aflame, I shall exit the Governor's boat and cling to its far side; my swimming skill fails me."

"Rest assured, Yosel, you shall not be placed at risk..." De Graaf turned to his men, "...on pain of death."

"Much obliged."

"I there anything more, then?" asked De Graaf.

"Aye, there is," said Yosel. "A captain who served with the Viceroy will be in the Governor's boat. He is charged with identifying Valdez." He turned to address Stevens, "You shall need to cover your head."

"So I shall."

"Is that all, then?" De Graaf asked again.

"Yes," replied Yosel, consciously choosing to conceal one critical point—an unwelcome 'welcoming' party would be waiting at the beach for De Graaf's return...led by Captain Connachan.

———

Alone in his office, Governor Acuña awaited the arrival of General Serezo, who would lead the exchange of gold doubloons for the release of Viceroy Valdez. He could ill afford to have the transaction fail. Nor could there be any loose ends. The General was key to both. This meeting was the last step to ensure General Serezo was on the same page.

Acuña grasped an olive jar containing a well-aged French wine. He withdrew the cork and poured two cups. The knock he was expecting came as he headed back to his desk.

"The General, sir," announced the guard.

"Enter, please," Acuña replied.

Serezo walked in, removing his black, feathered tricorn and bowing slightly in the process. "Your Excellency," he said.

Acuña approached, offering one of the cups. "Welcome, General. Let us begin with a fine wine, newly arrived from Burgundy." Serezo accepted it. Acuña extended his arm, "Please, have a seat."

General Serezo waited for the Governor to take his first. Acuña continued, "Since we are soon to launch our campaign to free the Viceroy, I thought it best we cover two key points, neither of which is to be shared beyond these walls."

"By all means." Serezo sipped his wine.

"First, I need some assurance that you and your men shall not fail. What final measures you are taking to ensure your success."

Serezo straightened up and leaned forward, placing his cup on the desk. "You are already aware that we shall have pistols at the ready, though hidden. If there is to be any deceit on the part of the pyrates, we shall put a swift end to them."

"Without endangering the Viceroy, of course."

Yes, of course."

"And if these pyrates are armed as well?"

"I have selected my finest marksmen. We shall enjoy that advantage. Each one shall have four pistols, two hidden on their person and two at their feet."

"Excellent," replied Acuña.

"With regard to the doubloons," continued Serezo, "we shall have only a top layer of them, below which are pieces of gold-painted lead."

Acuña paused, wondering how long it might take for the pyrates to discover the deception. It could easily lead to unfortunate consequences for the Viceroy. "I cannot approve such a ploy, General. There is too much at stake to take such a risk."

"As you wish." Serezo reached for and sipped his wine.

Acuña was shocked the General had caved without a challenge.

Serezo went on, "There is one final measure. I have arranged for a ship to intercept the pyrates following their departure—once the Viceroy is safely in our hands, of course."

Acuña considered that. Though he liked the idea, he worried the pyrates might discover the deceit in advance, thereby placing the Viceroy's safety at risk. In the end, he was fine letting the pyrates have the doubloons; no doubt most would later be recovered as a result of their being minted with an identifying mark. Besides, King Philip clearly valued Valdez more than he valued the gold. "No, General. I cannot approve this measure either. We must take no action whatsoever that might threaten the Viceroy's life."

Serezo didn't bother to contest this point either. "As you wish," he replied again, and sipped more wine.

"The second matter I wish to discuss is Tesorero Sanchez' representative—the Jew. He is unknown to me."

"To me as well, Governor."

"He is truly under orders from no one."

"Just so."

"Which makes him a loose end if, for any reason, you fail to execute the mission." Acuña had carefully chosen these words in advance. He didn't wish to directly order the execution of the Jew but believed the General would understand his intent, both by implication and by his use of the word 'execute'.

For a brief moment, Serezo looked questioningly at Acuña, saying nothing. He spoke cautiously, "Am I to understand…"

Acuña raised his hand to silence Serezo. "You understand completely, General." He rose, to avoid any further discussion on the matter and risk being tainted with ordering the killing.

General Serezo understood the meeting was over. He returned his cup to the desk and rose. "Thank you, Your Excellency. I assure you, we shall return the Viceroy in good health."

Serezo smiled as he left the Governor's residence. He was no fool. He'd fully expected Acuña to turn down his proposals to use lead coins and have a ship available to capture the pyrates. After all, political animals like Acuña seldom heeded the advice of their military leaders. The two proposals were merely a ploy. If the mission proved unsuccessful, the Governor's refusal to accept his proposals provided him the ability to lay blame at Acuña's feet. He was confident his own derrière was now sufficiently covered. He grinned at the thought that he might well be a more adept political beast than even the Governor. His smile quickly dissolved as he contemplated the execution of the Jew.

———

"You cannot be serious, Garret," William said in frustration. "We cannot seize the doubloons, nor De Graaf, with the expectation of turning them over to the Spanish for good favor. The crew will have none of it. The Queen herself might bloody well suspect we are working in concert with the Spanish."

"You understand, William, that if we do not act in this manner, we shall forever be branded as pyrates—by both Spain *and* England. The navies of both countries would spare nothing to seek us out." Garret was just as exasperated as William. Her feelings for him were strong, yet she couldn't let them subvert her intentions. She needed to convince him of her approach based on its merits.

William persisted, "Surely you must recognize we shall be the target of the English navy anyway, once *Mercilus* lands at Deptford. And the Spanish may well seek us out for our raid on Captain Drago's vessel, or for any future assault on a Spanish merchant. Have we not already accepted that we must now fly the red flag? There is no having it any other way. We are either all-in or not at all."

Deep inside, Garret sensed William was right. Still, agreeing to virtually fly the red was being forced on her by circumstances. It haunted her from the very moment she suggested an openness to stealing the King's doubloons. She would literally be flying colors other than those of England. What would her grandfather think if he were still alive? Or Admiral Drake, for that matter? Would they feel she was turning her back on England? And what of Queen Elizabeth, the woman she most admired, and with whom she shared a most uncommon thing—the leadership of men? It was something they'd bonded over. Would virtually flying the red mean losing Her Majesty's grace and friendship for all time? The thought pained her. Yet any relationship they'd once enjoyed was likely to dissolve anyway, given her ships' attack on *Mercilus*. The only thing now offering her any comfort was her agreement with William that he, and they, would never again assault an English-flagged vessel. She hung her head, recognizing this was indeed the moment. She was…finally…irreversibly…crossing over.

"You are most convincing, William. Let it be so, then. But not a red flag. Let us distinguish ourselves by flying a flag with no color—a *black* flag."

XXXI

If there was a moon, no one could see it. The stars, too, were beaten back by dark-hearted clouds. Black water swelled and eased gently beneath the longboat. Yosel sat near the bow as oars dipped and pulled in unison, offering up the soft gurgle of water rushing by. There was no other noise; the Governor's men had been instructed to remain silent.

Six soldiers rowed. Four other passengers sat near the stern: General Serezo, leader of Cartageña's military forces; Capitán Rivera, former second-in-command to Viceroy Valdez and the man charged with identifying him; Señor Ortega, whom Yosel had until recently known only as the Phantom; and Ayudante Vegas, Ortega's secret go-between with King Philip. Eleven men in total, but only the Jew knew all of what was expected to transpire this night.

Yosel wore a black coat and hat. His white bandana was tucked carefully inside the hat, hidden from view. A small dagger was sheathed and tucked into his trousers at the small of his back, though he had no desire nor intention to use it. He watched as Cartageña's lights blinked and disappeared as the boat passed a jut of land well beyond the harbor.

All of the planning he, De Graaf and the Phantom had done was about to unfold into a series of actions with admittedly uncertain consequences. Yet there was one measure of which even De Graaf was completely unaware—Yosel's plan for Captain Connachan to ambush the pyrate once he and his men rowed ashore with the King's doubloons. Yosel's sharp fear at being in the middle of this treacherous exchange was dulled by the knowledge that he'd separately alerted both

De Graaf and Connachan concerning his safety. He would be easily identified by his currently obscured white clothing and bandana.

He dearly hoped everything would go as planned. If so, he would soon be a free man, with the money needed to begin a new life in Cartageña. His indebtedness to Connachan for having saved his life would be dissolved. And he owed nothing to De Graaf. The pyrate might not survive the night anyway. That would be best, he thought, since he worried about having turned coat on the man by having arranged for Connachan to ambush him.

The quiet and calming sound of the water relaxed him. He prayed silently to a God he had no prior relationship with, asking for safety in his pursuit of the freedom to make his own choices in life—to define who he truly was, unencumbered by the demands of others. All of that possibility was perhaps only an hour or two away. He could virtually taste its sweetness.

With Cartageña now out of sight, Yosel turned to look at the sea beyond the boat's bow—nothing but black water with diminishing flecks of white reflecting off the water from the jeweled city's dwindling lights. It was a perfect night to mark the changing of his world…for all time.

———

Drifting silently, covered by a cloak of black canvas, the longboat containing De Graaf and seven others moved only with the water's flow, balanced by oars to maintain its direction. It was in a flanking position, sufficiently beyond the point where the two other boats would meet: De Graaf's approach-boat, on which Stevens served as the Viceroy's imposter; and the Governor's boat, carrying Yosel, the

Phantom, and the King's doubloons. De Graaf peered through one of the breathing holes in the canvas that had begun laying just a touch heavier with the onset of a drizzled rain. In the distance, he caught a lantern being lit in the Governor's boat as it neared Stevens' approach-boat well outside view of Cartageña's harbor.

De Graaf smiled inwardly at the thought that the Phantom was onboard the Governor's boat. It presented the opportunity to eliminate the Cartageñian. He was convinced the man intended to have him killed later on, to cover the tracks of his own involvement in the ransom scheme. By doing away with the Phantom, he could avoid that potential outcome…and having to share the ransom doubloons with him. Things couldn't have worked out any better if he himself had planned the Governor's strategy for the exchange.

He reached for and grasped his pistol, just as comfort. He liked the smooth feel of the grip's rounded, wooden heel at the base of his palm. The instrument would soon separate the Phantom from the doubloons he so deeply cherished, assuming the man didn't drown first.

De Graaf's pyrates hunched silently, uncomfortably, beneath the increasingly suffocating canvas. Their gently swaying boat was constructed of a hardwood that hurt to sit on for any length of time. That never seemed a problem when their attention was distracted by their rowing. But having sat in a crouching position for almost an hour, dripping sweat in the stifling heat and humidity created by the cloaking canvas, there was nothing else to focus on but their own discomfort. Still, the prize they anticipated was more than sufficient consolation. From time to time, each of them would glance De Graaf's way, hoping he might soon give the order. They were well-armed and anxious for the chance to wreak havoc on the Governor's men.

———

Seventeen men, and one woman, began settling into their hiding positions just beyond the tree line, a good twenty-five yards removed from the waterline where De Graaf's boats would later grind ashore, according to Yosel's map. Their own boats were already pulled up and hidden among the trees. Dark clothing and faces blackened by dubbin provided all the camouflage they should need to avoid detection as De Graaf's pyrates arrived.

Garret, William, Musa, Caber and the rest now readied their weapons. Each bore a cutlass, pistol, crossbow, quiver of arrows, and at least one dagger. The only exception was Musa. He'd chosen his executioner's axe over a cutlass, anxious to add more notches along its handle.

Not wanting their voices to carry, either across the water or inland, Garret ordered that only whispers or hand signals be used to communicate. They could ill afford to draw the attention of any of De Graaf's men who might have stayed behind at their encampment.

Garret strolled over to where Musa was fastidiously sharpening his axe. "Musa," she whispered.

"Aye Cap'n."

"You can now proceed along the pathway. No more than fifty paces. If one of De Graaf's men approaches from behind, you have my permission to add a notch to your axe." Musa smiled. "But if there is more than one, signal us with your bird call."

"Please Cap'n, let me judge whether I might handle them on my own." It was Garret's turn to smile. She had no lack of confidence in her fiercest warrior.

Garret and William had gone over their order of battle several times since receiving Yosel's message, refining it where they saw potential flaws or opportunities. The men were to wait patiently until De Graaf and his pyrates landed and were heading up the beach. Hopefully, their two boats would arrive together. The pyrates would then be closely gathered, making themselves high-percentage targets.

Garret organized three five-man units, each separated by five to ten yards. She, William and Caber were positioned in the middle of their unit—center, left and right, respectively. Once De Graaf's pyrates disembarked, they would each assign specific targets to the others in their unit. Garret's unit would take the targets in the center, William's those on the left, and Caber's the right.

The two men furthest from the center of a unit would wait to fire their crossbows until after the first volley, in an effort to minimize any lull in fire. All of them had been instructed to avoid aiming at any man dressed entirely in white, in deference to Yosel's desire for safety.

Garret had also made it clear that regardless of where De Graaf was positioned, he was to be hers alone. But she would not take his life with a crossbow. She sought a more personalized encounter, to avenge his brutal assault on Jorge Valdez.

She was well aware this was her second time carrying out a personal vendetta. Her first was the decimation of Santiago del Príncipe, in retribution for the slaughter of her crewmates who'd joined her in an innocent search for water. She thought about one other matter that still demanded she exact revenge—the assassination of her first lover, Ambassador Pantas, by the Spanish spy, de Cuero. His day too would come, she thought.

Garret returned her thoughts to the plan at hand. The first wave would be the crossbows. Four rounds, in rapid sequence. Given the short distance, they should be both accurate and lethal. Garret and her men would then charge the beach, with the aim of finishing off anyone still breathing.

Her master gunner had already spread a line of gunpowder in the jungle behind them, in an arc some forty yards in length, with the path to De Graaf's encampment at its center. If the sound of battle were to bring reinforcements from the encampment, the gunner would set fire to the powder. The flames would force them off the path and into thick vegetation, which they'd have to hack their way through in order to circumvent the fire. That would buy Garret and her men more time to secure the doubloons, scuttle the pyrates' longboats and depart.

Despite all her planning, Garret's mind was still consumed by doubt, wondering whether she had missed anything. As comfortable as she was with her strategy and tactics, she recognized that no plan was foolproof. She and her men would need to adapt to any unanticipated actions. Her only offset to unexpected events going unnoticed was a man named Woodman, whose sole task was to be her observer. The man was known for his keen sense of observation and awareness. Though not actually attached to Garret's unit, he was stationed behind her with the responsibility to immediately draw her attention to anything unfolding unexpectedly.

They waited quietly. Patiently. Garret's thoughts turned to William. This would be their first action together without a letter of marque from the Queen—in other words, as full-blown pyrates. She shook her head lightly at how far the two of them had come since their days as midshipmen. No longer operating under the orders of others, their future now lay in their own hands. In that respect, they were no different than wolves, who roamed freely and took what they needed to survive whenever opportunities presented themselves.

She felt a sudden need to establish some principles—a code by which they and their men would agree to be governed. After all, even wolves had a code by which the pack would live and operate. The first item that came to mind, one she and William had already agreed to, was that they would never attack an English vessel—merchant or military; unless it attacked first, of course. She knew there were other items to consider, including the sharing of prizes. She would give it all more thought once their work here was done.

———

Seated at the stern of the approach-boat, First Mate Stevens' right leg bounced up and down rapidly. His adrenaline pulsated within. He relished this role—posing as Viceroy Valdez and leading the assault. His five-man crew rowed normally toward the lantern-lit boat they'd spotted, confident it was the Governor's. Each crewman had been selected because he was a capable swimmer, a surprisingly uncommon skill among pyrates.

A thin trail of gunpowder ran down the middle of the boat. Four unconnected lines stretched out to the sides. There was just enough powder to establish a quick flame yet not enough to cause an explosion that might blow the boat to shreds. The initial flames would burst straight up in a near-triangle, given the boat's curvature. A medium fuse and the disconnected lines would allow the crew sufficient time to evacuate and push their boat forward before it was completely engulfed. In no time, roaring flames would be racing toward the Governor's men, causing the desired chaos.

Timing was critical. They needed to be close enough to the Governor's boat for their ploy to have full effect—forcing the Governor's men to scramble, and hopefully abandon their own boat.

There was no actual intent to set the Governor's boat aflame; that would only complicate the capture of the doubloons. For that reason, two thick trailing ropes were attached to the rear oarlocks on either side, enabling Stevens' men in the water to hold back their flaming boat from contacting the Governor's.

All of Stevens' men wore white headbands to distinguish themselves from any of the Governor's men who might also end up in the dark water. Hopefully, that would keep them safe from the pistol shots De Graaf's crew would fire from their currently hidden boat. Stevens' own white bandana was hidden beneath the black hood concealing his true identity. A white rope was tied loosely around the hood, at his neck. That and his double-breasted, brass-buttoned coat were intended to make the Governor's men believe he was indeed Viceroy Valdez.

"Signal the boat," ordered Stevens. His man at the bow lit the lantern, opening and closing its darkened front-piece three times, sending out bursts of light. The response from the Governor's boat came swiftly, as three distinct flashes.

"Ready the approach," whispered Stevens. "Bow-first to their broadside." From that direction, all of the Governor's men would clearly see the flames coming straight at them. It would take only one jumping overboard to drive most, if not all of them, to follow suit. Stevens wondered whether any could even swim. If they couldn't, it would make his job that much easier.

All of it would now unfold in mere minutes. Stevens' heart raced faster than his leg bounced.

XXXII

"Stevens has exchanged lights," De Graaf whispered to his men under their cloaked boat. "Row hardy. With stealth." He planned to guide them into position behind the stern of the Governor's longboat, confident the attention of Governor Acuña's men would now be entirely focused on Master's Mate Stevens' approach-boat. There was no room for error; stealth was essential to success. He would slink as close as possible but minimize the risk of being discovered. As soon as Stevens set the approach-boat aflame, his own men would row full-on toward the Governor's boat, using their pistols to exterminate everyone on board…excluding Yosel.

General Serezo watched the pyrate boat delivering the Viceroy closing in. "Cease rowing," he ordered, adding in a lower voice, "Pistols at the ready. Fire on my order."

Governor Acuña's words scrolled through his mind—'*take no risk whatsoever with the life of the Viceroy*'. Serezo shook his head. '*The Governor be damned*,' he thought. '*Risk is the very nature of military exercises. Actions are dictated by events unfolding on the battlefield, not by the wishes of some politician far removed from any peril.*' Facing only a handful of pyrates, he would open fire the moment he judged his men could easily dispense with them.

He noted a man at the stern wearing a hood over his head. A white rope hung 'round his neck. His hands were behind his back. '*That must be the Viceroy*,' he thought. He whispered to his men, "Do not shoot the man at the stern. Do you understand?" Several whispered back in acknowledgement. Judging the risk to the Viceroy was tolerable, he would shortly order his men to fire. He thanked God there were so few pyrates. '*How foolish they are,*' he thought. '*But then, pyrates aren't known for their intellect—with the exception of El Draque, perhaps.*'

Serezo watched in surprise and frustration as the pyrate boat altered its bearing, bringing its bow head-on to his broadside—an impossible angle for his men to hit all their targets. And it was now coming fast.

Beneath the hood denoting himself as the Viceroy, beads of anxiety-sweat covered Master's Mate Stevens' forehead. He judged his boat was almost close enough to set it aflame. "Three more strokes, mates. Full and hard. Then jump," he ordered.

The mate charged with lighting the short fuse placed one end near the lantern just as unexpected shots echoed from the Governor's boat. The two men nearest the bow were hit hard. Another, lightly grazed, immediately rose and jumped overboard.

"Damnation!" blurted the lantern bearer, finding himself fully exposed. Fumbling to insert the fuse into the lantern, a pistol ball hit and traveled through his cheek, shattering teeth. A spurt of blood followed it out the other side. The lantern fell, breaking its glass and setting the gunpowder ablaze. The powerful explosion blew the remaining crew overboard. Flames leaped in every direction.

Propelled over the stern, Stevens' flaming imposter's coat was doused by smothering water. The weight of it pulled him downward. Struggling to stay his descent, he freed himself from the deadly cloak, yanked off his hood, and discarded the rope encircling his neck. He kicked and flailed upward, gasping for air as he breached the surface.

"Maldición!" swore General Serezo, watching the blast send the hooded man overboard. Not knowing whether the Viceroy could even swim, he dropped his pistol and dove into the water, intent on rescuing him.

The flaming pyrate boat was now only two yards from the Governor's. A soldier stretched out his oar, hoping to stop or redirect it but the oncoming flames were bending his way, fanned by the breeze. Señor Ortega watched in frozen fear as two soldiers exited the boat to escape the flames. Ayudante Vegas ducked.

Yosel jumped overboard, shedding his coat and hat. He pulled tightly on his white bandana—the flag intended to preserve his existence. He grabbed onto the far side of the Governor's boat.

"Harder, you bilge rats. Harder," De Graaf screamed. His men had thrown off their canvas cloak at the first sound of pistol shots and were now rowing furiously toward the stern of the Governor's boat. "Hard to port," De Graaf yelled, seeking to gain a broadside position for a better firing angle. "Fire at will!" he roared as the boat turned.

Ten pistol shots echoed across the water. Only two hit the Governor's men. The sound and fury of the shots, and the now-breaching flames, created all the chaos De Graaf needed.

Unable to swim, Ortega and Ayudante Vegas pressed themselves hard against the longboat's bottom as breeze-bent flames streamed over the stern. Another soldier jumped overboard. Capitán Rivera and the remaining two soldiers fired back at dark targets.

A second round of shots peppered the Governor's boat and the surrounding water. Rivera, stunned by the unexpected appearance of a second pyrate boat, heard De Graaf directing some of his men to resume rowing; others to reload. "Malditos bastardos!" Rivera shouted at General Serezo's men who'd abandoned the Governor's boat. Flames licked hard at the sides and flowed across the top. Nothing inside told him it was better to stand and fight than retreat. "Man the oars. Row back, hard," he screamed at the two remaining soldiers. He glanced at General Serezo, now swimming beyond the rear of the flaming pyrate boat in an apparent attempt to save the Viceroy. He hoped to retrieve both of them later…if he himself were to survive this onslaught.

A soldier in the Governor's boat whacked his oar at Yosel, causing him to lose his grip. The boat began cruising away. Yosel's worst fear washed over him with the waves—he was alone in open water, incapable of reaching the distant shore.

De Graaf and his men were still several lengths from the Governor's boat when he heard Yosel's distressed call for help. He spotted the Jew's bobbing white bandana about twenty yards away. '*The gold or the Jew?*' he asked himself. It wasn't a choice, really—pyrates were treasure hunters, not life-savers. He looked away, ordering his men to pursue the gold doubloons. If Yosel were still alive once the gold was secured, he would return for him.

Head up, Yosel flailed toward De Graaf's boat, hoping to remain afloat long enough to reach it. His heart stopped as he saw it turn to intercept the Governor's rapidly retreating longboat.

Treading water, General Serezo searched for the hooded Viceroy with the white rope at his neck. But all he could make out in the dark were a few heads with white bandanas. Had the Viceroy drowned? He feared the worst.

Looking back, he watched the Governor's longboat in retreat. It was under a barrage of pistol fire emanating from a second pyrate boat whose men seemed to draw their form from the blackness of the night. Rivera and the others would be lucky to survive, he thought.

The screams of drowning men virtually smothered the pop of pistol shots. '*Damn them all*,' thought Serezo, recognizing he was now at the mercy of the sea. He made one last scan for the Viceroy. Still nothing. Taking a long, full breath and arcing forward, he pushed his head below the surface. His hands reached down for his boots, to free them from his feet. His body descended rapidly into the black depths. One boot, finally off, flooded with water, joining him in a race to the bottom. With the water's surface stretching away and his lungs threatening to burst, he finally managed to free his foot from the second boot. He waved his arms from up to down and kicked furiously, driving himself ever upward. His lungs forced open his mouth in desperation before his head cleared the surface. Finally breaching it, he choked and spewed salt water, gasping and gulping precious air.

Breathing deeply and treading water, General Serezo surveyed the scene. The pyrate boat engulfed in flame was losing a winless battle. Pistol shots from the second pyrate boat impeded Capitán Rivera's retreat. It seemed almost certain the Capitán would soon be overtaken. '*God save him*,' thought Serezo, though he doubted that was possible. '*More likely those specially minted gold doubloons will soon taste the filth of pyrates' hands; maybe even Rivera's blood.*'

Scanning one last time for the Viceroy, Serezo could see no sign the man was alive. He considered his options. Only one made any sense. He shed the rest of his clothing, put his head into the water, and began swimming toward the nearest point of land, angling his direction to account for the current. He prayed the Governor wouldn't hang him for losing both the gold and the Viceroy.

———

Garret heard far-off pistol shots echo across the sea. She glimpsed a glowing light, followed abruptly by a powerful bang. Perhaps De Graaf's exchange wasn't going as planned. She found herself hoping that, whatever had just transpired, the bloody pyrate would seize the gold. Otherwise, what was her purpose here?

She found it odd to be thinking this way—hoping her archenemy, and brutal attacker of her lover, would be successful in capturing the King's doubloons. How many more difficult, complex situations would she find herself facing, she wondered, now that she, too, was effectively embracing life as a pyrate.

William lay his crossbow on the ground, left his place, and walked over to Garret. He knelt beside her, speaking softly, "The bell has tolled. Let us hope De Graaf returns with gold in hand."

Garret nodded. "I find myself strangely hoping for his success."

"If he does succeed, it shall be for the last time."

"Let us not count our own success before all the sand has fallen."

"Just so," William acknowledged.

Garret sensed there was something more on his mind. "What is it, William? You seem hesitant to ask."

"I have been pondering the distribution of the gold. Since some of our crew is not here, is it fair that they receive the same share as those who are? Should we not give a greater share to those placing their lives in danger?"

Garret hadn't considered anything but equal shares. After all, her crewmembers, and Drake's before her, had always received the same portion. Still, she saw William's point. If these men with her didn't receive a better share, would they then choose to remain behind on the next assault, preferring all the reward with none of the risk? That was not a workable model going forward. "Fair point," she replied. "Perhaps a double share for each of these men."

"Let it be so, then. Shall I pass the word?"

Garret chuckled, "We are already dividing plunder we don't yet possess."

"It shall soon be ours. I have no doubt. We have planned well."

"Plans often unravel as events unfold, William."

———

"The white! The white!" Capitán Rivera yelled frantically as the incoming pistol fire momentarily ceased. One of the two soldiers onboard the beleaguered Governor's boat grabbed the white cloth and waved it vigorously.

"Those in the water," De Graaf pointed and shouted. His crew finished reloading and redirected their shots at a few men who'd earlier evacuated the Governor's vessel. Pistol shots whizzed through the water, some finding their mark. The shooting ended quickly.

'*Finally*,' thought De Graaf, '*The doubloons are mine*.' "Pistols at the ready," he ordered.

Within moments, De Graaf and his pyrates drew alongside the Governor's boat and grabbed hold, pulling it close. Senor Ortega sensed the irony in the gentle lapping of the water between the boats; it belied the sharp tension of the moment. He could see the shivering uncertainty in the eyes of Capitán Rivera, Ayudante Vegas, and the two remaining soldiers. But he himself feared nothing. After all, De Graaf was his partner in this ruse.

Though appalled by their treachery in ambushing him with a second boat, Capitán Rivera had no desire to antagonize the pyrates. "Por favor," he said to De Graaf, "take the chests." He pointed to them. The two soldiers quickly latched onto the handles and passed one chest across to De Graaf's boat. The vessels rocked heavily as the weight transferred. The pyrates opened the chest. Rivera watched as De Graaf withdrew one of the neatly stacked doubloons and held it high for his men to see, displaying the side with the Crusader's Cross. "God is finally with us, my friends," he laughed. His men cheered raucously.

When the pyrates' celebration finally quieted, Rivera spoke again, "What of the Viceroy?"

De Graaf looked his way, saying nothing. He raised his pistol, aiming it at Rivera's chest. The color drained from Rivera's face. De Graaf quickly redirected his weapon…and then fired it. The ball entered Señor Ortega's forehead. His eyes wide with shock, Ortega's body fell back against the side of the boat. It was the last thing Capitán Rivera saw, as another pyrate's bullet struck his temple.

"Discard the bodies," De Graaf ordered, once all the Governor's men were down. "Our mates in the water need the space."

Bleeding profusely but barely conscious as the pyrates shoved his body overboard, Ayudante Vegas felt the dimming of the spark within. His dying thought was of the pieces of eight buried in the woods behind his home, no longer of any value to him.

Their work done, the pyrates redirected their own boat, and the Governor's, to retrieve their fellow brigands.

Yosel had earlier spotted the floating carnage that was once the pyrates' approach-boat. Flailing away, he inexplicably managed to reach it. Small, non-threatening flames still emanated from its stern. He grabbed desperately onto its side. Though it sank a little under his weight, it didn't fully give way. '*I am saved,*' he thought, '*…a second time. Perhaps there is a God after all.*' Seeing De Graaf and his men begin to search for survivors, he screamed out to them.

General Serezo was a capable swimmer. He'd already put a good distance between himself and the three vessels. Once the shooting ended, he stopped to tread water and look back. The pyrates appeared to be searching for men in the water. Behind them, he noticed the dwindling flames of the boat that once carried the Viceroy. '*Damn them all to Hell,*' he thought. He turned and resumed swimming. His muscles were strained but his mind was unrestricted, filling with comforting thoughts of revenge.

———

The distant pistol shots were their signal. De Graaf's men who'd stayed behind at their encampment, gathered their weapons and headed along the path toward the landing site. They were to meet De Graaf's returning boats as reinforcements, in the event their fellow pyrates were being pursued by soldiers. Their jovial voices carried far ahead of them, making it obvious to Garret and her men that they were approaching. "Damnation," She whispered to herself. She hadn't anticipated having a group show up before the real action even started.

It was impossible to determine just how many were coming. But it was definitely more than a few, of that she was certain. She motioned her men to join her in heading down the path, hoping there would be enough time to deal with those approaching before De Graaf arrived. It needed to be done quickly…and silently.

Musa was already in position, much further up the path. Hearing the pyrates approaching in numbers, he signaled for support with his bird call. He intended to attack from the rear, so he concealed himself behind a thick tree and waited.

The pyrates came roughly two aside—each with a cutlass, and all bearing at least one pistol in their bandoliers, as far as he could tell. Four pyrates walked by but he couldn't be certain that was all of them. His breathing was slow and measured as they passed, oblivious to his presence. Two were talking. Two carried and sipped from tankards. Running his thumb along the blade of his trusted executioner's axe, he smiled. It had never been sharper…on either side of its head. He gripped the handle lovingly with two oversized hands.

Two more pyrates passed. Musa glanced back, to see whether more were coming. He spotted none. Once the last two were several yards beyond him, he stepped silently onto the path, crouching low and closing the gap with a rapid series of steps. The whoosh of his axe was undoubtedly the last thing heard by the trailing pyrate on the right, his head having cleanly fled the rest of his body. The axe came to an abrupt halt in the shoulder of the pyrate next to his now-headless mate. He screamed in agony, stumbling and falling to the ground. The four pyrates in front turned, spilling tankards and grasping cutlasses. Musa swung again at the two men closest to him, knocking the cutlass from one's hand. The other backed out of the way but now pointed his blade forward. It quivered, no doubt shaken by Musa's intimidating size and painted face. The big man brought his axe swiftly back into position, readying his next deadly sweep. Arrows suddenly whizzed past him while others hit their intended marks, studding the two pyrates at the front and forcing them to their knees.

The pyrate who'd lost his sword at the swing of Musa's axe quickly drew a pistol from his bandolier and scrambled to set it. He managed to fire off a shot but the arrow that suddenly entered his lower back forced the pistol slightly upward. The ball hit Musa in his upper left shoulder, wrenching it backward. With the axe still in his right hand, Musa gathered himself for another swing. But there was suddenly no need. One of Garret's men reached the shooter from behind and slashed a dagger across his throat.

Musa turned back to the wounded pyrate writhing in misery on the ground. He crushed his boot-heel hard onto the man's head, cracking his skull. The misery ended.

Several more of Garret's men appeared. One bladed an already downed man, expediting his voyage to Hell.

William approached Garret, still scanning the bodies. "Most

unfortunate," he said, shaking his head. "We should have scouted the encampment."

"Agreed," replied Garret, "although there was risk in that." She looked back toward shore. "We have to assume De Graaf heard the pistol shot. He will be on alert. He may even elect not to land here. All we can do at this point is resume our positions and hope for the best."

"It now seems foolish that we left our pistols behind. We could certainly use them."

"I suppose. We should grab the pistols these pyrates carried. Perhaps there are more weapons at their camp. Send four of the men to search."

"Aye, sir."

Garret suddenly felt William's words seemed odd—calling her 'sir'. Though proper when they were privateers, and she was his commander, they were now pyrates. Partners really. She had no true standing that warranted his use of the word 'sir'. That would have to change, she thought.

William sent four men back to the pyrates' camp, to gather anything of use. Garret and the rest returned to their positions at the landing site. '*If De Graaf still choses to land here,*' she thought, '*it will no longer be an ambush.*'

———

"There can be no doubt," insisted Master's Mate Stevens, still wiping the water from his face after being pulled into De Graaf's boat. "It came from the direction of our camp." The pyrates were debating the origin of the pistol shot they'd heard. Though listening intently for more, there was only the one. "Perhaps the Governor's men have stumbled across it," Stevens concluded.

"Unlikely," replied De Graaf. "Just one shot. More likely a drunken mate targeting a squirrel." The men in both boats continued listening for more shots. None followed.

De Graaf looked in the general direction of the landing site where his men onshore were to light a fire, to guide them in. There was no flame yet. No problem, he thought, he would head that way and take his chances. Once they neared the beach, he would keep a keen eye on it, just in case something was afoot. "Maintain course," he ordered.

Garret and her men looked on quietly as De Graaf's two boats approached. She breathed in deeply and exhaled slowly, trying to ease the tension within. But it refused to be tempered, rising instead with each wave delivering her archenemy to the edge of battle.

She scanned both vessels in search of Yosel, who was supposedly dressed entirely in white. But from her viewpoint and distance, there were too many men crammed together, all wearing white bandanas. There was no guarantee Yosel was even among them.

Her eyes were soon drawn to the unmistakable hulk at the stern of the nearest boat—DeGraaf. He appeared to be scanning the shoreline. Garret lowered her head slowly. "Down and tight," she ordered her men. "They are watching."

While lying prone at the edge of the trees, it struck Garret that De Graaf would be expecting the men from his camp to meet him on the beach. If none were present, it might generate suspicion. She instructed the four men closest to her, "Walk onto the beach, take seated positions, and refrain from presenting your blackened faces to open water." She didn't want De Graaf sensing they weren't his crewmates; nothing should seem unordinary.

Her men strolled onto the beach, heads down, concealing their crossbows and arrows. They sat and conversed, as they imagined De Graaf's men would have, and did their best to keep their faces concealed.

Now a mere forty yards from shore, De Graaf was more suspicious than ever. The men onshore hadn't set a fire to guide him. Nor were they standing to greet him. And there were only four of them, all seated and showing no interest. "Damnation. Ready your weapons," he instructed, his voice low enough to avoid skimming ashore."

Despite growing evidence of an ambush, De Graaf still held hope that he was wrong. An added worry was that his crew had virtually exhausted their powder in suppressing and finishing off the Governor's men. It would be primarily swords and daggers against whatever weapons these vultures on the beach possessed.

His boat slowed, its oars falling silent as the pyrates gathered their weapons. De Graaf carefully scanned the woods for signs of any men who were not on the beach itself.

"I see only the four men," whispered Stevens.

"It does not mean others are not there," he whispered back.

The men on the sand finally rose but refused to face the oncoming boats. De Graaf was now certain treachery was afoot. "Hard to starboard," he yelled. The scraping of wood and splashing of water accompanied the crew's scramble. The two boats began turning but the ever-increasing thrust of the waves propelled them incessantly toward shore.

Garret recognized the need to act immediately, despite it being impossible to assign specific targets. '*If Yosel is among these pyrates, then God be with him*', she thought. '*And with us.*'

"Fire!" she yelled.

Crossbows streamed six menacing arrows at the pyrates, followed by a second wave and then a third, as Garret's dug-in men alternated shooting and reloading. Those already on the beach retrieved the crossbows at their feet and participated in the hunt. The arrows' effectiveness was enhanced by De Graaf's boats having angled almost broadside in their abortive effort to change course. Impaled pyrates screamed in agony. Others dove into the water, to avoid being targeted. A few fired back with errant pistol shots. All had abandoned their oars. Both boats, pushed by surging water, were now within twenty yards of shore.

One final wave of arrows showered the pyrates before Garret and her men rushed the shoreline. They splashed into calf-deep water, a few carrying loaded crossbows. Musa hurled his lengthy axe into the side of De Graaf's boat, opening a gaping hole. Water gushed in. The remaining pyrates jumped out, some firing reloaded pistols and hitting two good targets. Crossbows drove arrows in the opposite direction, now with greater effectiveness. Clashing cutlasses unleashed spewing blood from glancing blows. The churning water all around grew red, though the darkness swallowed the color.

De Graaf's crew, outnumbered and losing, began throwing aside their weapons, raising hands in surrender…even Stevens. De Graaf was having none of it. "Fight, you bastards," he yelled. His men weren't inclined to follow the order; they preferred living over dying.

Standing in shin-high water, De Graaf watched as Garret

headed his way, her eyes locked on his. He hadn't expected this but he welcomed the moment. *'Revenge for Harker's death will soon be mine,'* he thought.

The fighting all around ceased. There were no voices, only the outburst of waves attacking the shore. Two gladiators stood motionless in the water, facing each other, one a hulking, menacing figure, the other diminutive by comparison. Though most regarded Garret as one of the finest swordsmen they knew, De Graaf was easily twice her size in weight. No one could envision her defeating him, especially with the water hindering her principal advantages—speed and movement. But De Graaf himself was in water that at times covered his knees.

Swaying in the midst of a wave, De Graaf scanned the assembly of men, thinking they would now witness his might and mastery of the Witch…and tell the tale for years to come.

"You cannot win this day," Garret called out to him over the crash of waves. "It shall end badly for you no matter what." She paused, cutlass at the ready. "Present your sword and suffer your fate." Two of her men aimed their crossbows at him.

De Graaf stared at Connachan. Her willingness to die for a cause was unfathomable, though begrudgingly admirable. He sensed her strength wasn't drawn from within but rather from her men's resolve. Not one of them had surrendered. They seemed inspired by her willingness to sacrifice all. If he were to end her, surely they would end him.

Soaking wet, with blood dripping down his face and arms, De Graaf weighed his potential loss of life and treasure against the slaying of the Witch. Outnumbered and virtually abandoned by his men, he recognized the futility. This was not to be his night. He decided to bargain, knowing full well Connachan wasn't yet fully, truly, a pyrate. He could draw on whatever good still resided within her—whatever sense of honor remained. "This treasure is mine," he shouted, "Planned and earned. What manner of man, or woman, would steal it from me?" He glared at Garret, daring her to prove her integrity.

William Tovery looked on, knowing precisely what De Graaf sought to accomplish with his words. *'How will Garret respond,'* he wondered, *'As the high-integrity privateer she'd always been, or as the newly minted pyrate who'd finally crossed over that fine line?'* He watched as Garret stood firm, legs apart and cutlass ready. Though wet, bleeding, and undersized, she was nonetheless ready to take on the intimidating pyrate in a fight to the death. It occurred to William just how much he admired her strength of character in this moment—and in many moments before, for that matter. *'God be with her,'* he thought.

"Your treasure is ill-gotten," Garret yelled over the sound of surging waves. "Your men have paid for it with their lives, as have mine." She pointed her cutlass at a dead body now floating in the water nearby. "We shall be relieving you of its heavy burden." One of Garret's men laughed at her response. A couple snickered.

De Graaf said nothing. Garret met and locked onto his eyes, her face serious and unyielding. "I say again, present your cutlass." As she uttered the words, she realized she was pitting her own life against the possibility of slaying the dragon whose actions had led to the death of her lover, Jorge. Yet De Graaf's hesitation suggested he might actually choose to surrender. If he did, she knew she would have to honor that. Though she longed to taste his blood, doing so after he surrendered might cause her to lose the respect of the witnesses to the confrontation. She was suddenly confused about her desired progression of events.

The King of pyrates forced her hand, tossing his weapon into the water, harshly. "Let us find another day to settle our grievances."

Convinced the action had finally concluded, Yosel raised his head above the side of the second boat, in which he'd remained hidden. He knelt and raised his arms in surrender. Garret's men headed toward the drifting vessel. They grabbed the rope hanging over the side and began pulling it toward the mass of bloodied bodies now chasing each other onto the beach.

———

They remained standing in her stateroom. "You cannot be serious," said Elizabeth.

"I am afraid so, Your Majesty," Lieutenant Ward responded. He was reporting on the incident in which Captain James Wenman was slain in battle. "It was most definitely Captain Connachan's ship."

"*Pandora?*"

"The very same, yes."

The Queen finally sat, shaking her head in saddened disbelief. The young woman who'd been so loyal to Admiral Drake, the one she admired and even used as her own personal agent, had somehow turned to the dark side—a damn pyrate!

Ward added his final thoughts, "The only thing absent was a crimson flag."

—————

Alone in her cabin, Garret gazed out the stern windows, wondering what exactly she would write. And where to start. She turned and walked to her desk. Taking her seat, she withdrew the quill from the ink and placed her left hand near the top of the parchment. She began writing,

> *Isla Tortuga*
> *29 June 1599*
>
> *My Dearest Thomas,*
> *I am afraid I am no longer the woman you may remember so fondly*

END

NOTES

A few of the characters in Pyrate Assassin are people who actually
lived in the period of interest:

- 'Drake' aka 'Admiral Drake' aka 'the Admiral', are references
  to the legendary Sir Francis Drake. None of the words/quotes
  attributed to him herein were things he actually ever said, as far
  as I know. I simply made them up.

- Thomas Drake was a real brother of the Admiral, though all of
  the events he's involved in here are fictitious.

- Queen Elizabeth, of course, is Queen Elizabeth I. Again, all of
  the events she's involved in here are fictitious, as are the words
  attributed to her.

- King Philip, of course, is King Philip II of Spain. Here again,
  only fictitious events and words.

- Governor Pedro de Acuña y De los Monteros, was the
  Governor of Cartageña from 1593-1601. Again, the words and
  events attributed to him are all fictitious.

Every other character in the book is purely fictitious.

The Inagua Islands and Isla Tortuga are real islands in the Caribbean.

Santiago del Príncipe was a real village at the time. Santo Pedro is
purely fictitious.

CHARACTERS

<u>Principal Characters</u>

Garret Connachan: Captain of the flagship *Pandora*

William Tovery: Captain of *Orion*

De Graaf, Yaugaan: Captain of the ship *Cutthroat* and partner of Harker

Ortega: Felipe de Heredia y Ortega aka 'The Phantom' aka Fantasma aka The Shadow; a wealthy Cartageñian

Scrapper / Scorpio / Kat: London street urchin rescued by Garret

Yosel: *A member of De Graaf's crew and willing spy for Garret following her having rescued him from drowning.*

<u>Secondary Characters</u>

King Philip II: King of Spain

Queen Elizabeth I: Queen of England

Abeo: Ortega's Black Master-of-Staff

Acuña: Pedro de Acuña y De los Monteros, Actual Governor of Cartageña (1593-1601) – but fictitious events

Ayudante Vegas, Pedro: Ayudante de Campo (Aide-de-Camp) to a Spanish General/senior military advisor to King Philip II; chosen by Ortega as his go-between with the King

Blair, Henry: Garret's Master's Mate

Caber: Member of Garret's crew

Catherine/Cath:	Server at the Gente de Mar and niece of its owner, Prince
Drake/'El Draque':	Admiral; Garret's former captain/mentor (*deceased*)
Jorge Valdez de Barragan:	aka: **the Viceroy**. Maestre de Campo and Spanish Viceroy for Military Affairs in the Southern Seas, based in the Inaguas (*deceased*)
Le Pen, Alain:	French pyrate captain
Musa:	Member of Garret's crew; a giant
Prince:	Owner of the Gente de Mar tavern on Isla Tortuga
Rivera:	Don Francisco Rivera de Mendoza, Viceroy Valdez' First Lieutenant
Serezo, Gonzalo:	General in charge of all military affairs in Cartageña
Stevens:	Harker's Master's Mate
Thomas:	Drake's brother; Garret's and William's former fellow midshipman
Wenman, James:	Captain of the warship *Mercilus*, sent to Isla Tortuga to deliver Thomas' message to Garret

<u>**Incidental Characters**</u>

Attila:	A pyrate captain of Dutch descent, based on Isla Tortuga

Babu / Babatundé: A friend of Abeo and slave, assigned to the construction of the Governor's residence in Cartageña

Beauclere: A pyrate captain of French descent, based on Isla Tortuga

Bora: A pyrate/former slave who accompanies Yosel to Cartageña

De Cuero, Rodrigo: King Philip's spy and assassin. Assassinated Ambassador Pantas.

Dodd: A tavern-goer in Santo Pedro

Drago, Luis: Captain of a Portuguese merchant ship captured by William Tovery and befriended by him.

Fernando: A Spanish guard/soldier with whom Abeo shares the secret of the ransom scheme

Harker: The former King of Pirates; De Graaf's former Captain and Partner (*deceased*)

Jimenez: Captain, Santo de Cristo

La Roja, Juan: Captain of the *Visser*, attacked by De Graaf

Manuel: A Christian seaman captured by De Graaf on his first assault as a pyrate captain

Pantas: Indonesian Ambassador; Garret's first lover (deceased/assassinated)

Poole: Helmsman on Captain James Wenman's ship, Mercilus

Prouten, Charles: Drake's one-time Master's Mate and occasional mentor to Garret

<u>**Incidental Characters**</u> (continued)

Snadden: Assistant to Dr. Stafford on the *Mercilus*

Stafford: Doctor on Captain James Wenman's ship, *Mercilus*

Vegas: Ayudante de Campo (Aide-de-Camp) to a Spanish General/senior military advisor to King Philip II; chosen by Ortega as his go-between with the King

Wakefield: William Tovery's Master's Mate

Ward, Lieutenant: Captain James Wenman's Master's Mate

Watts: A tavern-goer in Santo Pedro

Woodman: Garret's observer in the assault on De Graaf's men at their landing site

PRONUNCIATIONS

For what it's worth, here are my interpretations of the pronunciations of various names and places:

Abeo:	A-bay´-o
Acuna:	A-koon´-ya
Attila:	A-till´-a
Beauclere:	Bo-klair´
Caber:	Kay´-bur
Connachan:	Kawn´-a-han
De Graaf:	De Grawf˝
Drake:	Draik
Elizabeth:	E-liz´-a-beth
Jorge:	Hor´-hay
Musa:	Moo´-sa
Ortega:	Or-tay' ga
Pantas:	Pawn´-tus
Philip:	Fill´-ip
Tovery:	To´-ver-ee
Valdez:	Vall-dez´
Vegas:	Vay´-gahs
Wenman:	Wen´-mun
Cardiff:	Kar´-diff
Cartageña:	Kar-tuh-hay´-nya
El Escorial:	El Es-cor-rey-all´

Inagua:	In-aw´-gwa
Santo Pedro:	San´-to Pay´-dro
Santiago del Príncipe:	San-ti-a´-go dell Prin´-cip
Tortuga:	Tor-too´-guh

Gente de Mar: Zhawnt-de Mawr

SHIPS

Cutthroat
Captain: Yaugaan De Graaf
Originally a Spanish warship, it was captured by Harker & De Graaf in their assault of Nombre de Dios

Death's Head
Original Captain: Harker
His second ship, originally a Spanish Merchant—*Espíritu de los Santos*
Now Captained by De Graaf

Demise
Captain: Attila
A pyrate ship based at Isla Tortuga

Mercilus
Captain: James Wenman
An English warship sent to Isla Tortuga to deliver a message from Queen Elizabeth to Garret Connachan, or her partner, Captain William Tovery

Orion
Captain: William Tovery
One of Garret's private fleet of three ships. William took it on after his original ship, *Athena,* was commandeered by Captain James McBride

Pandora
Captain: Garret Connachan
The flagship of Garret's private fleet of three ships

Santo de Cristo
Captain: Jimenez
A Spanish merchant vessel attacked by De Graaf

Visser
Captain: Juan la Roja
A fishing vessel attacked by De Graaf as a set-up to defraud King Philip

LOCATIONS

Cardiff: England

Cartageña: Columbia

Hispaniola: West Indies island split politically into Haiti & the Dominican Republic

Inaguas: South Sea islands (One big, one Small)

Isla Tortuga: Tortuga Island, north of Hispaniola (now Haiti)

London: England

Nombre de Dios: Panamanian settlement titled by Drake as 'The Treasurehouse of the World'

Porto Bello: Panamanian settlement emerging as Spain's favored location for storing their treasure.

Santo Pedro: Fictitious village not far from Cartagena

Santiago del Principe: Home of those who massacred Garret's men

Spanish Main: The eastern coast of Central & South America

PLACES

Orion's Tavern: In London

Gente de Mar: A tavern on Isla Tortuga

ix

ACKNOWLEDGMENTS

I am extremely grateful for the contributions of those listed below…

Don Drucker, my decades-long consigliere, provided his typical unvarnished feedback. I love him for that. RIP.

Natalia de Oliveira Dal' Evedove, of One Demi-Goddess Books, provided perspectives I would never have seen. I am so grateful for her guidance.

Inspiration for the series comes from my pyrate-loving friends on Facebook: Adam Morrow (Shipwrecked with Captain Marrow); Mark Forget (Festival Des Pyrates); Dave Carroll, co-author of <u>Thatcher: The Unauthorized Biography of Blackbeard the Pyrate</u>. I also have to recognize several Facebook Groups, including Pirates; Pirate Nation; Rum-Runners Cove, Hoist the Colors, Pirate Enthusiasts; The Republic of Pirates; World Pirate Party; World Wide Pirate Community and others. The group administrators and members are valued for sharing their insight, research, context and humor.

A special shout-out to Edgar Barragan, aka Commodore Crimson, and his Crimson Pyrates & Privateers (also on Facebook). This nonprofit organization's quest is to rebalance the lines of plunder by drawing on those who have so much, to assist those who've suffered without.

A portion of the proceeds from this Series supports Edgar's foundation.

My thanks to Page Turner Awards, whose support and guidance led to this novel's selection as a Finalist for their 2022 Writing Award.

Thanks in memoriam to Roger C. Ambrose, who did the original design for the first four novels in my Pyrate Series. And thanks to James R. Whirlow, who made publishing the novel possible by picking up the torch and lighting the design cannon following Roger's passing.

Finally, a special thanks to JerichoWriters.com. Their website, and the aspiring writers who participate in their forums, have helped immensely, schooling me on writing and pointing me to needed resources.

I feel blessed to have all of you in my life

Pyrate: Black Flag

I

It rose defiantly from midnight blue water, its soaring cliffs of gray rock emerging as though cast out by those who ruled the depths of the Caribbean Sea.

"The Spanish call it Isla del Diablo," Drago shouted, trying hard to be heard above the howling wind and thundering waves. "A sailor's worst nightmare," he added.

Master's Mate Blair didn't need any explanation. The sight alone spoke to the treachery of this barren place. "Note the shoals!" He called out to the helmsman. He needn't have worried, however; the showering, windswept spray from crashing waves gave the island's dangerous barrier all the visibility it needed. Many of the craggy pillars of charcoal-colored stone disappeared with the water's rush, only to resurface as menacing, inanimate soldiers defending their island. They seemed eager to rip the bottom from any vessel foolish enough to approach, inviting the wind and water to hoist and toss its carcass onto the pebbled shore.

With the sails skillfully trimmed and anchors at the ready, the crew of the former privateering ship *Pandora* looked on in silence, mesmerized by the deathly images. Blair could read it in their eyes—the sense that Captain Garret Connachan had lost her bloody mind. He, too, questioned her sensibility, praying she had no intent to challenge this ominous gray demon.

"Steady as she goes Master Blair," Garret yelled forcefully, above the clamor of the water's collisions with the jagged rocks.

"Mother of Satan," Blair mumbled to himself.

Pandora continued paralleling the coastline, bearing lethal cargo she sought to unload—human cargo of the vilest form.

———

The hulking pyrate sat knees-bent on the damp floor of the cargo-hold, where water beaded and dripped like a ship's sweat. *Pandora's* extreme pitch and roll forced his rusting shackles to etch blood-bearing furrows on his wrists and ankles. The wrist-manacles did the most damage; their maker never imagined them being worn by a man with such massive forearms. Still, Yauggan De Graaf barely noticed the sting. His body already bore the scars of a man who devoured pain for a living.

"Damn you!" he yelled at the sudden bite. The oversized gray rat retreated quickly at the kick of his leg. "I have enough to worry about, varmint."

Alone and weaponless, De Graaf fully expected a merciless fate. He had no doubt Captain Connachan had cheerfully considered several options to exact her revenge. After all, she'd already proven herself to be the witch he always knew her as.

Despite the presence onboard of a known executioner—the behemoth Musa—De Graaf doubted beheading was the Witch's preference. Too quick a death. That was precisely why he'd decided it would be his favored demise, if given a choice. But that was unlikely. No doubt Connachan wanted him to suffer at length.

'*A drowning at sea would be more to her liking,*' he thought. Being thrown overboard in chains would yield a slower, more miserable death. Still, there was only momentary exhibition in that. Hanging was much more likely. Not only did it take longer, but it brought with it the spectacle of a jerking body and the public shame of defecation.

The more he thought about it, the more he worried the Witch might even resort to keelhauling—scraping his body around and under the ship's hull. It was a punishment he, himself, once meted out to the captain of the *Santo De Cristo*. He had to admit, her doing that seemed eerily poetic. But he didn't think Connachan had the stomach for watching a slab of bloody flesh and organs drip all over *Pandora's* deck at the finish. That sight had left many of his own hardened crew forcing out their innards.

'*Whatever the Witch chooses,*' De Graaf thought, '*I shall die with honor.*' It was the only way the most feared pyrate in the Caribbean should go. Having blazed brightly, being snuffed out within minutes seemed far better than growing old, dissolving like a crumbled ember in a wasting fire. That morbid thought brought him momentary warmth in this dark, foul hold, fighting off diseased and hungry rats.

———

The architecture, vibrance and vivid colors of Cartagena never failed to captivate first-time visitors to Spain's Caribbean jewel. But in this moment, there was no charm whatsoever in Governor Acuña's opulent office. He and General Serezo stood on either side of the gold-embossed ebony table that comfortably seated sixteen. It was here that the two men commonly planned activities requiring military support, including the General's participation in several construction projects authorized by King Philip. Many of those projects were intended to enhance the city's defenses, including an impregnable wall and military installations. The building of the Governor's palatial new residence was also underway.

Despite all their past collaboration, Governor Acuña was now furious with Serezo. Together they'd planned the exchange of doubloons for Viceroy Valdez, one of the King's closest personal friends. Valdez was believed to have been kidnapped and held for ransom by English pyrates led by a woman many referred to as The Witch. The General had assured the Governor that his men would safely secure the Viceroy's return. But now here he was, delivering news of the failure; news that threatened Governor Acuña's recall by the King himself. Dreams of his new palace behind gated walls seemed to be dissolving into the nightmare of a walled prison cell.

"I gave you complete control and unlimited resources, General," he screamed. "Only sheer incompetence could have produced such a result." He pounded his right fist hard on the table, causing his silver cup to jump. The port within erupted like a miniature volcano. Acuña's Spittle flew between them, losing propulsion and falling harmlessly on the black tabletop.

Serezo remained stoic, stone-faced and stone-bodied, as would any man of enormous pride. He offered no defense, nor resistance. Acuña sensed it was because the General understood this anger was appropriate, given the circumstances. Were their positions reversed, he was certain Serezo would mete out the same level of verbal violence.

The Governor finally sat, looking away and pondering his next steps. There was no reversing the damage that was done. So it was now critical that he control the narrative. That, and lay blame elsewhere. A politician must never accept responsibility; it would be career-ending. Only unseasoned politicians might be altruistic enough to fall into the trap of opening themselves up to blame. Not him. He was a seasoned politico, fully capable of engineering outcomes that burnished his already much-revered status. The only real questions were where the blame would be placed, and how the supporting framework would be engineered.

As to the first question…laying blame…he thought of the men who'd participated in the exchange. Best to blame someone of note who had perished in the effort, since they wouldn't be around to mount a defense. Don Francisco Rivera De Mendoza came to mind first. As Viceroy Valdez' second-in-command, he'd been brought in to identify the Viceroy during the ransom exchange.

The other man of any consequence was Felipe De Heredia y Ortega. He was a wealthy financier. Being a man of prominence in Cartagena, the Viceroy's captor (the Witch) had apparently reached out to Ortega for aide in getting their ransom request to King Philip.

The more he thought about these two men, the more Governor Acuña preferred blaming Ortega. After all, blaming Rivera might raise the ire of the military. Ortega, on the other hand, had no defenders; just haters who envied his wealth. In fact, most of the merchants in the city resented the man for his prior dealings with them. That was because Ortega always seemed to come away with the advantage. Yes, thought

Acuña, Ortega would be the better of the two to take the fall.

Still, General Serezo, silent and motionless, required punishment. He'd been in charge of the ransom exchange. A modest imprisonment would probably suffice, thought Acuña. He was confident Serezo would accept that penalty, since he ultimately needed the Governor on his side if he were to continue in his current, highly elevated role.

Acuña finally rose. "Guards," he called. Two soldiers entered momentarily. "Escort the General to the penitenciario. He is to be held there pending further word from me."

Serezo didn't resist. He slowly unsheathed his cutlass with his left hand, offering it up to the Governor, pommel first. "As you wish, Governor. I shall await your call." He bowed briefly before turning to exit with the guards on either side. The two soldiers held the General in high regard. But orders were orders. Their surprise at these particular orders appeared mollified by the General's own behavior.

As the men left, Acuña sat back down. He now needed to flesh out the story that would point to Ortega's fault for the failed exchange, the principal result of which was the Viceroy's apparent death. General Serezo had expressed absolute certainty that Valdez had drowned. The man's death at the hand of The Witch would be a far more difficult message to deliver to King Philip than the loss of his forty thousand doubloons.

———

It was clear the Witch was taking no chances. She and six of her men circled him, pistols drawn and aimed in De Graaf's direction. He watched the remaining crew members drop the barrel of water, food supplies, a knife, an unloaded pistol, gunpowder, a long-coat, a sheet of canvas and a variety of tools at the edge of the foliage. They'd earlier left a roped canvas bag containing pistol balls about fifty yards away, near the far end of the narrow, pebble-strewn beach. With the supplies unloaded, the men headed back to their longboat on the far side of the island, from where they'd all made the approach. The water conditions there were slightly more forgiving, though the rocky barrier ensured their approach was harrowing enough.

No one in his right mind would elect to land on this God-forsaken island, thought De Graaf. He wasn't expecting any visitors. Not live ones, that is. Dead ones, on the other hand, had floated ashore from the remains of ships that unintendedly challenged the deadly shoals from time to time. Scattered, disjointed remains of a few skeletons still lingered about. De Graaf understood those bones were likely to be his only human companionship while he lived out his remaining days here. His reality was now clear—the Witch intended his death to be a more prolonged experience than he ever anticipated.

Garret pointed her pistol to the rocks at De Graaf's feet. "You shall make your final peace here," she called out above the noise of the pounding surf. "Fair punishment for the brutal slaying of Viceroy Jorge Valdez."

"The bloody bastard was still alive when I left him," De Graaf shouted back.

"His death was imminent," Garret countered.

"So you claim," came the reply, accompanied by a wad of spit directed her way.

Garret felt a sudden urge to gut the man here and now. It was almost as though he knew she'd been forced to take Valdez' life herself, to end his misery. She took a deep breath and held back, having earlier concluded that a long and lonely existence on this isolated speck of land would inflict the maximum aggregate pain on the virtual killer of her former lover. Both physical and mental pain. "This place is the Devil's hunting ground," she responded. "You shall meet him here in good time, but not before daily regretting having caused the Viceroy's death."

"God damn you and all your ancestors, Witch!"

"I am afraid God is not on your side, De Graaf. He will surely have no mercy on your rotting soul."

De Graaf gazed at his foreboding surroundings. This long, narrow stretch of pebbled beach was surrounded almost entirely by towering stone cliffs. The grayness seemed to seep into and chill the deepest depths of his body. He peered into Garret's eyes in a bloodthirsty stare. "My men shall not take kindly to your actions here. I can already see them ravaging you like wolves craving female flesh."

Captain William Tovery, Garret's partner, drew his cutlass quickly and stepped forward, threatening to slice a few more scars on De Graaf's corpus; soon-to-be corpse.

"No," shouted Garret, extending her arm. "Leave him be. He is not deserving of the quick release I gave Jorge."

William hesitated before lowering his sword. His eyes never left the pyrate's face.

De Graaf grinned back, "You are a sorry want of a man," he taunted.

William's rage flared. He darted toward his target. Garret jabbed out her leg, tripping him as he went. He fell forward, scraping on the gravel. De Graaf roared with laughter.

William rose and glared back at Garret. "Damn you."

"Stand down, William. This is not your call to make." She turned to walk away. De Graaf laughed in his gravelly voice and spit in William's direction. William scowled, spit at the ground, and then turned to follow Garret. The other men backed up, keeping their pistols pointed at De Graaf.

"Shoot me," De Graaf yelled. "Shoot me now," he dared them. There was no response. He took an aggressive step toward them. Three pistols fired nervously. One shot whizzed past him. Another sliced his ear. The third bit the top of his shoulder. He stumbled backward from the third hit but smiled broadly, defiantly. "You are all cowards," he laughed.

Garret's men continued walking backward, training pistols on the wounded beast. He shouted once more at Garret, "You shall regret this, Witch. You can be certain of that."

One of Garret's men chose to fire a warning shot in the air as the group proceeded back to the head of the trail they'd crafted on the way here. De Graaf thrust his right hand hard into the air. "Damn you all, you bastards. When I get off this island, you are all dead men."

William trailed Garret along the narrow path. "You realize there is no assurance he will die here," he grumbled.

Garret stopped and turned to face him. "Leave it be, William. The deed is done. God will have his way with the beast." She turned back and continued walking.

After several paces, William continued, "I do worry about his crew. We can expect them to react with force."

"They won't even know what has become of him," replied Garret. "Or that we played a role in his disappearance. His only men who witnessed our ambush were with him at the time. And they're all gone."

"Except the Jew."

"I trust Yosel implicitly. He was the one who informed me of De Graaf's scheme."

"Which only makes him a traitor to his former captain. Who is to say he will not betray you?"

"Leave it be, William."

"You realize you are assuming there was no one from his campsite who may have remained behind, observing our ambush under cover of the jungle."

Garret paused. It was a fair point. "Perhaps it does suggest careful vigilance on Tortuga."

William accepted her concession. He changed course, "I am most anxious to be back there. Mostly for the food."

Garret nodded. "I too am famished." She stopped for a moment and leaned in close, whispering in his ear to avoid being overheard, "Before we get back, we must settle on the distribution of the King's doubloons among the crew."

"And where to secure our own," William whispered back. They shared a common concern…*Pandora* was not the ideal location to hide their portion of King Philip's forty thousand doubloons.

———

X

De Graaf sat on the gravel, pressing his hand hard against his shoulder to stem the bleeding. "Damn the Witch," he mumbled. He thought back to his earliest days alongside Connachan. She'd joined Drake's fleet as a midshipman, disguised as male. De Graaf wasn't sure whether Drake knew of her ruse back then. But years later, when he appointed her captain, he'd come clean with the crew. Ever since then, De Graaf was convinced the girl had seduced or bewitched Drake, to gain her promotion—hence the nickname "The Witch". It spread rapidly among her detractors.

Though any woman's presence onboard ship was a bad omen, De Graaf grudgingly admired Connachan's mastery with a sword. It was said she'd been finely tutored in military arts by a retired officer, after being expelled from a private academy for knifing a classmate. Her defenders claimed she was avenging the rape of her friend.

He thought back to the night of his assault on her ship, *Pandora*. He and his partner picked seven men to assist them in their effort to kidnap Viceroy Valdez and kill the Witch. Valdez was a valuable hostage for whom King Philip was likely to pay an enormous ransom. But the assault ended in the Viceroy's death…and Garret's killing of De Graaf's partner, something he'd vowed to avenge. Having escaped the carnage that night, he'd taken the Viceroy's ear and ring as trophies. The latter had been given to Valdez by King Philip himself, on his appointment to Viceroy.

It was those damned trophies that ultimately led to his being here, De Graaf thought. He'd used them to convince King Philip his beloved friend and Viceroy was still alive, and could be freed for a healthy ransom. The forty thousand doubloons had been handed over by

Governor Acuna's men, but then promptly lost to Connachan in an ambush. He suspected one of his own men had informed the Witch of his plan.

If he were ever to get off this damned island, he thought, he would rain bloody Hell on her, that bastard William Tovery, and the traitor within his own crew.

———

The fourth novel in my Pyrate Series, 'Pyrate – Black Flag, is coming soon. Click 'Follow the Author' on my Pyrate Rising or Pyrate Assassin Amazon book page if you'd like to be automatically notified of its release.

You can also visit:

- *My website: pyratepubs.com*
- *My Facebook Page: Pyrate Publishing*
- *My other Facebook Page: Pirate Card Enthusiast*